A Taste of Death and Honey

SHARON BAYLISS

Copyright © 2019 Sharon Bayliss

All rights reserved. No part of this publication may be reproduced, distributed, or transmitted in any form or by any means, including photocopying, recording, or other electronic or mechanical methods, without the prior written permission of the publisher, except in the case of brief quotations embodied in critical reviews and certain other noncommercial uses permitted by copyright law.

Published October 2019 by Animus Ferrum Publishing
Mishawaka, Indiana
http://www.animusferrum.com/

ANIMUS FERRUM
PUBLISHING

ISBN: 978-1-948661-66-9 - ebook
ISBN: 978-1-948661-67-6 – paperback

Format design graphics by Curiosity Quills Press

This is a work of fiction. Names, characters, places, and incidents either are the product of the author's imagination or are used fictitiously. Any resemblance to actual persons, living or dead, or locales is entirely coincidental.

To my sons, who bring the vibrance and hope of spring to every day of my life.

"You can cut all the flowers but you cannot keep spring from coming."
— *Pablo Neruda*

CHAPTER ONE

Wind moaned through the greenbelt, whipping and twisting the plastic shopping bags stuck in the trees. Samantha Carthage played with Imogene's long black curls, relishing the warmth and weight of Imogene's head resting on her stomach. Samantha's own hair had grown long and intermingled with Imogene's. The blackest black and lightest blonde looked so perfect together. She wanted to braid their hair together into one strand.

Another gust of stubborn winter air caused an army of discarded fast food containers to tumble across their patch of fresh green clover. Samantha ran her fingers along the goose bumps that erupted on Imogene's brown skin.

"You don't have to pretend it's not cold," Samantha said. "We can go inside."

"*Inside?*" Imogene sat up and widened her amber eyes in a look of mock horror.

Samantha laughed. "Okay, you're right."

Imogene held her hair back with one hand to keep it from whipping in the breeze and leaned down to kiss Samantha. Samantha thought Imogene always tasted like honey. Imogene would roll her eyes and say that on her best days she might taste like toothpaste or cinnamon gum, but no, she tasted like honey. Always.

"It's not cold," Imogene said. "It's the most beautiful day of the year."

Samantha knew Imogene meant this as a compliment for her, and not the day. Wizard spring had long since begun—spanning forty-five days before and after the equinox—and they defiantly wore sandals, but no one could call the cold, gray day beautiful.

However, Samantha could not imagine a day better than that particular March 4th. Over a year ago, when the summer wizards had determined her magical date to be March 4th, they labeled her as "too cold"… on the wrong side of the equinox they had explained. So, at first, she didn't like her date. Too warm for the winter. Too cold for the summer. She didn't have a home anywhere.

But, she didn't feel that way anymore. March 4th hovered in the gray area between winter and spring, but that's why she loved it. March 4th *breaks* the winter. The first flowers raise their heads. The world feels the sun and has hope, knowing winter will soon end. That moment was *her* moment.

Though much of the grass remained dead from winter, they had found a spot where the ground had erupted in a lush carpet of clover. Samantha could smell the life bursting from the earth, ready to replace every touch of gray with green after green after green.

Imogene stood up and pulled Samantha up with her. "Let's not go inside. Let's just go farther and farther away until they drag us back."

"Yes."

Imogene ran deeper into the greenbelt surrounding the neighborhood that contained Jefferson Parish Children's Shelter. Discarded syringes, condom wrappers, and other filth littered the thin, trashed-out greenbelt. But spring didn't care. Spring blossomed around Imogene as she half walked, half skipped along. Greens glowed brighter. Tiny, timid flowers opened.

"I can't believe Officer Pike didn't see us leave campus. I thought for sure, he would catch us," Samantha said.

"I guess the gods wanted us to have a happy day," Imogene said.

Imogene always looked happy. Samantha saw the weariness of a hard life in Imogene's eyes, but her lips always lingered on the edge of a smile. She seemed to know something no one else did, about how it would all turn out okay in the end. Around Imogene, Samantha felt that way, too.

Samantha would never forgive her mother for neglecting her and leaving her, but she took her last words to her to heart. *Dance then, wherever you may be.* That described Imogene perfectly. She could find beauty anywhere. She could make this trashed-out greenbelt with graffiti covered rocks feel like Eden.

"Oh, no," Imogene said.

Imogene kneeled and her long black curls fell to the ground covering whatever she cradled in her hands.

Samantha also kneeled in the carpet of dense green moss that had erupted from nowhere, and gently pulled Imogene's hair to the side so she could see what she held. Imogene had a baby bird in her hands. The poor bird looked crushed on one side, and Samantha could see some reddish purple guts spilling out. Ants feasting on the creature now walked up Imogene's forearms. Samantha tried to brush them off.

"Put it down," she said, trying not to swat the disgusting thing out of her hands. "It's already dead."

"I'm not sure."

"It's definitely dead." Samantha pulled Imogene's hair away from the dead thing. She wanted to jump up and down going "ew, ew, ew, ew, ew, ew, ew" and then drag Imogene to a vat of hand sanitizer. But Samantha knew Imogene wouldn't appreciate her finding the "beautiful" cycle of life and death icky.

"I feel more powerful when I'm with you," Imogene said. Despite the tenderness of the statement, Imogene didn't look at Samantha as she spoke. She never took her eyes off the bird. "I wonder…"

"What?"

Imogene closed her hands around the bird and closed her eyes. She looked like a child praying at the edge of her bed. Samantha watched flyaway strands of Imogene's hair twist and twirl in the breeze and listened to the sound of wind and cars on the nearby highway, wondering how long Imogene planned on kneeling there in silence.

Then Samantha heard chirping.

Imogene laughed breathlessly and opened her hands to reveal a whole, living baby bird, shaking the ants off of its wings. She held it up to Samantha in her cupped hands as if offering a present. Samantha didn't know if Imogene wanted her to take it, but she didn't dare touch the thing. When Samantha didn't respond, Imogene set the bird on the ground and watched it hop away. Her usual smile looked pale in comparison to the beaming white-toothed smile she sported now. Imogene stood up and threw herself into Samantha's arms, giggling like a small child on Christmas morning.

Samantha squeezed her back, but now she felt a chill even with Imogene pressed against her.

"Imogene…" she said.

Imogene pulled back and looked ready to do a cartwheel. "I did it. I finally did it. I've gotten close before."

Tears hung from Imogene's eyelashes. Samantha could guess the time she had "gotten close." However, Imogene had never told Samantha that part of the story. Meddling with life and death was forbidden. Besides, wizards couldn't raise the dead. They just couldn't. Everyone knew that.

"You can't do that," Samantha said. "It's not possible."

"You just saw me do it."

"God. What are you?"

"Please don't look at me like that."

"I'm just… surprised."

Imogene wrapped her arms around Samantha and whispered close to Samantha's ear. "You're the reason I could finally do it. Because you make me happy," she said.

"Me too," Samantha said. The two words sounded didn't seem like enough. "I love you," she added.

They hadn't said "I love you" before, and with every silent second that passed, Samantha's stomach turned into a tighter ball. *Why doesn't she say something?* Imogene had grown so still and quiet in Samantha's arms she wondered if she had stopped breathing. Samantha wished she could reach back and grab those three words, go back to a place before she had ruined that perfect moment. Samantha took a deep breath of Imogene's hair, hair that somehow always smelled like rain.

When Imogene finally moved she pulled back enough to look Samantha in the eye. Samantha didn't know what expression she expected, maybe pity, maybe embarrassment, maybe happy speechlessness, but Imogene looked distracted. She looked *through* Samantha instead of at her. Her perpetually happy face that overflowed with joy a moment ago now seemed cast in shadow.

"Are you okay?"

When Samantha spoke, Imogene directed her gaze back to her and she smiled. As always, her smile had that faint hint of a secret, but a darker one this time.

Samantha shivered. Clouds must have rolled in because it seemed so much darker and colder than it had a moment ago. Samantha looked up, but didn't see any new clouds or a low flying plane blocking the sun, just the same white sky. She couldn't stop herself from shivering now. The air felt cold, but also painfully dry and empty. Even with a deep breath, she didn't seem to get enough oxygen. The air, once filled with the smells of new grass and the sounds of the highway, had emptied as if a pocket of deep space had passed over them.

"What is going on?" Samantha asked, rubbing her arms, which burned from the cold. Imogene continued to stare, her eyes not focused on anything. "Are you okay?" she asked again.

"Yes. I'm okay. I'm wonderful." Imogene blinked and snapped out of her reverie. She looked at Samantha now as if she had just now noticed her presence. She smiled and then kissed her, in a gentle, lingering way, far slower than usual.

Then, Imogene turned and ran. Punch drunk from the kiss, it took Samantha a moment to follow.

"Imogene," she cried.

Imogene followed all sorts of strange things. Butterflies. Rainbows. Sunsets. Thunderstorms. She might run toward anything at any moment. But something about this felt different. It felt wrong.

Imogene had tossed her sandals and Samantha jumped past them to continue her pursuit. Imogene ran faster barefoot, and Samantha only glimpsed the occasional curtain of black hair, passing through the gray Spanish moss.

"Stop!" Samantha cried.

Samantha heard highway noise and as she passed through the trees, she found herself only a few steps from the interstate. Samantha skidded to a stop in the broken glass-laced gravel on the side of the road. Part of her wanted to continue to follow Imogene onto the asphalt, but she couldn't will her body to do it. Imogene stopped. The wind stopped. Everything stopped. Except for the cars.

Imogene stood in the middle of the highway and turned back to look at Samantha. Imogene kept her eyes locked on Samantha's while an eighteen-wheeler plowed into her at highway speed.

Time hung in the air. In the space of an instant, Imogene became nothing but a mass of black hair and red blood smeared across the highway. Samantha ran toward Imogene's body. She heard tires squealing and horns honking, but she didn't take her eyes off of Imogene.

Samantha only recognized Imogene's hair. The truck had crushed her body and left nothing more than a mess of torn flesh. Imogene could not have turned into this alien creature in the space of a few seconds. How could her life have been so fragile?

Samantha felt hands on her, and the distant sound of a woman whispering to her in a thick Louisiana accent. The woman tried to pull her out of the highway. Samantha's body grew cold from the inside out. "I can save her," she croaked. "I can save her."

The Mundanes trying to help her ignored her mutterings as madness, but she had seen Imogene reverse death only moments ago. Spring witches could give life. They could resurrect the dead.

But, even as she screamed it, she knew she could not. If she had ever had such power, she didn't have it now. Even on good days, Samantha wasn't special. She was March 4th. Not hot enough, not cold enough, and not balanced enough. And, she certainly had no power over death. And she couldn't remember ever feeling less powerful than she did right then.

The strange woman had pulled her into a hug on the side of the highway and stroked her hair to try and calm her. Samantha pressed her face into the stranger's T-shirt and did her best to remember the taste of honey and the smell of rain.

CHAPTER TWO

David Vandergraff had visited New York City once before. On a sales trip in August of 2001, only weeks before the fated terrorist attack. He remembered his eyes were constantly drawn to the Twin Towers. A bit of sunlight would glint on their silver face, drawing his attention. He remembered staring at the towers as he walked down the busy sidewalk and nearly getting run over by a bus. The clouds reflecting on the towers mesmerized him for some reason. Now he couldn't help but wonder… did he know? If he had known he was a wizard at the time, would he have recognized the premonition? Could he have done anything to stop it?

Now that he walked down the busy street, once again staring up at massive buildings like a yokel, he realized the arrogance of assuming he could have stopped the attack. None of the many other wizards in New York had stopped it. Wizards didn't have the power to stop any of the countless horrible things happening in the world every day. If they did, then why wouldn't they?

On his last trip, he spent a lot of time staring at the towers, and also a lot of time staring at people. Although different from the world he knew, New York had seemed familiar. Everywhere he turned he thought he saw someone he knew.

He had the same feeling this time, but now he knew he didn't see forgotten college classmates or other random acquaintances. He saw wizards. He counted nine on the subway ride from the airport to the hotel. Still a small percentage since he must have passed thousands of people, but he could go months without seeing another wizard in Houston, except, of course, the ones he shared a house with.

In New York, he saw them everywhere and they saw him too. They might make eye contact for a moment or two and then pass by. The local wizards seemed used to seeing their own kind. David wanted to go shake hands with all of them. Maybe it was a Southern thing, but they felt like long-lost family members. Considering the interrelation of wizards, he probably did have distant relatives among the crowd. However, David knew no good would come from adding any additional wizards to his life, especially not wizards like him.

Most wizards related to David were probably winter wizards, the ones often seen in magical stories feeding sweet princesses poison apples, releasing flying monkeys, and terrorizing poor little Harry Potter.

David knew dark wizards were like snakes, not all of them were venomous, but it was still good sense to avoid poking at them with sticks. The dark wizards he saw on the streets of New York fell into two distinct categories—either well dressed in expensive clothes and chatting away to themselves on Bluetooth, or unfortunate individuals, who smelled of urine and also chattered away to themselves... but with no one on the other line.

"Good morning," David said into his phone as he swilled the bitter coffee he had made in the bathroom of the minuscule motel room. The room didn't have the luxury of tables or chairs and he had to drink his coffee on the edge of the bed.

"You know, it's an hour earlier here," Amanda said back.

"I see that you're still mad."

"I'm not mad," she grumbled.

"Considering my track record, I can understand why you don't like me leaving home."

"Are you bringing home any additional children?"

"I doubt it."

"What do you mean, you doubt it? You're not sure?" Her tone mixed levity and venom.

"I'm *definitely* not bringing home any additional children. I just don't know what I'm bringing home."

"Yeah, that's what makes me nervous."

"How are you feeling?"

"Still fine, David."

He could imagine her rolling her eyes. He was afraid to believe the cancer was gone. The tide had turned so quickly, he feared any day they would get a call from the doctor saying he had made a mistake. Maybe the doctor confused her chart with someone else's. He couldn't handle having hope and then having to lose it all again.

"How are the kids?" he asked.

"Alive."

"Well, that's good. You've met the minimum standard for parenting."

"I try."

David paused and examined the sticky black goo at the bottom of his coffee cup. "You know we need this."

"No, we don't. We've made it this far. We'll just keep going."

David paused. "I don't like being this guy. I want a life where I can pay for more than rent and groceries without going into debt."

"I know. Just please promise me you'll be careful. Read every word of anything you're asked to sign. And follow your gut. You have the ability to sense dark magic at work if you *pay attention*. If something feels wrong, it probably is."

"I've got it under control."

"Okay," she said doubtfully.

"Are you drinking coffee right now?"

"It's before 10 a.m. and I'm not dead, so yes."

"What does it taste like?"

"Is this like the coffee version of phone sex?"

"Yes."

"It tastes like coffee, David."

"You're no fun."

"It tastes like freshly brewed café au lait served during a summer rainstorm in the Florida Keys."

"I love you."

"I love you, too."

The estate lawyer's office had a certain X-Men villain feel—everything a shade of black, white, or gray, including the floor, which looked like solid mercury. The ceilings weren't unusually high, but David's footsteps echoed as if he walked through a large chamber. He shivered and would swear they had the air conditioner on, strange for a day with melting patches of snow on the edges of the sidewalks. He felt fortunate he'd chosen to wear a suit.

"Mr. Vandergraff?"

The young man who came out to greet him didn't look like a super villain, but David could tell he was a dark wizard. He appeared about a decade younger than David and wore so much gray David figured he either hated color or couldn't see it. He looked at David through wire-rimmed glasses.

"I'm Peter Sherman, an associate partner. I'm handling Rachel Colter's estate." Mr. Sherman reached out to shake

David's hand.

As a businessman, David always believed he had impeccable instincts about people. As a wizard, he knew he had *more* than good instincts. With a simple handshake, David could *feel* that person's intentions and could sense malice or deception.

David didn't sense anything unusual from Mr. Sherman's handshake. Mr. Sherman really didn't *see* David; he saw the paperwork and lawyer's fees David represented. Mr. Sherman's had no motive other than to fill in all the boxes and get this meeting completed as accurately and efficiently as possible. David could see how Mr. Sherman had the capacity for evil since he seemed to value paperwork more than people, but he had a convenient and helpful evil for the present situation. David could get this done and get out of here without hassle.

"Thank you for coming in," Mr. Sherman said. "I'm sure it was an inconvenience." He said it as if he read from a script. "But the terms of the will specifically stated that the estate should be dispersed in person."

"May I ask how she died?"

"She drove her car into the Hudson."

"On purpose?"

"It appears so. The police say she never pressed the brake."

"That's horrible."

David wished he felt more surprised. Rachel Colter had been the sister of Whitman Colter, the man who had raped and abused David's children for many years. Rachel killed her brother—her talisman—even though she knew it would destroy her. The last time David saw her, she spoke nonsense and muttered the lyrics to *Auld Lang Syne*. She had refused help, but David wished he had done more. Rachel deserved better than dying alone at the bottom of a river. *Hell*, everyone did.

Mr. Sherman turned away from David, signaling that the question and answer portion of the meeting had ended. David followed him into his office—predictably bland and even colder than the lobby. David sat in one of the chairs opposite the desk and suppressed a shiver.

"May I offer you refreshment?" Mr. Sherman asked.

David considered asking for coffee, the hotter the better, but resisted. He rubbed his hands together to warm them instead.

"No thanks, I'd just like to get this done quickly."

Mr. Sherman nodded. "Yes, sir. As soon as Mr. Colter arrives we'll get started."

The statement hung in the air for a moment. The words made no sense to David, but Mr. Sherman had certainly said them. David knew Rachel's brother, Whitman Colter, was dead. He had seen his body. And Rachel had no other family. He knew she had never married, had no other siblings, and her only daughter had died, as well as her parents. The words, "Mr. Colter" entered his ears and then spread through his body like poison. "I'm sorry, who?"

"Mr. Colter," Mr. Sherman said again.

Mr. Sherman did look at David now. He squinted at him and sniffed the air twice. David guessed the man somehow sensed danger. He appraised David as if assessing risk, figuring how the shift in mood would impact the bottom line. David couldn't guess what scent he might give off for this little weasel to sniff at, but he felt as if he glowed, or the opposite of glowing. Sucking in light. He only needed to hear the words "Mr. Colter," and now the man had said them twice.

"Is there a problem? You weren't aware there was a second beneficiary?"

"I don't understand who you're referring to."

Before he could explain, the receptionist chimed in on the intercom. "A Mr. Colter is here for you."

Now David had heard the words spoken three times and he felt like a black hole. His human non-magical self knew Whitman Colter could not be alive. But he had already been wrong about that once, and his magical self did not trust his own memories.

As his heart raced with nerves, he felt an unexpected twinge of excitement. David had a realization that felt cold, but also pleasant, like a crisp cool winter night. He wanted Whitman Colter to walk through that door, because when he did, he would kill him. Right here, right now. He would get the justice he thought he would never get.

David stood up and picked a heavy clock off the desk and pictured it cracking Colter's skull. He felt like two people, one that could kill without hesitation, and another person watching, terrified… appalled, that he could turn to murder so quickly. But Whitman Colter was no ordinary man. He deserved death.

Two things happened at once. The clock David had picked up flew out of his hand and across the room as if someone had turned on a giant magnet. And a man appeared in the doorway. *Him.* He recognized the stark black hair and black eyes. Even the magic in the room felt as dark and limitless as the West Texas sky the man had once lived under.

Even with the clock somehow tugged from his hand, he prepared to strike. He advanced, but the sensible second David watching him saw something that made him pause. He didn't see the bedraggled, withered heap of a man he had found in the desert. He saw a Whitman Colter standing tall, fresh, young, and strong. Somehow he had regenerated himself into a younger body. Replenished and ready to live his horrible life all over. Then his second, sensible self tapped him politely on the shoulder. When he realized the normal, human explanation he felt ridiculous.

"You're his son," David said.

The *other* Mr. Colter didn't say anything. He glared at David. His black eyes flickered with danger, but David sensed no recognition in his gaze.

"Mr. Vandergraff, please sit down."

The weasel-like Mr. Sherman had become much more venomous. He picked up the now broken clock and glared up at David.

"I am deducting this from my expenses," Mr. Sherman said.

David wanted to argue because technically Mr. Sherman broke the clock when he presumably propelled it out of David's hand with magic, but David would have happily broken it on that man's head if he had gotten the chance.

"Sit down, gentlemen," Mr. Sherman said. He had a red glint in his eyes and David couldn't tell if the glint came from him or something reflecting off his glasses.

"From your reaction, I assume introductions aren't necessary," Mr. Sherman said.

David didn't know what to say. He had almost murdered a complete stranger. From the darkness in the room, David guessed this boy was as evil as his father, but he didn't know for sure. He didn't care to find out either. He just wanted to get away from him.

"Uh," the other Mr. Colter said. "No, I don't know this man. How did you know my aunt? Were you her boyfriend or something?"

Mr. Sherman looked furious. More personal issues to get in the way. "If you two want to fight over the money, you can do so on your own time. Half goes to Zander Colter, half goes to David Vandergraff. The terms are clear and they will not be disputed in my office. If Ms. Colter had ordered all of her money to be dumped into the sewer, I would do it. Once the deceased has passed, the time for argument has passed as well." Mr. Sherman lost his previous blandness and stared them both down without flinching. A lawyer for dark wizards likely didn't intimidate easily, even by a Colter and a Vandergraff.

"I have a few questions," Zander said.

"I said there would be no discussion," Mr. Sherman said.

Zander glared at Mr. Sherman, and then also took a

sideways glance at the broken clock, and then at David, who shifted his glare to a pen on the desk to avoid meeting his eyes.

"The estate has been liquefied and split 50/50. You will each inherit $3,616,310.24, to the penny."

"Oh my God," Zander said.

David gasped too. He had not known what to expect. Rachel had been a successful investment banker and he knew she had money, but that amount of money would change his life. As long as he invested the money wisely—which he would—he would not have to worry about money for the rest of his life. He would stay in a real hotel tonight and eat steak for dinner. Then he would go out any buy his wife and kids presents.

Mr. Sherman pushed two pieces of paper across the table to each of them and then pushed two pens toward them in one simultaneous, almost choreographed motion. David's heart rate spiked. A dark wizard pushing a contract across the table should always cause suspicion, but this felt like more than suspicion. He felt bile rise in his throat and his vision went blurry for a moment. In his head, he heard Amanda's words. *If something feels wrong, it probably is.*

David realized he had held his breath again and he exhaled deeply. He could feel evil in the room because of the people in it, but it didn't mean anything about the contract. He had almost murdered someone. He sat next to the youthful doppelganger of the man he hated more than anything. Naturally, he felt off. So what if he had to share the money with Colter's son? As far as David knew, Zander had nothing to do with what happened to Crystal or his kids. They would take their shares and go their separate ways. No big deal.

Even still, he read every word of that contract, like he promised Amanda, though it appeared the same as the contract the lawyer had already emailed him. Reading every word took willpower. Mr. Sherman glared at him the whole time and the silence and coldness in the room felt like death. He would give anything to leave that room, but he forced himself to endure.

Zander read every word too, his black eyes alight with excitement. But they also had a searching quality, as if he read each word twice, looking for something between the letters.

Despite all the attention the men showed to the contact, it appeared as boilerplate as his lawyer had said. David didn't have to do anything special to receive the money and he could do whatever he wanted with it. If he showed up and had the documentation to prove his identity, he could take the money home.

Only the requirement to come in person seemed strange. He hadn't thought much of it when he got the call. He would get a substantial inheritance, and didn't know anything about estate law. Getting on a plane to New York to collect didn't seem like a big deal. But now, the requirement seemed much more dangerous. Rachel wanted them to come in person, which meant she wanted them to meet. That seemed cruel and unnecessary, even for a dark witch. But he didn't worry about the "cruel" part, he worried about the "unnecessary" part. Rachel didn't strike him as the type of person who did things without a reason.

David looked up and realized Zander had signed his page and now watched him.

Those black eyes.

David signed his name.

He felt no sense of doom, or no *increased* sense of doom, when he signed his name. He didn't care why Rachel had wanted them to meet. In some ways, he considered her a friend, but he barely knew her and she had recently chosen to drive her car into a river. Who knew what might have gone through her head. He just wanted to go home to his family. He had changed Xavier and Evangeline's last name to Vandergraff a long time ago, and he never wanted to hear the word "Colter" again.

"Thank you, Mr. Sherman," David said. "I am sorry about the clock."

Zander glanced at the clock again and opened his mouth to say something, but appeared to change his mind.

Mr. Sherman spared a few more words about the details of how the funds would be dispersed, and about taxes and such. When Mr. Sherman got up to walk them out, David looked at his watch. The whole meeting had lasted less than ten minutes.

If he and Zander left at the same time they'd end up in the elevator together, so David veered toward the restroom. For some reason, Zander took an odd verge at the same time and knocked into his side. It must have looked odd to Mr. Sherman, the two men slamming together like two pool balls ignoring the laws of physics.

David loathed touching Zander. His body seemed unnaturally cold and solid. Zander couldn't have hit him hard, but David's arm pulsed with pain anyway.

Zander muttered, "Sorry."

David didn't even spare him a cold glare; he darted toward the bathroom without looking back.

Once inside, he breathed a heavily potpourried sigh of relief. The receptionist and Mr. Sherman would think he had food poisoning, but he didn't care. He promised himself he'd stay in the bathroom at least twenty minutes. In that time, Zander would catch a train or call a cab and leave his life forever. Figuring he'd make use of his time, he reached for his phone to call Amanda and give her the good news.

He reached into his pocket and noticed something missing. His wallet. He had had his wallet during the meeting… he took his identification out.

That son of a bitch.

Zander must have slammed into him so he could pick his pocket.

CHAPTER THREE

David burst out of the bathroom as dramatically as he had entered. He didn't see Zander in the lobby. He couldn't believe his audacity, or more, his pettiness. Why would a man who had just inherited three million dollars pick a pocket? He had the bad feeling Zander hadn't done it to snag the forty dollars or so David had, or to take a quick shopping spree before David canceled his credit cards. David's heart rate spiked thinking about the other things in his wallet. Namely, his driver's license with his home address. Pictures of his kids.

On the thirtieth floor, David had no choice but to wait for the elevator. Even the agonizingly slow elevator would take less time than running thirty flights of stairs. When the door finally opened, he pressed the close door button multiple times in rapid succession. The woman already in the elevator stepped away from him. On the way down, the elevator stopped two more times, and David wanted to curse every person who came in and slowed him down. When they finally made it to the ground floor, David knocked into two people as he ran out, but he didn't have time to worry about it.

He scanned the first floor for that stark black hair, but didn't see him. He tried to get a lock on that dark energy, but it just swirled around his own head. The phrase "blind with rage" took on a literal meaning. How could he find someone else's dark magic when he himself swam in it? He ran out the front doors and into the cold March air, which smelled of exhaust and exotic spices from nearby food carts.

He darted his head in all directions. Zander had a short head start, but he couldn't have gone far. David didn't see a subway entrance near here. He could have ducked into a shop, but which one? David tried not to panic. He would find him sooner or later. If David concentrated, he could sniff out other wizards like a bloodhound, and he couldn't miss that cloud of cold darkness surrounding Zander.

"Hey," Zander said.

David spun around and slipped in a patch of melting snow before steadying himself. Zander leaned against the building behind him, as if waiting for David to find him. Apparently David couldn't sniff out darkness as well as he thought. Or maybe Zander could cloak himself. In any case, the bastard stood right behind him.

David lunged at him and pinned him against the wall. He wanted to strangle him. But he also felt eyes on him. They stood in the middle of a public street in the middle of the day. He released Zander from his grip and stepped back slightly. If he had been an animal, his teeth would have been bared. As a human man, he had to settle for the most menacing glare he could muster.

"Please don't hurt me," Zander said. "I'll give you your wallet back." He didn't sound terrified, but he did sound... human. And so young. Zander was a fully-grown man, taller than David, but he couldn't be much older than his own kids.

To his magical senses, Zander felt like a swirling mass of evil, and it surprised him to find that he had nearly throttled a human boy.

Zander pressed David's wallet into his hand. "I didn't take anything."

David took a quick glance into his wallet and checked the contents.

"Then, why did you take it?" His voice still sounded like a growl.

"So you would come after me."

"What?" David hissed.

"You didn't seem interested in talking to me after the meeting. You couldn't get away fast enough. I had to do something… or you'd be gone forever."

"What?" David asked again.

"I just want to talk. It won't take long."

"No," David said.

"Why not?" he asked, looking young again, as if David had denied him a toy he had asked for.

"What the fuck do you want to talk about?"

Zander winced a bit at David's harsh words.

"I just wanted to know if you knew my parents. You must have at least known my aunt, and that's more than I can say. I never knew anything about my family at all until I found out I had an aunt, who is apparently rich… but also dead."

"How old are you?"

"Twenty."

"So he must have had you before he met Crystal."

"You mean my father? You know him? Who is Crystal?"

David paused and considered the young man. He didn't sense any deception. But even if David could stomach looking at his face for the space of a cup of coffee, he didn't know anything, at least not anything Zander would want to know.

"I don't have any family," Zander continued. "What about you? Are *we* related?"

"I'm sorry you don't have any family, but I'm afraid you still don't. To tell you the truth, you're lucky you don't know your family. You really dodged a bullet, trust me on that. Take your money and go back to your life."

"No, you have to give me more than that. Who are you? Why did my aunt leave you money if you're not family?"

"I'm sorry. I'm done here. Good luck to you." David turned around.

"You can't just leave," Zander said.

"Yes, I can," David muttered and walked away.

"6675 Tremont Lane, Unit 475. Houston, Texas. 77845."

David froze. He turned back around. "What did you just say?"

"I gave you your wallet back, but it already gave me what I needed to know. Your driver's license had your name and address. You can leave, but I'll just find you again."

David clenched his jaw. The sensible side of him knew that, evil or not, assuming this kid told the truth, he had no clue what he threatened or what it would mean to David. He had no idea that a man who looks very much like him had brutally abused two of David's children for many years. He had no idea what trauma showing up at his doorstep might cause. He didn't understand the danger of threatening the Vandergraff family.

David thought he saw a bit of Zander's smugness melt when he saw the look in David's eyes, but he still looked resolved.

"If you come anywhere near my family, I'll kill you. That's a promise." He had gone past the blind rage now. However, aside from the real Whitman Colter, he doubted he could kill a man, even if he wanted to. One violent act could strip his tenuous humanity away completely. As a husband and a father, he couldn't risk it.

"I don't know why you hate me so much," Zander said, again in that weary, human tone. "But just give me a few minutes of your time, and then you'll never see me again."

David didn't see that he had a choice. Zander might show

up at his door whether he talked to him or not, but if David didn't give him this little chat he knew he would. He tried to talk himself into rational thought. David wouldn't want someone to judge him by the actions of *his* father. Zander's story made sense. He just wanted to know where he came from. David had nothing but bad news for him, and he would try to share as little as possible. In part to spare Zander's feelings, but mostly because he didn't want to tell that story, especially to a stranger, even if that stranger did have a stake in it.

No matter how hard he tried to muster sensible thinking, he couldn't shake the feeling that a cloud of the darkest evil hovered around Zander. He heard Amanda's words once again. *If something feels wrong, it probably is.*

David agreed to go to a Starbucks with Zander. And as he sat across from him with his Americano he considered the extreme strangeness of having coffee with Whitman Colter's son in a Starbucks in New York City. An event so ridiculous, he felt as if God had gone on vacation and set fate to "random."

David wanted to get this over with. No long-winded question and answer session. And he wanted to stay in control of the conversation. So, he just started talking.

"As you already know, my name is David Vandergraff. Rachel Colter was a friend of mine. I didn't expect her to leave me money, but my family fell on hard times, and as far as I know she doesn't have any other family, and not much in the way of friends. So, she thought of me in her will, I guess.

Rachel was an investment banker here in New York City. She was very smart and a great businesswoman. She was never married. She had a daughter, but regretfully, she died years ago.

"Your father, Rachel's brother, was named Whitman Colter. I'm afraid he also passed away in 2013. I'm sorry to say he was a criminal and died at the hands of police when he resisted arrest."

He had lied at the end, but that story would hold up if Zander checked the official police records.

"That's really all I know. I'm afraid I'm not aware of you having any other family. But again, I don't know everything. You're probably better off talking to Mr. Sherman. I'm sorry, I'm sure it's a disappointment."

Zander had lapped up his every word, clutching a tall drip coffee he hadn't even tasted. He didn't say anything now, just waited. David suspected he could talk until his voice went out and it wouldn't satisfy Zander.

David could empathize a bit. Amanda had removed large portions of his memory. She had removed painful, dark memories of an abusive father, but he still felt violated at the loss. He could feel the absence inside him. David could imagine knowing nothing about your family had to feel similar.

"You're not really done, are you?" Zander asked.

"I'm afraid so. Honestly, I don't know what else to say. Like I said, I'm sure this is a disappointment, but it's all I've got for you."

"No, no, no. I know there is more. There has to be *more*."

Something about his words and the shine in his eyes gave David a powerful sense of déjà vu. David wondered if déjà vu had a real magical meaning, not a trick of the mind but an actual connection between two moments in time that had some significant link to each other. A vivid image of Crystal filled his mind. He could smell the sandalwood in her hair. He could hear the wind whipping around them in another, very different moment many years ago.

Now David wanted to leave even more. He felt as if Crystal's spirit had washed right through him. He rubbed his face trying to rid himself of her phantom scent.

"She has nothing to do with this. He was born before her time. They never even met."

"What?"

David didn't realize he had spoken his internal monologue aloud. A sparkly, fuzzy Crystal feeling clouded his brain. That, and the intense washes of rage he had felt ever since he met this man, left him feeling every minute of every day of his of his forty-four years weighing on his chest.

He had to leave, but he knew Zander wouldn't let him, and he had no idea what to say to get him off his back and away from his family.

"You want to know the truth? Your father raped my children and killed their mother. And you look exactly like him. So, I don't want to talk to you anymore."

Zander stared at him, mouth parted, but not saying anything. David may not have gotten rid of him, but he had stunned him. Taking his chance, he got up to leave and didn't look back.

CHAPTER FOUR

The world continued to turn, but left Samantha behind, stranded in a netherworld where time didn't exist anymore. But, no matter how ghostly she felt, the shelter workers expected her to go to school. And eat. And shower. Her caregivers had given her space at first, but grew impatient. So, she had seen her friend smeared across the highway. Get over it already. Of course, they didn't know Imogene had been more than a friend. And, if they didn't scrunch their nose at her for falling in love with a girl, they still wouldn't believe her. They would say she hadn't known her for long enough, or they were too young, to really be in love. So, she didn't say anything. Really. Nothing. She only spoke enough to avoid angering shelter workers and teachers. Just enough to slide by under the radar.

She spent all of her time thinking about Imogene, even though this hurt so much she could hardly breathe. She forced herself to do it. Imogene didn't have a family, and the system had tossed her around too much to make many real friends. If Samantha didn't remember Imogene, she would cease to exist. And, no one with that much life—enough that it spilled out to cure the death of others—deserved a fate as Mundane as death.

If Samantha couldn't bring her back to life, she would keep her memory alive. She would force Imogene's face to haunt her.

At night she would lie in bed, running through every memory she had of her. She would panic when she forgot something—like the shape of her toenails or what she had said that made them laugh right before they had kissed the first time. She also forced herself to think about their future. How they vowed to run away together if either of their caseworkers transferred them to different homes. About all the places they planned to visit together when they aged out of the system. New York. Rome. Tokyo. And, everything in between.

She pictured her there, in the future. On windswept white-sand beaches, in the ruins of a Mayan village, and planting vegetables in the garden of their house. She pictured her old, with white strands in her black hair and crinkles at the edges of her eyes. Those images, although beautiful, caused her so much pain, it took all her willpower to keep from trying to forget. To maybe try a pain-reduction spell like the ones her parents had fallen victim to. But, if she did, Imogene would disappear.

On the spring equinox, she wandered away from school at lunch with no plan in mind. She wanted to experience the springtime. The magnolias on the streets had erupted in fragrant flowers, and honeysuckle draped the fences. The air felt perfect, drenched in the rich smell of soil and flowers, as if the air had turned to warm honey. The sun warmed her bare shoulders. For the first time since Imogene died, she tasted a tiny bit of hope. She felt Imogene's presence with her as she walked. Imogene was the spring. And spring was everywhere. Touching her skin. Filling her vision. Inhaled into her lungs.

So, she wandered and didn't stop wandering. She and Imogene had vowed to run away together if anyone ever tried to separate her. They had never imagined death would cause the separation, but she would keep her vow. She would never return to the shelter, or to anywhere else she couldn't be free.

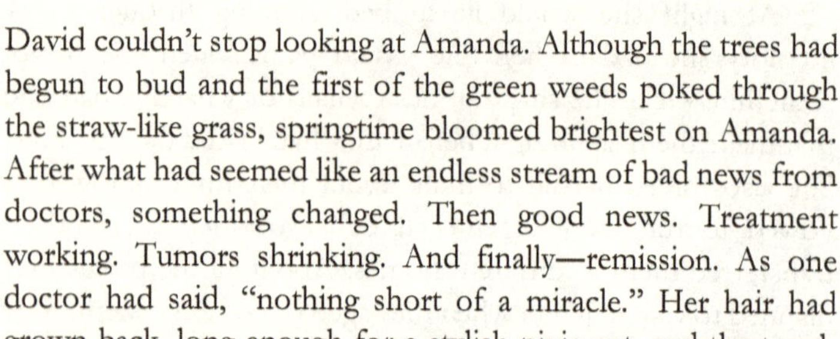

David couldn't stop looking at Amanda. Although the trees had begun to bud and the first of the green weeds poked through the straw-like grass, springtime bloomed brightest on Amanda. After what had seemed like an endless stream of bad news from doctors, something changed. Then good news. Treatment working. Tumors shrinking. And finally—remission. As one doctor had said, "nothing short of a miracle." Her hair had grown back, long enough for a stylish pixie cut, and the touch of pink on her lips and cheeks had now returned.

"For Christ's sake, she's fifteen years old and she still can't stay out of mud puddles," Amanda said. "Emmy!" she shouted. "Stop that." Despite her outburst, Amanda didn't look the least bit bothered. She smiled and took a deep breath. David inhaled too. The air smelled like the dust of fresh rain.

"Do you remember when she used to go out in storms to collect worms and frogs?" Amanda asked. "She would bring them back inside in Solo cups and then forget about it. I've seen a lot more dead frogs and worms than I would like. Then I would get mad at her and she'd just cry because her frogs died and we'd have to have a funeral."

David nodded and watched with rapt attention while Amanda tucked a stray hair behind her ear.

"Stop staring at me," she said, shoving him away gently. "It's creepy."

"I'll stare at you if I want to."

"I like this place. It's not quite what I expected, but I like it."

"What did you expect?"

"I don't know. Something closer to an H-E-B, maybe. You're not expecting me to farm my own food are you?"

"We're twenty minutes from a grocery store, you won't have to churn your own butter. You'd be useless in a zombie apocalypse, you know. And I like this place. It has good energy."

"Good energy? Listen to you all sounding like some kind of wizard… I agree though."

"Our back patio will face west so we can sit out there and drink margaritas and watch the sunset. And that field over there is about to be full of bluebonnets."

"Mmm," she purred. "You had me at 'margaritas.' It sounds like the perfect place to grow old and drunk together."

"That's exactly what I was thinking." He had been smiling so wide his face hurt. "For clients, I usually commit to project completion in six months. But I think I can manage three."

"Eeee." She squealed in an uncharacteristic fashion. "It's going to be incredible." She rested her head on his shoulder.

Emmy came over with Evangeline trailing behind her. "I think we should have a moat with sharks that shoot lasers," Emmy said.

"Done," David said.

"I think we should also build Evangeline's lizard it's own house so I don't have to live with it anymore," Emmy added.

Evangeline smirked.

"Okay. What kind of house would your lizard like?" David asked Evangeline.

"Stop saying yes to everything," Amanda said. "She's probably not joking."

Patrick and Xavier came up, returning from investigating the small creek that ran through the land. Xavier sneezed five times in a row.

"You okay?" David asked.

"I don't think Xavier can live here," Patrick said. "He's allergic to all the pretty flowers."

Xavier looked as if he would say something and then sneezed again. "There's so many *plants* here," he said finally.

"I know what you mean," Amanda said. "I think I can taste the pollen in the air. I can feel it suffocating me, like a yellow plague. Look, it's already made our car yellow."

"My eyebrows are itchy," Emmy added.

"Yeah, I know," David said. "Springtime, yuck. Flowers, eeeew. You guys are impossible."

"Your son can barely breathe," Amanda said.

"He's fine."

"Can I help you build the house?" Xavier asked. He looked at David. Despite the redness and excessive blinking of his eyes, he looked much more present than usual. "If you want, I could come work for you."

Play it cool. Play it cool. Visions of "Vandergraff and Son" danced in his head. He couldn't help from smiling like a kid at Disneyland at this suggestion. "Yeah. Of course."

"So I can quit school?" Xavier asked.

"Well… no. But you can work for me on the weekends if you want. I'll pay you."

"I guess," Xavier said with a shrug. *Well, that excitement died fast.*

"We can talk about plans when we get home," David said. "You know, real ones. No sharks with lasers, but I do want your input."

They headed back to their new Cadillac Escalade that smelled of fresh leather and plastic.

"For the record, I would be awesome in a zombie apocalypse," Amanda muttered. "*Awesome.* We would be the last family alive. You would be *lucky* to have me."

Three months ago, Amanda had struggled through the worst Christmas of her life. Unlike previous years, David and the kids did all of the decorating, which didn't take long in their tiny apartment. After years of buying a tree for a large house, David hadn't learned to pick out a smaller tree and he found himself constantly getting smacked in the face by branches as he walked around his living room.

Chemotherapy had weakened Amanda, so David

understood why Amanda didn't want to come along to pick out the tree, or go present shopping. But when they brought in their one remaining box of Christmas ornaments from storage, Amanda left the room.

He instructed the kids to start decorating and followed her into their bedroom. She had taken off her wig and crawled under the covers, wrapping the blankets around her head instead.

"Are you okay?"

"Fine. Just tired."

"Are you sure?"

"Yes, I'm sure I'm tired."

"We can wait to decorate the tree until you feel up to it."

"Please don't. Just get it over with now."

He sat on the edge of the bed and put his hand on her blanket cocoon.

"I'm really fine, David. Just go. Help the kids."

"I don't want you to miss decorating the tree."

"I know what you're thinking and please don't say it."

"What?"

She rolled over to look at him, careful to keep her bald head covered in the comforter. "You're thinking this is the last time I'll ever get to decorate a Christmas tree, and I'm missing my last chance."

"No, I wasn't thinking that. I would never think that."

"Well, that's what I was thinking. And I'd rather not. I don't want to have a *last* Christmas."

"This isn't your last Christmas."

"You're right. My last Christmas was last year. Actually, that one sucked too. I'll take the year before that. That was my last Christmas. And it was nice. I'm not going to have some crappy, depressing Christmas this year where everything I do is the last time. Last time I make cookies. Last time I wrap presents. Last time I decorate a tree. I'm not going to go through that."

David inhaled a shaky breath and his head throbbed.

Hearing her talk like that always made his head hurt, as if the information damaged his brain. His throat constricted and he didn't know if he might cry or vomit. Even though he never complained to her aloud, he felt pathetic. *She* suffered real pain, but he couldn't even think about it without feeling ill.

"I don't think this is going to be your last Christmas. You'll have so many more Christmases you'll be bored of it by the end. You'll be wrapping presents for your great-grandchildren someday."

"Go away, David."

"I'm sorry. That was the wrong thing to say. But I believe it."

"Yeah well, you're an idiot. And you can't accept me dying. I understand that, but it doesn't change anything. I'm not afraid of dying, David. I just don't want to make it any harder than it has to be, okay? I feel better if I accept it, instead of constantly lying to myself like you do. If that works for you, fine. But it doesn't work for me. So just respect my wishes."

David's throat had stiffened, so he chose not to respond. He laid his hand on her cheek, his fingers stroking her bald head. She squeezed his hand back, and he left.

CHAPTER FIVE

David tossed his muddy work boots onto the balcony of their apartment. Over the past few weeks, he hadn't been home as much as he would have liked, but he had a good reason. From dawn until after dark, he supervised the construction of their new home. Despite their cramped quarters, no one wanted to move twice in the space of a few months, so they stayed in the apartment until they finished the house. So David wasted no time. Within a week, he had worked with an architect to design their dream home. And now construction had begun.

David closed the sliding door and grabbed a plate of stir-fry that had gone cold on the stove. He sat in the living room where his kids messed with their various new electronic devices. He could smell the fresh scent of plastic and Styrofoam packaging.

"Okay, you know the drill. You have to tell me one thing about your day," David said. "Emmy, do you want to go first?"

"I don't know why I have to play this game," Emmy said from her spot where she lay on the dull carpet looking at her phone. "I've been talking since I got home. You just haven't been here to hear any of it."

"You have to play because he's trying to train you to tell him *only one* thing about your day," Patrick said.

"That's not true, Emmy," David said.

"Okay, my one thing is… Aiden H. should not wear skinny jeans," she proclaimed. "He looked horrible."

"Thank you, Emmy," David said. "Duly noted. Patrick?"

"The guidance counselor came to talk to our class today, talked about the stuff we'd need on our college application to stand out. And then I realized… I'm completely ordinary and uninteresting in every way."

"You know perfectly well that you're anything but ordinary," Amanda interjected from where she hid behind a laptop at the dining room table. Amanda had turned shopping for furniture and picking out tile into a full-time job, and had various samples and catalogs from the hardware store splayed across the table. "You're just ordinary by Mundane standards.

"Thanks, Mom. That's very helpful."

"Evangeline?" David prompted.

"Force equals mass times acceleration," she said. Evangeline was the only person in the family not permanently attached to two or three electronic devices. She sat cross-legged on the floor, surrounded by papers and books.

"You're just reading from your homework," Emmy said.

"It works for me," David said. "Thank you, Evangeline. Xavier?"

Xavier didn't respond and continued to stare at a commercial for breakfast cereal playing on the television.

"Xavier?" David repeated.

"What?" he asked.

"Just tell him the sky was blue today so we can all go on with our lives," Emmy said.

"Oh," he said. He squinted at the ceiling as if the events of the day appeared as distant as the constellations. "I saw a Tesla Roadster," Xavier said. "Brand new. Still with dealer plates.

Silver."

"That's pretty cool," David said.

"I think I saw that too," Patrick said. "When I went out to lunch. Where did you see it?"

"The middle school," Xavier said. "When we picked up Eve."

"Some rich person must have gotten lost," David said.

"Yeah, like we did," Emmy said. "What kind of millionaires live in crappy apartments?"

"It won't be much longer," David said.

While Amanda showered David lay in bed with his laptop, browsing through possible faucets and showerheads. He could work on their new house for every waking moment and not get bored.

Then he scrolled through e-mails from various subcontractors and deleted the intermixed spam. His cursor hovered over an email from Peter Sherman, Attorney at Law. He almost deleted it with the spam. He had gotten his money, and couldn't imagine what else this man would want.

Dear Mr. Vandergraff,

I have an important message from Ms. Rachel Colter. I can share this message with you for an additional fee of $1000. Upon receipt of the funds via wire transfer, I will send the message immediately.

Regards,

Peter Sherman

p.sherman@rothandmorganestatelaw.com

"Son of a bitch," David shouted at the screen. "You dirty, rotten, disgusting, bastard."

Amanda opened the bathroom door. "What are you yelling about?"

David turned the laptop screen toward her and placed it on the bed for her to read.

"That nasty little creep," Amanda said. "It's people like him who give dark wizards a bad name," she said, applying lotion to her hands. She used to buy that pricey lotion before they lost their money, and the flowery smell transported him back in time.

David could think of lots of things dark wizards did to give them "a bad name" much worse than swindling, but he agreed this was particularly weasel-ish

"I'm just going to ignore it," David said.

"Why don't you just negotiate him down?" Amanda asked.

"No, I'm not paying anything."

"You don't want to know what she said?"

"If there was an important message, he should have given it to me when I flew to New York to meet with him. It's not like he forgot. He didn't strike me as the absent-minded type."

"I agree he's trying to milk extra cash out of you. But that doesn't mean the message isn't real. This has always seemed too good to be true. I know something else is going on with this inheritance, and I want to know what it is."

"You want me to give him money just to send me a message he should have given me anyway?"

"Please."

The next morning, David did as Amanda asked. He called and negotiated down to $250, about half an hour of a lawyer's fee. He wondered if Zander had also gotten a message and what he had paid for it. That poor kid thirsted for information. Mr. Sherman could have gotten him to pay much more.

Mr. Sherman sent him a .pdf file. David opened the file and saw a scanned image of what looked like a word scribbled onto a cocktail napkin.

Sacrifice.

"Oh come on. Is that really it?" Amanda said. "That doesn't even look like a woman's handwriting."

"Well, it looks like I was swindled," David said, although the word felt heavy in his brain. Those nine letters danced in his stomach, making him feel sick. "I guess I'm just like Jack with his magic beans," David said with a weak laugh, trying to ignore the darkness creeping into his gut.

"Jack's beans *did* grow into a beanstalk," Amanda said.

"So, the moral of the story is 'buy magic beans'?"

Amanda laughed, but her laugh didn't sound convincing either. She ran her finger over the words on the screen like how she might stroke a baby's head.

Emmy winced as she heard crunching. She put her pillow over her face, but could still hear the horrible crunching sound of Evangeline's lizard crushing cricket bodies in its jaw. For Christmas, Evangeline had asked their parents for only one thing… a bearded dragon, which she named Annabel Lee, after some Edgar Allan Poe poem. Emmy would miss Evangeline when they got their own rooms, but she would not miss the damn lizard that made their whole room smell like lizard pee.

She hated the lizard and watching it eat live crickets, but she had grown used to it. But something felt odd to her this time. So she took away the pillow and looked over at the terrarium. She felt cold, as if something watched her. Something so dark she could hardly breathe. But she only saw her sister.

Evangeline had her hands cupped in front her, like she was praying, but Emmy guessed she held one of the crickets. However, she didn't know why Evangeline had closed her eyes with such reverence, as if she had kneeled to pray at the altar after communion.

"What are you doing?" Emmy asked.

Evangeline didn't open her eyes. "Practicing," she said.

Then, she opened her cupped hands and opened her eyes to look inside. She laid an unmoving cricket on the table. She examined it, poked it with one finger, and then smiled.

Emmy felt the cold feeling return. Her stomach lurched as if she had reached the plummet on a roller coaster.

Evangeline looked up at Emmy and smiled.

For once in her life, Emmy didn't want to say anything. She wished she hadn't seen it, although Evangeline knew she saw. Perhaps she had intended to demonstrate her nifty little skill.

Evangeline took two more crickets out of her box and handed one to the lizard and put the other one back in her own cupped hands as she had before.

"Don't," Emmy said.

The gross little creatures were doomed to death anyway. That's why she had bought them at the weirdo pet store. But that didn't stop it from seeming so… so wrong.

Evangeline did as Emmy asked and put the cricket back on the table, where it leapt at the wall and fell behind the bed.

Emmy flinched. "Great. Now that damn thing will keep me up all night."

"You were the one who asked me not to kill it."

Emmy swallowed hard. "How long have you been able to do that?"

Evangeline looked as if she couldn't stop herself from smiling. She *had* wanted to show off for Emmy.

"Maybe always," Evangeline said. "But I didn't know how." She paused. "If you don't like it, I don't have to do it in front of you."

"Have you done this before? Like… on anything bigger?"

"You mean like, a person?"

"Well… no… have you done it to a person?"

"No. But I think I could. I saw it once."

"You saw what?"

"Life in a person. I could just reach in and snuff it out like pinching out a candle. But, with a person it's harder. I need to practice with small things first."

"First? Who are you planning to kill?"

She shrugged as if Emmy had asked her what she wanted to eat for dinner. "I don't know," she said. "Caroline maybe. Or, anyone who tries to hurt me. If I got good at it, you know, it would be easy. If anyone got close to me I could just kill them if I wanted to. No one could hurt me, or you. Or anybody I cared about."

Emmy didn't argue. She had a point. And after everything she had experienced, Emmy could imagine why Evangeline thought she needed the power to kill someone with a touch.

But, it felt so damn cold in that room. And, she'd only killed a cricket.

CHAPTER SIX

Samantha wrapped a baby blanket around her head like a burka and huddled inside a Little League dugout. She had taken the blanket from the donations closet of the last shelter where she had stayed. A pinkish gray—once true pink—blanket with lambs. It reminded Samantha of her mother, but she didn't know why. Perhaps her mother had once wrapped her in a similar blanket.

She rested her head on the wall of the dugout and closed her eyes. She should try to find food, but she just wanted to rest. Finding an enclosed place to sleep had become a luxury. She didn't like begging. She hated feeling on display like that. Vulnerable. She'd rather be hungry. Besides she had found a new kind of hungry—a hunger that felt more like nausea and pain. She knew she needed food, but it didn't sound appealing.

She had experienced hunger before. When her parents started fading away, she often went without food, and no money in the bank account to buy any. But if she got too hungry, she would go to the Vandergraff's house. They always had food. She had already tried this on a cold and rainy day when she would have done anything for a warm, dry bed. She tried calling Emmy and then Patrick. But she had either remembered their numbers wrong, or they had been disconnected. Her parents' old friends would take her in, or at least give her a meal, but she didn't remember their phone numbers or their addresses. She only remembered useless things like the ugly frog statue her mom's friend had in her yard. Not the street they lived on. Houston seemed impossibly far away anyway.

She could go back to the shelter, but then again, it meant people would look at her and talk to her. She wanted privacy. She wanted to rest.

She heard the swing of the gate to the baseball field and her eyes shot open. She tugged her blanket tighter, wishing for a real invisibility cloak. If she stayed quiet, they might not notice her. Anyone might open that gate. Maybe afternoon practice had started. Or a maintenance worker needed to work on the field.

A man appeared in the entrance of the dugout. He walked directly to where she hid, which could only mean he had come for her specifically. She could tell he was a wizard, which could explain why he found her so quickly and easily. Who knows, maybe had had set up some magical snare to trap wandering witches here. She sat in a perfect cage with him blocking the only entrance. Instead of fear, she felt frustrated. She only wanted to sleep.

She couldn't immediately tell what kind of wizard he was, which probably meant an equinox wizard. Solstice wizards—winter and summer—blared their identity with as much subtlety as Las Vegas. Equinox wizards—fall and spring—had more complexity.

He dropped a white fast-food bag on the bench and fished in his pocket. Intricate tattoos covered his forearms and he had a pipe stuck in the back pocket of jeans worn from true wear, not the "distressed" jeans you buy in the store.

He pulled a small white piece of paper out of his pocket. It looked like a receipt from a convenience store. He looked down at something scrawled on the receipt and said, "Samantha Carthage?"

Samantha didn't reply. Did he have her name written on that receipt? She stayed still and silent, as if he might go away if she didn't move.

"Are you hungry?" he asked.

Samantha continued to stay still as a rabbit trying to hide from a fox.

He handed the white bag to her as if he also considered her a skittish little rabbit. He approached her slowly, put the bag on the bench next to her, and backed away, showing her his hands as he did so.

Samantha grimaced at the bag. Burger King. "I don't eat meat," she said.

"Okay, no problem," he said. He pulled the burger out of the bag, unwrapped it, and opened the bun to let the patty fall to the dirt in a splash of mayonnaise and lettuce. He put the bun back together, wrapped it in its foil, and handed it back to her.

She reached into the bag and selected a single fry. As soon as the grease hit her lips, she dug in for another handful and ate like an animal, licking the salt and grease off her fingers.

"You are Samantha Carthage, right?" the man asked again. He sat next to her now, but left a wide breadth between them.

"How do you know my name?"

"I know the names of all the wizards in my area," he said. "I'm Carlos."

Samantha didn't believe in french fry fairies who showed up when she got hungry and wanted nothing in return. She bit into the now mayonnaise and lettuce sandwich, the food simultaneously making her feel stronger and like she needed to throw up.

Carlos pulled the pipe out of his back pocket and filled it with some purple herbs she didn't recognize. He lit the pipe and the smoke smelled like a combination of cloves and burning hair. He held the pipe out to her in offering, but she crinkled her nose and shook her head.

"Smart girl," he said. He puffed on his pipe waiting for her to finish eating. She could see his tattoos closer now, and saw he had intricate tree branches covering each arm with words interwoven into braches. On his left arm, Samantha found the words, "Exodus 20:5," hiding in the brambles. On his right, he had the names, "Isabella," and "Elena." He must have seen her looking, because he said, "I have a baby sister about your age." He pointed to "Elena." "She likes meat though. Refused to eat anything *but* cheeseburgers from ages five through seven."

"I know what you're doing. You're telling me about your little sister so you'll seem less threatening. Just tell me what you want."

"You're clever. And bold. I didn't know that about you. Or… perhaps you've recently changed."

"You don't know anything about me," she said. Not as a comeback, a statement of fact.

"Do you know what I am?"

"Fall, I think."

"Yes, but more than that. I'm an oracle. I know about lots of things."

Samantha smirked. "So, you want to tell me my future? I don't care about my future." She hadn't considered the truth of the statement until she said it aloud. She didn't plan to kill herself, but she didn't care what happened next. She had lost everyone she had ever cared about. She lived moment to moment, caring only about food and safe places to sleep because biology required her to care about those things. The future didn't exist at all.

"Maybe not," Carlos said. "But there are some things you care very much about, even if they are recently passed."

"If you're trying to sell me a prophecy, you can probably tell I don't have any money."

"I don't care about money."

"What do you care about?"

"Lots of things," he said.

Samantha had removed the blanket from her head and now squeezed it in a tight ball in her hand.

"I can tell you about Imogene Grey."

Samantha had expected that, but hearing her name hit her like an electric shock, both painful and exhilarating. She loved hearing her name on someone else's lips. Someone in the world knew her name and remembered her.

"You're a little late, don't you think? I don't need any prophecies about Imogene. If you can see the future, why didn't you show up six weeks ago? You could have told us not to go into the Greenbelt that day. You. Are. Too. Late."

He tapped the ashes out his pipe. "That wouldn't have done you any good, I'm afraid."

"What do you mean?"

"Because Imogene was murdered. With a killing curse. A very powerful one. Staying home may have kept her alive slightly longer, but with a curse like that..." He whistled. "It would catch her, more sooner than later."

Samantha hung on his every word. She didn't want to care what this man had to say, but it felt so true. No one runs in front of an eighteen-wheeler for no reason. Samantha had thought perhaps Imogene's dangerous resurrection spell had gone wrong somehow, that death needed the final say, one way or another. But Carlos's words felt so true. Someone had *taken* Imogene from her. Ripped her from the world. Not by an accident of magic, but as a conscious, destructive act. That's how it felt.

"Who? Why?"

"I can't read events like reading a book, because the words are always moving around. And usually it's not words at all, but pictures. Or sometimes less than pictures, just the flowing of magical energies that are invisible to almost everyone else."

"You're saying you don't know?"

"I know where the spell originated. A violent, powerful spell of that magnitude is impossible not to notice. I know where it came from, but not exactly who. And I can't tell you why. I can only point you in the right direction."

"Where?"

"Does the name Vandergraff mean anything to you?"

Samantha had decided Carlos wouldn't hurt her, but she definitely did not like him. So damn smug. He had this half-smile as if he knew everything that had ever happened and everything that would ever happen and found it all fucking hilarious. He knew the name Vandergraff meant something to her, and enjoyed watching her reaction.

Samantha scrunched her nose at him. "You're saying a Vandergraff killed Imogene?" she asked flatly. "Which one? You know what, it doesn't matter. None of them would have any reason to kill Imogene. I doubt any of them even know she exists. You're just messing with me."

"You don't believe me?"

"I don't know."

"Like I told you, it's messy. I know the spell came from them, but that's all I know."

"So, are you just a really bad oracle then?"

He smiled, more of a sinister Cheshire cat look than anything pleasant. "I'm one of the best in the world," he said. "I'm an artist of fate. A true masterpiece is greater than the artist. Even the man with the brush can only see the strokes one at a time."

"Well, if you think you're getting any money, or anything else out of me, you can't even read what's right in front of you."

"I don't want anything."

"So, you just go around giving away free information and cheeseburgers to people out of the goodness of your heart? Nobody does that. Everybody wants something in return."

"Now, Samantha, you know that's not true. Every day, all across the world, people do good things and ask nothing in return. Sure, perhaps they do good deeds to please their God or so they hate themselves a little less, but for nothing as foul and common as money."

"Then why are you doing it? To please your God or because you hate yourself?"

"I want to do right by the world."

Samantha wiped grease off her fingers with a napkin. Even with food in her belly, she felt lightheaded, but maybe less because of hunger and more because of what he had said.

"When a wizard disrupts the balance with something as wretched as a killing spell, it's always my concern. I want to return the balance, that is all. I do want something from you, but it's nothing you need to worry about. I simply want you do continue on the course of your life. Doing what you would normally do."

"You mean I'm one of the strokes of your brush."

He half-smiled again. "It doesn't matter what I want. Imogene didn't deserve to die as she did. Justice is another word for balance. And we want the same thing."

He pulled his wallet out of his pocket and pulled out two crisp hundred dollar bills and pressed them into Samantha's hand.

"I'm afraid I can't afford a plane ticket, but this should be more than enough for bus fare and food so you don't starve before you get there. There is a Motel 6 by the Greyhound station. It's not nice, but it's safe. Lots of families. Stay there tonight, and leave in the morning."

"You want me to go to Houston?"

"No, *you* want to go to Houston."

"I don't know where they live now."

"Either you'll find them, or they'll find you. I'm not worried about that."

Carlos got up. "See ya," he said and headed out of the dugout. At the last moment, he turned around and looked her in the eye. "You'll be okay, you know. Maybe not right away, but you'll be all right. You're going to live a good life, Samantha."

She didn't want him to know how much it meant to her, so she waited until he had left before she let the tears fall. Again his words felt so true, magically so, as if they imprinted themselves onto time. And for the first time since Imogene died, she noticed now much she wanted his words to be true.

CHAPTER SEVEN

After the workers had left for the day, David watched the sun set over the newly erupted field of bluebonnets behind their new home. He would spend the rest of his life here. Here he would grow old with Amanda. His grandkids would visit. He couldn't imagine anything better.

He had never felt happier in his entire life. This seemed strange to him. Before his marriage fell apart and before he learned the truth about what happened to Xavier and Evangeline, he had lived what seemed like an idyllic life. But a life full of holes and lies. His memories. His children. Always waiting for Amanda to learn about his affair, never knowing if she would still love him. But now, he had everything, in all its horrible truth. He had suffered for it, nearly lost it several times over, and that made the happiness so much stronger.

David stared back at the skeleton frame of his new home cast against the setting sun, cheerfully ticking off to-do items in his head. Thinking of who he would need to contact tomorrow, and what jobs he would have to oversee, when he heard the crackle of gravel. He shrugged involuntarily as a sudden, but a stabbing burst of fear crawled up his neck.

Despite the unexplained fear, he expected to see Patrick's car on the unfinished driveway. He didn't think Patrick and Xavier planned to come by after school today, but he could have forgotten.

He didn't see a car at all. The disturbed gravel sounded more like footsteps.

"Mr. Vandergraff?"

David swirled his head around. He had snuck up on him once again. Zander Colter. He should have sensed his presence by more than the sound of his feet on gravel. He should have *felt* him coming. How did he keep sneaking up on him? Zander stood by David's work truck, which now read "Texas Star Construction Management." He had left his name out of his new company name on purpose, but Zander found him anyway.

David could feel his adrenaline levels rising. He clenched his teeth together and swallowed.

"It's just me," Zander said, as if that would bring some comfort.

"What the fuck are you doing here?" David had noticed his prevalence of f-bombs increased in this boy's presence. "How did you find me?" He looked at the skeleton of his new home, wishing he could hide it from view.

Zander shrugged. "I know you didn't want me to come to your house where your kids are. So I came here instead. I waited until you were alone."

"Why?" David demanded. "I told you to stay away from my family."

"I have."

David advanced toward him. In the setting sun, he saw a glint of gold out of the corner of his eye. It reminded him of when he saw the Expedition glinting in the West Texas sun, and the fear he had felt then. Instead he saw Zander's car—a brand new silver Tesla Roadster. Why did that seem familiar?

David's mouth went dry. Xavier had seen a silver Tesla

Roadster parked outside the middle school. Patrick had seen it too.

"You're stalking my children," David said in a hissing whisper. "Why are you stalking my children?"

David didn't care to hear the answer. He felt cold, black magic cracking and splitting inside him.

"Not stalking," Zander held his hands up in surrender and backed away. "I'm just… that's what I'm here to talk to you about." Zander's black eyes widened, and David knew he must have looked as angry as he felt. "Hey…" he croaked. "I didn't do anything. I didn't talk to any of them. They didn't see me."

Despite having no formal training in either offensive or defensive magic, he knew a lot on instinct. He'd only experienced one magical attack, at least only one he could remember. But in the shadow of Zander's black eyes, that fight seemed weak in comparison. Thea Prescott, a petite summer witch trying to defend herself against an attack he didn't plan to make. And even then, she didn't want to hurt him at all. She *wanted* him to kill her.

Even with this flash of doubt, David didn't back down. Zander had backed up against David's truck, but that didn't stop David from getting within arms reach of him. The human part of David thought about punching him in the face, but David's instinct told him he should aim a magical attack at the heart.

David thrust his hand into Zander's chest with enough force he thought he might have broken some bones in his hand. But the attack had little to do with the hit. Zander looked stronger than David, and certainly younger. He could take him on physical strength.

David knew for a good attack, you didn't try to stifle the rage and fear as you would in most situations. You wanted to really feel it. To feel every single facet of your anger. To taste the anger in your mouth. To smell the adrenaline radiating off of you. He thought about Whitman Colter, and the things he had done to his kids. And he thought about all the things he feared Zander might do. And he let himself *really* feel it. He wanted to harm Zander, but he didn't anticipate how much bringing up this rage would hurt himself. His face felt hot and swollen as if he wanted to cry and vomit at the same time. And then he released all that rage through his hand and into Zander's body.

The rush of the magical attack left David stunned for a minute. His vision went white as if hit in the head, and he had a sudden feeling of complete disorientation. He couldn't tell the difference between the earth and the sky. But the feeling passed, and left him with only a tingling in his arms and an erratic, racing heartbeat.

And a body.

Zander had slid down the truck and now leaned against the wheel, completely still. Other than his complete stillness, he looked fine. No blood. No bruises.

A different fear raced through David now. He hadn't meant to kill him. The thought had never crossed his mind. For that moment in New York, when he thought Zander was his father, he did want to kill him. He knew he would have. But since he realized his stupid mistake, he knew he couldn't kill him. He wanted to intimidate him, scare him off. He didn't know what he had wanted to do. He had no plan. He just had rage.

With his heart vibrating in his rib cage, he kneeled next to Zander. He reached out to feel for a pulse, but then pulled his hand back. He didn't want to leave any more fingerprints or DNA than he had to. As soon as that thought sprung into his mind, the reality of what he had done intensified, like a cold ball of ice building behind his skull.

He positioned the back of his hand in front of Zander's mouth to feel for breath. When he didn't feel anything, he no longer cared about leaving evidence and clutched him by the shoulders and shook him. Zander did nothing but slump onto the clay earth. He touched his wrists looking for a pulse, and when he found nothing, he went straight to the source, pressing his hand against Zander's heart as he had when he had attacked. But this time he willed it to beat. He prayed to God and simultaneously tried to summon his own magic to get it moving. But as soon as he tried, he knew his magic didn't work that way. It reminded him of trying to melt ice with more ice.

"No," he screamed at Zander, as if he could yell at him back to life, and he slapped him in the face.

In the midst of his panic, he had a rational thought. A human man could not kill another human man by placing his hand on his chest. Maybe Zander had a heart condition. Or asthma and had stopped breathing.

David closed his eyes and tried to remember the papers he had seen Patrick with last summer. Patrick had trained as a lifeguard, and unlike David, knew CPR. David vaguely remembered a CPR class he took after they had Jude. He tried not to over think it, and went to work. He pressed into Zander's chest with both hands, unsure of how hard to push. After a few tries, he pushed harder, and stopped to pinch his nose shut and blow in his mouth as he'd seen in movies.

"Please come back," he said. "Please. Come on."

He continued for a long time, his actions becoming more and more forceful until he heard Zander's ribs crack under his compressions.

The sound of the crack seemed like the final blow. David pulled out his phone to call 9-1-1 and saw the time. 6:32 p.m. How much time had passed since Zander had died? The last workers left at six, and he appeared a few minutes after. So, thirty minutes? At least twenty minutes? He should have called 9-1-1 right away. Why hadn't he? Because he didn't want to get caught? Because he thought he could take it back? So foolish. David knew he had murdered this man, but no Mundane court could convict him. What would the coroner call the cause of death? From a Mundane perspective, David only gave him a good shove in the chest.

If the paramedics came, they would cart him off to the morgue. He had no family. No one to claim him. The coroner would probably say he had some heart defect that caused it to stop beating for no reason and he'd end up in some unmarked government grave.

No matter what David did now, Zander would remain dead. Perhaps some wizards could will a man back to life, but not David. He couldn't will him back to life, so he closed his eyes and focused on finding another answer. Rachel's image popped into his head. Rachel Colter. Zander's aunt. If she had foreseen this, she might have planned a way to stop it, to save her only kin. David thought about his own unhelpful message, and wondered if Rachel had left one for Zander too.

David fished around in Zander's pockets, and sure enough, he carried it around with him too—the scanned image of a few words.

Then David heard the faintest sigh, and then a cough.

"Oh thank God," David said. David had nothing to do with Zander coming back to life after so long. He had no one to thank *but* God.

Despite hating him enough to take his life moments ago, he gathered Zander up in his arms like his own child. He coughed again and groaned, clutching his chest, and David remembered he had broken his rib. Zander came to his senses, and scuttled away from David like a limping spider, wheezing as we went, and cowered when David reached out to him again.

"It's okay. I'm sorry," David said. "I'm not going to hurt you… I mean I'm not going to hurt you again. You need to go to the hospital. I'll take you."

Zander shook his head and drug himself away, grass stains and dirt caking his jeans.

"It was an accident," David said. He had wanted to attack him, to hurt him. But he hadn't wanted to kill him. Although, now he supposed he hadn't. Clearly he hadn't. "Please, let me help you."

"Don't touch me," Zander said. David felt relieved to hear a real sentence come out of his mouth, despite how raspy it sounded. He had to admit, the word "zombie" had surfaced in his mind. Back from the dead maybe, but he could talk.

"Okay, no problem," David said, holding his hands up in surrender as Zander had before he attacked him. "If you don't want me to drive you, I'll just call an ambulance."

"No," Zander said. He sat now, hunched over with his hand on his chest. "No hospitals. No doctors."

"Why not?"

"No doctors," he wheezed again. "I'm fine. Leave me alone."

"I can't do that." His words sounded distant and quiet as if they hadn't come from him. "I can't let you leave."

CHAPTER EIGHT

Samantha used Carlos' money to get on a bus, but not to Houston. At least not right away. She went to a Chinese Buffet and ate until she felt sick. Then she bought a bag of lemon chocolate truffles at the CVS. She couldn't eat anymore now, but she had spent a lot of time on the streets thinking about chocolate. Beds, showers, heaters, and chocolate. With her chocolate in hand, she checked into a hotel, showered, and fell asleep immediately among the fresh, clean sheets.

The next morning, she headed to the Home Depot. As expected, the garden center burst with green ready for spring planting. People streamed in and out, wheeling large carts of soil and potted plants. She wished she could spend hours there, just smelling everything. The smell of fresh soil and pungent herbs made her think of her mom. She used to smell like that all spring. Samantha selected one robust looking rosemary plant and headed back to the bus stop.

She let the plant sit on her lap as she rode. The smell of the rosemary invaded her senses and made her eyes water. Rosemary was Samantha's middle name. Her mother had named her for an evergreen because they survived even the coldest, darkest winters. They thrived in eternal greenness, unbothered by snow and ice.

She didn't understand how she could love and hate her parents so much at the same time. Their weakness had killed them. They fell victim to an insatiable need for pleasure. They weren't evergreens at all. They wanted springtime to last all year, and they died for it. So stupid. So weak. But she missed them so much.

Every time she tried to sleep, she could hear her mother singing, "This little light of mine." She sang it to Samantha every night for all of her childhood. Now Samantha repeated it as a prayer in her own head every night. This little light of mine. I'm going to let it shine. Let it shine. Let it shine. Let it shine.

She had made a mistake thinking of the song while smelling rosemary. She now wept quietly in the middle of the bus full of people. Fortunately, people preferred to look away from her and pretend she didn't exist. She preferred it that way too.

She got off the bus, clutching her rosemary plant and walked through the New Orleans neighborhood where she had lived with her aunt until Samantha didn't interest her anymore and she boarded a plane for India or somewhere. Samantha's aunt had already had her parents cremated before she arrived. She never saw their bodies. Never got closure. Just her aunt's assurances that "their earthly vessels had perished but they still flourished in eternal springtime."

Her aunt had hosted a small funeral when Samantha arrived, which seemed mostly like an excuse to drink wine. The grown-ups barely talked about her parents until they had the actual ceremony. Then they mixed the ashes with the earth and planted evergreens. Samantha had chosen rosemary. One plant for each of her parents. No one else seemed interested in the ritual and they left Samantha to do the planting. She had made a point to mix the soil well so her parents' ashes would mix too. They would have wanted that. Of all their faults, a lack of love wasn't one of them. They loved each other completely and they would have wanted to be together in death. Finally no space between them. No difference between one and the other. In death they got it. As dirt, you couldn't tell where one ended and the other began.

Someone else had probably moved into her aunt's house, but Samantha didn't care. The rosemary plants in the backyard represented her parents, and she would visit them whenever she pleased. She marched through the backyard gate as if she owned the home and no one stopped her. The overgrown yard might have meant no one new had moved in yet. The St. Augustine crowded around the lonely rosemary bushes, swallowing them. But Samantha knew when winter came, the lush grass would retreat and the only the rosemary would stand tall.

Samantha didn't have Imogene's ashes. They had pumped Imogene's remains full of chemicals and left her rot in some random government cemetery. A foul end for a spring witch. But the real Imogene had long since left her body and it didn't matter where that rotting flesh resided. Imogene resided everywhere and nowhere at once. She didn't need her ashes to call her spirit.

She should have also bought a garden spade at Home Depot. But it felt good to get her hands in the dirt. It felt real. She loved the smell of the dirt and the grass. She broke a sweat pulling out the stubborn grass to expose a patch of soil. But the soil itself felt warm and supple, and teemed with earthworms. She smiled, remembering how her mother always talked to the earthworms and thanked them for their service to the soil.

After she placed the plant and refilled the soil, she spoke aloud the words from Shakespeare, "There's rosemary, that's for remembrance; pray you, love, remember." Her aunt had used that same quote during the funeral, but it fell flat now. She knew she should speak aloud to Imogene. Her own words, not something recited from a standard spring funeral ceremony, but she felt so drained, so empty. She knew if she spoke from the heart, she would cry, and she was so tired of crying.

She looked at the small plant among the thick St. Augustine and thought it looked underwhelming. Imogene deserved so much more. She had thought this would give her some closure, but she only felt angrier. The fragrance of rosemary had seeped into her hands and taunted her now.

Dirt caked her nails and her hands burned with tiny scrapes from her effort. Her hands felt cold and hot at the same time. She didn't know if her hands burned from digging through the soil, or if magic accumulated there.

She kneeled next to her freshly planted rosemary again and placed her hands at the base. She felt the tingling, burning sensation transfer from her fingers into the plant. The leaves lengthened and grew greener. And the scent increased too. The rich rosemary fragrance made her eyes burn. She thought she might gag.

Then delicate purple flowers erupted from the branches. The flowers looked a bit too small and too pale. Proper spring wizards didn't mess with the life cycle of plants. "Just because you can, doesn't mean you should," her mother used to say. "The flowers know when to open. You don't know better." If you caused flowers to bloom at the wrong time or a plant to grow too fast, it would struggle and suffer. Nature knows better.

But she didn't care much about life cycles at the moment, and she continued on to her mother and father's plants and did the same. By the last plant, her mother's, she had gotten the hang of it, and the flowers bloomed larger and a deep purple. She liked the way the purple stood out among the green lawn, but she regretted using her magic in this way. This would cause these plants to struggle and possibly die—a foul memorial. But she needed somewhere for the tingling magic in her hands to go.

The show of flowers only provided brief relief. As the backyard gate swung shut behind her, she felt the burning in her fingers again. She didn't want to make flowers. She wanted to spill fire from her hands. She wanted everything to burn. That's why she had manipulated the plants. She didn't want pretty purple flowers, she wanted death. She wanted to hurt the plants. To manipulate them. Control them.

She laughed at herself a bit. Spring wizards were so weak. She wanted to kill something and she couldn't do better than making plants flower too early and disrupt their life cycle and growth. If she wanted justice, she would need a killer.

CHAPTER NINE

avid woke with Amanda clutching his arm. Her pose
appeared strangely defensive against a sleeping man.
"Are you okay?" she asked, her voice much more
tender than her clutch implied.

"What?"

"You said your brother's name, and then you rolled over
and smacked me."

"Oh… sorry. James keeps flicking pennies at me while I
sleep."

Amanda looked around the room. "You mean in a dream?"

"Well, he's dead Amanda."

"I know… that's not what I mean."

"He used to mess with me while I slept. Stick things in my
ears. Draw on my face. Stuff like that. I keep dreaming he's still
doing it."

David sat up and looked at the bedside clock. He had barely
slept that night and hadn't planned on sleeping at all. He only
wanted to wait for his alarm clock to sound so he could leave
again. He didn't want to leave the kid alone in the shed all night,
but he didn't want to disappear in the middle of the night either.

He didn't want to involve Amanda in what had turned into several felonies and he didn't want to lie. Lying about where he went at night reeked of an affair, and he didn't want her to even consider it.

"I need to go." He turned to her and kissed her on the cheek. "Are you okay making sure the kids get to school?"

"It's before 7 a.m., David, where are you going?"

"The job site. Got people coming at eight and I need to get ready for them."

David sped all the way to the job site. He had placed an entrapment spell on Zander. He had once tried it once on a dog in the neighborhood that kept getting out of his yard and attacking other dogs. The spell appeared humane and effective. The dog simply forgot how to get around the fence. But Zander had a lot more intelligence than a dog.

David unlocked the tool shed and found Zander where he left him. The events of the night before seemed so strange and distant he thought he might have imagined them. But unfortunately, he hadn't. Zander leaned against the side of the shed and sat up straight when David came in. He blinked and held up his hand to block the stream of morning light that had flooded the dark shed.

David handed him a bottle of water, a granola bar, and a bag of frozen corn.

Zander looked at the corn, and then back at David—his hands shaking. Perhaps the bag of frozen corn made David appear even more psycho.

"It's for your rib. I couldn't find an ice pack."

Zander gingerly put the corn on his side, watching David, like he waited for him to strike.

"There's a Porta-Potty outside if you want to go to the bathroom."

Zander took a small sip of water and winced, clutching his broken rib. "What did I do wrong?" he asked.

The question made David's stomach drop. Again he sounded so young when he asked, like a punished child. Also, David didn't know how to answer the question.

"I can't let you leave until I know you'll stay away from my children."

"I'll try."

"You'll *try?*" David kicked some spare tools in Zander's direction and Zander flinched. David flinched too, sickened at himself. This all felt so wrong. Zander's dark eyes had reddened, either from crying all night or the dust in the shed.

"Why don't you fight back?" David asked. "Why did you just let me attack you last night? There was no counterattack at all, at least not that I felt. Why did you just me do that to you?"

"I don't understand what you did to me," he stammered. "When you came at me… I wasn't worried at first. I mean, you didn't have a weapon. And I thought I could take you if it came to blows. I didn't see how you could hurt me… until I saw your eyes. I've never seen someone look like that. And then… it was just pain. The worst pain I can imagine. Not physical pain either… it was more like… fear. What did you do me?"

"I…" David trailed off. Once again, he felt like a complete fool. He had missed the most obvious thing in the world. Because of his appearance and his family, David had seen nothing but a powerful dark wizard when Zander walked into the room. But that didn't mean Zander knew what he was. Even wizards don't always tell their children the truth. And Zander said he had no family. If Mundanes had raised him, he didn't have a clue.

David looked at the boy, despite his size, looking much smaller, huddled in the corner, cowering away from David. In Starbucks, the *question* had reminded him of Crystal. He wanted to know *more*. Like Crystal, part of him knew something was different about him, but he didn't know what. And like Crystal, he sensed David had the answer. David had never told her.

Zander's father Whitman had led her into the clutches of dark magic.

"Did you take my message?" Zander asked. "The one from my aunt?"

David had forgotten all about it, but he had taken the message. David pulled the crumpled paper out of his back pocket and opened it without offering it to Zander.

Save his baby girl.

David's one-word message had alarmed him… but these four words sucked all the moisture out of his body. He thought he could hear his brain contract.

"What does this mean?" David asked. He threw the paper in Zander's direction and it fluttered down among the sawdust hanging in the air. "What does it mean?" he shouted again.

"I don't know," Zander said. "But it's why I'm here. I thought maybe the 'him' was you. I thought you needed my help."

"Well… you're wrong. I don't need your help. And I don't need you anywhere near my daughters, *especially* not Evangeline. She doesn't need saving, and if she did, *you* would not be the one to save her. *You* should never be within fifty miles of her."

David heard a loud clang on the outside of the shed. His heart rate spiked. He had canceled all the work for the day.

"Don't speak. Don't move," David said to Zander. He drew magic out of himself and into the words to make it a spell. He didn't know if it had worked, but Zander didn't budge.

David opened the door to the tool shed and something small and shiny hit him in the face. David looked down to see a shiny copper penny gleaming in the dust and Patrick staring at him.

"Did you just throw a penny at me?" David asked.

"I thought you were dead or something," Patrick said. "I tried to use a penny to open the lock, but then I realized the door wasn't even locked, it was just stuck somehow. And you didn't hear me when I called your name."

David felt a bit impressed with his own handiwork at "sealing" the shed. He kneeled down to pick up the penny and watched it gleam in his palm.

"What the hell are you doing and why didn't you answer me when I called your name?"

"You're supposed to be in school."

"School hasn't started yet. I've still got about forty-five minutes."

"So what are you doing here?"

"I came here to tell you to stop doing whatever you're doing. If you continue on this path, you will create an unfavorable turn in fate."

"Are you being serious right now?"

"Who is in that shed with you?"

"No one."

"There is powerful magic in that shed, and it's not yours. Not even close. If it's not a person, it's some other magical object. But I assume it's a person, because it drove here." He pointed to the Tesla, now dimmer from a night of dust from the worksite. "And if I couldn't already tell that, now I'm certain because you worked so hard to keep people out. Who the hell is in that shed?"

"Patrick… I need you to trust me. I don't want you involved. Please leave."

"No, I need you to trust *me*, and do what I say."

"*Excuse* me?"

"I'm not leaving. Punish me if you want, but I'm not leaving until you tell me."

David rubbed his eyes, itchy from the pollen and dust in the air. Patrick acted like a different person, older and more self-assured.

"You recognize the car?" David asked.

"I've seen it around."

David told him about who owned the car and about how he had followed Patrick and the others. Patrick listened with his mouth in a hard line.

"Xavier said he saw the car parked at the middle school," Patrick said. "Evangeline is the only one of us who goes to the middle school. He was watching her." Patrick paused. "You should have told us. I could have helped you hunt him down. Although it looks like you didn't need any help."

"I don't want you involved, Patrick."

"We're a family. We're in this together. That's what families do."

"Lock people in sheds?" David asked.

"If necessary."

"I appreciate that but… I don't want your help with this."

"Do you think we should kill him?"

David's stomach lurched as he had a powerful déjà vu moment to a similar moment in time. Jude had made the exact same offer—to kill Whitman Colter because David could not.

He had had the same thought himself—if Zander wouldn't stay away from Evangeline, he would have to die… for good this time—but as soon as he heard the words on his son's lips, he heard the darkness in them.

"No," David said. "You were right the first time. I'm going down the wrong path. I'm going to let him leave. Okay?"

Patrick stared at him, then looked at the shed. "Can I talk to him?"

"No."

"I just want to see what he looks like. That way I can watch out for him. You're not there to watch out for everybody at school. That's my job."

"That's not your responsibility either."

"Sure it is."

David looked down at the penny in his hand and thought about how protective he had felt of his younger brother, and how he had failed to protect him so many times over. "Okay. I guess it wouldn't hurt for you to see him."

David pushed the shed door back open and gestured for Patrick to go in and he followed behind him. Zander stood now, although stooped from his broken rib. It appears he had gotten up to retrieve his message, because he held it in his hands, the paper now smudged with grease from landing on some tools.

"This is Zander Colter," David said.

Patrick stared at him for a long time.

"Patrick?" David asked.

"What?"

"You've been staring at him for almost a full minute without saying anything."

"Have I?"

"Something wrong?"

Patrick finally looked at David. "Does anyone else know he's here?"

"No. Why?"

"People know I'm here," Zander added. "They will notice if I disappear. They'll come looking for me."

Zander's shaky voice gave away his lie. Zander had already told David he had no one and nowhere to go. Already a ghost.

"I've done it before and it worked really well. I can do it again. I can send him away."

"Like you did with Jude and Caroline."

"Yes."

The penny in David's hand suddenly burned hot. He dropped it on the floor of the shed, rubbed his hand on his jeans, and then picked it back up. "That's a really good idea," David said. The words on Zander's letter gnawed at his brain, but he ignored them. If Evangeline or Emmy needed saving, they had him for that.

Patrick moved toward Zander. Zander backed away and grabbed a wrench.

"Don't you dare," David said. The wrench flew out of Zander's hand and hit the side of the shed with a much louder clang than the penny.

"Please don't hurt me," Zander said.

"I'm not going to hurt you, I just need to touch you," Patrick said.

"What?" Zander asked.

"I got it," David said. David had gotten good at keeping Zander from escaping and he knew he could take it another step. Zander's knees buckled under him, and he cowered on all fours. He couldn't raise his head to look at them.

"Go ahead," David said. "He can't move."

CHAPTER TEN

"Yes, this is Amanda Vandergraff," Amanda yelled into the phone over Emmy's chatter. "Louisiana what? Emmy shh."

"Oh my God, Eve, your lizard just peed on the kitchen counter."

"She has a name," Evangeline said.

"Girls, shh. Evangeline, clean up that pee. And use disinfectant. No, that's dish soap. Emmy, help her."

"It's not *my* lizard."

"I'm sorry, what?" Amanda said into the phone. "Let me go somewhere quieter. Okay, go ahead. What did you say?"

"I'm from the LHRYP, the Louisiana Homeless and Runaway Youth Program." The man had a mild Spanish accent.

"Okay… how can I help you?"

"My name is Anthony. I'm a caseworker at the Healing House Shelter, and I'm calling about Samantha Carthage, do you know her?"

"Um… yes. What is this about?"

Emmy squealed from the kitchen.

"Hang on," Amanda said into the phone, and then covered

the mouthpiece with her hand. She raged back into the kitchen. "For the love of God, shut up! This is an important call. And Emmy, it's urine, not battery acid. Get over yourself."

"Is everything okay?" said the man on the other line, and Amanda realized she had taken her hand off the receiver for the "urine, not battery acid" line.

"Yes, I'm so sorry. Please continue."

"This is one of the numbers Samantha left. Is she available by chance? Or are you able to get a message to her?"

"She gave you my phone number?"

"Yes, ma'am."

"No, I haven't seen her in over a year. I'm sorry. Did you say you're from a homeless shelter? She was supposed to be with her aunt. Where is she now?"

"I'm afraid I don't know. She left the shelter two weeks ago. That's why I'm calling you now. If you hear from her, will you contact me?"

"Hang on, there is no way she gave you my number. It changed. We turned off our cell phones off for a while. When we got new service, we had new numbers."

"I don't know, ma'am. Maybe your old number forwards to your new one."

"I… I don't remember. I'll keep a look out for her. Can you do the same? Tell me if you find her?"

"Sure."

"Finally," Amanda said, as soon as David walked through the door.

He dropped his keys and wallet on the side table. "What do you mean 'finally'? It's 10 a.m. I'm usually not back until after dark."

"There is something I need to do today," Amanda said,

almost bouncing. She looked as if she could stay awake for days. "So you need to watch the kids. Patrick will take Xavier and Evangeline home with him as usual. But Emmy has play practice after school, so you'll have to pick her up from the high school at six thirty. And get dinner."

"Where are you going?"

"Just trust me. I support you on all *your* crazy ideas."

"No, you don't."

"Samantha is missing."

"Who?"

"*Who?* What's the matter with you? Samantha Carthage."

"I'm sorry… I remember her. I just… that came out of left field."

"Are you okay?" She squinted at him.

"Fine. Just tired. You know I slept like crap last night. Samantha is missing? Is she okay?"

"I don't know, David. She's *missing*. I didn't mess with your brain today, what's your excuse?"

"God. That's awful. Do the kids know?"

"No. I thought it would be best not to tell them. I don't want them to worry. I mean she's probably fine. She probably ran away. No big deal. I just… really want to find her. Like a magical impulse. I don't even want to go to sleep. I feel like I should leave right now."

David rubbed his eyes with his thumb and his forefinger. His head hurt. His full brain couldn't process any more. "Are you sure that's a good idea? To follow a magical impulse? I know I did… but it didn't work out very well."

"It could have worked out worse."

"Well… yeah."

"I'm going David. I'm not asking you if I *can* go. I'm going. This is not a discussion, it's just your notification."

"I don't want you to go." The statement came out as pathetic and tired as he felt. "What if something happens to you?"

"I'm going to be fine. It's not like that. I just think she needs help." She hugged him and leaned into his chest. "I know we've run into complicated spellwork, but most of the time spells like this are pretty simple. If you really want someone, you can call them."

"Why in the hell would she want you?" It came out meaner than he had wanted, but it was a good question. Even if she needed help, the mother of her rapist wasn't the best choice.

"I don't know, David. But I'm going to find out."

Amanda didn't excel at following random magical impulses as much as some of her family members. She didn't like going anywhere without entering an address into her GPS first. She didn't think she could find the hair salon she visited every other month or the post office closest to their house without GPS. She didn't think she could find anything without a mechanical voice telling her where to go.

With her jaw clenched, she stopped at a Starbucks in Baytown and sipped her espresso roast, waiting for a good idea. She considered which would embarrass her more—returning home after only a few hours and admit she had failed at magic or drive all the way to Louisiana, hoping for a sign of something, and then turn around and go all the way back home.

She stared out the window and watched the endless line of cars drum through the drive-through. Amanda always had mixed feelings about the spring, especially days like this. Midseventies with the sun at a perfect tilt, so the sunshine warmed you down to your core but didn't make you hot. Days like this always made her feel as if she should be doing something better. Her kids should fly kites or paddle a canoe, not stay inside playing video games.

When the kids were little, the bluebonnets carpeting the sides of the road taunted her every morning. Every time those beautiful little devils showed themselves, she knew she would have to drag her kids out to take the obligatory Texas bluebonnet photos. And, they would complain their clothes itched, and someone would always find their way into a fire ant hill or get stung by a bee, and all for maybe—if they were lucky—one photo with them all looking at the camera and not scowling. Springtime reminded her of everything she wanted to be, but had never become.

She decided to get another coffee—something stronger this time. She ordered a double espresso with foam.

"Amanda," called the young woman making drinks.

Amanda picked up her drink but then stopped and turned around. "This isn't mine," she said.

"You're not Amanda?" the girl asked.

"I am… but that's not what the drink says." Amanda held it out for the girl to see.

"Um… yes, it does," the girl said.

Amanda looked at the black letters scrawled across the side of her cup. "No… it says Greyhound. That's not even close to Amanda."

"What?"

"Greyhound," Amanda said again.

"Are you looking for the Greyhound station?" the woman shouted over the hiss of the steamer.

"No. It says Greyhound on my cup."

"You're almost there—just on the wrong side of the highway. At the next light, take a U-turn under the overpass and start going westbound, but don't get on the interstate, keep right, and you'll see the big Greyhound sign."

Amanda backed away toward the door while the barista gave her a strange look.

Amanda got behind the wheel of her new BMW, her heart

racing. She looked at her cup again. It said Greyhound, clear as anything. Perhaps magic was easier to use than she thought. For David and Emmy they would follow vague feelings, but Amanda got specific directions from her Starbucks barista. It seemed too easy. She didn't feel directed by her own magic, but by some outside force that had grown impatient with her and had to spell out her directions word for word.

She followed the barista's directions to the other side of the highway and found the Greyhound station as described. She hoped the magic didn't expect her to get on a bus and leave her BMW in the parking lot.

She waited in the short line and then approached the tired looking woman behind the counter, who barely glanced at her.

"Hi. I'm looking for my… daughter," she said, trying out a story she had formulated in line. "I think she's coming in today from… New Orleans… but her phone is dead. And I'm not sure when she's coming in or if this is the right station. Maybe you could help me, her name is Samantha Carthage."

"Mrs. Vandergraff?"

Amanda turned around and dropped her purse. She had found exactly what she had been looking for, but her mouth gaped.

"Oh my God," Amanda said, reaching down to pick up her purse off the scuff-marked floor.

Samantha looked at the woman behind the counter and then back at Amanda, hugging elbows that looked pointier than they had the last time she had seen her. She looked… wilted. Too pale and her hair could do with a good brushing. Dirt had turned the tops of her feet gray and she had amended her plastic flip-flops with duct tape. Amanda thought she looked like a homeless person and as soon as she thought it she felt foolish. Of course… she *was* a homeless person. At least that's what the man on the phone had said.

"Can I get you some breakfast?" Amanda asked.

"I don't understand. Did you come here to pick me up?"

"It appears so."

"How did you know I would be here?"

"That's a difficult question for me to answer."

Samantha stared at her absently, and Amanda worried something about her had broken. Maybe she had gone the way of her parents.

"I don't need your pity," Samantha said.

"I beg to differ," Amanda said, looking her up and down. "But I'm not the type to pity people. Are you going to come with me or not?"

"I don't know."

"You're a child and you're alone and homeless and hungry. If you think I'm just going to leave you in a bus station in Baytown, you've got another thing coming, young lady. Now get in the car."

"You know, you're mean when you're trying to be nice," Samantha said.

Amanda smiled. Good. She had her wits about her.

"Do you have bags?"

Samantha held up the canvas grocery bag she had slung around her shoulder. "Just this."

CHAPTER ELEVEN

Zander's head throbbed with hunger and exhaustion and his hands trembled on the steering wheel, but he couldn't stop driving. He feared he couldn't stop the car to go to the bathroom. He would vow to take the next exit and somehow forget his plans right before he made the turn. He mouth felt so dry and he had dirt on his face, but he couldn't stop. He couldn't get off the interstate. He knew people reacted in strange ways to trauma, but this seemed especially bizarre. He feared he had really lost his mind now. Or maybe the doctors had been right and he had always been crazy.

Eventually, the inevitable happened, and the car alarmed him that he only had a few miles left before his charge depleted. He had found his way into the middle of nowhere. Even stranded, he felt relieved. He could get out of the car and pee. And he could unglue his stiff fingers from the wheel.

When the Tesla spluttered to a stop, he coasted onto the shoulder. He let out a sigh of relief when he put the car in park. He didn't know where he had ended up. Somewhere in Louisiana. Despite the manic driving, he made the choice to drive home, which in his case, wasn't a place, but a person.

After he'd taken a few moments to pee and chug his water bottle, he knew he needed to call a tow truck before his cell battery went dead too. He should… but he didn't. He wanted to talk to someone else. His finger hovered over the screen for a while before he pushed call. He sat there in silent panic as the phone rang, trying to will the right person to answer.

"Jefferson Parish Children's Shelter. This is Patty. How can I help you?"

"Hi Patty… I don't know if you remember me. I used to live there. My name is Stephen Becker." He picked the name of another boy his age. The most inoffensive one he could think of. Stephen had been polite and well-mannered, but also bland. Way too boring to have done anything interesting after Zander had left.

Zander heard her typing, perhaps looking up the name of the unmemorable boy.

"Okay, yes. Hi, Stephen," Patty said. "How can I help you?"

"I was hoping to speak with one of the residents."

"Perhaps, but we have an official process you have to go through. You remember. But it's no big deal. I'll just need to verify your identity."

Zander didn't remember. No one had ever tried to call him. He guessed it made sense. They did have lots of security procedures.

"What's the name of the resident?" Patty asked.

He knew he wouldn't pass any identity test she threw at him, but he would try to fake it as long as he could.

"Imogene Grey," he said.

The clicking of Patty typing on the other line stopped. Silence hung on the line. He thought he could hear the woman's heart beating.

"Is this… Zander Colter?" she said softly.

Zander hung up the phone.

"Shit," he muttered to himself.

Zander had stayed in a lot of places, but never made a friend. Not really. He played with the other kids and he liked some of them fine, but he had never belonged. He didn't know why he felt that. He looked like all the other kids.

But on the first day at Jefferson Parish Children's Shelter he met someone he liked, and not who he would have expected. While he unpacked his clothes in his new room, a little girl peered at him from around the door. She had mismatched socks on her hands, and a green T-shirt tied around her head like a bandana.

"Hi," Zander said.

"Do you want to see my castle?"

"Okay."

Playing princesses with a little girl might not give the other kids the best first impression. But he didn't care much anymore. He followed her into the girls' room. She led him to the closet and opened the door.

"This is the secret passageway," she said.

Zander followed her obediently. She sat in a nest made out clothes and bath towels, and pulled Zander down with her. He sat across from her, with his legs crossed, his backpack clutched in his hands

"I'm Imogene," she said. "What's your name?"

"Zander."

"I'm six and a half."

"I'm nine."

"That's pretty big."

Zander shrugged. "I guess so."

"Are you going to live here with Miss Cathy and Mr. Ray?"

Zander nodded.

Imogene smiled. "You can be my big brother."

"So, if this is your castle. Are you a princess?" He gestured toward her bizarre headdress.

She rolled her eyes. "Nooo. I'm a dragon."

"Oh, right. What do I get to be?"

"You're a wizard," she said.

"Okay." He pulled a pencil out of his backpack.

"What's that?"

"My magic wand of course."

She laughed. "You're silly. Wizards don't need wands."

Despite his exhaustion, David couldn't sleep. He had thought he could get a nap in before the kids came home, but he could only stare at the ceiling. He could hear his brain buzzing. Patrick's spell had sent Jude and Caroline away. No one had seen or heard from them in almost a year. That seemed like the best alternative to David anyway. Jude was his son, and he loved him. But he also loved his other children and didn't want them anywhere near Jude. He wanted Jude to be okay, but also far from the people he loved. He assumed he and Caroline lived out of state somewhere, perhaps not like a *normal* young couple, but normal enough. Maybe he really loved her, and if he did, David thought that might him happy, and maybe it would make them both better people.

However, he couldn't sleep. He didn't trust Zander would stay away, and the unanswered questions nagged at his brain. Nothing with Zander felt settled.

After several hours of not sleeping, he came up with an idea that made him feel better. He had a private investigator who helped him investigate Julie Prescott's disappearance, and he had the money to pay him to do whatever he wanted, including following Zander Colter.

CHAPTER TWELVE

Amanda sipped more coffee while she watched Samantha eat eggs and strawberry waffles at Waffle House.

"So, how have you been?" Amanda asked.

Samantha glanced up at her with a scowl. "Not the best."

"Sure…" Amanda said.

"You're not going to eat anything?" Samantha asked.

"Not at the Waffle House."

"But you eat sometimes right?"

"Of course."

"You look really skinny."

"So do you."

Samantha shrugged her bony shoulders.

"I had cancer," Amanda said. "What's your excuse?"

Samantha stopped shoveling food into her mouth for a moment and looked up at her. "Oh. I'm so sorry."

"It's okay. The cancer is gone now."

"That's good." Samantha drank half of her orange juice in one gulp. "Poverty," she said.

"What?"

"My excuse for being skinny."

"That's a good excuse."

"So was yours."

Amanda glanced at the menu. Maybe food would make this conversation less awkward. The coffee didn't cut it. If they both shoved food in their faces, they wouldn't have to talk.

"Do you want my bacon?" Samantha asked. "I told her I didn't want it but she brought it anyway."

Amanda accepted the piece of bacon from Samantha's plate. "So I guess you're some kind of vegan now?"

"No." The syrup had spilled into Samantha's eggs, but she didn't seem to care. "I'm a lacto-ovo vegetarian," she continued.

"What is that?"

"It means no killing. But I'll eat animal products. Like milk and eggs."

"Aren't eggs unborn chicken fetuses?"

"The eggs we eat are unfertilized. They would never become chickens. Why do you even care? You kill Bambi for sport. Why are you hassling me about eggs?"

"I don't know. You're right. I'm sorry. And, no I don't kill baby deer for fun."

"Just Bambi's mom."

"Yeah, I guess so." Amanda tapped her nails on the table and then stopped herself. Samantha already ate so fast she might choke, even without Amanda rushing her. Besides… Amanda didn't know what to do next. An awkward conversation at Waffle House seemed less awkward than bringing her home.

"So how did you find me? Did *he* tell you I would be here?"

"Who?"

"Carlos."

"I don't know who that is."

"He gave me money and told me to get on the bus to Houston. He said you would find me. Well not you exactly. A Vandergraff. I didn't really expect you. But maybe I did. I wanted a—"

Samantha stopped midsentence and at first Amanda thought she might have choked.

"You wanted a what?"

"A killer."

Amanda raised an eyebrow. "What?"

"We shouldn't talk about it here."

Had she heard her right? In any case, she agreed that they shouldn't discuss it here.

"So if Carlos didn't send you, how did you know to come?"

"I don't know. I got a call yesterday from someone with some homeless youth program said you were missing."

"That's weird."

"Why?"

"I left the shelter three weeks ago, I don't know why they'd wait this long to call. Besides, I never gave anyone your number. I also never talked to anyone at any homeless youth program."

Amanda tapped her nails again, scowling at a coffee stain on her napkin. She didn't like magical forces driving her actions, but she preferred that over a man on the phone conning her the old fashioned way.

"Maybe Carlos called you. Was it a man?"

Amanda nodded with her nose scrunched. "I don't understand who this person is. Do you know him?"

"I'd never met him before he gave me money and told me to come here."

"Why would a random man want me to pick you up from a Greyhound station? It seems like he went to a lot of effort to make that happen."

"I don't know. All I know is what he told me. He's a fall wizard. And he thinks he can manipulate fate."

"What does that mean?"

"I'm not sure exactly. He talked about people like they were pawns in a chess game. He's playing chess, I guess."

"I don't like that. I don't appreciate being played with."

Samantha shrugged. "Neither do I, but I do appreciate the breakfast."

"Well… you're welcome. I don't mean to say I'm not happy to help you. I am. If this Carlos person wanted me to help you, all he had to do was ask. I didn't need to be tricked."

"Do you know the name Imogene Grey?" Samantha asked abruptly. She also stopped eating and looked up at Amanda. She clutched her fork with unexpected malice.

"No," Amanda said. "Should I?"

Samantha stared at her for several seconds. She could have counted Amanda's eyelashes. Amanda guessed she searched for lies. She wouldn't find any.

"Okay," Samantha said finally.

They didn't speak for a long time in the car. Amanda wished finding Samantha would have taken longer. She had run out of time to figure out what to do next. Amanda saw Samantha clutching her thin arms and she turned off the air conditioner.

"Whatever you couldn't say in the restaurant. I suppose you could say it now," Amanda prodded.

Samantha inhaled and put her hand to her mouth as if she wanted to catch the sob before it burst out. But, she failed. Her face contorted in tears.

"Why are you crying?"

Samantha took several deep breaths as if she thought oxygen could vaporize tears. Her face went still again. She shook her head.

"Okay," Amanda said. "It's okay. We don't have to talk."

"Yes, we do. That's why I'm here. I think that's why I'm here. You can help me."

"I can," Amanda said. "I can give you money, help you find a place to stay…"

"That's not the help I mean."

"Okay…"

"What do you know about killing curses?" Samantha asked,

staring at her dirty nails.

"I don't know anything about killing curses." Amanda said it too curtly, it sounded like a lie, but she told the truth. Her parents didn't teach her comparatively harmless magic, but they certainly didn't teach her killing curses. "Is that what you meant when you said you were looking for a killer? You think all winter wizards are killers?"

"No."

"Why are you asking?" she asked more gently. "Is there a deer you want dead?" Her attempt at humor fell flat.

"Before I asked you about Imogene Grey. She was my girlfriend. I was in love with her. And she was killed by a killing curse. I want revenge."

Amanda adjusted her sunglasses, processing all of that information. "I'm so sorry. Who killed her?" she finally asked.

"I don't know."

"How do you know it was a killing curse?"

Samantha rested her head against the window. "I'm just really tired," she said. "I don't want to talk about it anymore."

"Okay."

CHAPTER THIRTEEN

"You're home," Patrick said as he tossed his backpack on the couch. "Dad said you were driving to Austin to find some kind of special granite for the countertops in the house." Amanda pursed her lips, simultaneously annoyed and impressed with David's detailed lie.

"Well, I found it. Turns out they have that kind of granite in Houston. It was easier to find than I expected. A little too easy, really."

"Okay," Patrick said, as he headed for the refrigerator. Xavier ate plain slices of bread out of the bag.

Evangeline walked toward her room and Amanda grabbed her arm. "Where are you going?"

"My room," she said with a menacing scowl.

Amanda dropped her arm. "Sorry. Just hang out here for a minute, okay?"

"Why?"

"Because I need you to take some clothes down to the laundry room."

"I *just* got home. And why me?"

"Do this for me now and I won't make you do any more chores for three days."

Evangeline sneered, but seemed to agree to the terms, because she took off with a basket of dirty clothes from the hamper.

"What do I have to do to get that deal?" Patrick asked. "One load of laundry and you leave me alone for three days?"

"So Patrick, how was your day?" Amanda asked, ignoring his question.

"Fine." He cracked open a Dr. Pepper.

"Good."

"You know, I never asked you whatever happened with you and Samantha. Did she break up with you?"

"What? That's random." He blushed.

"I was just so caught up with the cancer stuff, I wasn't paying much attention. I'm sorry."

"It's fine, Mom, you had cancer. And I don't feel like having six months worth of heart-to-hearts now to make up for it."

"Xavier, I see what you're doing," Amanda said. "No video games until you do your homework. Why do I have to tell you that every day?"

"I wasn't," Xavier protested, holding his Xbox controller. "I just want to watch TV."

"Fine, but not too loud. Patrick, wait." She grabbed Patrick's arm as he tried to use the brief distraction to make an exit. "I really need to talk to you."

"What?"

"I asked you about Samantha because she's here."

"What do you mean?"

"She's in our apartment."

Patrick looked around the living room/kitchen.

"She's asleep in Emmy's bed."

"Are you sure?"

"Of course I'm *sure*."

Patrick put his soda down and stared at her open mouthed. Even Xavier had forgotten to turn on the TV. "Why?" he said finally.

"She was homeless."

"Homeless?"

"Yes. So I brought her here. Just until I figure out what to do with her. We'll probably help her get an apartment or something."

"When were you going to tell me this?"

"I'm telling you now."

"She was really homeless? Is she okay?"

"She seems tired and stressed, but she'll be fine I'm sure. I also, I wanted you to know up front, she's a lesbian now."

"What?"

"She had a girlfriend… but she died. Samantha thinks it was a killing curse."

"Okay… okay… that's a lot of information." He rubbed his scalp as if he needed to massage his brain.

"Is it okay she's here?"

"Of course. It's good. I'm glad."

Patrick fished his keys out of his backpack and headed for the door.

"Where are you going? I thought you said it was okay."

"It is okay. It's great. I'm great. I'm just going out… maybe forever."

"Patrick, I'm sorry. Which part upsets you? Is it the lesbian thing?"

"I'm not upset. I'm just leaving."

Emmy stared at Samantha sleeping in her bed, wearing her clothes. Something about the blonde intruder sleeping in her bed reminded her of Goldilocks. Emmy had the urge to poke her to make sure she was real. She rolled over and Emmy considered running back out of the room before she woke up, but Samantha opened her eyes and saw her before she had a chance to run.

"Emmy?"

Emmy sat on the edge of the bed next to her, and Samantha propped herself up on her elbows. She had grown thinner and paler, and Emmy's shirt hung around her collarbones. She had shadows under her eyes.

"Hey," Samantha said.

"Hey."

"Is it okay I'm sleeping in your bed?"

"Sure."

Samantha sat up and gave Emmy a bony, but warm hug. "I missed you."

"I missed you too."

"How long was I asleep?"

"I don't know. How long have you been here?"

Samantha shrugged. "I don't know. It was daytime," she said vaguely. "Your bed is just so comfortable."

"Is it?"

"You have no idea how nice it is to have your own bed. And it's so clean." She picked up the pillow and buried her face in it to smell it. "Reminds me of my mom."

"I think everything in here smells like the lizard."

She smiled. "I guessed that wasn't yours."

"My mom said you were homeless. Why didn't you just come here sooner?"

"I don't know. Maybe I should have." She crawled out from her cocoon of blankets and sat cross-legged next to Emmy. "But it's not like I'm going to stay."

"Why not? Where are you going to go?"

"I don't know. I'll figure something out."

"You'd rather sleep under a bridge than stay here?"

"That's not what I mean."

"We have money now. We can give you some. Can you get an apartment when you're under eighteen?"

"I don't know, but I'm not legally emancipated. I'm supposed to be in the system. But I don't want to be anymore."

She picked up a brush off the end table. "Can I use your brush?"

"It's Evangeline's. But yeah."

"I am here for a reason."

"Revenge against the person who killed your girlfriend."

"How did you know that?"

"Because my mom told me in one very alarming run-on sentence as soon as I walked in the door."

"Does that bother you?"

"Which part?"

"The girlfriend part."

"I'm not a freaking caveman. And I'm not surprised."

"Really? I didn't even know."

"Well, I guess I'm smarter than you."

Samantha smiled and continued to work at a stubborn tangle with Evangeline's brush. Emmy made a mental note to pick out the blonde hairs before Evangeline saw it and cursed them both.

"Is Patrick here?"

"No. Not at this moment. He might be a little less okay with the lesbian thing. Not because he has an issue with in general… but because, you know… he's not a woman."

"He shouldn't be upset about that."

"I don't know if he is. He's just acting weird. Who the hell knows what his problem is."

"I didn't mean to drive him out of his own house."

"You didn't. It's not your fault he's a weirdo."

"I guess not."

"What was her name?"

Samantha swallowed and placed the brush back down. Emmy could tell by the look on her face she had loved her. She looked pained, as if thinking of her name made a point of light burn into her brain.

"Imogene," she whispered. "Imogene Grey."

"That's a pretty name."

"Did you know her?" Samantha looked at her pointedly now. Her green eyes a little red, gaze boring into Emmys.

"No… of course not. Should I?"

"No." Samantha examined the frayed tips of her hair. "I can't think of any reason why you would. No one knew her. At least not really. She had no family. She moved around too much to have many friends."

"Do you have a picture of her?"

"No." Samantha pressed her hand against her mouth as she winced as if another laser had hit her brain.

Emmy hugged her. "I'm sorry. And if you think someone killed her, we will assassinate the bastard."

CHAPTER FOURTEEN

Zander remembered Imogene liked looking at the sky. She would lie on her back and look up and pretend the sky was another world, where the clouds were mountains surrounded by blue ocean. She would point at certain clouds where she would like to live.

He couldn't see the other world as easily. He thought the clouds looked like clouds. But sometimes, he could see it. Especially during the sunset. The clouds streaked with red and pink and orange looked like a desert landscape. But not a dry, barren one, but a golden landscape of milk and honey where you could run forever and never get tired. At times like that, Imogene would look up and see a golden palace in the sky, and he could see it too.

He didn't know how he ended up with a little girl as a best friend. But the other boys didn't like him anyway. They thought he was weird, and they were right.

"That's where my mom lives," Imogene said, pointing to an impressive spire of clouds on the verge of brewing into a storm. "She has a pool filled with feathers. And seven unicorns."

"What are the unicorns' names?"

"Now how would I know that?"

Zander laughed. "You're right. Stupid question."

"What about your mom?"

"I don't know how many unicorns she has."

"For real. Did you parents die or were you taken away?"

"My mom died. I never knew my dad."

"Me too."

"Do you remember your mom?" Zander asked.

"I don't have to remember her. I talk to her all the time."

"You'll have to show me how you do that."

"I'll ask her the names of her unicorns. If you want to know."

"Okay. I want to know."

"Do you want me to ask her about your mom?"

Zander paused, working out a lump in his throat. "No," he said finally.

Zander looked up at the sky from the same spot. The sun burrowed under a deep blanket of clouds, making the sky a flat whitish gray. He tried to imagine what the little girl Imogene would say about a sky like that. Perhaps she would think it looked like a giant ice rink in the sky, ready for twirling and dancing… if she even knew what an ice rink looked like. A recent storm had shaken tiny white flower petals from the trees, creating a scattering of white on the ground, furthering the illusion of cold and snow.

His new jacket smelled strongly of leather. He tugged on it and looked back at the sky warily. Apparently, leather jackets couldn't get wet. He vowed to avoid buying them in the future. Any jacket you couldn't wear while standing in the rain was a waste of jacket. He thought all clothes were a waste of money to some extent, and he half hated himself for how much he had spent on this outfit. He wouldn't tell Imogene.

He watched tiny droplets hit the sleeves of his jacket. He already felt foolish for waiting so long; he would feel more foolish standing in the rain letting the water destroy his $500 jacket. But what if he left to protect his stupid jacket and she arrived a few minutes later?

The rain came down harder now, making a pitter-patter sound on the leather. He looked at his phone, to check the date for probably the thirtieth time, and raindrops dribbled down his screen. He shoved the phone back in his pocket and walked back toward the road, figuring he could wait for a few more hours in his car. If she came, she would have to park along the road too. He would see her.

Zander got in his car and listened to the sound of the rain on the roof of the car. He squinted through rain streaking down the window.

He woke later to late day sun streaming into his car. He cursed himself for falling asleep. She could have come and left. Why would she have thought to look for him inside a brand new Tesla? The sun lit up the wet highway making it look like a river of gold.

He felt a tickle of the back of his neck and turned. He half expected to see her waiting for him in his tiny backseat. It sounded like something she might do. Crawl in his car and wait for him to wake up, and then flick his ear to startle him. But the car remained empty and he must have imagined the sensation on his neck. He brushed his neck and shoulders checking for spiders.

He got out of the car and the sudden warmth nearly knocked him down. The sunshine had squelched the cold air that had blown in with the rain shower. The air smelled fresh and cleansed from the rain. He couldn't smell the refineries or the distant sulfur mine. Raindrops trickled from the leaves of the trees, and more white petals had fallen. The petals had danced along rivulets of rainwater, creating swirls and patterns.

Coming here might have been worth it for this moment. He had nowhere else to go anyway. He had no one else he wanted to see. And the money had driven away the need to search for a job or an apartment. He could drive around staying in hotels for as long as he wanted. He had nowhere to go, except to Imogene.

She would love this moment, especially the sun glinting on the highway and the flower petals floating on tiny rivers. And her sky had returned. The clouds had parted and turned gold. He had thought he heard her walking toward him so many times that day, he no longer trusted his instinct, but he felt as if he might see her at any moment. She would walk down the highway toward him, the sun gleaming on her black curls. Even when she grew up, she never lost the smile she had as a little girl—a smile of complete abandon. She had never once tried to hide a smile or stifle a laugh. She let it come. She would smile at him like that. Any minute.

With every step forward, he smiled, thinking he might see her. He felt as if he did see her… but for only a split second—a trick of the light and shadows, or a rustle of a bush. The glare of the sun on the road caused him to squint and every dark silhouette could have been her… *was* her… for a brief moment.

He blinked several times in rapid succession, trying to rid himself of the strange sensation. His brain had turned funny. He hadn't had a proper night's sleep or non-fast-food meal since he had spent almost two days locked in a shed. But he had to be here *today*.

He saw the glint of something brighter gold on the highway ahead of him, something manmade that didn't belong.

He came closer and saw it wasn't gold at all, just glinting in the sunlight like the road. A small wooden cross, painted purple and decorated with fading stickers of flowers and butterflies, as if decorated by children. Purple glitter sparkled on the leaves and dirt around the cross where it had shed from the well-glittered cross.

He kneeled down next to the cross, so he could straighten it. Then he saw the words written on the cross.

RIP Imogene

As rare as the name was, he did not consider it could be his Imogene, not until he saw her face. A pale, lifeless facsimile of the face he kept expecting to see. He pulled a photograph out from a bed of wet leaves and shook the water off. He held a recent school photo of Imogene, looking as she did when he saw her last, but faded in the sun. Almost all color had washed from the photo. After a few more weeks in the sun and rain her face would disappear.

Even with the photo, he couldn't believe it. The fear seeped in gradually, first tasting like metal in the back of his throat, then like pain behind his nose. His lungs turned to lead, and he couldn't breathe. He couldn't remember how to breathe. So instead of breathing, he wept.

After sleeping all day, Samantha had trouble sleeping that night. Amanda had adorned the lumpy and frayed couch with silky brown and black throw pillows that looked expensive and had a plasticy new smell. She stayed up and messed around on Amanda's laptop. She hadn't used a computer in so long, and she hadn't used a nice one in even longer. This computer moved as fast as she could think.

She entered "Imogene Grey" into every search engine and always came up with nothing. Just lists of names that happened to include "Imogene" and "Grey." She got a hit from ancestry.com for an "Imogen Gray" who had lived in the 1800s. Instead of finding answers, she drowned in meaningless links and ads for car insurance and wrinkle creams. Pointless things filled the world and according to the internet, Imogene Grey had never existed at all. An empty future of doing horrible things like checking e-mail and paying electric bills weighed on her. All those inane things seemed so impossible and pointless without

Imogene. She didn't know what scared her more—thinking she might never get over Imogene, or thinking she might. That one day she might forget.

Tired of the tiny apartment, she put on Emmy's sweater jacket, warm and soft and smelling like dryer sheets, and went outside to sit on the stairs. The world fell quiet in the middle of the night. Even in Houston, with traffic sounds and lights everywhere, no one moved around the apartment complex. So peaceful.

She heard the apartment door open behind her, breaking her silent reverie.

"You're not leaving are you?"

Samantha gasped, which made her feel foolish, but he had grown so much taller. Patrick came over, wearing pajama pants and a Houston Astros T-Shirt.

"How did you know I came out here?"

"I heard the front door open… I wasn't asleep."

"No, I'm not leaving. Just wanted to get some air."

He sat next to her on the step, avoiding her eyes.

"Wow," she said.

"What?"

"You're just really tall."

"Um… thank you?"

"You're welcome."

"I'm sorry I haven't talked to you until now."

"You were very sneaky. I didn't even know you came home."

"I live here. I have to come back eventually."

"Do you want me to leave? I know I have no business here."

"No, of course not. I'm glad you're here. I wouldn't let you leave until you had someplace to go."

"Someplace to go," she repeated, wrapping her mind around each strange word.

"Did I say the wrong thing?"

"No."

Patrick tapped his fingers on his knees.

"So you're not going to leave?"

"No. At least not right this second."

"Okay… well, then I'll see you tomorrow I guess. It's Easter tomorrow, so we're going to a thing."

"Oh, right."

"Okay, tomorrow."

"Yep."

"Good night."

"You too."

Patrick got back up and smiled at her awkwardly and went back inside.

CHAPTER FIFTEEN

"It makes no sense for me to go without you," David said. He put his hands in the pockets of his freshly pressed khaki pants and then arranged the sleeves of a button-down shirt he hadn't worn in a long time.

Amanda stared at him as if the careful crease in his pants offended her.

"Somebody needs to stay home with Xavier and Evangeline," she said.

"Well, it could be me. Or they could stay here alone. Or they could come with us. That's not a good excuse."

"They turned their back on me," Amanda said. "They weren't there when I needed them most. I don't forgive so easily."

"You forgave me."

"No, I didn't."

"I see… good to know. But you tolerate me. Dare I say… you might even like me."

Amanda gave him an eye roll that reminded him of Emmy.

"So, if you can not forgive me and share a bed with me, then you can have Easter supper with your brother and your parents."

"Just leave it, David. I'm not going."

"Why would I go if you're not? They hate me."

"They don't hate you. Well… my parents hate you. Carson and Jess don't. Not really."

"You could at least come to church first."

"I don't want to be one of those people that only goes to church on Easter and Christmas."

"So it's better to not go at all?"

"Yes."

"That makes no sense to me."

Amanda shrugged and turned back to flipping through Facebook on her Kindle, as if to imply the conversation had ended.

"To tell you the truth, I'm surprised you don't want to go back to church now."

"Why is that?" she asked, not looking up at him.

"Because you're *alive*. The odds were against you and you lived. I know a cynic could easily say it had nothing to do with prayer, but personally I think it's close enough to a miracle to at least give God the benefit of the doubt. The least we could do is go to church on Easter."

Amanda continued to stare at the tablet, but she had stopped moving through her newsfeed. She stared at the table as if she could see through it and stared at something far away.

"The way I see it, a lot of bad things have happened to our family," David continued, unsure why she stayed silent. "But considering the alternatives, things have worked out okay. I mean God only has so much to work with here. I think He's done pretty good by us on the whole. I mean, you're *alive*," he stated again, feeling as of he shouldn't need anything else to win the argument. To him, her life proved God didn't *completely* hate him.

"That wasn't God," Amanda said in a strange, distant voice.

"What do you mean?"

"God didn't save me."

"Okay, and you're so sure of this because…"

"Just forget it. It's not important."

"It sounds pretty important."

"Is there still coffee left?"

"Amanda."

Amanda kept her back to him as she refilled her cup. "Just go to church if you want to go to church," Amanda said.

"I do want to go to church. I really want to go. I've done some things I'm not proud of lately… and I'd really like to find my way back to the light."

She turned around now. "What have you done you're not proud of?"

"I should have told you sooner. The only reason I didn't was because… telling someone else made it real, I guess. I'd rather pretend it never happened."

"Jesus, David. What are you talking about?"

He looked around the living area. "Let me tell you in our bedroom."

"Okay."

David followed her into the bedroom. She set her coffee on the bedside table and sat on the bed, looking up at David, waiting.

He sat beside her and told her everything that had happened with Zander. How he may have killed him with magic. How he had kept him prisoner and planned to kill him. How he might have killed him if Patrick hadn't interrupted him. She listened with her hand on his leg.

When he finished, she took a sip of her coffee and put it back down before speaking. "You should have told me."

"I know."

She squeezed his leg. "You've been with me through so much darkness these past months. You were there when I was sick and ugly and dying, and you didn't even bat an eye. I think

I can handle a little light murder and kidnapping for you."

David chuckled put his arm around her. "You were never ugly."

"I guess there are some benefits to having a husband that's a big fat liar."

He chuckled and kissed her on the forehead.

"Look at me." She took his face in her hand and made him look in her eyes. "You're a good man. Maybe not in a Captain America way, but a good man nonetheless. You would never hurt anyone just for the sake of hurting them. You're only dangerous when you're protecting your family. I don't know whether or not it's okay with God or not, but it's certainly okay with me."

"The thing is, I feel guilty about what I did to him, but like a coward at the same time. I couldn't kill him. I'm not sure if I ever could ever kill anyone. I'm not even good at being evil. Somehow I managed to be evil and a coward all at the same time."

Last Christmas, David woke to find his bed empty. He found Amanda in the living room, rearranging the ornaments on the Christmas tree, her face red and wet.

"You're crying."

She stood up straighter and wiped her cheeks with her hands. "You're very observant."

"You don't have to hide out here. You can cry in front of me, you know."

"I don't want to upset you."

"I'm your husband, not your child."

"I lied to you before."

"About what?"

"When I said I wasn't afraid of dying. I'm so scared, David. I don't want to die."

"You're not going to die," he said, moving close to her on instinct. "You'll make it through this."

"See, that's why I can't talk to you," she turned back toward the tree to deflect his comforting hug.

"What do you mean?"

"You just keep saying everything will be fine. That I'm strong. That I can beat this. That's all you say, over and over. I hate it."

"What is wrong with saying that?"

"It's not true. None of it. I'm not strong. If I ever was, I'm not anymore. I'm so tired of fighting. I'm going to die, and I'm terrified."

"You're—"

"And I'm so sick of people talking about *fighting* cancer. They act like if I just *fight* harder, I can beat it. What fucking fight? I have no control over this. I *wish* all I had to do was fight. *That* I can do. They act like if you're tough enough and brave enough, you can live forever. It's such bullshit."

"I—"

"Stop. Don't say anything. Whatever you're going to say is wrong."

"I'm sorry."

"You don't have to apologize. It's not your fault. I know you're scared too."

"I am. But… I don't want you to protect me. I want to protect *you*. Make you feel better if you're sad."

"You do. Sometimes, when I can't sleep, I crawl into your arms while you're asleep. And I feel better. But only for a little while. Then being close to you just reminds me of everything I'm going to lose. I can't even stand to feel happy anymore. It hurts so much. I love my stupid, pathetic little life. Stupid things, like drinking coffee in the morning and lying in bed watching TV with you at night. It may not seem like it all the time, but I love it. Why can't God just give me that? Every other stupid person in the world gets to have that. Why not me? Why do I have to lose everything?"

"I don't know."

"What if there's nothing? No God. No Heaven. All that waits for me is just… nothing. It's just all over. I won't even get to keep my memories of my life. It's just all gone."

"Have you lost your faith?"

"No… I don't know."

"I decided a long time ago that doubting whether or not God was real didn't make Him any more or less real. So what's the point? Not knowing is just part of being human. You can't know. It's not possible. So don't try. Just… hope."

"I do hope. I hope so badly that someday I'll get to see you again in Heaven. Or Hell. I don't even care. I just don't want to know there will ever be a last time I'll see your face. I don't want to know my brain will die and I'll forget every moment we ever spent together. So all I do is pray there is more than this. That I'll find you again. That I'll find my babies again."

"You will."

"I don't want to die, David. Please don't let me die."

"I would do anything to stop it."

"But you can't."

"Don't give up," he said. He wanted to shout at her and hold her all at once. "You can't give up hope."

"David, that is exactly what I asked you not to do. No bullshit about hope. I'm sick of it."

"Hope isn't bullshit. Especially not for a witch. I know wizards can't raise the dead, but you're not dead, Amanda. Even Mundanes have a better chance of beating cancer if they have hope—studies have shown that. And you're a witch Amanda. Your hope really means something. Don't lose it."

"I already told you. I'm not strong enough. I can't go through all of this and muster magical, life-giving hope at the same time. I'm that kind of wizard."

CHAPTER SIXTEEN

On Easter morning, the Vandergraffs got all fancy for church, well most of them, anyway. They invited Samantha, but she declined. She had gone to church with Emmy before, and it didn't bother her, but things had changed. She felt as if she fit in less than before. Patrick and Emmy both looked about ten years older. Patrick in a real honest-to-God suit, and Emmy in heels and a paisley dress. Samantha had no clothes like that, and didn't feel like looking too tall and too thin in Emmy's clothes, or like a 40-year-old woman in Amanda's.

"You should come," David said to his two children still barefoot and wearing pajama pants while he stood in the doorway.

"They don't want us there," Evangeline said.

"I don't care."

"Well, *I* don't want me there either," she said.

David sighed and stared out into the parking lot.

"I could stay with them," Amanda offered.

Samantha followed David's gaze. She saw nothing but sunshine and blue skies reflecting in car windows. And the chatter of other people dressed for Easter Sunday. Clicking heels. Children talking. It all seemed harmless, but David's nervousness had infected her. She didn't see whatever scared him and that scared her all the more.

"I just convinced you to go," David said to Amanda. "If anyone should stay, it should be me."

"Oh my *God*," Emmy said. "What is the matter with you guys? They're not babies. You can leave them alone for a few hours. You do it all the time. What's going on?"

"You're right," Amanda said. "Let's go." She tugged on David's arm.

"Don't answer the door," David said, looking at Evangeline and Xavier.

Samantha seemed invisible to him, but that didn't bother her. Right before turning to leave, David looked at her. "Don't let them answer the door. Watch them."

Samantha nodded, but she didn't like the strange request. Xavier was older than her, and she didn't think he'd appreciate a babysitter. Not that Evangeline would either. She couldn't imagine what David thought would happen to them on a random Sunday morning, but if a monster did come to the door, she would hide behind the winter solstice witch—the youngest and shortest. Emmy had told her everything—how Patrick and Evangeline were honest-to-god event wizards. She found that impressive, but terrifying.

Samantha closed the door and turned around to face Evangeline and Xavier. She had considered accepting the invitation to church because she didn't want to stay home with these two. But she would hate brunch with the Oppenheimers more. Everyone knew who she was and they'd look at her and *know* and *stare* and it would suck.

"Who or what does he think is going to come to the door?" Samantha asked, turning both deadbolts.

"I don't know," Xavier said. "Paranoid, I guess."

She had asked him a question, but the sound of his voice still stunned Samantha. She couldn't remember him ever speaking to her directly before.

"They didn't take the flowers," Evangeline said, pointing to the potted Easter lilies that cluttered the dining table, all wrapped in gleaming purple foil. They made the whole apartment smell like a garden, which apparently offended Evangeline because she made a face as if she had tasted sour milk.

"Why would they take them?" Samantha asked.

"I don't know," Evangeline said. "I thought that's what they were for. For Easter church."

"They bought them from the church," Samantha explained. "They're not going to take them back."

"Why did they buy them?" Evangeline said.

"It's a fundraiser, I think," Samantha said, recalling going to church with Emmy on Easter one year.

"So the more flowers you buy, the more God likes you?" Xavier said with a half-grin.

Wow. He talked and almost told a joke. And almost smiled. He had turned into a different person than the one she met two years ago.

"Something like that," Samantha said.

"I guess that explains why they bought so many," Xavier said.

Evangeline plucked a large petal off one of the lilies and examined it.

"Don't do that," Samantha said.

"What?"

"Don't pick the petals off flowers. It's disrespectful."

Samantha thought for a second she might get cursed for telling her what to do, but Evangeline cocked her head and looked at her.

"Sorry," she said, finally. "Honestly, I don't see what the big deal is about flowers. They die so easily. Especially after they've been cut."

Samantha's heart rate rose. The way Evangeline said *cut* bit at her, but she didn't know whether or not Evangeline meant to threaten her or make an obvious observation about flowers.

Evangeline took the petal she had already plucked and held in her closed fist. When she opened her hand and revealed a desiccated petal. Dry. Brown. She dropped the now dead petal into the trashcan.

She could have crushed the delicate petal in her hands… but it looked as if she had done so much more. She hadn't crushed the petal… it had died.

"Don't do that," Xavier said. His voice made Samantha jump. So cold and dry now, not the almost lighthearted person who had spoken before. Samantha wondered if she could still choose brunch with the Oppenheimers, then she realized what she should have known as soon as Emmy told her about Evangeline.

"It's you," Samantha said suddenly. "*You're* the Vandergraff I'm looking for."

"I'm the Vandergraff you're looking for, for what?" Evangeline asked mildly.

"I should have guessed it when Emmy said you were a winter solstice witch."

Evangeline pursed her lips and gestured for Samantha to continue.

"Do you know what happened to my girlfriend, Evangeline?"

"I live here and I'm not deaf," Evangeline said.

"Right. Well, that's why I'm here. To see you. I just didn't realize it before now."

Samantha stopped and looked at Xavier who eyed her over a bowl of Honey Nut Cheerios. She needed to talk to Evangeline alone. She didn't know him at all, but she doubted he would support her idea. He got mad when she killed the flower petal.

"You want me to kill someone for you?" Evangeline asked. Samantha couldn't read her tone, as she couldn't when she had made the comment about flowers.

"What?" Xavier asked.

"Yes," Samantha said. As soon as she said it, her mouth went dry. Saying it aloud made it seem so absurd. So horrible. But why lie? She wanted justice.

"You can't be serious," Xavier said, standing up. Samantha took a step back even though Xavier didn't move any closer to her. He had grown taller also, and his magic seemed bigger too.

"I'm serious," Samantha said. "They took the only reason I had for living. The only thing that made me happy. And they're going to get away with it. I can't let that happen."

"She's not an assassin for hire," Xavier said. "She's not doing it."

Evangeline glared at her brother. Samantha remembered what her mother had once said, that solstice wizards have a lot of power, but they could be manipulated easily. They're all brawn, no brains. And Samantha could see how she could work their dynamic to her advantage.

"Why not?" Samantha asked Xavier, ignoring Evangeline.

"Because she knows better than that," he said.

Perfect.

"Shut up, Xavier," Evangeline said. "Quit speaking for me."

In some ways, these two might have come from another planet, but some parts of human nature couldn't be overcome. A girl like Evangeline would never appreciate her big brother telling her what to do.

"I'll do it," Evangeline said.

"No, you won't," Xavier said.

"Yes, I will."

She could feel their magic intensify. Like the air had gotten loud. She pulled on her earlobe trying to get her ears to work properly. If they fought, she should get out of the crossfire.

"You can't stop me," Evangeline said.

Xavier didn't respond. He kept his mouth in a firm line, glaring at his sister.

"How would you?" Evangeline asked him. It seemed as if she poked a lion with a stick. But no matter how they might look on the outside, Samantha knew Evangeline had the bigger claws.

"Come here," Evangeline said.

It took Samantha a second to realize Evangeline spoke to her. She approached Evangeline cautiously. She had a darkness radiating from her Samantha hadn't experienced before. She had plenty of experience with dark wizards, but they weren't all like this. For example, Emmy's magic seemed dry and cold. It had a pleasant crispness to it. Refreshing.

This felt like fear. Evangeline's magic loomed in front of her and behind at once, as if she might bite at her heels or swoop down at her from above.

"I need your help," Evangeline said. "You need to send my magic out to your target."

"I guess I should have said... I don't know who the target is. I don't know who killed her."

Evangeline cocked her head to the side. "Well, that's different then. But it shouldn't be a problem."

Xavier made an exasperating grunting sound as if actual words couldn't express the extent of his disapproval. "Oh, come on. That is sloppy magic. How would that even work?"

"You're thinking like a Mundane," Evangeline said to Xavier. "She doesn't need to know *who* killed her." She turned to Samantha now. "It's not about the who it's about the what. You want to attack *what* took her away from you. You want to trade death for death. Your feelings are strong enough to guide the magic."

"I'm not sure," Samantha said. Common sense agreed with Xavier, but as a solstice witch, Evangeline understood magic in a way they could not.

Evangeline held her hand out to Samantha, the same small hand had brought death to a flower petal, but she reached for it anyway.

Xavier grabbed Samantha's wrist before she could touch Evangeline and clutched it painfully. She pulled away from him, but she struggled to move her arm. She gasped as she felt her arm grow cold and numb—deadened and alive with pain at the same time as if her nerves froze.

Xavier released his grasp. "I didn't mean to do that," he said. "I'm sorry."

Samantha rubbed her arm and shook her hand out, trying to rid herself of the sensation.

"Don't touch me," Samantha said in a fiercer tone than she expected.

She placed her own hand over the red handprint he had left.

"Just go away, Xavier," Evangeline said. "Go play video games some more. It's the only thing you're good at. You *suck* at magic. Just because you can't cast a spell right and end up hurting the wrong people, doesn't mean I will. I know what I'm doing."

Samantha felt as if her heart beat in her face. Xavier glared at his sister. He crossed his arms across his chest and Samantha knew that meant Evangeline had won the argument. At least, he had surrendered.

The nerves in her right hand continued to prickle and her hand shook as she held it out for Evangeline this time, red hand mark blazing.

"I'm ready," Samantha said, lying. "So you say I just need to think about what happened?"

"Think about what killed her. I know it's harder when you don't have a face or a name."

"No, I think I've got it." Samantha thought about the feeling that came over her right before Imogene ran off. The cold, darkness passing over them. In her experience, most spells weren't that visceral, but she had never felt a killing spell. Or perhaps she had—the darkness that had passed over them before Imogene died.

Evangeline took her hand and Samantha was surprised her hand felt like… a hand. After Xavier's burning touch and all the dark energy radiating from Evangeline, she had prepared herself for something more malicious. For a second the whole thing seemed ridiculous. Despite practicing magic her entire life, her spells working surprised her. And this one seemed especially far-fetched. She would hold hands with this person and they would bring death to someone?

"Ready?" Evangeline asked.

Samantha nodded. What she had felt from Xavier had felt like a little prick compared to Evangeline. She gave Samantha what she had asked for. Death. Samantha tried to release her hand, but Evangeline squeezed it tighter.

Samantha grabbed at her neck with her other hand. Her throat felt as if it closed up. She had asked for death and she would get it. She hadn't thought about the danger of touching someone as they cast a killing spell. It now all seemed so stupid. She might as well have committed suicide. Black marks spotted her vision and she tasted the metallic twang of blood in her mouth. She didn't understand how she still stood. She didn't feel as if she had control over her body at all. She pictured herself suspended in air, hanging limp like a body swinging from a noose.

She thought about Imogene and she felt a taste of hope. She believed in an afterlife. She didn't believe in the clouds and harps version of Heaven. Her parents said humans couldn't comprehend the afterlife, and shouldn't waste time trying. But it existed, and waited for her. Maybe if she thought hard enough of Imogene, she would go to her, somehow their spirits would find each other on the next plane.

She no longer felt limp and the room spun. She could hardly tell the ceiling from the floor. She touched her hand to her cheek and realized someone had slapped her.

Xavier came out of nowhere and grabbed her jaw and turned her to face him. Then he slapped her again.

"Stop," she said weakly.

"You're supposed to send the magic *out*," he said. "Quit dying and do what you're told."

Xavier's face quivered in front of her as if her eyeballs vibrated.

"Okay," she said. Or, maybe she said nothing, but she thought it. Death had seemed welcoming for a moment; there would be no justice in that. Only more death at the hands of a killer who would never see justice. She had to stay alive long enough to get her revenge.

She replayed the moments of Imogene's death in her head and the images came easily, as if she transported back in time. Watching Imogene running toward the highway, feeling as helpless as she had then. But this time, time moved slowly. Her hair flowing behind her, appearing suspended in zero gravity. Samantha would live in that moment forever. Watching her run to the highway. That moment would never end. It stretched all the way to eternity, and Samantha would never run fast enough. No matter how slowly Imogene moved, Samantha moved slower.

The rich, earthy smell of potting soil brought her back to her surroundings. Her legs had given way and she had brought one of the lilies down with her. She propped herself up on her elbows, surrounded in dirt and petals.

"Are you alive?" Evangeline asked.

The brother and sister kneeled on either side of her staring at her.

"I guess so," Samantha said. An answer as pointless as the question. As she tried to sit up, the room spun once again and she held her head between her two hands trying to get gravity to act normal. Her head throbbed in pain. She felt as if she opened her mouth again she would vomit.

"Don't touch me," Samantha said, swatting her hands around her face and hitting nothing. She ventured another attempt at opening her eyes and saw neither of them had reached out to touch her anyway. To their credit, they looked concerned. Evangeline had her had her arms wrapped around herself and she picked at her elbow.

"No one is touching you," Xavier said.

Samantha gasped. She didn't trust her eyes, but she had already seen Evangeline do it once.

"The flowers are dying," Samantha said.

Evangeline and Xavier turned to look at the flowers on the table.

The once bright white lilies yellowed and withered. The long, slender petals browned and curled at the ends and then fell, cluttering the table, and some falling to the floor. The flowers smelled different now. A sweetness intermingled with rotting replaced the fresh flower scent from moments ago.

Xavier sighed and then stood up.

"I'd help you up, but I've have to touch you," he said and walked off without offering a hand.

Samantha sat up and shook the potting soil out of her hair. Xavier came back with a garbage bag and threw the dead lilies in the bag. He seemed calmer with something specific to do. Evangeline sat next to Samantha and watched him for a moment, and then got up herself. She came back with a broom and dustpan and swept up the soil and dried flower petals from around Samantha.

CHAPTER SEVENTEEN

Eloise and Erastus Oppenheimer both had light blond hair and fair skin, so David had always thought they looked ghostly. However, in old age, they looked more eerie as if they had wandered in from behind the veil. Eloise had grown thinner, and her stark white hair had thinned as well, but she moved like a young woman. Erastus walked with a cane and his white hair now covered his entire body. Reddish rims around his blue eyes made them look especially piercing when he stared David down as they approached.

Even with seemingly thousands of people streaming through the foyer, and a roar of friendly greetings and organ music, Erastus had managed to pick out David from all the way down the walk and stare at him unblinkingly for several minutes as they walked closer. Jess and Carson also greeted them in the foyer, along with their three oldest children—the younger two probably in daycare. Their kids looked so much older, David might have guessed that they'd raised a crop of completely different, but similar-looking children. Their oldest, Ashlynn, was the same age as Evangeline and looked alarmingly grown-up in makeup and high heels.

Erastus stopped glaring at David to address his daughter for the first time in over a year. "Why did you cut your pretty hair?" he asked. "You look like a boy."

Amanda gave him a tight-lipped scowl. "It fell out during chemotherapy, *Dad.*"

"I think it looks very nice," Eloise said, reaching out to rearrange a strand even though Amanda looked mad enough to bite. "Stylish. Like on the television."

"Thank you," Amanda said.

"How much did your haircut cost?" Eloise asked.

"I don't know mom, $75?"

She gasped and put her hand to her heart. "That's obscene. Sandy at Great Clips does my hair. $6.99. She can do that same cut you have for $6.99."

"I'm not sure if that's true, but okay."

"Please," she said, waving a dismissive hand at Amanda. "You really think the homosexual who cuts your hair is more than *ten* times better than my Sandy?" Eloise asked.

Amanda gritted her teeth and turned toward David, giving him an, *I told you this was a bad idea* glare.

"Look at these two," Eloise said, ignoring Amanda's scowl and kissing Emmy on the cheek. "What a lovely young lady you've become. And look at you in your tie," she said to Patrick. "You look just like a man."

"Where is my grandson?" Erastus asked.

"He's right here," Amanda said, nodding toward Patrick.

"No, not that one. Where's Jude?"

"College," Amanda said.

"Don't tell me 'college,'" Erastus said. "It's Easter Sunday. That's a family day. Do they now hold classes on Easter Sunday? I wouldn't be surprised, the way the world is these days." He tapped his cane on the floor as if to add an exclamation point to his sentence.

"He has a test tomorrow," Amanda said. "Had to study."

"Oh, I see now. You're lying." Erastus pointed a knobby finger at Amanda.

"The service is going to start in two minutes," Carson said. "And last year on Easter Sunday, it was standing room only, so…" He took his mother's arm and led her into the church to put an end to the conversation.

After a large Easter dinner of honey baked ham at Jess and Carson's house, David sat in the living room in the hopes of having a moment of reprieve. He called Xavier, as Evangeline preferred to pretend phones didn't exist.

"What?" Xavier said on the other line.

"When I call you, I'd really prefer it if you didn't answer with 'what?'"

"Okay."

"Am I interrupting something important?"

"It's kind of important."

"If it's anything other than a video game, I'll give you a million dollars."

"Well, in that case, it's something else," he said over the sound of digital gunfire.

"What is your sister doing?"

"I don't know."

"Well… have you at least seen her lately? Is she in the apartment?"

"Where else would she be?"

Erastus entered the room, clacking his cane on the hardwood, and keeping David in scope the whole time with those pale watery eyes.

"All right then," David said into the phone. "I'll let you get back to killing zombies, or Nazis, or zombie Nazis, or whatever. We'll be leaving here very soon."

"Okay," Xavier said again and hung up.

Erastus sat on the cream colored couch next to David with a grunt.

"Was that your girlfriend?" he asked.

"No," David said. "It was my son."

"Ah, the bastard."

David shook his head, but ignored the comment. "From the way you've been staring me down all morning, I assume you've come in here to threaten me in some way."

"Naw."

"Really?" he asked with a tight smile. "Last I heard, you planned to kill me on sight."

"Well, my sweet little girl asked me very nicely not to. In truth, what she said was 'listen old man, you lay a finger on my husband and I'll cut you.'" He laughed his big, ground shaking laugh. "I still think she should have divorced you, but I've always respected the big brass balls on that girl."

Erastus gestured for David to come closer and David leaned about an inch toward him. He smelled like wintergreen and stale coffee. "But I could you know," he whispered. "I could kill you without a blink. It would be very easy." He laughed again, as if he had shared a dirty joke and not a death threat.

"I thought you didn't practice magic," David said.

He laughed again. "You think I mean by magic?" He stopped laughing and looked David in the eye, his expression taking an abrupt shift toward darkness. "Killing spells are for *cowards*," he said, spraying him with spit as he emphasized the last word. "That's what wizards do. Too prissy to get their hands dirty. Too cowardly to face their victim. I'll tell you how you kill a man," he said, pointing a hairy finger at David. "You look that man in the eyes and you pull the trigger. You watch as the life drains from him. You *own* it. You *experience* it. That's the only way to truly respect the power of death. You face it. You speak to it. You smell it. You taste it. Anything else disrespects man, life, death, God, and everything else."

"Or you could just not kill anyone," David said.

Erastus laughed again. "Your generation is so soft. I was in

'Nam. I know death. And I saw a lot of cowardly killing. Dropping bombs. Placing mines. Not me. I was a sniper. You think the men I killed didn't deserve to die?"

"I have no idea."

"Yeah, well," he said, waving a dismissive hand. "You couldn't do it."

"No, I couldn't. And I don't think that's a bad thing."

"Being a practicing dark wizard is bad enough, you're not even a good one. That's the only Godly purpose men like us can have. We do the tough jobs. The things the others can't stomach. Things that can rip the soul to pieces but still need to be done. That's why God placed us on this earth. If you can't do that, then you're nothing but a demon."

Patrick wandered over clutching a Solo cup and sat in the over-sized sofa chair across from them. David gave him a warning look, trying to tell him to hide out elsewhere, but Patrick didn't seem to notice. Erastus turned his milky eyes over to his grandson.

"Patrick," David said, trying to shift the conversation. "Why don't you tell Grandpa what you're thinking about majoring in?"

"I haven't decided," Patrick said.

"I thought you were going to go for pre-med," David said.

Patrick shrugged. "Maybe. I'm not sure."

"What did you think of the service?" David asked, continuing his push for small talk. "I thought it was nice. I liked the preacher."

Patrick shrugged. "If you really think about it, the Easter story is pretty dark and violent. And kind of gross."

"But it has a happy ending," David said.

Patrick squinted at him. "Do you believe that? That Jesus really rose from the dead?"

"I don't know," David said. His attempt at small talk had failed. How did he end up talking about religion of all things? "I don't think it matters though."

"It doesn't matter whether or not Jesus really rose from the dead? I think that's pretty critical, actually."

David considered the question. "I think the important part is when he died on the cross. He suffered terrible pain for what he believed in. He was afraid and he was alone. But he did it anyway… because of love. And in doing so, he became more immortal than any other human being that's ever lived."

Patrick nodded and picked at his cup. It pleased David that he came up with an intelligent enough answer to satisfy Patrick—the child most likely to outwit him.

"You should pay attention to the Easter story, son," Erastus said. "Your kind probably nailed him to that cross that day. *You* come from a nasty breed," Erastus said, pointing his cane at Patrick. "On your father's side for sure. You sure as hell didn't get it from me."

"Hey," David said. "That's not okay. He's your grandson. He hasn't done anything wrong." David defended Patrick automatically, but he didn't understand the insult. What did he mean by nasty breed? Wizards? He had that on both sides, and he directed his words toward Patrick.

"Oh, I think Patrick can take care of himself. Isn't that right, Patrick?"

"I don't know what you're talking about, Grandpa," he said.

"Just promise me this, son. If the time comes, you kill me like a man. No sorcery. Look me in the eye and take my life. And don't send one of your assassins either. I want you to do it."

"My assassins?" Patrick looked at David and had a hesitant smile, as if unsure whether or not his grandfather had told a joke he didn't get.

"All right, that's enough," David said. He grabbed Patrick's arm and led him out of the room.

"Do you think he's gone senile or something?" Patrick asked.

"I don't know. I'm sorry."

Amanda helped Carson wash dishes after dinner for something to do with her hands. Her mother had helped alongside them, but got tired and went to go lie down, and Jess watched the kids, so Amanda only had to deal with her brother, the least of the evils, perhaps. He had tried. He visited her in the hospital. He invited her over for all the holidays that had passed since they had been estranged, but she'd always used cancer as an excuse, even when she felt up to it. If he couldn't come visit her through cancer treatment, she wouldn't drag her exhausted, nauseous self over to his house for some obligatory holiday invite.

"I'm really glad you came," Carson said, taking a dish from her hand and drying it.

"I'm here because David wanted to come. And because I wanted to go to church on Easter."

"Well, I'm glad you wanted to do that."

"Just so we're clear, you didn't save my soul or anything. God and I are just fine."

"Okay."

"How are Mom and Dad? You would tell me if one of them was sick or something, wouldn't you?"

"They're fine. Healthy. They don't practice magic, so…"

"So, they'll live forever? I forgot all Mundanes lived forever. Thanks for reminding me." She attacked a plate with a sponge, making an unnecessary squeaking noise.

"You know what I mean."

"Not really."

"They were really happy to learn the cancer is gone. They were worried about you."

"Yeah, I could tell by the way they never contacted me or visited me in the hospital."

"I told them they should. They just didn't want to encourage you."

"Encourage me to *what* exactly?"

He didn't reply, and took the plate she attacked with the sponge. "I think this is clean," he said. "You're going to wear a hole in the porcelain."

She held up a small plate. "Can these go in the dishwasher?" she asked with a tone more aggressive than necessary for the question.

"I'm not sure. To be safe, let's not."

Amanda rinsed off the remnants of chocolate cream pie, ignoring the hot water biting her skin.

"I just want you to know, I love you anyway," Carson said.

"You love me *anyway*? You are such a jerk."

Carson put his hands in the air and opened his mouth in theatrical speechlessness. "My unconditional love for you makes me a jerk? Seriously, Amanda?"

"When you say it like that it does. You clearly don't understand unconditional love."

"Oh, don't I?" he said with a cold chuckle. "What exactly am I getting wrong?"

"Unconditional love isn't loving someone *in spite* of who they are, it's loving them *because* of who they are."

"Now you're the one being patronizing. Acting like I don't understand love. What, you think you love your family better than I love mine? That I'm not doing it right or something?"

"No, I'm not saying that."

"Obviously anything I say is going to piss you off, so what's the point?"

"I don't know. You're the one who invited me here. Where do you put these crystal goblets?"

Carson took the goblet from her. "Just put them here for now, they go in the cabinet."

"I shouldn't have said you didn't understand love," Amanda said, keeping her eyes the lemon-scented bubbles she had accumulated in the sink in front of her. "But you don't understand winter magic. You don't understand it, so you hate it."

Carson paused for a moment before he spoke. "What's to understand?"

"Chemotherapy is like dying so you can live. It kills you cell by cell in the hopes the tumors will die as well. It's *poison* you willingly pump into your veins every week. It made me feel sicker than I ever thought possible. Sick enough that sometimes I forgot why I wanted to live in the first place."

"I'm sorry."

"No," she said, waving away his platitude. "Just listen to me. I'm telling you it wasn't life that saved me. It was death. Poisonous, toxic, death pumped into my veins. In the end, healing wasn't about life. It was about death. Instead of running from death, I had to drink it."

"Okay. So what are you saying?"

"I'm saying that destruction has a purpose in the world, and you shouldn't be so afraid of it."

"It may have a place in the world. But it doesn't have a place in my own home. Or in my own children."

Amanda chuckled. "Yeah, well, it's there if you like it or not. You have five children, and four of them are winter. You really think none of them are ever going to figure it out? Hell, probably at least one or two of them already have."

"You don't know my children."

"No, I don't. You've made sure of it. But I know teenagers, and I know winter wizards, and I know you're kidding yourself."

"No, you're kidding yourself if you think dark wizards don't have a choice. We can still be good Christians and good people. That's the choice we've made. Your family made a different choice."

"For the record, we are good Christians and good people. We just also happen to be wizards. We chose to be proud of who we are."

"And what about Jude? You're proud of him? Do you even

know where he is?"

"You fucking asshole. How dare you throw that in my face?"

"I'll keep praying for you, Amanda."

"Oh, really? Well, I'll keep praying for *you*."

Amanda shoved a clean serving platter into Carson's hands.

"Calm down, you're going to break my china."

"You're right. I think we're done here. I wouldn't want to break your pretty plates."

"Don't leave." He grabbed her arm. "Please don't leave it like this," he said in a softer tone. He caught her gaze and screamed words she couldn't hear with his bright blue eyes.

"Leave *what* like this?"

"Well… you know, us. You're my sister and I love you. I need to make things right before…"

"Before what? If you cared about making amends with me before I died, you would have visited me on my actual deathbed. The cancer could always come back, but for now I'm in the clear. You're a little late to make amends."

"You never know when things might change."

"I said we're done here. Where is my family? We're leaving. Happy Easter."

Emmy listened as Ashlynn swiped through pictures of her spring break church retreat. She had a lot of pictures of her new boyfriend and she gave Emmy a play by play of every moment they had spent together. When did Ashlynn become so boring?

They used to be best friends, with matching best friend lockets and everything. They looked similar, so they would always tell people they were twins even though Emmy was a year and a half older. Now that Emmy knew about wizards, she could see that she and Ashlynn had winter magic in common too. She had a nice crisp, dry cold magic radiating from her. However, it seemed Ashlynn remained oblivious.

Emmy would want to know. She would want to know every stupid little thing she cared about didn't matter, just boring, Mundane shit. She would want to know she missed a whole other magical world hanging right in front of her face—or closer than that—living *inside* her. It would be cruel to let her go on not knowing, living a boring Mundane life when she could have so much more.

However, Emmy had already heard the sound of Mom's voice rising downstairs and figured they didn't have much time for that discussion. She couldn't casually mention the existence of magic. *BTW—Magic is real. And you're a witch. One of the bad kind. But, it's not really that bad. Well, it kind of is. But not all the time…*

"Can I ask you something?" Emmy said.

"Sure."

"What did your parents tell you, about why they stopped talking to us?"

Ashlynn puckered her lips, as if to protest talking about something other than her boyfriend.

"I don't know. You know parents. Some stupid drama." She smiled to herself as she continued to look at her pictures.

"So they didn't explain it at all? Why didn't you ask them?"

"Well, *your* mom decided to stop coming to see us," she said, swinging her legs around to sit next to Emmy on the side of the bed. "We invited you to Christmas and you didn't come. She's the one that's mad at my dad. I don't know why, and I don't care. Whatever it is, it's stupid."

"*Your* dad bailed on her when she was sick."

The door to Ashlynn's room opened and Aunt Jess entered, her long paisley skirt rustling around her. "Hi, girls. What are you doing?"

"Nothing, Mom," Ashlynn said.

"Emmy, can I see you for a second?" Jess asked.

Emmy looked at Ashlynn, wondering if she had heard her wrong.

"Me?" she asked.

"What do you want, Mom?" Ashlynn interjected.

"I just want to show Emmy something. It will only take a minute."

Emmy followed Aunt Jess out of Ashlynn's room and into her little cousin's empty bedroom next door. Emmy stepped on a truck and it made a siren sound. Aunt Jess ignored the offending toy and grabbed Emmy's arm so hard it hurt. Emmy tried to pull away. Aunt Jess had always seemed so kind. She had warm chocolate eyes and cute little freckles. Seeing her turn aggressive scared Emmy.

"Let go of me," Emmy pleaded. "Don't hurt me."

"What did you do?"

"Nothing. I didn't tell her anything." Emmy said, but her aunt looked at her with confusion. "Aunt Jess, please, you're hurting me."

Aunt Jess released Emmy's arm, leaving a red mark behind. "I'm sorry, honey. I'm just scared."

"What are you talking about?"

"You're playing with some very dangerous magic."

"I don't know what you're talking about," Emmy said. She didn't feel as if she could do anything particularly interesting, let alone dangerous.

"Maybe not you, but there is powerful dark magic coming from your family you'd have to be blind to miss. It may not be you. I think it might be the *girl*. The one your father had with that other woman."

"Her *name* is Evangeline."

"I'm sure it wasn't you, Emmy. You're a good girl."

"What makes you think Evangeline's casting dangerous spells? Have you ever even officially met her? You don't know anything about our family anymore."

"I know Samantha's friend died from a killing spell. And that draws attention. You don't see killing spells very often, even among dark wizards. Too difficult. Too risky."

Emmy paused a moment, distracted by curiosity. "Hang on. How did you know about that? Did my parents tell you?"

Aunt Jess raised her eyebrows. "I'm an autumn witch, honey. It's my job to know about these things. I'm always watching."

"Well… that's really creepy."

She had a brief flicker of a smile, and then her face went cold again. "You don't understand," she whispered the words and looked around her. "I have very good reasons for keeping my children away from magic, and it's probably not the reasons you think."

"Okay… then why?"

"Magic disrupts the balance… specifically powerful solstice magic. It calls attention to you. If you don't practice, they won't come after you."

"Who won't come after you?"

"You're a good girl, Emmy."

"Stop saying that."

"When they come, just run. They won't follow."

"Aunt Jess, who is coming?"

"Leave your family and run."

"I would never leave my family."

"Just run."

"What is this? Some kind of vague fall witch prophecy?"

"I have five children, Emmy, and four of them are winter. I'm on your side. Please trust me. I don't want you to be hurt, just like I don't want my own children to be hurt. Just run. They won't follow if you don't practice." Aunt Jess pulled her into an aggressive hug and kissed her on the side of her face. "Goodbye sweetheart," she said. "You'll be okay. You're a good girl."

"I told you to stop saying that."

"Emmy, where are you? We're leaving now," Mom yelled from downstairs. Emmy answered the call, happy for an excuse to turn away from Aunt Jess and run down the stairs. At the bottom, she looked up and wished she had said goodbye to Ashlynn, but Mom grabbed her by the arm to pull her into the humid air.

"Dad and Patrick are already in the car. Come on. We're going home."

CHAPTER EIGHTEEN

I t took the rest of the Vandergraffs a long time to come back to the apartment, but Samantha didn't mind too much. She lay on the couch and stared at the ceiling and tried to focus on remembering which way was up. She thought she might vomit if she moved too fast, but she gradually felt better. She had a headache and felt lightheaded, but she no longer expected her heart to stop beating at any moment.

Xavier and Evangeline weren't so bad when they weren't casting spells through her body. Evangeline brought her a glass of water and then ignored her, which Samantha preferred over the type of freak out that might have come from Emmy and Patrick. Although she did think Xavier kept an eye on her. Or Samantha just happened to lie near his video game console in the living room. He played for the rest of the afternoon, as Evangeline had dared him to do before.

When Samantha heard the jiggle of the lock at the front door, she sat up and tried to compose herself. She took a deep breath to stifle the wave of nausea.

Amanda came in carrying two more potted lilies, fresh and alive. Patrick followed her with a dish wrapped in foil looking angry and handsome in his shirt and tie. He glanced at Amanda before moving past his mother into the kitchen to put the food away.

"So, what did you guys do while we were gone?" Amanda asked.

Samantha and Xavier both said, "nothing," in unison, which probably seemed super suspicious. They glared at each other, both blaming the other for replying so quickly.

Amanda looked at both of them with narrowed eyes. "Okay," she said finally. "Weren't there more lilies here?" she asked putting the other two down on the now empty dining table. She looked around the apartment.

"Xavier threw them away," Evangeline said. She had appeared from the doorway of her bedroom where she had lurked for the past hour.

"Why would you do such a thing?" Amanda asked, turning on Xavier.

He glared at Evangeline and then opened his mouth to explain, but no explanation came out.

"Allergies," Samantha said. "They were giving him allergies."

"Why didn't you just say something?" Amanda said. She took the two lilies she had brought in and took them back outside and placed them outside the door. Amanda stayed in the doorway and said, "What are you two looking at?"

Samantha could see Amanda's face turn serious, but she couldn't see what she looked at. Samantha stood up and walked toward the door. She felt as if she walked across the deck of a ship, but she managed not to vomit or faint on her way to the door.

She clung on the doorframe and watched David kneeling, watching something fluttering on the ground on the landing outside their apartment door. Emmy stood over him, watching as well.

"I think he's having a stroke or something," Emmy said. "He just keeps staring at them."

"Staring at what?" Amanda asked.

"Butterflies," Emmy explained. "Three dead butterflies."

"That ones not dead," Amanda said, and she nudged the fluttering one with her shoe. "Oh, well, there it goes." The fluttering one lay still, its purple wings brilliant in the sun.

Samantha walked over and kneeled across from David, grateful for a chance to sit. She felt Emmy's eyes on her as she steadied herself.

Samantha didn't know why she felt compelled to test out her skills, but she knew what Imogene would do in the situation, so she did the same. She nudged the purple butterfly into her cupped hands. For the past few hours, keeping herself alive seemed like enough work, and she doubted she had any extra life available to share, even enough for the tiny creature. But she could try.

She opened her hands. At first she thought the wings had fluttered again, but it was only the wind. The wind ruffled the wings and then a larger gust sent the dead insect tumbling across the cement landing, away from Samantha. She looked up and everyone watched it as it tumbled away and off the side, getting one last taste of flight in death as it floated down to the ground.

Patrick, Evangeline, and Xavier had come outside too and watched the butterfly fall. Samantha eyed Evangeline for her reaction. She clutched her arms around her chest again, looking much more like a little girl. Samantha had never seen Evangeline look that afraid.

Later Amanda went "angry shopping" as David had called it and he stayed engrossed in his laptop, so Samantha took her opportunity to corner Xavier in the kitchen.

"Are we the three butterflies?" Samantha whispered, as she poured herself a glass of water. "What does that mean?"

"Nothing. They're butterflies," Xavier said without looking

up at her. "Maybe they were flying too close and got caught in Evangeline's spell or maybe it was a coincidence."

"You're probably right. It was just really creepy. There were three of us. And three dead butterflies. If it's not us, then who?"

"No one. No one is a butterfly. We're people." Xavier glanced over at David, who sat at the dining table staring at his laptop.

"Well, yeah. I know that. It's *symbolism*."

"And technically, I was just there. I didn't participate in the spell." Xavier watched as Patrick emerged from him room, having shed his church clothes in exchange for a T-shirt and shorts.

"Yes, you did. You helped me. If you hadn't been there to slap me back to my senses, it might not have worked. And I might have died. So… thank you, by the way."

"Quit talking to me. People are going to think we're friends."

"How horrifying for you."

Samantha followed Xavier's glance to Patrick. He remained engrossed in his phone, too engrossed, as if he made a point to ignore them.

"I'll stop," Samantha said, but Xavier had already left the kitchen.

David's vision kept blurring as he read the words on his laptop screen. He bit the inside of his lip so hard, he tasted blood. He had to bite his lip to stop himself from letting loose a string of curses in front of his children. None of them had noticed he had glared at his laptop screen without typing for several minutes while tapping the dining table with his pen.

His private investigator had followed Zander and confirmed that he did leave the state, but only got as far as Louisiana and then stopped, not nearly far enough. He had assumed Patrick's spell would have sent him to the airport to get on a plane to Australia or something similar. It would take a powerful wizard to resist a fall equinox wizard.

However, Zander's current whereabouts weren't David's biggest concern. Despite all the horrible things that David had imagined about this young man, the PI's information shocked him.

Zander had lived in a juvenile detention center from the ages of fifteen through eighteen. The PI had explained that this particular facility served the "criminally insane" —too dangerous to be around other children in foster care. Zander only walked free now because he had committed his crime as a minor and the psychiatrists had deemed him mentally incompetent.

At fifteen, the courts convicted Zander of homicide—specifically the murder of one of his foster siblings, a baby girl.

The son of a bitch murdered a baby.

CHAPTER NINETEEN

Patrick cringed as he loaded bags of soil and compost into the trunk of his new car. The nerves threading through his spine felt as if they snapped one by one. Caroline's torture had left him with nagging pains that wouldn't go away. He had gotten used to clenching his jaw and trying to ignore it.

"I hope you weren't too attached to your new car smell," Samantha said, misinterpreting the look on his face.

Thunder rumbled and Patrick looked up. "Overrated," he said as he closed the trunk. They both climbed into the front seat and Patrick pulled out of the Home Depot parking lot. He turned on the air conditioner high to combat the murky humidity clinging to him.

"Thanks again for doing this," Samantha said. "I miss having a garden."

"It's no problem."

"My mom used to make a fertilizer brew every spring. Grass clippings, fruit peelings, and plenty of spring magic. It worked amazingly. Could make anything grow. To me, *that* is what springtime smells like. Orange peels and fresh grass. Delicious."

"Do you need grass clippings and orange peels?"

"It's okay. I don't have time to brew anything. I need to get these in the ground right away."

Samantha held up the paper grocery bag she had stashed at her feet.

"Did you just buy that? I didn't notice."

"No."

"Then where did you get it?"

"The garbage."

"What?"

"They are the Easter lilies Xavier threw away yesterday."

"Oh, okay…"

"Evangeline was talking about how flowers die easily, and that's not really true. The petals themselves are fragile…" She took a small dirty bulb out of the bag and held it up. "But the bulbs are not. That's one of the reasons why the lily is a symbol for Easter in the first place. Resurrection."

Patrick watched Samantha wander around the land around their new home site, examining spots of soil. A cottonwood tree shed tufts of cotton that floated through the air, making it look as if Samantha wandered through a springtime snowfall. He tried not to stare at her too much, although it seemed more awkward to stare at the ground or the sky. He forgot where he would naturally be looking without Samantha there.

She had grown more beautiful, although he couldn't say why he thought that. She didn't look good in an objective way. Her hair that once looked like spun silk had now frayed and looked tattered as if she'd stopped brushing it. Two very long years reflected in her eyes—time when she's suffered, grown, and changed, and became a different person.

"I like this spot," Samantha said.

Patrick walked toward her to examine the spot of ground she had chosen. Other plants liked the spot. It overflowed with bright green grass and small purple flowers. Bees buzzed around his ears.

"Are you sure this is okay?" Samantha asked.

"I don't see why not." Patrick hadn't asked his parents whether or not Samantha could plant lilies on their property, but mostly because he had skipped his last class of the day so he could take her.

Samantha tried to help bring over bags of soil and compost, and she was stronger than she looked. Patrick took the big bags, and he felt as if his back might snap as he slung them over his shoulder. White spots swam in his vision. Samantha swung the smaller bag of compost over her shoulder like a feather pillow.

He used the shovel to break ground for Samantha's garden, and she cared for her mangled lily bulbs, untangling and trimming the roots like a child's hair.

"You've changed a lot you know," she said.

"Have I?"

"Everyone in your family has changed some since I saw them last. And I've changed. But you've changed the most. Why is that?"

"I don't know how to answer that," Patrick answered, wiping sweat out of his eyes.

"Something about you is fundamentally different. But I can't put my finger on it."

"*Fundamentally* different? I doubt that."

Samantha shrugged.

"Is it *bad* different?"

"Change isn't always good, but at least it's change."

"It's hard to argue with that logic."

"Then don't."

Patrick shrugged and went back to shoveling.

"I think that's good," Samantha said. "I don't need a very large bed."

Patrick tried not to act too relieved. He put his shovel down and rubbed the base of his back before helping her rip into the bags of soil and place them over the bed.

After that, she shooed him away because she wanted to plant the bulbs herself. He didn't argue. In part, because he needed to drink some water and catch his breath, but also because he trusted her with the actual plants. She was spring. He was fall. He had no use touching plants. If the symbolism behind the seasons held true, he would kill them, or at least mark the beginning of their slow demise.

The hovering gray clouds threatened rain, but also brought cooler air. Maybe the fresh cool air would make Patrick smell better by the time they got in the car. Of course, Samantha had spread compost with her bare hands, so stinkiness didn't seem high on her list of concerns. When she finished, she sat with her knees folded under her staring at the patch of dirt they had created. She wiped beads of sweat off her forehead, leaving a swipe of dirt across her forehead to match the dirt caked on her hands and forearms.

He tried again not to stare. Dirt suited her, that and the flush of red on her cheeks from the work and the heat, the sweat running down her chest, and the cottonwood tuffs adorning her hair, she looked stunning.

However, Samantha didn't seem to notice him staring. She stared at the bed, as if literally waiting for grass to grow.

"How long will it take?" Patrick asked. As far as he knew, she might say *seconds* or *weeks*.

"You're supposed to plant bulbs in the fall. They bide their time all winter and then burst out of the ground in the spring."

Everything she said about the seasons always sounded so sexy.

"But it's already spring," she continued. "We're going against the natural order of things. But we're wizards. That's what we do… go against the natural order."

"Well why didn't we plant flowers that are meant to be planted in the spring? Wouldn't that have been easier?"

She didn't answer. Instead she reached over and grabbed his

hand, now sweaty and raw from the shoveling. Her hands felt warm and gritty. She pulled him over to her.

"What are you doing?" he asked, trying to sound casual. In honesty, his heart had plunged into overdrive. She was gay, which unexpectedly, had felt like a relief. He could spend time with her and stare and her without having to do anything about it. The perfect coward's love affair.

"I'm casting a spell to make them grow," Samantha answered. "I thought you could help me."

"I'm fall. How can I cast a growing spell? Everything starts to die in the fall. Leaves turning brown and falling off, and all that stuff."

"Don't be so negative. You're alive aren't you?"

"Yeah…"

"Well then you must have some power of life in there you can share with the flowers… or I just wanted a reason to hold your hand."

She gave him a cock-eyed smile, which Patrick didn't return. He didn't intend to glare at her, but he must have, because her smile faded and she dropped his hand.

"No, I can help," he said. "I mean, I can try. If you think it will help. I don't want to accidentally kill your flowers."

She smiled. "I trust you. The worst you can do is nothing at all."

Patrick doubted that, but he'd never tried a spell like this.

"So what do I do?"

"It's like most other kinds of spells. Concentrate on what you want to happen. Really visualize it. You'll be specifically harnessing the life inside you… which everyone has of course, even Mundanes, plants, and bugs. Everything. Spring wizards are just the best at using it. But you can use it too… especially you," she added.

"I guess Emmy told you what I was."

"A fall equinox wizard," she said nodding. "I almost

guessed that myself when I checked your date, but I wasn't confident enough to say so. It's a pretty big deal."

He shrugged. "If I even am one."

"Don't shrug like that."

"Like what?"

"You *know* you're an equinox wizard, I can tell. So don't pretend you're not sure. You're way more than you used to be, and you were always a little smug."

Patrick scoffed. He had never felt smug. Smugness implied confidence. Granted, he did feel more powerful now, but that made him worry more about making a mistake.

"Are we going to do this thing, or what?"

Samantha held out her hand to him again, and he took it. Less taken off guard this time, but his heart rate increased.

"Give it a minute. Really focus on it."

Patrick closed his eyes, but chanced a few peeks at Samantha who had her eyes closed too. He could feel her hand growing warmer as if she did manage to increase the life inside her. The sensation intoxicated him. The warmth radiating from her hand made everything wonderful. The pain in his jaw and in his back turned into a pleasant warmth, the smell of sweat and dirt became as delicious as melted chocolate, even the scene in front of him came alive. Millions of colors he had never seen before danced in the flowers and the sky and in Samantha's skin and hair. Even the pounding of his heart felt good. Instead of anxiety, the racing heart rate reminded him of all the life he had in him, and the miracle of how mere cells and blood and hair became so much more with the power of life.

Samantha dropped his hand and he wanted to grab it again, to bring back the magical feeling.

"Are you okay?" she asked.

"Fine," Patrick answered.

His ears and eyes felt too hot and he couldn't imagine what he might look like, probably bright red.

"I know you weren't doing anything," Samantha said, but she didn't sound angry. She rolled her eyes.

"I'm sorry. I just don't think I can. Did it work?" He glanced at the bed of dirt.

"I don't know," Samantha said. "It's too soon to tell." She skimmed the top of the soil with her fingers as if she did half expect to see green bubs popping through the soil.

"How long?"

"I don't know," she said again, an edge to her voice this time.

Patrick noticed the grass around the bed had thickened and glowed with a shade of green he'd never seen until moments before when the whole world had a million extra colors. The purple flowers that had once dotted the grass behind them had turned into a lush carpet, so bright they looked unreal. From what he could tell the spell had worked on the grass, on the flowers, and possibly on him. But not the lilies.

"Why don't you tell me if they'll grow," Samantha said, suddenly angry. "Don't fall wizards know everything?"

"No," Patrick said. "All other kinds of wizards think we can predict winning lotto numbers and stuff. I don't know much about fall magic, but I know it doesn't work like that. Was there some specific question you wanted to ask me?"

"What do you mean?"

"That's always what other wizards want from fall wizards right? Some kind of prediction or prophecy."

"No, I don't think we *want* them. Fall wizards just like to give them."

He smiled. "Well, not me. Besides, no one can really tell the future, even wizards. And if they say so, they're lying."

"I don't think that's true."

"Fall wizards are really just very good guessers. We can't actually *see* the future, we're just really good at anticipating what will happen. We can see the world in a grander way. We can see forces at play that are invisible to others. We know what people are likely to do even if they don't know it themselves. So our predictions are just extremely educated guesses."

"Yeah… you're really smug."

"I'm saying I *can't* tell the future. Even if I think I know the future, I could always be wrong."

"Have you been wrong before?"

"Sort of," he said. "The prophecy itself isn't wrong, but the interpretation could be wrong. I am wrong all the time."

"Do you *want* to be wrong?"

"Why would I want to be wrong?"

"I've just never heard a man brag so much about his ability to be wrong about stuff. It's suspicious."

He laughed. "Well… yeah. I want to be wrong sometimes."

"Because you know something bad is going to happen?"

"That's not what I mean. It's just… what's the point of anything if you know how it's all going to turn out? Knowing the future kills all hope. Hope can only exist when you don't know what's going to happen. There is always a chance something amazing could happen tomorrow. If you were going to die in a week, would you want to know? What's the point? It would just ruin your last week on earth."

"*Am* I going to die in a week?"

"No, of course not."

"Are *you* going to die in a week?"

"No. No one is going to die in a week. Well, I mean lots of people are going to die in a week, but not necessarily anyone we know. It was just an example."

She leaned in and kissed him, which totally took him off guard. Probably because she said it earlier, but he thought she tasted like fresh cut grass and oranges. Her lips fit in with his perfectly, as if they could anticipate each other's actions and didn't take a wrong move.

She pulled back and smiled at him.

"Did you know that was going to happen?"

"I did not."

"There you go. The world is still full of beautiful chaos." She fluttered her hands in the air on the world "chaos," as if she shooed away invisible butterflies.

Samantha leaned in to him again, catching his lips in another supernaturally delicious kiss. Then she crawled on top of him, and wrapped her legs around his waist. He pushed her off of him, more roughly than he had meant to.

She glared at him open-mouthed from the patch of too-green grass next to him.

"What are you doing?" Patrick asked.

"What does it look like I'm doing? I *was* making out with you."

"You can't."

"Why the hell not?"

It seemed so obvious to Patrick, he didn't know where to begin. The *reasons.* "I thought you were gay," he said, choosing the easiest reason first.

"I like both."

"You can't do that."

"Yes, I can."

"Are you sure?"

She laughed with an exasperated tone. "Yeah, I'm sure, Patrick."

"Is that really something you want, after everything that happened?"

"Oh, I get it. Because of what Jude did to me, I should never want to have sex again, right? I'm permanently damaged and incapable of actually *wanting* someone."

"Of course not. That's not what I meant…What about Imogene? I mean she just died."

"Oh my God," she said standing up. "Two for two. You really know how to kill the mood. Yeah, she's dead Patrick," she said with tears brimming out her eyes. "You don't think I know that? You find it necessary to remind me?"

"I…"

"She's dead, and a lot of the time, I wish I was dead too. I find one thing that makes me feel a little more alive, and you take it away from me."

"I…"

"Fall wizards are the worst," she said. "No wonder you're so rare, how do you even reproduce when you're such a buzzkill?"

She grabbed her sandals and walked away, and Patrick followed her, not sure how she planned on storming away if he was her ride.

"You know, I'm a big girl. If I say I want something, then I do. You don't have to try and protect me from my own silly desires."

"Okay, I'm sorry."

"Take me home… back," she said, amending her statement.

CHAPTER TWENTY

Zander remembered the feeling of small hands shaking him. Imogene's black hair dangling in his face. One of her hot tears dripped on his forehead.

"Hey… what's wrong?"

"You have to come. Help me please."

He crawled out of bed and followed her. The house had a strange nightmarish feeling about it. A coldness hung in the air. An absence. He had no idea how to describe it, but it felt sinister. The image of Imogene's little figure darting through the house, her oversized white T-shirt glowing in the darkness, had burned into his memory.

Apparently, he didn't move fast enough, because she stopped to grab his hand and pull him along. She had done this before. If she wanted him to look at an interesting bug or some imagination game required immediate attention. But this time, she clutched his fingers so tightly, they felt like all bone. He had no idea someone so small could have so much strength.

She pulled him into the nursery room and pointed at the crib.

"She's not breathing," Imogene said.

Zander's stomach lurched as he looked at the tiny unmoving figure in the crib.

"She always cries at night, and I come in and sing to her," Imogene said. "But I woke up and it was too quiet. Too quiet."

Zander's mouth tasted like blood, and he realized he had bitten into the side of his cheek. The sinister cold absence came from this room. Death.

Imogene had crawled up onto a toy box she had placed by the crib and reached into take the baby. She thrust the child into Zander's arm.

She was cold. Still.

"I sang to her before I went to bed, and she was fine. What happened? What did I do?"

Zander's arms shook. Even if the child had lost the warmth of life, she couldn't have become so cold. Even wrapped in blankets, she seemed frigid.

"I almost brought her back. I got so close. I just couldn't ignite enough fire. Help me, Zander. Help me."

"What?"

"You're a wizard. You're a special wizard. Help me relight her fire."

"Imogene…" his voice broke. "That's just a fantasy. I can't do anything. We have to wake Miss Cathy. We have to call an ambulance."

"No! No ambulance!" She squealed it so loud, he knew she had probably woken some of the others. "They'll just put a blanket over her face," Imogene said quietly. "They'll put a blanket over her and she'll be gone forever. They can't help her. The Mundanes can't help her. Please Zander, just try."

A light turned on down the hall.

"No," Imogene gasped. "That's Miss Cathy. She'll call the Mundanes."

Imogene snatched the infant back from Zander and ran out of the room. Zander followed her without thinking. He followed her out the back door and out of the backyard gate, his bare feet burning in the cold.

"Imogene. Stop," he called. Once the shock of finding himself outside wore off, he caught up to her and grabbed her by the shoulders. "What are you doing? I'm sorry, it's too late. It's too late. It's not your fault, but there's nothing you can do now."

"That's not true! I made her breathe again. But I couldn't keep the light burning."

"That's not possible."

"Shut up. Shut up. Why are you being so stupid? Why won't you help me?"

"I…"

"You can see if you really look. You can already see. Can't you see what's missing?"

"Give her to me."

"Are you going to take her to Miss Cathy?"

"No," Zander said, although he didn't have a different plan.

Imogene passed the child to Zander's arms. They made the transition carefully, though he couldn't harm the infant anymore.

Zander looked at the tiny doll-like face, made more doll-like by its stillness and coldness. "That's not fair," Zander said. "That she should die before she even lives. It's wrong."

"Make it right," Imogene said, her voice trembling in the cold. She too had bare legs and feet.

"I don't know how."

"It's like praying. Have you ever prayed before?"

"Yes. But I'm not sure it works. At least not for stuff like this."

"Yes, it does. Everybody has a little light. If the light is too weak and it's too windy, it can just blow out. You only have to relight it again."

"Where do I put the match?" To outside ears, it may have

sounded like an absurd question, as if he mocked her. But the way she described it… it made sense. Like relighting a pilot light that had gone out. As long as he could find the gas to light, he could turn her back on. Half of him felt ridiculous for thinking it, but his other half felt as if his own light had turned on. Or the light had always existed, but kept shrouded. He now had enough light for the both of them.

Imogene took his question as seriously as he meant it. "That's the hard part. The soul is not in a certain place in the body. It's everywhere. It's inside her and outside her and in you and me, and in everything."

Zander shook his head. He brought the infant's body closer to his chest, holding her tightly, hoping perhaps some of his life might bleed into her. He didn't have time for Imogene's riddles. He felt as if the "gas" he had to light wouldn't last. He only had a certain amount of time to ignite it or it would be lost forever.

"What the hell are you doing?" asked Mr. Ray. He had come around the house with a flashlight, apparently following the trail of open doors they had left.

"No!" Imogene said. "Run!"

Zander followed the little girl's command, even though he knew he would get in massive trouble. Somehow he had accidentally kidnapped a baby and a little girl, and he couldn't explain why. But something drove him. Something made sense to him that he knew Mr. Ray, Miss Cathy, or anyone else in the world wouldn't get. He didn't have the words for it.

Now in the lead, Zander tugged Imogene along by the hand, with the infant clutched to his chest. They cut through another yard toward the little city park. He didn't have a plan. He needed a moment alone with the infant.

He ducked under the playscape to hide, ramming his head on the overhang, forgetting how tall he had gotten. But he hardly noticed the ringing in his head. He pulled the child close to him again, pressing her against his chest, putting her heart close to his heart. Imogene said something, but she sounded distant. He had to concentrate. He let the light from his own body seep into the small body. The child's body grew warmer and had the faintest tremble like a distant roar of thunder. He had to do more. He had more light as his disposal. He had more light than what lived inside him. The light lived everywhere. He could see it now—a giant web of light pulsing through everything around him. Little flickers of tiny animals and bugs, glowing masses of it coming from the houses around him. Veins of light running down plants. And the most surprising, running through things that weren't alive at all. Flickers of sparkly light floated through empty air like clouds.

But Imogene shined the brightest of all. How had he not noticed it before? She glowed as brightly as he did. Her light had depth and gravity. More than the light that blazed from sun or fire, her light was *life*.

"Help me," he said. "We can do it together."

Imogene didn't need much convincing. She wrapped her arms around him, sandwiching the baby between them. And just like that, Zander didn't feel cold anymore. And the cuts and scrapes on his feet didn't hurt. He didn't need a body; he could float into the sky if he wanted to. Visit Heaven at any moment. He didn't have to wait to die.

He felt the child stirring, perhaps not a physical stirring. A tiny flicker and a humming, almost indiscernible. Then he heard the cry. Not the loud, juicy cry he had gotten used to drowning out with a pillow over his ears every night. A quiet, strangled cry. Dry and animal, but a cry.

Imogene squealed. She took the baby from Zander and held her to her chest, tears steaming down her face again. "You did it. You did it."

"Wait, I don't know if it's done yet." He had the feeling the fire hadn't quite, *caught*. They had given her a taste of their own life, but he didn't know if it would stick to her when they parted.

Awestruck by the new lights all around him, he had failed to notice the Mundane ones. Mr. Ray and Miss Cathy's flashlights drowned them and behind them the red and blue twirl of a police car.

Imogene turned to run, but they had trapped themselves under the playscape. Imogene could only kick at Miss Cathy. She hissed and snarled like a feral cat. Finally, Miss Cathy pulled the baby out, too-roughly Zander thought, from Imogene's little arms.

"Dear Lord, she's ice cold," Miss Cathy said. "What have you done? Oh God, oh God. You killed her."

"No, wait," Zander said. "We need more time. We can bring her back. We just need more time."

Zander's claims didn't make an impact on Miss Cathy, she ran toward the police car in her muddy house shoes, screaming for him to call an ambulance.

Zander sat in his car until the sun set, and all the shimmery gold on the highway had gone. Then the highway became nothing more than headlights and taillights streaming by, cars and trucks careening toward who knows where. In such a hurry to get... somewhere.

He had entered the phone number for the shelter into his phone a few times, but couldn't bring himself to hit send. He couldn't think of anything more terrifying than the sound of ringing on the other end—a distant trilling death march toward a truth he didn't want to hear.

"Children's Services. This is Stacy."

"Is she dead?" Zander asked in a scratchy voice.

Stacy remained silent on the other line.

"Just tell me if she's dead. That's all I want to know. Dead or alive. Tell me."

"Is this Zander Colter?"

"Tell me."

"I'm so sorry."

"No… no… no," Zander said. "You're wrong. You have to be wrong." He couldn't stop his voice from breaking, from crying on the phone with this random woman. "How?"

"She skipped school and got hit by an eighteen wheeler when she was trying to cross the highway."

"No… no. That didn't happen."

"I'm sorry. That's all I can tell you. I shouldn't even tell you that."

"How could you let this happen? You were supposed to be taking care of her."

"She snuck out all the time and ran around everywhere. It was a wonder it didn't happen sooner."

"You were supposed to take care of her."

"I'm sorry. I have to hang up now."

"When did it happen?"

"March 4th."

"March 4th?" Another wave of tears hit him, and the shelter worker might not understand him. "But I was free. I was… I could have protected her. I could have stopped it. That was weeks ago. I was free. I was…" In New York collecting his money. Vile, rotten money.

"I'm sorry, Zander."

The shelter worker hung up the phone and he dropped his phone on the floor of his car.

"I'll give it back," he said to no one. God he supposed. "I don't want the money. I'm sorry I took it. I'll give it back."

"Zander?"

Zander didn't look at the nurse. He continued staring at the pattern of bumps on the wall. He would do whatever she asked though. Resisting only wasted energy.

"It's time to see Dr. Suri."

Zander stood up from his chair with a scraping sound and followed the nurse, staring at the ice cream cones pattern on her scrubs. The nurse opened the door to Dr. Suri's office and Zander went inside and went to his chair. He had given up on trying to say the right things to Dr. Suri. He could not explain his behavior on the night the baby died. He had tried telling the truth and tried lying and tried a variation of non-committal explanations like "I don't remember" and "maybe I was sleepwalking." All of which got him diagnosed with a schizophreniform disorder, which Zander took to mean they thought he was crazy, or at least they didn't understand him, and had to pick something to diagnose him with so they could lock him up.

He had also learned that no amount of non-crazy behavior could get him released from the hospital. The nurses and doctors praised his good behavior, treatment compliance, and good relations with residents and staff. It didn't matter. They didn't trust him around other children in a foster home or shelter, so he couldn't leave, not until he turned eighteen.

It turned out the doctors had concerns about more than the night in question. When he first entered the hospital, they asked him questions about other things, like his relationship with Imogene.

"We're friends," he had explained. "I know we're not the same age, but we get along. I'm like her big brother."

"What do you do when you're together?"

"Talk. Sometimes we play games. I look after her when we're away from the shelter. I keep her safe."

"What do you talk about?"

"I don't know. She does most of the talking. She's a kid, so she talks about kid stuff. She tells stories and asks questions and just says whatever she's thinking. I don't know how to answer these questions. We just talk like normal people talk."

"Zander, Imogene Grey doesn't talk."

"What do you mean?"

"She has trauma-induced mutism. She hasn't spoken since she entered foster care."

"Well, that's just not true."

"Have you ever heard her speak to anyone else? Caregivers? Other residents?"

Zander shook his head. The doctor must want to trick him.

"Have you?" the doctor prompted again.

"Yeah. Of course I have. I'm sure I have."

"Can you think of an example?"

"She *talks*. She never shuts up."

The doctor frowned but he raised his eyebrows and nodded, jotting down notes.

Almost two years later, Zander once again entered Dr. Suri's office at 10 a.m. on a Wednesday, as usual. He sat in the same chair, ready to say the same nothing. But when he looked up, someone else sat in Dr. Suri's desk, smiling at him.

"Imogene?"

Zander looked around the room and found it empty except for the smiling girl sitting in the overlarge desk chair. Well, that answered some questions for him. He was crazy. Stark raving insane. At least know he knew for sure.

Imogene got up from behind the desk and jumped into his lap, giving him a surprisingly forceful hug for a figment of his imagination. She also smelled real, of rain or fresh dirt, as if the outdoors followed her everywhere. She giggled in his ear, as if she couldn't contain her happiness. Then she pulled up another chair and sat next to him on his side of the desk.

Delusion or not, he smiled when he saw her. Somehow her hallucination had grown up. She had left behind the frizzy-haired little girl that constantly had dirt on her face. She had done something with her hair that turned it into neat curls that glistened like black glass. She grinned, sitting right on the edge of her chair as if she might dive into his lap again at any moment.

"Surprise," Imogene said, bouncing in her chair. "I'm here."

"I am… surprised."

Her smile faded and she leaned closer to him, her warm honey colored eyes and thick lashes blinking right in his face.

"Are you okay?" she asked. "Something's wrong with your eyes."

He didn't know how to answer her question. He hadn't worried about being "okay" for a while. He just *was*.

"My eyes?"

"They're not sparkling." She sat back in her chair and nodded to herself. "They make you take drugs, don't they? That's what's making you like this."

"Clearly they're not giving me enough."

"Why do you say that?"

"Well… because you're a hallucination."

She laughed, but with her brow furrowed. "Seriously? Zander, I didn't do all that work to get in here just for you to think I'm not really here." She swatted him gently on the cheek. "I'm as real as you are. It sounds like the drugs are making you crazy and not the other way around," she said, her cheerful demeanor melting into concern. She took his face in her hands and looked him in the eyes again. "Please believe I'm really here."

"If you're real, explain how you got here. Why didn't the nurse see you just now?"

"She wasn't looking properly." Imogene looked down at her hands. "It was a lot of work to get here. Lots of confusion and concealment spells on lots of people. And I'll still probably be caught. At the very least, I don't have much time. It's easy to trick Mundanes, but I'm not invisible, and they have eyes. One wrong move, and it's over."

"Please stop talking like that. You're almost grown. If you talk about magic and spells, they'll think you're crazy too. I don't want you to end up like me."

"I don't talk much to the Mundanes."

"No, you don't. And they all think I'm crazy because I claim you talk to me."

"They do?" Imogene continued looking at her hands. "I'm sorry, Zander. This is all my fault." A tear slipped down her cheek, and Zander reached over to wipe it away. When he did, she looked up at him and smiled, taking his hand. "Don't let them kill your spirit, Zander. Please. You have such a beautiful spirit. And it's still in there, waiting to be let free. And I talk now. I just pretend like I'm talking to you. And I can talk to other people. It's getting easier. But I still don't like it. I would rather talk to you."

"You really are here, aren't you?"

"*Yes.* You know how good I was at sneaking out of the shelter. I'm sneaky."

"You look different. You look… pretty. Really pretty."

She rolled her eyes. "You don't have to sound so surprised."

"I'm not… I just… you look nice."

"And you look like a grown-up. Like a *man*." She laughed.

"Is that funny?"

"Very funny."

"I'm glad I'm amusing to you."

"You look very handsome. But you've always been handsome. All the girls at the shelter had a crush on you. And they hated me because they wanted to be your girlfriend and you ignored them. You only paid attention to crazy little Imogene."

"The other girls were boring."

"Their Mundanes. It's not their fault." Imogene looked away from him. "I'm sorry. I'll stop talking about magic. I know you don't like it."

She grabbed his hand, as if dangling off the edge of a cliff.

"I'm trying to figure out a good way to sneak you out of here. Would you want that?"

"They won't let me go back to foster care."

"You won't go back. You're almost eighteen now. You'll just be free. And you'll take me with you."

"Imogene…"

"This is my fault. And I want to make it right. And more than that, I want you back." Another tear line appeared on her cheek. "You're my home."

"I'm nothing to you. I'm not your real brother. I'm not your family. I'm just some guy."

"Not to me. And being family isn't about having the same parents or anything. Family can be anybody. It can be two random people."

"I want that more than anything. I want to leave with you."

"Then we will."

"It won't work."

"It *will*. We're going to go *everywhere*. And do *everything*. It will be the best life ever."

"Yeah," he said, starting to believe it. They would go to all the places they saw on television, like New York and Paris and Hawaii. And he would be with his family, his other. He knew how she felt. He had never felt as related to anyone, including his own mother.

Imogene sat up straight and turned her head, as if she had heard something Zander hadn't. "Dr. Suri has remembered his appointment now. I could only distract him for so long. I have to go."

"No. Please don't go."

"I'll come back. I'll come back for you."

"Imogene."

"I love you, Zander."

CHAPTER TWENTY-ONE

"So do you forgive me, or am I just your ride to visit your garden?" Patrick asked, as they parked back at the home site three days later.

"A little bit of both, I guess. It's not entirely your fault you're an idiot. It's in your nature."

"Thank you?"

She smiled. "You're welcome."

Samantha walked over to their garden bed and Patrick's heart rate spiked. He had planned to apologize in the form of making a move on her this time since she seemed on board with the idea. But the thought made him want to take off running across the field.

"I really thought they would grow," she said, looking down at the garden bed. A few tiny sprouts of weed had poked through, but no sign of lilies.

"It's only been a few days. I'm no gardener, but I'm pretty sure these things take longer than that."

She sighed. "Maybe the bulbs are dead too. Lilies may seem like they come back from the dead, but of course, they don't really. Nothing does."

She clutched her elbows and hunched slightly, as if she shielded herself from a winter wind that didn't exist.

"All we know is that when something dies, it changes," Patrick said. "It can never go back to what it was before."

"I'm not really upset about the flowers."

"Well, I figured as much."

"Not that flowers don't deserve to be cried over."

She sniffed and wiped her eye.

"I never said anything about what happened to your girlfriend. And I should have. I'm sorry. Sorry for not saying anything… and sorry it happened."

"You don't have to say that. Everyone says, "I'm sorry." It doesn't mean anything. It's just what people say."

"Maybe. But that doesn't make it less true."

He pulled her into his arms, and she nuzzled her face into his shoulder. He could feel the warmth and wetness of her face as she continued to cry. He slid his fingers through her long, damaged hair, working his way through tangles.

"You smell nice," she said.

"Thanks. It's probably laundry detergent."

She laughed. "Well, it's nice." She looked up at him as if she might kiss him again, but then she scrunched up her nose.

Yikes. That's not the face you want a girl to make when they're considering kissing you.

"What?"

"You're right. I can't do this." She stepped away from him. A tiny step, but she might as well have catapulted halfway across the earth.

"Okay," Patrick said.

"It's not what you think," she said. "I just can't look at you without thinking about her. Which makes no sense at all. I can't imagine any two people so different. You act different, and you could hardly look more different. I think it's your eyes. You have the same eyes."

"Really?"

"Like dark honey, almost reddish. So unusual, and so strange to see on both of you. But it's good. Like you saved a piece of her somehow."

Her description of the honey red eyes reminded him of a powerful image he had seen once before. He realized why the story of Imogene's death had bothered him so much when his mother told him… why he had felt so unsettled.

It seemed as if the falling cottonwood suspended in the air as everything came together, all the pieces fitting into one horrible puzzle. He wished the scene would freeze. The air so clean and fragrant, you could drink it. Samantha's crisp scent lingering close to him. He collected all of it, and he felt as if he'd bottled the moment in his mind to reproduce at any moment.

"Imogene… she was a spring witch?" he asked.

"Yes. An incredible one."

"What did she look like?"

"Why?"

"I'm just curious."

"Black hair. Dark skin. And the eyes, like I said, amber like honey. She was so beautiful."

The description could fit any number of people, but his gut told him that it didn't. Now it all made sense. He had seen Imogene in his vision.

"What day did she die?"

"March 4th," Samantha croaked.

Samantha's date—a horrible offense. And it was no accident. He had chosen that date because he had been thinking about her.

"Samantha," he said.

"Yes?"

"There is something I need to tell you."

"Okay…"

"I killed Imogene."

CHAPTER TWENTY-TWO

On March 4th, Julie Prescott did something she had never done before. She skipped school. She walked right out of class and no one said a word. She waved and smiled at teachers and the parking lot monitor. Then she got on her bike and rode away. No one tried to stop her. They trusted her.

She had never ridden her bike for as far as she planned on riding today. Her heart beating madly from nerves before she'd made it through her first mile, but after a while, the ride felt great. Her thighs burned with effort, but a good burn. She wanted to feel something, and she loved having a destination and a plan. With every pump of her legs, she got closer.

She went off course a few times, and had moments of panic, but would find her way again. Eventually, she had to will herself to keep on course. Riding off to nowhere tempted her more than she had ever imagined. She had already gone this far, why not keep going? Bike away and never go back. She would feel the burn in her thighs and the cool breeze in her face and pretend there nothing else existed in the world. She flew away.

When she arrived at the park, her legs felt like jelly. She

thought she might fall down as soon as she climbed off her bike. She would ask them for a ride back to school, but she knew her mom had placed a repulsion spell around their home and school to keep the Vandergraffs away. Patrick and Evangeline had enough magic to combat it, but she wouldn't ask them to go through that just for a ride.

"Hey," Julie said as she parked her bike on the rack. She had this perma-smile plastered on her face Patrick thought looked awkward, like a Barbie doll tired of smiling but couldn't get her face to move.

"Hi," he said.

"Hi," Evangeline echoed.

Julie continued to smile as they shared a moment of uncomfortable silence.

"We shouldn't stand in a circle. You know, just in case," Patrick said, and he backed away from the two girls, doing some weird spin, as if he could somehow confuse magic.

"You're probably right," Evangeline said.

Patrick stared at ants walking up the bark of a tree. He didn't imagine it. The whole forest understood that three of the four events stood together. Birds cried, frogs sang, and the leaves themselves quivered. All too loud for a fresh, peaceful, March day.

"So, you're not going to look at us?" Evangeline asked.

"It's very hard to talk to two people without standing in a circle," Patrick said.

Julie giggled. "We're still in a circle. You're just facing the wrong way."

Patrick turned around. Julie grinned at him from where she had perched on a fallen tree branch. He hadn't seen her since they rode in an ambulance together last summer. But when he managed to track her down and ask for her help, she didn't think twice. She ditched school and met them without hesitation. She looked much better than when he'd seen her last. She sparkled again. And, looked like a tree fairy as she smiled at him and waited for instructions. She plucked petals off a purple wildflower.

"Just stop worrying about what shape we're standing in, and tell us what to do," Evangeline said.

He didn't know if he loved or hated being in charge. But fall wizards always had to have two minds about everything. Nothing could be simple. Or easy. Perhaps the girls gave him control because of his age. These girls weren't the type to let a man tell them what to do. Most likely, they deferred to him because he was fall. He would know what to do. Two steps ahead all the time.

"Um…" Patrick said. "Well, I hadn't gotten that far yet. I wanted your opinion."

"What did you see, exactly?" Julie asked. Her smile faded and she placed the now petalless flower down by her side. Her smile had shifted into an odd grimace, as if she prepared for him to hit her. She didn't want to know the answer to her question.

"I've learned not to worry too much about the details of the vision," Patrick said. "It's all symbols. It can be misleading. But, I think I know what's going to happen. Ca… She will finally find the spring equinox wizard she's looking for. Very soon." He had avoided saying her name and it reminded him of the whole he-who-should-not-be-named thing with Voldemort. He would not give Caroline the same power and intrigue. "Caroline," he added awkwardly at the end. Evangeline and Julie both squinted at him funny.

"Yeah, I kind of figured that's who you meant," Julie said. "But thank you for clarifying."

Oh good, summer witches are capable of sarcasm. Or maybe more politeness. Hard to tell.

"Why did it take her so long?" Julie asked. "Where has she been?"

"I cast a spell to send her away, her and Jude. It worked for a long time, but now I think it's worn off."

"And you think she's about to get her spring magic, to complete the four events," Julie said.

Patrick nodded. "I'm just not sure if knowing that will help anything. If I foresee something, does that mean it's already too late?"

Julie and Evangeline didn't answer, they blinked at him. They both had green eyes that looked as if they could see through your skin. Odd that anything would be similar about fundamental opposites. Aside from looking healthier and happier, Julie looked more like Caroline. Probably because she looked older. Evangeline looked older too, but he saw her every day and didn't notice.

"Well, of course we can stop her, right?" Julie said. "Why wouldn't we?"

Traditional good guy arrogance. Or, maybe just hope.

Patrick looked at Evangeline for another perspective.

"It doesn't matter whether we can or not," Evangeline said. "All that matters is whether or not we want to try. And, we do of course." She said it with a hint of an eye roll. Of course her boring fall older brother had to overthink everything all the time.

"That's not what I meant exactly. Of course I want to try. What I'm wondering is if there is any use in trying to stop her from finding the spring wizard? Or should we assume she will, and come up with some other way to bring her down?"

"If you can't change fate, then what's the point of having visions at all?" Julie asked.

"I wonder that myself all the time," Patrick said.

"This is pointless," Evangeline said. "All we have to do is try. If it doesn't work, it doesn't work. But I think we have a good shot. She is probably using a siren spell to call the spring equinox wizard like she did with us, but we can use our magic to repel the spring wizard. Even if she stole some of our magic, we *are* us. Our spell will kick her spell's ass. And, if that doesn't work, we'll just kill her."

Patrick looked at Julie. She had that frozen deer look the summer wizards get. He thought he could understand a bit of what she might have felt. Part of her wanted to say, "How dare you, that's my sister!" and curse Evangeline for even suggesting it. And, the other part of her loved the idea. Patrick could guess this because he felt this way about Jude.

"No," Julie said, sounding appalled. Maybe as a good witch, she only had the first thought. "I'm not using my magic to kill anyone. Ever. For any reason."

Evangeline glared at her, but didn't argue.

Wanting to bring the conversation back from murdering people, Patrick interjected. "All right then, we're agreed... I guess. We'll cast a spell with the intention of countering Caroline's siren spell. A repulsion."

"I think it's best if we keep our intentions as simple as possible," Evangeline said. "Three different kinds of magic might need to work in different ways. I say we just cast a spell to keep Caroline from finding a spring equinox witch or wizard. Ever. Period."

"You think that's going to kill her, don't you?" Julie said, standing up. "Because that's the easiest way for that spell to work. If she's dead, she can't find a spring equinox wizard."

"What is with you? You should want her dead more than anyone. And, have you considered that by killing her, we could save other people she plans to hurt in the future? You summer wizards are so dense. You think you're doing the right thing, but all you're doing is the easy thing. By not killing her, you're just causing other people pain. Maybe even death. If you want to do what's right, you should do anything you can to prevent that."

Please don't curse each other. Please don't curse each other. Patrick had no intention of jumping in the middle of that particular fight. Although, he guessed that unlike their respective brothers, who had gotten in a spectacular duel last summer that almost killed all of them, the girls had better sense. Besides, he could tell they respected each other. Perhaps because they were both solstice witches, or from facing a hardship together. But, they had a bond, even though it made little sense.

"The right thing is not the easy thing," Julie said crossing her arms, her eyes greener as they got red with tears. "Doing the right thing is hard. There is no thing that is the easy thing."

"I honestly wasn't suggesting we kill her anyway. That's just what you heard. All I said was that we should keep the spell simple." Evangeline's voice turned kinder. "If I wanted to kill your sister, I wouldn't do it from far away with a vague spell. I would do it up close, so I could see the life leave her eyes."

Patrick didn't know if she meant to comfort her or frighten her, but it did ring true.

"What do you think, Patrick?" Julie asked, wiping tears from her cheeks. "What spell should we do?"

Evangeline turned to look at him, too. He could swear the trees looked at him.

Dammit.

"I… I think what Evangeline said made sense. We keep it simple. We'll cast a spell to keep Caroline from finding the spring equinox witch or wizard. Maybe, it would be less dangerous if we focus on keeping her from finding the specific one she's hunting now, instead of adding that she never finds one. It would take a long time for her to find another one. And, if our spell works, we can always cast it again."

"Okay, I like that," Julie said. "We'll keep her from finding the spring equinox wizard she seeks. I want to focus my spell on helping the spring witch or wizard. Protecting them from Caroline. Protecting them from pain. If the spell has good intentions, it will do good things."

Well, maybe in her case.

Evangeline nodded and she reached out to take Julie's hand, and then Evangeline reached her hand out to him and Julie followed suit.

Patrick stared at them. "Seriously? We're going to hold hands to form a circle? Why don't we just bulldoze the forest right now?"

"Come on, Patrick," Evangeline said. "Quit being such a baby."

Patrick took Evangeline's hand and then Julie's. He could feel the power of their circle, but it felt more comfortable than he had expected. After all, the last time he had experienced both of their magic at once it had nearly stopped his heart and caused him to bite off his tongue. The previously overly-loud forest became quiet. He felt power surging through him, but it didn't feel dangerous. It felt as if it would keep him alive forever. He could do anything. Fly. Travel through time. Survive a bullet to the head. He felt limitless. He probably smiled like an idiot, but it didn't matter how stupid he looked because both the girls had their eyes closed.

He closed his eyes too. Working together, they found the spring equinox easily. Their magic cried out for that missing piece, spanning out across miles seeking it. And, then he could see her. A pretty girl, with dark skin and eyes a strange amber color that almost looked red. She smiled at him, as if he was the home she had never found. Now that he'd seen her, he knew he could find her if he wanted. He could put the keys in the ignition of his car and it would go to her. But, that's how Caroline found the three of them. Instead, he'd have to do what his instinct fought against. In order to protect her, he'd have to stay away from her. Probably forever.

Caroline will never hurt you, he thought. And, because his heart swelled to know she existed, he added, *No one will ever hurt you. You will be happy for the rest of your life.*

Samantha took shallow breaths. The world, once brimming with oxygen from the fresh green around her, had grown cold and the infinite expanse of air didn't seem like enough.

"No, you didn't," she stammered, unsure of what else to say. "You didn't even know she existed. You didn't know anything about her until I told you." Maybe she had misheard him. His words made no sense.

Patrick's honey brown eyes watered. He bit his lip as if to keep it from trembling.

"The spell… it didn't do what we wanted. We didn't intend to hurt Imogene. We were trying to protect her. But now I see how the spell worked…" He covered his mouth for a moment, and then continued in a constricted voice. "I wanted her to be safe from Caroline. To be happy… for the rest of her life…" Patrick buried his face in his hands now. "I promise Samantha… we never intended. God… I am so sorry. I…" He collapsed to his knees, kneeling before her.

She felt numb. Like ice or worse. Ice felt cold. It burned. She felt nothing. Like dead flesh. Part of her wanted to take him in her arms and hold him until he stopped shaking. Kiss his neck and run her fingers through his hair and tell him it would all be okay. But the other part of her wanted to kill him. To watch his blood splatter on the pink primroses at his feet.

As soon as she thought it, the dark truth came to her… she had already killed him. She and Evangeline had cast a killing spell directed at Imogene's killer. Sooner or later, the spell would hit its mark.

"You said 'we,'" Samantha whispered. "You didn't cast the spell alone?"

He shook his head, with his hand covering his mouth. "Me. Evangeline. Julie."

"Julie?"

"Julie Prescott, the summer solstice witch. Three out of four of the events. Imogene must have been the fourth. We just didn't want Caroline to find her. We didn't want her to have the power of all four events. That's all…"

Samantha kneeled down to face him. "You should have been more careful," she spat. "You were careless. The three of you have so much power, you shouldn't have cast any spell…and one as vague as that? You killed her. You motherfucker. This is all your fault."

She shoved him and he fell backward onto the ground.

"I know," he said.

Samantha had lost the numbness, but now she had to hold her arms to keep them from shaking. To keep her from clawing out his eyes or ripping out his hair. "You're so stupid," she said. "How could you?"

"I'm so sorry. I… I would do anything to take it back. I would. I would give my own life to bring her back."

"Yeah… you will," she said. "But it won't bring her back. I'll just lose both of you."

"What do you mean?"

"I cast a killing curse. *We* cast a killing curse. Me and Evangeline. To kill Imogene's killer. You're already dead."

"Evangeline?"

"Yes. She helped me cast the killing spell."

Samantha turned toward the thicket of cedars behind the home site, walking quickly, tears burning in her eyes.

"Where are you going?"

"Don't follow me," she shouted.

CHAPTER TWENTY-THREE

Tropical Storm Levi came to Zander's hospital in the summer of 2013. They didn't evacuate, but the residents needed to take shelter inside the stairwells. He remembered how hot it had felt. They had turned off the air conditioner and the unmoving air in the stairwell heated quickly. People always got excited and loud during a storm, and in the stairwell, their yells and cries echoed. He hated all of it.

When the lights went out, everyone screamed in delighted horror. Flashlights and lanterns turned on, saving him from the oppressive darkness, but he thought if he didn't leave the stairwell, the walls would crush him. Or all the oxygen would deplete and his lungs would collapse. The fear felt incredibly real, and far more dangerous than any bit of rain and wind outside.

The moment he felt the urge to run coincided with the only opportunity he would ever have to run. Everything had fallen into place. As one of the most well-behaved and sanest residents, the staff had their attention away from Zander. In that moment, the two staff within sight ran up the stairs to help restrain someone. He also knew he had a minute or two before the generators would kick on and the alarms on the doors would turn back on.

He didn't care about getting in trouble. When they found him outside, he would tell the truth and say he had a panic attack in the stairwell. He was crazy, after all.

He ran down the stairs and thought he heard someone shouting after him, but he ignored it. On the bottom floor, he thrust his weight against the emergency exit door. He couldn't open it, but not because of a lock. No alarm blared when he managed to crack the door enough to see the light outside. Wind whistled through the tiny crack and he felt water creeping in and soaking his socks. He figured he couldn't open the door because of the wind and water. He continued to push on the door until it flew open. The wind and rain had stopped, as if someone had hit a giant off switch in the sky.

Imogene stood in the parking lot and smiled as if they had arranged to meet there. And she might as well have stood in the middle of a battlefield. A tree branch had already smashed one of the cars in the lot and an increasing tide of water tugged at the wheels. Once the wind picked back up, anything could hit her. Broken glass. The metal sheeting that had come off the roof. Another tree branch. Hell, maybe the cars would rush toward her as the water rose.

But she didn't seem concerned. She continued to smile at the sight of him. The rain on her skin and hair glimmered even through several miles of clouds blocked the sun. She looked nothing like a little girl anymore. She had a power and confidence about her, he couldn't understand. Like before, he assumed he imagined her there. A real flesh and blood girl couldn't have stood against that storm. Even though he might have hallucinated her, he clutched the side of the building and reached out a hand to her.

"Come inside," he said. "Hurry. It's not safe."

She waded in the flood water toward him. She reached her

hand toward him, but stopped several feet away so he would have to leave the wall to reach her. She meant to rescue him, and not the other way around.

"It's okay," she said. "We're safe."

"We have to get inside. This must be the eye of the storm or something. It will start again." Now he had made it outside, his powerful urge to get outside had faded and he felt exposed and vulnerable. He couldn't remember why he had felt so desperate to get out here in the first place.

"I told you I would come back for you. Here I am. And here you are. Outside of these walls. You can come with me now."

"But the storm… we won't get far."

"I hate to use Mother Nature in such a violent way, but it had to be done. No one will be hurt, just some wind and water damage."

"Are you saying you *caused* the storm?" He raised his voice as if speaking over the howling winds, even though the air had become still. "You're insane," he said, in a tone more sad than cruel. "You're going to get hurt. Please just come inside with me, before the wind starts again."

"Most of the time, nature is beautiful, nurturing, and incredibly patient, but she can also muster a power and fury than could tear down Hell itself. Nature only allows humanity because of her kindness, she has the power to obliterate all mankind creates." She held up her hands in demonstration.

Her wild mess of hair fluttered again in the wind. The storm would come back at any moment. "Please," Zander said. "I don't want you to get hurt. I don't want to lose you."

"We won't get hurt Zander. I already walked through the storm to get to you. We can walk back out."

Zander left the safety of his wall and walked over to Imogene to grab her hand. Instead, she wrapped both her arms around him. He didn't see any option that seemed good. He could leave with her and they would probably drown or he could take her back inside, hold her for the few minutes that the storm raged on, and then they'd take her away again.

"Please trust me," she said. "I'm not just any witch, I'm a very special witch. And you're a special wizard. We're so full of life death has to work very hard to take us. A little wind and rain can't hurt us."

He nuzzled his face in the softness of her hair. She smelled like the storm. Of dust and water and electricity. The blackness in the sky had grown darker and made the day look like night. The trees on the edge of the parking lot cracked and moaned.

He pulled her back toward the building.

"No," she said, pulling away. "We can run into the storm and the Mundanes can't follow. This is our only chance."

"I'm sorry, Imogene. I can't let you get hurt."

She leaned her weight away from him, pulling on his hands. She claimed she could muster up a storm and then walk right through it, but didn't have enough physical strength to resist his pull. He didn't want to drag her, so he picked her up. She thrashed and kicked, and he pulled her tighter against him.

"No," she said. In the rain he couldn't tell if she was crying, but her voice broke. "Please take me away. You promised."

"I love you, and I'm going to keep you safe."

"No. Please, no."

When he reached the door, the wind had increased enough that he could hardly open the door, especially while carrying the thrashing Imogene. He draped her over his shoulder and tugged against the ripping winds. He pulled open the door and got them both inside. With a howl, the door shut, leaving them in darkness.

He continued to clutch her and he heard a crash outside as if a car had careened into the side of the building.

"If you started the storm, then stop it," he said.

"It doesn't work like that," she said.

He took her hands and squeezed them in his own until they

stopped shaking. "I'll keep my promise. I'll take you away, but if we go now, they'll just follow us. We'll wait until we can really be free."

He couldn't see her well in the darkness, but she seemed to look away from him. "I made a storm for you. And you won't even take three more steps from the wall for me."

"On your eighteenth birthday. I'll come find you."

"That's too long. And what if they move me again? You won't know where to find me."

"Easy. We'll meet at our spot. The place we used to run away to. On your birthday."

CHAPTER TWENTY-FOUR

Patrick drove to the middle school in a state of muted terror. His knuckles ached from clutching the steering wheel. He never realized how dangerous driving was. The cars heading the other direction loomed far too close. One tiny flick of the wheel and they'd have a head on collision. A killing spell would likely take him that way. That's the leading cause of deaths among teenagers and it could happen so easily. Only a tiny twist in fate.

However, at the same time, every moment he didn't crash reinforced the possibility Samantha's killing spell hadn't worked. She and Evangeline had cast the spell four days ago. Since then, he had spent several hours driving around Houston. The spell had plenty of chances. As far as he could tell, their spell killed Imogene the same day, if not immediately. As he understood it, some spells—like fireworks—were duds.

He had met Samantha on his lunch period, so Evangeline was probably in class. He considered his options. He could try to use magic to call her so she would walk out. He could use a cloaking spell on himself to go in and get her. Or he could take the Mundane route and walk into the office and ask for her, making up some excuse.

He waited in the parking lot considering his options when he heard the loud buzzing of the passing period bell. He saw Evangeline break from the sea of students flooding out of the portable building and walk toward his car, tugging on the straps of her backpack.

Patrick jumped out of the car, feeling like one of the stereotypical kidnappers he saw in safety videos as a kid.

"Come on, get in the car," he said.

Evangeline did as he asked without comment, chunking her backpack in the backseat, and climbing into the passenger seat.

"How did you know to walk over here?" Patrick asked.

"I sensed a familiar presence," she said as Patrick pulled away from the school.

"How very Darth Vader of you."

"What?"

"Doesn't matter."

"So why are you here?" she asked, drinking from his water bottle. "Is everything okay?"

"Hang on, let me get somewhere safe. I can't talk to you while I'm driving."

"Why not?" she asked.

He pulled into the nearby Whataburger parking lot and told her what Samantha had told him with the car safely in park.

"Well," he finished. "Is she right? Did you cast a spell like that? Against us?"

Evangeline had her arms crossed over her chest and her eyebrows furrowed, looking more angry than anything else.

"Well?" he prompted again.

"Yes."

"But it must not have worked," Patrick said. "Because if it did, we would already be dead. Right?"

"A killing spell is a type of catalyst spell." Evangeline picked at a scab on her knee. "They don't usually work right away.

Sometimes they take years."

"Our spell killed Imogene right away."

"Well, it was cast by three out of four of the event wizards. My spell probably won't work as fast as a spell cast by all three of us. I'm not as powerful on my own. But… I don't think it will take years. Days. Weeks maybe."

"Okay, well then that's what we'll do."

"What?"

"All three of us will cast another spell to stop your killing spell. You said the three of us are more powerful than you alone, so we should be able to counter it."

"Maybe."

"What do you mean, *maybe*?"

"So, she's okay? You've talked to her?"

"Who?"

"Julie."

"No, I haven't talked to her yet. I just came right over here." Patrick took out his phone and dialed Julie's number. He winced and pulled the phone away as a horrible screeching sound came through the phone. He dropped his phone and it clattered between the driver's seat and the center console.

"Shit," he muttered.

"What the hell was that?"

"It sounded like a fax machine or something," Patrick said.

"What's a fax machine?" Evangeline asked.

"You try on your phone," Patrick said.

"I don't have it," she said.

"Why not?"

"We're not supposed to have them at school."

"And you have to be the only kid in the world who follows that rule."

"I doubt it would work on my phone anyway," Evangeline said. "It's probably part of the repulsion spell Julie's mom cast. That's why I don't mess with phones and stuff. Magic makes them go screwy."

"What if we just drive to her?" Patrick asked. "Will the spell let us?"

"Probably not. With the repulsion spell and the killing spell both working, we'll almost definitely die before we reach her. A car accident is probably the easiest way to die," she said, far too calmly.

"Yes, I'm aware of that. Okay, just get out."

"What?"

"Get out of the car. I'm not going to put you at risk."

"That doesn't matter. I'm at risk anyway. I could die in class."

"How?"

"I don't know. Stabbed in the eye with a pencil? Running with scissors? Julie is my friend," she concluded.

Patrick considered asking her what definition of "friend" classified them as BFFs, but she elaborated for him.

"We're the same," she said.

"Opposites, technically. Polar opposites."

"Besides, we have to all get together if we want to counter the killing spell, and we need to do that as quickly as possible. It would be stupid to do extra driving just to come back and get me."

"Put on your seatbelt."

"I'm already wearing my seatbelt."

Patrick tugged on it to check like they do on roller coasters.

"Do you mind?" she asked.

Patrick screeched to a halt in front of the Prescott's house. He cringed at the noise, not wanting to draw so much attention. As they had gotten closer, a loud ringing vibrated in his ears. He kept checking his ears to make sure blood didn't drip down them. He thought he tasted blood in his mouth and wondered if his brain melted. Evangeline covered her ears too, even though the sound was literally in her mind. He had to keep reminding himself the effect came from the repulsion spell—although that didn't mean it wasn't real. He didn't know if the repulsion could actually hurt them.

"No one is home," Evangeline shouted.

"You're sure?" he shouted back.

"Of course I'm sure. We could feel them easily if they were in there. She's probably still at school."

"No, school should be out by now. Something is wrong with Julie, Evangeline. I can sense it."

"Did you see a vision?"

"No. Stupid fucking visions. They never come when I need them." As soon as he said it… he had one. "Her bicycle."

"What about it?"

"I see it. Or I will see it."

"Where?"

"On the side of the road."

"What road?"

"Stop asking questions. I don't know."

"She rode her bike to meet us. Maybe she takes her bike to and from school. Where is the school? She might be on her way home."

Patrick had no idea what school she went to, but he pulled out his phone and found a high school three miles away.

The ringing in his ears decreased as they moved further from the house, but then increased again, as they got closer to the school. He pulled his car over, too disoriented by flashing visions in his mind to drive, especially in a high-risk situation.

Then he saw it. The bicycle, just as he had envisioned it, discarded on the side of the road, one wheel badly bent.

"No," Patrick said.

"Julie," Evangeline said.

They both jumped out of the car, leaving it parked oddly, not fully pulled onto the shoulder. Patrick ran toward the bicycle.

"Julie?" He called.

"There," Evangeline whispered. Patrick could tell by her tone that it wouldn't be good.

Julie lay in a thick carpet of wildflowers and overgrown grass and weeds, difficult to spot from the highway. He knew without moving any closer, without touching her, without checking for a pulse, she was dead. Although he never felt as good at sensing wizards as some of his relatives, he couldn't mistake the absence. All that bright, burning light had left her body. She blended with the flowers, rocks, and dirt. No light about her at all.

Evangeline ran to her and turned her over. Blood from a large head wound matted her once radiant blonde hair. Her arms fell in distorted angels as Evangeline cradled her body.

Evangeline looked up at him, for once, looking her age, and not like a terrifying, powerful witch, but a little girl wanting him to explain everything and make it okay.

"She's dead," she said. "Did I do this to her?"

Patrick didn't have a response. He felt like he was underwater, swimming through the humid air toward them.

Julie's blood spilled out on Evangeline's neck and chest, and he wanted to tell her to put her body down… holding her wouldn't help anything… no point getting her DNA and fingerprints all over her… but he couldn't do it.

Instead, he took Julie's small, cold hand in his own. "It's okay," he said. "We found you. You're not alone anymore." He had no idea why he said it. "We'll stay with you until help comes… then we have to go." He moved a piece of blood-stained hair out of Julie's eyes and called 9-1-1.

"Patrick," Evangeline. "I'm getting blood on your seat belt."

"It's okay." He kept his eyes on the road and didn't turn to look at her, mostly because he didn't want to take his eyes off the road for a second, but also because he didn't want to look again. Seeing her covered in blood made his stomach lurch. Even now, he could smell the metallic scent wafting off of her, intermingling with the spicy smell of her shampoo. She had Julie's blood on her neck and in a rust covered rim around the front of her white shirt. She had a swipe of blood across her cheek where she had used a bloody hand to tug her hair behind her ear. A red tinge tinted the tips of her long, dark hair.

"We should stop somewhere so I can clean up. I can't go in the house like this."

"I just need to get you home."

"Are you afraid we're going to die before we get there?" she asked.

"Well… yes, Evangeline, I am."

"I'm sorry."

"I just need to concentrate on driving right now."

Patrick didn't need to look at Evangeline to know what she felt. Her emotions wafted off of her. The air in the car felt cold and dry. He had the—perhaps ridiculous—fear that the rainwater running down the windows would turn to ice.

"I don't want to watch you die," Evangeline said. "I want to go next."

"Jesus, Evangeline, don't say things like that. Neither of us is going to die."

The rain picked up, as if to laugh at him, pelting the roof of his car and streaming down the front window.

"If you drive any slower, we're going to just be stopped," Evangeline said.

"Maybe we *should* stop until the rain passes."

"No, that would be the rational course."

"I don't understand."

"Right now my curse is bending fate, trying to find a way to kill us. Trying to get us in the right place at the right time. We can't stop the curse, but we may be able to dodge it for a while by acting against what fate wants us to do. If the rain makes it seem like we should stop, we should just drive all the faster."

Patrick shook his head and let out a long breath, trying to

keep himself from panicking. His hands shook and he struggled to breathe. If he had to die, he didn't want to die because he fell apart and had a panic attack in the middle of the highway during a storm.

"Julie died much like Imogene did," Patrick said. "Is that part of your spell? Some kind of eye-for-an-eye?"

"I could see how the magical forces could interpret it that way. But I can't guarantee that's how it will happen to us. If we stay away from roads, the curse can still get us, but it might take longer to weave it's way toward us."

When they pulled into a parking spot in the apartment lot, Patrick thought he might throw up. He opened the door and leaned out. Little white sparks hovered in his vision.

Evangeline appeared surrounded in the white fuzz of dizziness. She grabbed his forearm and Patrick saw the lines of bloody, rainwater running down her wrists. The deluge didn't seem to remove the blood, but spread it, washing reddish brown down her entire body.

"Are you okay?" She asked shaking his arm.

Patrick took a few deep breaths and nodded. "I'm not dying, if that's what you mean."

"Dad's car's not here. Do you think Amanda is home?"

Patrick looked around for her car and then remembered she kept her new BMW in a closed garage.

"I don't know. She might be helping Dad with house stuff."

"I want to go inside. I want to change and take a shower."

Patrick nodded. She guided him out of the car by the arm like an old man.

"I'm fine," he said.

Evangeline jumped in the shower right away because she wanted to get Julie's blood off of her, but also because she wanted to cry without Patrick watching her. But though she wanted to cry, she couldn't do it. All the tears had gotten stuck in her head, making her brain feel too full. She let the water run down her face and pretended she could cry, watching the water turn pink around her feet. Evangeline dried herself off and put on new clothes in the tiny bathroom, careful to avoid the blood that had gotten on the floor and on the sink. Her wet, bloody clothes lay in a heap on the floor and now she'd have to touch them again and get her hands bloody again.

Evangeline gathered the bloody clothes in her hand, knowing she would have to change out of these clothes now too. A ruddy orange mark seeped onto her clean shirt.

She left the bathroom and froze. Amanda dropped shopping bags by the door. "Why aren't you in school?" she demanded, then her gaze turned to what she held in her hands.

Although Patrick hadn't gotten as bloody, he had already changed and showered too. "Mom, let me help you with these bags," he said trying to draw her attention away from Evangeline.

But Amanda advanced toward her. She took the clothes out of her hands, and then dropped them on the linoleum with a gasp as if Evangeline had handed her a snake. Amanda grabbed Evangeline's arms and examined them, and pulled aside her wet hair to reveal more of her skin, and found only old scars.

Evangeline pulled away. "I'm fine. It's not mine."

"Patrick?" she asked, turning toward him.

"Not his either. We're fine." Evangeline looked down at the bloody heap. "I was just going to take them to the laundry room," she said as if that provided sufficient explanation.

Amanda grabbed a dish towel from the kitchen and ran it under warm water. She pulled Evangeline's hair off her neck again. "You just missed a spot," she said. Amanda wiped a patch of blood away from under her ear. The warm water on the soft cloth felt comforting, and she relaxed her clenched fists.

"Just tell me what happened."

David let Emmy and Xavier in the house and then slammed the door. The three of them left a pool of water in the entranceway—all dripping wet from the downpour. Emmy stomped as if she tried to deliberately leave mud on the floor.

"I'm going to kill him," Emmy said. "I'm going to murder his face."

David banged on the boys' room door, and Patrick opened it part of the way, glaring out at him. He wore pajama pants and looked at him as if it was six in the morning, not six in the evening.

"What the Hell, Patrick?" David asked. "Do you think I just bought you a car because I'm a really nice guy?"

"No."

"That's right. No. You have a car because you have responsibilities. What is the matter with you?"

"Oh… Xavier and Emmy."

"Oh right *them*," Emmy said.

"Emmy, just back off please," David said. "Go change into dry clothes." Emmy stayed put with her arms crossed over her chest. Xavier went into their shared room to get dry clothes and then came back out, knocking into Patrick. He headed into the bathroom and slammed the door.

"You were supposed to pick them up from school," David continued, turning back to Patrick. "Like you do *every single day*. And that's not all. Did you forget something else today?"

"What?"

"You'll never guess who I found at the home site. Do you want to guess?"

"Samantha?"

"Correct. She said you just left her there. She didn't want to see you, so I dropped her off at a hotel."

"She got mad at me and refused to get back in the car."

"I don't care. You don't just leave her there. At least call somebody else to pick her up, or give her money for a cab, or *something*."

"I'm sorry."

"I don't need an apology, I need an explanation."

"I guess I forgot. I'm not feeling well."

"Why didn't you just call me and ask me to pick them up? And why did you only pick up Evangeline? How could you remember to pick her up, but not the others?"

"She's sick too. She wanted me to come and get her."

David put his hand to his forehead and Patrick flinched as if he might get hit. David had indeed smacked his forehead harder than necessary. "You don't feel warm. It's probably just allergies."

"Maybe."

"You're grounded this weekend. If you don't want to use the car to pick up your siblings, you can't use it for anything else either."

"I don't have anywhere to go," Patrick said.

"David," Amanda said, coming in from outside with a basket of dry clothes that had gotten wet again on the walk over. "Stop yelling at him."

As soon as David looked away, Patrick closed the door again.

"Why are you doing laundry during a storm?" David asked. "Can't it wait?"

Amanda looked down at the tangle of clothes. "Not really," she said. "The two of you need to sit down. I have some bad news."

"Oh God. The cancer is back," Emmy said. The same thought had popped into David's head and the room swayed.

"No. No, honey. It's not about me," she said, putting the basket down on the kitchen counter. She gestured toward

Xavier, who had come out of the bathroom in dry clothes.

"So the cancer isn't back?" David asked.

"No. Just listen to me. Sit down." Amanda gestured toward the kitchen table.

"Me too?" Xavier asked.

"Yes, you too." The chairs scraped about the floor as the three of them sat as requested. Amanda took the fourth chair.

"Does this have something to do with why Patrick didn't pick us up?" Emmy asked.

"Yes, actually."

"What? Is he okay?" David asked. "If you know what's going on, why didn't you call me?"

"Just let me talk," Amanda said. "Patrick is fine. He just had a rough day." She took a deep breath. "I'm afraid Julie Prescott died today. Patrick and Evangeline found her body."

"What?" Emmy asked after a pause. "What happened to her?"

"She was hit by a car on the way home from school. It was a hit and run."

Emmy put her hands over her mouth to suppress a sob. Tears spilled down her cheeks. Hearing about the death of someone so young always hit hard, but David didn't expect her to react like that.

"Oh my God," Emmy said between sobs. "No."

Amanda reached out the to squeeze Emmy's hand. "I'm so sorry, sweetheart."

"That's horrible," David said. "After all she's been through… and then she's killed by a hit and run? It's just…"

"How did Eve and Patrick find her body?" Xavier asked, scowling.

"They had been going to meet her," Amanda said. "Apparently they had stayed in touch. I didn't know."

"Meet her for what?" Xavier asked.

"I… I don't know. He just said they were friends with her.

They were both upset. I didn't interrogate them about their friendship with Julie. Why does it matter? I'm telling you she died."

"It matters," Xavier said.

"Why does it matter?" David asked.

"They're event wizards," Xavier said and stopped talking as if he didn't need to say more. "What if they were casting spells?" he added finally.

"If they were before, then they're not now," David said. "Have some respect. Amanda just told you a girl we know died."

"The three of them shouldn't have been together," Xavier said.

Emmy stood up. "Mom, can I talk to you? *Privately?*"

"About what?" David asked.

"Don't you know what *privately* means?" Emmy asked.

Amanda stood up and squeezed David's shoulder to imply that she would tell him later, and she followed Emmy outside. Apparently, she didn't want Evangeline to know either if she avoided her own room.

Amanda followed Emmy out onto the landing. The landing of the stairs above protected them from the rain.

"Let me take Patrick's car," Emmy said. "Dad just grounded him anyway."

"What? What do you need car for? Besides, you don't have driver's license. What makes you think I would say yes to such a ridiculous request?"

"I'm old enough to get a learner's permit. And you know perfectly well I know how to drive. I am asking you for the car instead of sneaking out and taking it. You should be thanking me."

"Oh really? I should be thanking you?"

"I need to go see Nathan."

"Oh," Amanda said, pausing. The rain drummed on the gutter next to them. "You hadn't mentioned him in such a long time. I thought that was over."

Emmy crossed her arms over her chest. "Are you going to give me the keys or not?"

"That's why you got so upset. Not just about Julie, but because of Nathan. Because of how much it would hurt him to lose his sister."

"Yes, that's right." She held out her hand palm up, as if she expected Amanda to hand her the keys.

"I think it's sweet you want to be there for him. But no, I'm not giving my fifteen-year-old daughter car keys so she can go visit her boyfriend who is in college."

"He's not my boyfriend."

"What if I drive you?"

"Ugh. Mom. No."

"That's the only way it's happening, honey."

"I shouldn't have said anything. I was trying to be nice. Trying to make you not worry about me. I could have just left."

"I'm glad you told me."

Emmy let out a long sigh and looked up to the heavens as if to ask God why she had such a ridiculous mother.

"Okay. Fine. You can drive me. Just pretend you don't exist. And if any of his family is around don't try to kill them or anything."

"Yes, I think that would be very bad manners."

CHAPTER TWENTY-FIVE

Amanda convinced Emmy to wait until the weekend and told David Emmy wanted to go visit a friend who lived on the other side of town and he didn't question her. Emmy had Mundane friends she hung out with sometimes.

Another storm lingered on the horizon, a giant purple blue mass and Amanda drove right toward it. Texas managed to always be flooding or in drought, and usually dealing with both at once somehow.

"Do you want to talk about it?" Amanda asked Emmy, who thumbed through photos on Instagram.

"About what?"

"Nathan."

"There's not really anything to talk about."

"Did he break up with you?"

"We were never officially going out, and why do you just assume he broke up with me?"

"Okay. I'm sorry."

"I broke up with him," Emmy said, putting her phone down.

"May I ask why?"

"It's obvious, isn't it?"

"Not really."

"His father *murdered* my uncle. And he might have murdered Dad if he had been the one to get out of the car first. And he didn't even get punished for it."

"But what does that have to do with Nathan?"

"He didn't *do* anything about it. He could have told the police to support our story. He could at least have moved out or something. He just continued living with a murderer for the rest of the summer like nothing happened."

Amanda's knuckles ached and she realized she'd clutched the steering wheel too tightly. They had done the same thing when Jude raped Samantha. A whole lot of nothing.

"It's difficult when it's someone you love," Amanda said.

"Why are you defending him?"

"I— "

"Besides. That's not the only reason. His mom created this nasty repulsion spell. If I try to text him, it breaks my phone."

"Is that why we had to keep getting your battery replaced?"

"Yes."

Amanda shook her head. She wanted to demand phone repair money from Thea Prescott, but she might call it even if she taught her that nifty phone breaking spell.

"Visiting in person is actually easier," Emmy said. "A repulsion spell doesn't literally create a force field. I can go see him but things get in the way, like bad traffic, or car trouble."

Amanda eyed the storm again. It looked as if it could morph into a funnel cloud at any moment. "You could have told me before we started driving."

"We'll be okay. It will just take us twice as long to get there probably."

Amanda didn't like that she had so much experience driving to his apartment. "Are you having sex with him?" she asked.

"Mom," Emmy whined.

"It's a serious question. You're too young to have sex. But if you are, I want to know you're being responsible."

"We're not having sex," Emmy said. "We're barely talking. And I'm not having sex with anyone. I'm a virgin."

"Good for you."

"Uh… thanks? Can we stop talking about this?"

A wave of brake lights turned on in front of them and she had to slow to a complete stop. Amanda groaned. "That bitch."

Nathan opened the door and all of Emmy's insides contracted. Seeing him knocked all the air out of her, for two reasons. One—he looked amazing in his suit and tie, so handsome and grown-up. Two—he looked so sad, as if raising his head to look at her caused pain.

"Emmy," he said.

"Hi."

"What are you doing here?" He searched the parking lot behind her, and Emmy felt her cheeks burn. She shouldn't have come… especially today. She could guess why he was dressed like that. Julie's funeral.

"You called me," Emmy said.

Nathan pulled his phone out of his pocket and glanced at it, then chuckled at himself weakly. "Oh, that's not what you meant."

"No, it's not. I mean… maybe I was wrong. I'm not always sure…" She stopped herself from saying… *because I think about you constantly anyway. How am I supposed to know when it's real magic?* "I can go. This is not a good time," she said gesturing toward his outfit.

"No, don't go. You're not wrong." They shared a moment of awkward silence, and then Nathan gestured out to the parking lot. "Did you come with someone?"

He probably could sense the presence of a dark wizard lurking about.

"My mom," Emmy said, her cheeks burning again. He already considered her a little girl. Getting dropped off by her mom didn't help.

"You can invite her inside if you want. She doesn't have to sit in the car."

"Yes she does," Emmy said.

"Okay," Nathan said with a small smile. He stepped aside and gestured inside. "Come in."

She loved his apartment so much. He had all the windows open, so it smelled of the recent spring rain, intermingled with that inexplicable scent that was *him*. The closest description she could think of was hot orange spice tea.

"When do you have to leave... for the funeral?" Emmy asked.

"Half an hour ago would have been good."

"Oh." Emmy's mouth tasted like metal. Can you actually bleed from pain and awkwardness? It felt like the recurring dream where she can't move, can't speak. She had to watch the moment shatter to pieces in front of her. He'd leave and she'd never see him again. And her last memory of him would be this one, where he radiated so much pain and she couldn't take it away.

She felt her eyes burning with tears, and instead of falling apart in front of him, she followed her other instinct. She fell into his arms and he threaded his fingers into her hair and pressed her head against his chest. She let silent tears bleed into his fancy dress shirt and hoped she didn't leave mascara marks. She thought he might have been trembling, and she squeezed her arms around him to keep him still.

"I don't want to go," Nathan said.

"You should go. You'll regret it if you don't."

"Come with me."

Emmy pulled away and looked up at him to gauge his seriousness. Even though he stood tall, his light had faded so much, in Emmy's eyes, he might as well have fell to his knees.

"I don't think I should," she stammered. "It would make your family mad. I don't want to make them mad today."

"That's why I called you. At least, that's what I had been thinking all yesterday and today. How I wished you were here, how I wished you would go with me. And now here you are."

"I'm not dressed right."

Nathan stared back at her, mouth open. Emmy couldn't stand by his side at a funeral. If she so much as saw a single tear trickle down his cheek, she would lose her mind and sob for three days. She had always considered herself tough, but seeing Nathan cry, no… she couldn't handle that.

"I can stop by my house and change," she said.

Mom didn't like Emmy going to a place full of summer wizards, but she gave in. She even let Nathan pick her up. Not from their apartment… but from the nearest HEB parking lot.

They held the funeral at a massive church made of cut limestone and giant wooden arches that looked more like a castle than a church. Emmy couldn't imagine why they needed a church this big, but cars filled the parking lot and overflowed onto the grass. Everyone had loved Julie Prescott. And that surely intensified in death. When a boy at her school died in a car accident, the whole school went to his funeral, and people didn't like him that much. They couldn't stand it when someone that young died, even if they didn't know the person. Emmy could only imagine this would be amplified a million fold for Julie Prescott.

In life, Julie's endless admirers had given Emmy a bad teeth grinding habit, but now it brought her comfort. To Emmy, Julie's death seemed like a huge deal, and she appreciated that the rest of Houston felt the same way. And on a more selfish note, the people made it easier for her to blend in. Emmy could sense the vast majority of people there were Mundanes, but still more wizards than she had ever seen in one place. And not surprisingly, they all had warm energy.

Aside from a magical instinct that helped her identify wizards, she could spot them with her usual senses too. She sorted out that the wizards all dressed "wrong" for a funeral, at least wrong as far as she knew. Emmy wore a simple black dress, like most of the Mundanes. But the wizards dressed for Easter Sunday, not a funeral. Most of the women wore white or other light colors. The men wore more traditional suits, but not black. Lots of gray and blue and khaki. Nathan wore a gray suit and light blue tie. She wished he would have said something about her black dress, but it didn't matter. She blended in with the Mundanes, which worked out fine.

The summer wizards they passed began a predictable and almost amusing pattern. They would see Nathan, look very sad, walk toward him… then see Emmy clutching his arm, stare at her, and freeze. If Emmy had grieved someone she loved, she wouldn't want tons of random relatives and family friends to bombard her, so hopefully she did Nathan a favor by terrifying everyone he knew. He didn't seem to notice or care they kept their distance.

They entered the enormous sanctuary and found more white everywhere. Large white drapes hung from the cross and the rafters. White candles shimmered everywhere. And the smell of flowers overwhelmed her. White lilies covered everything. Aside from the large photo of Julie, and the glistening gold urn surrounded in a circle of candles, this looked more like a wedding than a funeral. Even though she didn't know Julie well, Emmy thought she would like it.

As they walked down the aisle, Emmy's gut clenched. She could handle random summer wizard strangers, but she wouldn't sit right next to Nathan's parents, and Lucas. She had once vowed to murder Nathan's father if she ever saw him again.

She wouldn't kill a man at his daughter's funeral, but he wouldn't shake his hand either.

However, whether for her benefit or his own reasons, Nathan led her into a pew about halfway to the back, far away from his family.

"Are you sure you want to sit here?" she asked. "I don't mind staying here if you want to go up front."

"No, I want to sit here with you."

"Okay."

Emmy had butterflies in her stomach, as if she prepared to go on stage for debate or theater. She didn't have to do anything except sit in this pew and hold Nathan's hand, but that seemed horrible enough. She didn't want to see any of this. She didn't want to hear people talk about Julie. She didn't want to stare at her bright smiling photo. She didn't want to cry in front of strangers. She didn't want strangers to cry in front of her. She didn't like all these Mundanes crying over someone they didn't understand, making comments about the strange funeral. If she didn't want these things, she could only imagine how Nathan might have felt.

Emmy stared at the glistening gold urn, her vision already blurry from tears. It looked like a massive, sparkling chrysalis. It made it seem like in a few days, when everyone had gone away, Julie would break out again with massive golden butterfly wings.

A man in a white robe began the service. Emmy couldn't tell if he was a Christian pastor or some kind of wizard priest… if those even existed. However, she sensed he was a wizard, whatever else he might be. He glowed like the other summer wizards, the effect more pronounced with his white robe. Between all the white, the inferno of burning candles, the glistening gold urn, the giant windows, and the abundance of summer wizards wearing white, the whole place already glowed as if they had walked into Heaven with Julie. The brightness offended her winter sensibilities, but was much easier to handle than usual. Julie's funeral should shine like the face of the sun.

The priest asked them to stand, and they began the service with "Morning Has Broken," which again made Emmy think they had confused Easter music with funeral music. Emmy couldn't imagine singing at a moment like this. She couldn't possibly croak out notes. Besides the words in the hymnal blurred from her already free flowing tears. Nathan didn't sing either, and she didn't want to look at him, afraid to see him crying too. She considered herself anything but a coward, but seeing Nathan cry terrified her.

They finally got to sit and Emmy let out a long breath, not realizing how tired she had gotten from standing there in silence, holding Nathan's hand.

The wizard preacher guy went to the pulpit and began to speak.

"O Great Spirit, Mother and Father of us all, we ask for your Blessings on this our Ceremony of Thanksgiving, and honoring and blessing of our beloved Julie.

"My dear, sweet Julie. You stand at a Gateway now. And we all stand with you. The light of these thousand souls stand beside you as you pass into the Summerland. You are not alone. Although we may pass years or even millennia apart, in death time is nothing, so we all march through the gateway together, hand-in-hand."

Emmy heard Nathan sniff and take a shaky breath, and she squeezed his hand with both of hers, even though one of them covered with her own tears and snot.

"A loss like this is unfair, and cannot possibly be understood, or perhaps even accepted in our limited state of flesh and bone. We are too small, too tethered to our earthly bodies to see more than the tragedy. The pain. The anger. And I will not ask you to feel otherwise.

"But I do ask you to have faith. A soul such as Julie's cannot be snuffed out by the mere loss of her flawed, limited, human body. The great Goddess Fire has released her from her tomb of flesh. The fire has turned her body to earth, her blood to water, her breath to air, and her spirit to unencumbered flame.

"She is not gone, but everywhere. She is the Air in the East, the Fire in the South, the Water in the West, and the Earth in the North."

They finished the service with "Because He Lives," another hymn Emmy recognized from Easter.

As people moved toward the exits, with red faces and smeared makeup, Emmy steeled herself to prepare to face the Prescotts. She would have to now.

"What next?" Emmy asked. "Will they scatter her ashes somewhere?"

"I want to go," he said in a raspy voice.

"Don't you have to see your parents? At least so they know you're here?"

"They know I'm here."

He took her hand and pulled her down the aisle and out into the lobby. He kept his head straight ahead, appearing to avoid looking anyone in the eye. She had to jog to keep up with him and had to direct her gaze toward her feet so she wouldn't wipe out in her heels.

She crawled into the passenger seat of his truck and watched as he laid his head in his hands against the steering wheel and cried.

CHAPTER TWENTY-SIX

Nathan sat on his couch back at his apartment, and Emmy sat next to him. She took his hand, but he didn't seem to notice.

He spoke for the first time since they drove away. "They say she's in the Summerland. Which is the same as Heaven, I guess."

"Do you believe that?" Emmy asked.

"Yes. I mean, I know it might not be true. That maybe after death there is just… nothing. But if that's true, I'll never know. I'll just die and that will be it. So, I figure I might as well believe."

"I'm sorry, I shouldn't have asked."

"It's okay. And for the record, if there is a Summerland, I definitely don't believe it's just for summer wizards. That's the stupidest thing I've ever heard. And if it was true, I don't think I'd want to go."

"I'd be happy to try and get you into Hell if you prefer," Emmy said. "I'll make a few calls."

Nathan laughed and dropped her hand. Using his own to wipe tears from his eyes.

"You know, the only thing that makes me feel better is knowing for her, this is all over," he said. "Whether she's in the

Summerland or just gone, no one can hurt her anymore. She's free from all of this."

Emmy took his hand back as soon as it got within reach.

"Why did you come here now?" he said.

"You said you wanted me to stay," she said.

"No, I mean why did you wait until now? It's like you only show up when things are terrible. Is that a winter witch thing? First, when Julie is missing. Then, when Julie is dead. What horrible, fucked-up thing has to happen for me to see you again?" He wriggled his hand free from hers.

Emmy opened her mouth to say something, but she didn't know what. As much as she hated to see him in pain, she felt worse to see him hurting because of her.

"You think I called you with magic?" he asked. "I did, but not just today. There have been so many times I've wished you would show up on my doorstop. *Really* wished it. *Commanded* it. But you didn't show. I wanted to take you to a football game. I wanted to see you on Christmas and New Years. I wanted to see you on my birthday, and on yours. I wanted to see you on your day, January 18th. And I wanted to see you on all the boring, ordinary days in between. Is that not good enough for you? Ordinary days? Or do you only like the horrible ones?"

"I want ordinary days," she said.

"I wanted to be with you when I was happy."

"You're making it seem like I just abandoned you," she said, regaining some strength. "That's not what happened. You said I was too young and you didn't want to be with me."

"No, that's not what I said. I said I didn't want to commit statutory rape. That doesn't mean I never wanted to see you again. That was your choice."

"Yeah, and I think you understand why I was mad at you. Your father *murdered* my uncle, *and* he got away with it."

"Well, what do you expect me to do about that?"

"I don't know, how about *anything*?"

"He was just trying to protect my mom."

He grabbed a water bottle from the fridge and took an angry chug. "You left me because of something that had nothing to do with either of us. And that's not fair. It's also stupid. If we're going to get mad at *each other* every time someone in our family does something horrible, you're right, we should just forget it."

Emmy felt her face get hot and she knew she would cry for about the millionth time today. Why couldn't she be more of an ice queen like her mother? She had to get the weepy thing from Dad.

"I'm sorry," she said, trying to talk without crying. "You're right."

"It's okay." Seeing her cry, he changed his demeanor. He sat back down next to her and put his arm over her shoulder, pulling her closer to him. "It's okay," he said again.

"I did want to be with you on the ordinary days," Emmy said. "I really did. I broke my phone so many times my parents didn't buy me a new one until they got the inheritance. I had no *phone*, Nathan. Because of you."

He chuckled. "That is pretty serious."

He ran his fingers through her hair as he held her face against his chest. Emmy didn't understand how deodorant and soap could smell so delicious. She could hear his heart beating.

"If I convinced my mom to lift the repulsion spell, would you try calling me again?"

"She won't lift the spell."

"Then we'll figure out a way around it. You're here now. It can be done."

Emmy nodded with her face pressed against his chest.

"But for now, I have to take you home before the monsters come looking for you."

CHAPTER TWENTY-SEVEN

Samantha didn't want to see Patrick, but she needed to know why he hadn't left for school this morning. Xavier opened the door in response to her knocking. He looked terrible. His eyes appeared sunken and glassy. *Oh God, it's already happened.*

"What happened?" she asked. Her voice sounded restricted as if someone stood behind her and strangled her while she talked.

"What do you mean?" Xavier asked.

"So everything is fine?"

"I guess so. Did you want to come in or something? Emmy's at school, but Patrick is here."

Samantha let out a relived sigh. Despite her anger, the thought of Patrick dying made her feel sick. His death wouldn't make her feel better about Imogene, not even close. Everything would be so much worse. She would lose one more person she cared about.

"So Patrick is okay? And your sister too?"

"Emmy?"

"No, Evangeline. She didn't go to school either."

"What are you, the truancy police? You're not in school either."

"But they're both here, in the apartment. They're okay."

"Yes. Patrick and Eve stayed home sick today."

"Oh God," Samantha said, putting her hand over her mouth. "Sick with what? What do they have?"

"A cold…" Xavier said, squinting at her.

"Like pneumonia?"

"No… honestly, I just think they're upset about Julie and faking being sick."

"Who is Julie?"

"Julie Prescott, that summer witch. She died. Patrick and Eve found her body."

Samantha's stomach flipped as if she had reached the top of a roller coaster. "The summer solstice witch?"

"Yes."

"Oh no. Oh God." Samantha walked inside and Xavier closed the door behind her.

"Did you know her?" Xavier asked.

"I killed her," Samantha said. "I killed a person."

Xavier shook his head and squinted at her again. "No… she was hit by a car."

"No, I killed her with a spell. The killing spell I cast with your sister."

Xavier's face turned yellower and paler. "I don't understand… you're saying Julie killed Imogene? Why would she do that? Can a summer witch even cast a killing spell by herself?"

Then Xavier's face froze. She could imagine a film of ice forming over his eyeballs.

"She didn't cast the spell by herself," Xavier said, his lips looking way too white.

He had figured it out. She silently cursed herself. She hadn't meant to come here and blab to everyone. For whatever reason, he already looked on the edge of death, and now she felt like she should grab his arm to keep him from passing out.

"I'm sorry," Samantha said, so quietly she almost didn't want him to hear her. "I have no business here, I'll go."

"You're not going anywhere," Xavier said. It looked as if his eyeballs vibrated. He grabbed her arm.

"What are doing?" Patrick asked, coming out of his room. "Let go of her."

Xavier dropped her arm. Both Evangeline and Patrick had emerged from their rooms, like lions circling.

"You were never sick at all," Xavier said. "You just wanted a reason to hide under your covers."

"How could you tell him?" Patrick asked Samantha.

"I didn't mean to. He figured it out."

Xavier moved toward Patrick and then punched him in the face. Samantha gasped. Patrick hunched over and cradled his cheek. He moved his jaw from side to side as if testing to see if it still worked.

"I should kill you," Xavier said.

"Go ahead," Patrick said, holding his cheek. "The waiting is the hardest part."

Xavier turned to his sister. He didn't hit her, but he curled his face into the most aggressive look of disgust Samantha had ever seen.

"You cast this spell," he said, practically snarling. "Stop it."

"I can't. You know I can't."

Then Xavier turned his snarl toward Samantha. "You stop it," he said. "You're spring."

"Maybe the spell didn't work," Samantha said. "It's been almost a week." However as soon as she saw the lilies she had known it had worked. And now Julie was dead... "The truth is... I've already tried to reverse the spell, and I failed."

"What do you mean?" Patrick asked.

"There were Easter lilies in the room... and when we cast

the spell, they all died," she said to Patrick, knowing the other two knew the story. "I regretted the spell as soon as I saw those lilies dying. So I planted them and used spring magic to try to get them to grow again. But as you saw, it didn't work."

"Could it though?" Patrick asked. "Could a spring wizard reverse a killing spell?"

"No," Evangeline said. "Spring wizards can't stop death. No one can stop death."

"Imogene could," Samantha said. "You killed the only person who could have saved you."

"No, she couldn't," Evangeline said, although her voice had lost some of its confidence.

"I saw her do it," Samantha said. "I watched her bring a dead bird back to life. She could do exactly what you can do. No, she could do something much harder. She was more powerful than you," she added.

"So if we found another spring equinox witch," Patrick interjected. "They could reverse the spell."

"What do you mean, another one?" Samantha asked. "You murdered the woman I loved so you could stop Caroline from finding her. Now you're telling me she could just move on to another one?"

"We *didn't* murder her to stop Caroline from finding her," Patrick said. "We were trying to protect her. We wanted to protect the next spring equinox witch she was going to find. We wanted to keep the spell conservative—as simple as possible."

Xavier scoffed.

"There can't be many more though," Evangeline said. "How many spring equinox wizards are there in the world?"

"One hundred and ninety-two," Patrick said.

"What?" Evangeline asked, breathless.

"How in the hell do you know that?" Samantha asked.

"I don't," Patrick said. "It's an educated guess. Seven billion people in the world. We believe that about .001% of them are wizards. So, that's 70,000 wizards in the world. If we assume roughly one out of every 365 wizards is a spring equinox wizard, then that comes out to 192, which is obviously a rough estimate."

"That's a lot though," Samantha said.

"Well, yeah," Patrick said. "It's rare, but it's not like event wizards are 'the chosen one.' Just rare."

"If that's 192 out of the whole world though," Evangeline said. "It's a lot less close by, right. How many in the U.S.?"

"Eight or Nine," Patrick said. "Assuming they're evenly distributed throughout the world."

"Eight or Nine?" Evangeline repeated. "That's so many."

"Not really," Patrick said. "Eight or Nine out of three hundred million is infinitesimal."

"Not if you're using a siren spell," Evangeline said. "It's not like Caroline is just knocking on doors asking for spring equinox wizards. She's using a very powerful siren spell to bring one to her. It may take a while for the spell to filter out such a low percentage of the population. But it will work, sooner or later. And, if you found the one equinox witch that was closest and stopped Caroline from finding her, you're only one-ninth of the way through."

"Which is exactly why we shouldn't try to find another spring equinox wizard," Patrick said. "If we did, we'd just be doing exactly what Caroline wants us to do. That's how siren spells work. A spring witch doesn't just plummet through the air and land on her front step. Fate brings her what she wants. And I'm not going to help the spell work by finding a spring equinox witch myself so Caroline can just swoop in and take her."

"Shut up about Caroline," Xavier said. "You're going to die. So what if Caroline finds the spring equinox wizard? How do you know she's still looking or even still alive? She and Jude just disappeared. It's been almost a year. And you still think she's going to show up any minute."

"Yeah, I do Xavier," Patrick said. "You don't understand her. She's patient. Just because she hasn't done anything yet, doesn't mean she won't. She'll wait until the right moment."

"But you banished her," Xavier said. "She can't come back."

"Banishment. Repulsion. Misdirection. All those spells are limited and they fade with time. Free will can beat them if the person is persistent enough."

"Leave springtime alone," Samantha said. "Quit trying to *use* us. Stay away from all of the spring equinox witches and wizards—all spring wizards for that matter. Even if you find one, you'll just end up hurting them," Samantha said. "Besides, Evangeline was right, a spring equinox wizard can't help you. A winter solstice witch cast the spell, and with all things equal, death beats life."

"Why?" Patrick asked.

"*Why?* Because it *does*," Samantha said. "Every living creature dies. In the end, death beats life. Every time."

"No it doesn't," Xavier said.

"What do you mean?"

"Life beats death," Xavier said. "Every *individual* creature dies, but before they do, those creatures have babies. And those babies have babies. Life continues. Life wins. It has for millions of years."

The hopeful and profound sentiment stunned Samantha, and she didn't respond right away.

"Well, yes," Samantha said. "After Patrick and Evangeline die, life in general will go on. But that doesn't really help us, does it?"

CHAPTER TWENTY-EIGHT

Emmy didn't have the chance to say goodbye to Julie at the funeral, and she felt compelled to do so. In part to pay her respects to Julie, but also because she didn't want to believe it. She wanted to go back to the memorial site and not find Julie's name. It would have all been a bad dream.

She walked through the lush green St. Augustine lawn, the heels of her sandals sinking into the soft earth. She took her shoes off and flicked the clumps of mud off before continuing barefoot. Water hung in the air suspended, like a zero gravity deluge. Her hair stuck to the sides of her face, and mud squished between her toes.

As she got closer to the urn garden, she stopped. Someone else sat by the avalanche of flowers at Julie's memorial. With a sick jolt, she thought it might be Caroline, but on second glance she saw a girl a couple years younger than she was. She sat with her legs folded under her in an impossible yoga pose, and strange white pieces of paper or fabric littered the grass around her.

She had pale skin, and her hair matched. If she hadn't been young, Emmy would have thought her hair was white, and not blonde. But, in contrast to the rest of her albinoness, her eyes were dark brown, almost black. And, her eyelashes were dark and long too, in contrast with the rest of her blondness. She was pretty, but in a strange way. Emmy couldn't decide if she wanted to stare at her because of her beauty or because she looked weird.

"I wouldn't come any closer," the girl said.

"Why not?" Emmy asked.

"I'm not supposed to be around people."

"That's weird," Emmy said. Ignoring the warning, Emmy walked closer to the girl, but had to stop. She had a sudden wave of nausea and put her hands on her knees. Her mouth filled with saliva. She took some deep breaths to stave off vomiting.

The deep breaths might not have been a good idea. The most noxious odor she'd ever encountered filled the air. The closest comparison might have been rotting road kill. It smelled like death. Odd thoughts scrolled through Emmy's head. Dead bodies surrounded her under the ground, but graveyards didn't actually smell bad, do they? Was the smell coming from that girl? How could a human person smell like that? Unless she's not a human person. Ghost? Zombie? This was a graveyard after all.

The scent molecules had gotten in her mouth and now she could *taste* death. She spit and coughed, and then retched.

"Just step back," the girl said.

Emmy's eyes burned, and she couldn't tell which way she had come from, but she stepped a few steps and the smell lifted. It lingered a bit in her nostrils and seemed stuck in her hair for all eternity. But she could smell the lawn and the flowers again.

"You're a winter witch," she said. "How did you know my sister? Or are you just here to make sure she's really dead?"

The girl didn't smirk or laugh. She stared at her with those black hole eyes. Emmy couldn't put her finger on it, but she found something distressing about those eyes and she made a point to look at her eyebrows instead.

"Your sister?" Emmy asked.

That could only mean one thing. Julie had two sisters—Caroline and the mysteriously missing Leona who Nathan had called a "siren." This must have been her. But Leona didn't match her expectations. Julie and the other summer wizards burned as if they walked around on fire all the time. Emmy had expected a siren to be worse. However, unlike Nathan's description, Leona didn't sparkle at all. She looked like her sisters in the face, but she didn't fit in.

"Leona Prescott?" Emmy asked with the same tone of incredulity she might have if she'd met the Easter bunny.

Leona nodded.

"You exist," Emmy said.

Leona raised an eyebrow. "Who are you?"

"Um… Emmy Vandergraff?" She didn't why she said it like a question. The question was not her name but… do you know who I am?

Leona nodded. "Nathan told me about you."

"He did?"

She nodded again, her expression flat.

"You weren't at the funeral," Emmy said.

"My parents didn't want me around all those people."

"Because you're a siren," Emmy said.

"That's right."

"What does that mean anyway?"

Leona fiddled with the frayed ends of her hair. She had grown her hair so long it skirted the grass.

"It means I give off pheromones."

"Like you can make people fall in love with you?"

She shrugged, looking at the tips of her hair wrapped around her fingers. "I can alter emotions and behavior in lots of ways. And I can't control it. People have died because of me," she said.

"That's a weird thing to tell someone you just met."

"Is it?" she asked. "I don't talk to many people."

Leona's cold disposition shifted. She pressed her lips together, and Emmy saw her pale skin had reddened around her eyes. She wiped tears off her face.

"But Julie would call me and visit me behind our parents back. They thought she was little miss perfect, but she didn't mind breaking the rules when the rules were wrong. My parents thought I was jealous of her since she was a solstice witch and everyone loved her. But I wasn't jealous, not really. The bright ones burn quick. All the event wizards, they're too powerful for this world, and they don't last long."

Emmy felt her gut tighten into knots, thinking of her brother and sister.

"I wasn't jealous of Julie's power," Leona said. "I was sad for her. She was a good person, and she deserved better than this."

"I agree." Emmy wanted to sit down next to her, but knew better now. She stayed put.

Leona picked a weed from the grass and held it in her palm. Emmy watched as misshapen white leaves sprouted all over it, and realized that these leaves surrounded Leona. Emmy ventured a few steps closer to grab one of the delicate white pieces and saw not a leaf, but a petal, at least in texture. The deformed petals looked more like a spitball than a flower.

"You're a spring witch," Emmy said.

Leona nodded, rifling through the lawn looking for a useful plant. Emmy assumed Leona would be summer like her family—an assumption she now realized was silly. Caroline was fall. Patrick was fall and came from two winter wizards.

"What is your date?" Emmy asked.

"March 18th."

"But that means you're on the wrong side of the equinox. For summer wizards… I mean."

Leona put down her latest weed and looked at Emmy.

"I mean, not even Caroline is on the wrong side of the

equinox," Emmy said.

"It's just a few days off," Leona said.

"Is that the real reason why they keep you locked up? Because you're a spring?"

"No."

"But they wouldn't be such jerks about it if you were on the "right side" of the equinox, would they?"

Leona didn't answer, she continued trying to make a weed bloom. Her next attempt came out better. A small bud formed on the tip of the weed and spread into a lopsided white rose. Leona put the deformed flower on her sister's grave.

"I'm not very good," she said. "No one ever taught me spring magic."

"Can I help?"

"Can you?" she asked with an eyebrow raised.

"Well, I don't know. But Nathan says I tend toward spring. I could try."

"I think he's right," Leona said, smiling at her.

Emmy walked to the other side of Julie's grave, keeping a wide breadth between them. She took a weed out of the lawn and held it her hand, feeling silly.

"You can come here now," Leona said. "I'm not afraid of you anymore."

"Really? I'm not going to throw up?"

"Probably not."

Emmy walked around the grave and kneeled next to Leona. Dirt and grass stains covered her white dress and her long blonde hair looked as if it weighed about a hundred pounds in the humidity. It stuck to her neck and arms like extra veins against her pale skin. She smelled strange—a bit like onions, with a hint of rotting plants. Maybe a touch of soured milk. But on the whole, it she could tolerate it.

Leona closed Emmy's hands to create a cocoon around the little weed and placed her hands over Emmy's. Emmy didn't know if it was the siren thing or an effect of the spring magic, but she felt this beautiful warmth, as if Leona dipped Emmy's hands in warm milk and honey. Her skin tingled as if her dead skin cells popped back to life.

Leona took her hands away and Emmy opened her cupped hands. At the base of one of the leaves on the sad little plant, little white fingers emerged, and then widened and opened to create a small, but flawless white lily.

"Wow," Emmy said.

"I think your magic did help," Leona said.

"I don't feel like I did anything." Emmy leaned over and placed the delicate little flower beside Julie's memorial.

Emmy rubbed her now smooth hands. Her dry and picked at cuticles had become soft and pink, with no more peeling dead skin. Even her nails seemed stronger and longer. She couldn't stop rubbing her hands together, feeling how her skin had seemed to turn to silk.

Emmy's phone rang. Xavier's name flashed on the display.

"Hello," Emmy said.

"Where are you?" he asked in a gravelly voice.

"Is Mom looking for me? How does she know I skipped drama practice? I'll be back at the school for her to pick me up at six."

"Come home now."

"Why?"

"Patrick and Eve are going to die."

"What did you say?"

"Patrick and Eve are going to die."

"Xavier…" She didn't understand the joke and she didn't like it. The bile rose in her throat again.

"Just come home now."

"Okay."

Xavier hung up the phone and Leona stared at Emmy, her glare caused a gross film to cover the back of her throat.

"Are you okay?" Leona asked.

"Sure. My brother is weird." Emmy got up and turned to leave, stomping her foot that had begun to tingle.

"It was nice meeting you," Leona said.

"You too. I'll see you later."

"When?"

"When what?"

"When will you see me?" Leona asked with big, expectant eyes.

"Oh… I don't know. Sometime, probably. Bye."

"Bye."

CHAPTER TWENTY-NINE

P atrick heard his mom yell his name from behind his closed door and he emerged from his room to find his entire family sitting in the living room and staring at him. They all looked angry, except Dad, who looked on the verge of tears. Evangeline sat at the end of the couch with her arms crossed and body facing away from Mom as much as she could without sitting backward and staring at the wall.

"Is what your brother just told me true?" Mom asked.

"What did he tell you?" he asked

Evangeline nodded, and Patrick took it to mean they all knew the truth.

Mom breathed in a strange jilting pattern, as if she had forgotten how to do it. "I… I don't even want to say it," she said. "Tell me she's wrong."

"I can't believe you told," Patrick said to Xavier.

"Grow up, Patrick," Mom said. "You're not children who are tattling on each other. How dare you keep this a secret from me? How dare you prevent me from trying to help?"

Patrick stared at the worn carpet. "There are several vague catalyst spells in play. It's hard to say what will happen."

"Answer me directly," Mom demanded. "Has a killing spell been directed at you and Evangeline?"

"It was an accident."

Mom put her hand to her mouth, which seemed as if it would make breathing harder. She shook her head, staring at the wall. Then she put her hand down and shook her head again, but this time like she tried to wake herself up.

Dad stared at him with reddened eyes.

"Okay. Don't worry," Mom said. "We'll fix this. I mean… it's crazy. You can't just *will* someone to die."

"You can," Evangeline said. "I did… Julie's already dead."

Mom put her whole face in her hands this time, rubbing her eyebrows as if that might somehow give her an idea.

"No, I've got it. I can fix this." Mom shook her head as she spoke, as if she didn't believe it herself. "We'll fix this. You're going to be fine. Just… okay." Mom looked around the room, seeming lost. "I have an idea… I do. We'll fix this," she said for the fourth time in the space of a minute. "Eve and Patrick, go in the boys' bedroom. I want you both in the same place so I can keep an eye on you."

"Can I get a book first? Can I get Anabel Lee?"

"No. Don't leave my sight. Just go in there."

"Mom, don't be insane," Patrick said. "I'll go with her to her room so she can have her stuff."

Patrick followed Eve to her room where she sat on her bed, petting the lizard. She looked like she held her breath.

"This isn't your fault," Patrick said. "You were just trying to help Samantha."

"Hmm," she responded, perhaps afraid to open her mouth all the way.

"I'm sure we can find a way to undo the spell."

She shook her head. "It is my fault," she said. "I wanted someone to kill, so I cast a stupid, lazy spell. I wanted to test my skills but on someone who deserved it. Not Julie." Her voice broke on the word "Julie." She took a moment to breathe and compose herself again. "But I imagined doing it in person. Any dark wizard can cast a vague killing spell out into the world. I can do so much more. I just wanted to do it in person, for real."

"That's why you're upset? Not because we're going to die, but because you didn't get to 'do it in person'?"

"Julie didn't deserve to die. She was a nice person, and a fantastic witch. She never got to realize her powers either. It's not fair. I just need to find Caroline. So I can kill her before I die."

Patrick sat next to Evangeline and the lizard wagged its tongue at him in warning.

"Don't you even care about dying?"

"Not really."

"Well you should," he said. "I care about you dying. Lots of people do."

"I just want to be able to finally try the spell before I die. But it has to be someone who deserves it. I am not a monster. There is no point in killing just to kill. I want to kill to make things right."

"I don't think you're going to die. We're going to find a way to stop it. But even if you were, wouldn't you rather die with a clean slate? An untainted soul?"

She glanced up and squinted at him.

"I already killed Julie *and* Imogene, and it's very, very bad luck to harm a spring wizard."

"Is it?"

She nodded. "Everyone knows that. If you kill a spring wizard… that's so bad. So unlucky. Even if we break the killing spell, we're going to be punished for what we did. She was even a spring equinox witch. That's so bad," she said again. "I'm going to die either way. I want to kill Caroline first. At least then I'll have done something useful before I die."

"If you want to kill someone, Caroline is a good choice. But

I'd rather you not kill anyone. I can't believe I even have to say that."

"You don't get it."

"No, I don't. I will never get that."

"I want to make things right. I've had this power all along, but I never realized it. I never *used* it. I could have killed my stepfather a hundred times over. But I didn't. I didn't do anything."

Patrick had never heard her mention her life before, and he found himself tongue-tied.

"You can't think like that," he said, finally. "You were just a kid. You're *still* a kid. And even if you weren't, it's not your responsibility. Those types of things just shouldn't happen. It's not your fault."

"I never said it was my fault," she spat. "I just should have done something. I'm a winter solstice witch. No one should be able to hurt me."

Patrick stared at the lizard while it continued to stare back at him with unblinking yellow eyes. His mouth felt dry.

"I'm not exactly an expert on the topic," he said. "But I know killing someone won't take away what happened to you. It won't make it right, won't take away the pain. I wish I knew what would, but I don't think there is anything."

Patrick wished he had something more hopeful to add, but his words had dried up like his tongue.

"Wow, that was the least comforting thing I could have possibly said, isn't it?" he asked.

Evangeline smiled. "No, it wasn't so bad. It was honest. I hate it when people try to comfort me anyway. Everything they say is always so stupid."

"I don't doubt that."

"If you're going to be honest with me, then be honest. You *know* you can't undo the spell. You *know* we're going to die. I've seen it in your eyes... for a long time now. Way before any of this."

Patrick didn't say anything. His dry mouth now seemed too wet. "You saw it in my eyes, huh?" he said, continuing to delay.

"Just tell me. How does it happen?"

Patrick took a deep breath. "Honestly, I have had visions of us dying, but they change, like fate is still trying to figure it out."

"What do you mean?"

"I've seen you drowning. I've seen you falling. I've seen you *jumping*. I've seen myself drowning. Burning. Bleeding. I've been having visions like that since last summer—when Julie went missing. And that makes sense. That's when the chain of events began. The chain of events that would lead to our death."

"But you said you saw me drowning, falling, and jumping. Couldn't it be jumping, then falling, then drowning? I could jump off something into water."

Patrick grimaced and shook his head. He wanted shake off her words. He hated how calmly she could speak about her own death. "I don't know. I'm saying it's not always the exact same scene. I've learned enough about by visions by now to know they are told in symbols. I'm not necessarily going to see the exact details of our deaths. Who knows, maybe that means the details are still to be determined, subject to change by fate. I can't tell you exactly when or where it's going to happen. Or how... or why. It's a lame skill I know."

CHAPTER THIRTY

Amanda did her best to open the front door quietly. She didn't want to wake the kids. Jess Oppenheimer stared in at her and David from the stoop, looking at them like strangers.

"Come in," Amanda said.

Jess stepped over the threshold. When Amanda closed the door behind her, Jess rubbed her arms though it wasn't cold. The weather had found that middle spot where they didn't need the heat or the air conditioner, and if anything, the room felt warm and stuffy.

"Are you okay?" Amanda asked.

"You called me here in the middle of the night and didn't say why," Jess said. "I'm not okay. I'm terrified. What is going on?"

"I'm sorry," Amanda said. "We just couldn't sleep without answers. And I thought maybe this way, we could be delicate about it."

"Answers?" She cringed. "That's why you wanted me, and not Carson. For some kind of psychic reading? At 2 a.m.? I have children at home."

"We wouldn't have called you if it wasn't important." Amanda swallowed and took a shaky breath.

Jess reached out and squeezed her hand. "Okay. What is it?"

"You can't tell anyone," Amanda said.

"Well, I'm going to tell Carson."

"You probably shouldn't."

"Why can't she tell him?" David asked. "What does it matter if people know?"

"*Because* killing spells are not the kind of thing you broadcast to the world."

Jess took a sharp intake of breath and backed a step toward the door. "I knew it," she said. "I knew it." She reached for the doorknob and Amanda grabbed her arm.

"Whatever it is," Jess said. "I'm not helping you." She held her head too high, as if feigning confidence she didn't have.

"No, you don't understand. We're the *victims*. Patrick and Evangeline," she said in a breathy whisper.

Jess gasped. "But they're children. Who would cast a killing spell against children?"

"*They* don't see them as children. Patrick and Evangeline are event wizards. The winter solstice and the fall equinox. You know how people feel threatened when event wizards are around. And two in the same house... it scares people." Her creative perversion of the truth impressed David.

"That's horrible," Jess said, too flatly, as if exterminating event wizards, even children, was only mildly upsetting... and not at all surprising. "I'm so sorry."

"No," David said. "Don't say *you're sorry* like they're already dead. How dare you?"

"He's my nephew. And my kind. I'd do anything to help him, I just don't know what I could do."

David chose to ignore that she left Evangeline out of the equation.

"But I can't do anything," she continued. "Is it even

possible to stop a killing spell? I don't know. I don't know anything about them."

"We just need information," Amanda said. "All we know is they think a killing spell has been cast against them. And it's already working. It killed Julie Prescott."

"Oh God," Jess said. "I saw that on the news. She was the summer solstice, wasn't she?"

"Any kind of information you have," Amanda continued. "A prophecy. Anything. If you could even just tell us if the spell is real. I've heard fall wizards can do that. They can see spells somehow. See magic."

Jess walked away from the door. She moved past them and into the living room, placing her purse on the coffee table and then staring at the carpet. "That's true," she said. "But it's not as simple as you make it sound."

"Nothing ever is," David said.

"Well, you're right," Jess said. "Magic is rarely simple. Especially powerful spells. But in this case… that's not a bad thing."

"Why?" Amanda asked.

"The more powerful and complicated the spell, the more likely something could go wrong."

"So that's possible?" David asked. His voice sounded too loud. He didn't want to wake the kids, although knowing them, at least two of them were already wide awake and listening to every word. "The spell could just not work?"

"Of course it's possible," Jess asked. "I'm more surprised when spells actually work, than when they fail."

"That's good," David said, nodding. "See," he said to Amanda. "If killing spells really worked, then why wouldn't wizards being dying off left and right?"

"Wizards *are* dying off left and right," Amanda said.

"You can see spells?"

They all turned to see Evangeline standing outside her door.

He hadn't noticed her open the door, or close it again. She held a yellowed paperback book in one hand, and had her lizard cradled in the other, and David guessed he had been right and she hadn't been sleeping.

"You must be Evangeline," Jess said. "I'm Jess."

It struck David that Jess and Carson had never met his other children.

"You didn't need to bring her here," Evangeline said. "Patrick can see spells. He can see spells even before they are cast. He knows we're going to die."

"There's nothing wrong with getting a second opinion," Amanda said. "The doctors said I was going to die too. And here I am."

"Well," Evangeline said to Jess. "Do you think I am going to die?" David hated the false bravado in her voice. The less afraid she seemed, the most afraid he believed she was.

Jess walked over to her and stopped a few feet away. "May I?" she asked, raising her hands.

"You're afraid of me, aren't you?" Evangeline asked.

"People are often afraid of what they don't understand," Jess said.

"So, then you *are* afraid of me."

"Yes," Jess said. "But I'm more afraid *for* you."

"Patrick doesn't have to touch people to see their spells."

"That's very impressive. I won't touch you if you don't want me to."

"No. It's okay," she said with a shrug.

Despite the permission, Jess approached her at a glacial pace, which made the interaction seem all the more awkward. David stood a few steps away in a protective hover, although he knew Jess was in far more danger than Evangeline.

Jess brushed Eve's long hair off her shoulders and laid her hands on them. The muscles in Jess's jaw tensed, especially noticeable in one of the calmest people David knew. He thought of what had happened to Penelope—when he accidentally struck her with dark magic when she tried to "read" him. But Jess lived surrounded by winter wizards. She could handle herself. But none of her family members had Evangeline's power. He felt protective of both of them.

"For what it's worth," Jess said to Evangeline, with her hands on her shoulders. "You're dangerous, but not because you're a bad person. Your magic is dangerous, but you're not. At least... you don't have to be. You just have a lot of negative energy. And a lot of negative samskaras—which is like a spiritual scar. But unlike real scars, samskaras aren't stuck forever. They can be changed."

"Just tell us what we want to know," David said, pacing in short circles.

Jess took her hands off Evangeline's shoulders and rearranged her hair the way she had it before, which David considered unnecessary touching, especially to someone she had called dangerous.

Jess rubbed her arms and David wondered if she felt colder after touching his daughter.

"Dammit, Jess, quit stalling," David said.

"I'm not stalling," she said and then negated that statement by closing her eyes and taking an excessively long exhale.

"Jess, have my children been hit with a killing spell?"

"I'm trying to decide what to say."

"What is there to decide?" David demanded. "It's a yes or no question."

"Winter wizards always want a yes or no," Jess shot back. "They want it all to be black or white. I know you think fall wizards are just trying to aggravate you by not giving you the simple answer you want, but we're not. Simple answers don't exist. If any so-called oracle gives you a simple answer, then they're lying to you. If you want the truth, then you can't have simple. You can't have it both ways."

"For the love of God, Jess," Amanda said. "Just give us your cryptic fall witch bullshit then. Just give us *something*."

"If she wasn't a winter solstice witch, I would be 100% certain she's been hit with a killing spell. A very powerful one. Death is... right behind her. But because of the nature of her magic, I can't be sure if death follows her, or if she *is* death. There is just... so much death in this house. I could feel it when you visited for Easter. It's toxic. And it's worse now than it was before. An impending killing spell would explain that. But other things might explain it too. So, there you have it, my cryptic fall witch bullshit. Good enough?"

"I would appreciate it if you would care a little more about the death of my children," David said.

"I care very much," Jess said. "I care about all of you. But what's done is done. It's too late now."

"Just get out," David said. "Get out of my house. I wouldn't want the death getting all over your warm, gooey yoga energy."

"David," Amanda said touching his elbow. "You wanted the truth."

"I wanted answers," David said. "And she didn't give me any."

"Yes, I did," Jess said. "You just don't want to listen."

"Get out."

"Okay," Jess said. She gave Amanda a hug, and gave David a meek smile. "I love you both," Jess said. "I really hope I'm wrong." She looked back at Evangeline before she picked up her purse and went out the door.

David knew how it felt to fear for the life of someone he loved. He had experienced that more times than he liked to count. He knew the panicked adrenaline-fueled fear that caused him to act without thinking. He knew the terrible absence of having a missing child. The horrible nagging, and not knowing.

But the most difficult type of all these flavors of fear was the lack of control. When he watched Amanda's health decline.

He could support her. He could take care of her, but he couldn't save her. He hovered between desperation and numbness.

He felt similar now, although the numbness felt more pronounced. At least with Amanda's cancer, he could consult with doctors. He could hear test results, view MRI scans, and listen to the prognosis. None of that had felt comforting at the time, but in retrospect, he had appreciated the concreteness of it all. He could see the enemy, right there on the MRI.

With the killing spell directed at his children, he felt lost. He didn't know how afraid to feel because it didn't seem real. As Amanda had said, *you can't will someone to die.* It didn't work like that. However, the chances Julie, a healthy, resilient girl, would coincidentally die in the same week the spell was cast against her… it didn't seem likely. Especially after she had survived much worse perils than biking home form school.

He had no information at all. No prognosis, no expectations, and no treatment plan. He wanted that the most. Chemotherapy. Surgery. Sometimes the treatments seemed worse than the disease, but it gave them a way to fight.

David took a sip of his coffee but it had gone cold as he stared at the clock willing it to move faster. Amanda had finally gone to bed, probably because he kept nagging her to do so. Although she had only agreed to sleep on the floor next to Patrick. He had this irrational fear if she didn't get enough sleep or drink enough water, or something else simple, the cancer might come back. He had also agreed to keep watch for the both of them. Although he had no idea what he should watch for. The cloaked figure of Death peering through the windows?

He had waited for 7 a.m., 8 a.m. in New York. As soon as the clock changed to seven, he looked at a business card he had stuffed in his wallet and called the office of Peter Sherman, the estate lawyer. The receptionist transferred him.

"Mr. Vandergraff, how can I help you?" His voice on the other line sounded distant and bored.

"I need to hire you. Not as a lawyer, but as a wizard."

All night, David's hands had reached for the business card. As a wizard, that provided reason enough. His subconscious knew what to do, even if he had no idea why.

"I don't understand," Mr. Sherman said.

"If you can give me the answers I need… if you can help me, I'll pay *anything*."

Mr. Sherman stayed quiet on the line for a moment. "Go on."

"I need to reverse or stop a killing spell."

Mr. Sherman took another pause. At least he didn't gasp or shout, although he didn't seem like the gasping and shouting type.

"Sir, my specialty is working with people who are already dead. Handling their affairs. The only thing I know about killing spells is even the darkest wizards know better than to cast one. I'd be happy to help the subject of the spell with planning their last will and…"

"Can they be stopped?" David interrupted.

"Perhaps. I wouldn't be the right person to ask."

"Who is the right person to ask?"

"Who do you *want* to ask?" Mr. Sherman parroted back.

David's eye ticked in frustration, and he rubbed it to calm the tick.

"It's my children, Peter. Can I call you, Peter? I'm going to." He bared his teeth at the phone. "My son and daughter. They're sixteen and fourteen years old. They are going to die."

"Have you considered consulting with Zander Colter?"

"Why would I do that?" David yelled back.

"Because he's intended to save your baby girl. At least, that was my understanding of the message. As for your son, I'm not certain."

David stared at some crumbs on his keyboard. *Save his baby girl.* The baby *killer* would save his child?

"How would Rachel have even known this would happen?" David asked. "She wasn't a fall witch. It's my understanding that winter witches don't have that kind of skill."

"Don't underestimate the dead. They can see things you and I can't even imagine. For them, time is irrelevant. Past, future, present—it means nothing."

David squeezed the phone, wanting to strangle the voice on the other line. Why couldn't anyone give him straight answers? He suppressed a nagging voice reminding him that Jess and Mr. Sherman had given him an answer, just not the one he wanted.

"The dead see more than us, but also less at the same time," Mr. Sherman continued. "All of the frivolous details of life are stripped away, and they have a clear view of only the things that were important to them."

"Stop talking. I don't know how much time I have and I didn't call you for a philosophical discussion about dead people. None of this information is making me feel very generous. If you don't have anything helpful to add, I won't waste any more of your time."

"For my standard fee, I am more than happy to give it another try."

"Give *what* another try?"

"I'll consult with Ms. Colter and see if I can get her to add any more detail to her message. Even gleaning a word or two from the dead is difficult. And their messages are rarely specific. The full sentence I retrieved for Zander was far more than I'm usually able to provide."

It took a few more seconds after he finished speaking before David registered what he had said. His tongue felt numb and two sizes too big.

"Rachel didn't write those messages for us at all. You made them up yourself and then sold them to us."

"Why do you think I offered the message to you weeks after we met? If she had given me a message when she was alive, I would have shared it with you at our meeting."

"You swindled me. You son of a bitch."

Mr. Sherman appeared unbothered by David's accusation. "I assumed you understood," he said. "That's part of the service I provide. I'm an estate lawyer for wizards, and as such I can do more than prepare documents. The living hire me to help resolve their affairs after they have passed. Meet their final requests. And provide communication to their loved ones if needed."

David wanted to stay angry. But he wanted to believe Mr. Sherman more. Before he knew he was a wizard, he never believed mediums existed, but at the time he didn't believe wizards or magic existed either. And what Mr. Sherman had said about the dead seemed true. He had felt like he got messages from Crystal before and now he felt haunted by James. And neither of them offered useful or detailed instructions.

"Prove it," David said. "Prove you can really speak to the dead."

"I'm not going to be able to provide a demonstration over the phone. I'm not one of those fraud mediums you see on television who just tell you what you want to hear. It takes time and deep concentration. But it's worth it. The dead give fantastic advice. They are incapable of deception or malice. They can see the past, present, and future. And they are always driven by love. You see love is what makes us immortal. Our love lives after our bodies perish. It's the love I speak to. And as such, the words are always true and very important."

Mr. Sherman had found a new eloquence. Perhaps speaking to the dead was his true passion, the Mundane paperwork of managing estates, a necessary annoyance. David wanted to believe him. He wanted to believe he had spoken to Crystal and James, at least in their simplistic way. And he wanted to believe. If his love would live on, death didn't sound as frightening. It sounded blissful. A simple, truthful existence fueled by love itself.

"That's what you meant when you said you were the wrong person to ask about the killing spell," David said.

"That's right."

"So Rachel… being dead… might know how to stop a killing spell?"

"I don't want to bring you false hope. Generally speaking, magic can't be stopped once it's sent out into the world. However, skilled wizards can manipulate spells that have already been cast… in theory at least. But you have to outsmart the magic—know more than the magic knows—which may not be possible… for the living of course."

"Do it. Stop whatever you're doing and talk to Rachel. Money is no object."

Patrick could feel her magic hovering over him without opening his eyes. He had to admit it comforted him—his mother's crisp magical cloud keeping watch. A good winter, like silent snowfalls and the cold quiet of an early winter morning. He had known that presence all his life, even before he understood that he felt her magic.

Although he didn't mind her presence, he felt compelled to roll over to glare at her. The pain already made it impossible for him to get a good night's sleep, and he didn't need anything else making it harder.

"Are you going to watch me sleep all night?" Patrick asked.

"Probably."

"Because that's not creepy."

"Oh, so you can do it, but I can't?"

Patrick propped himself up on his elbow. "What do you mean?"

"When I was sick and I would sleep during the day, you

would come in and check on me. You'd put your hand over my mouth to see if I was still breathing. It was sweet. You have a good heart, Patrick."

"You're my mother. What kind of person would I be if I didn't care whether or not you lived or died?"

"You always have to be so rational about everything."

"I'm probably not going to die in my sleep you know. If killing spells are like all other kinds of spells, they have to work within the bounds of reality. I don't have a heart condition or anything like that. I won't die in my sleep unless an asteroid hits my bed."

"Or the apartment catches fire. Or a car drives through the wall. Both of those things have happened to us you know."

Patrick punched his pillow into a more comfortable shape. "I guess if I have to go, I wouldn't mind dying in my sleep."

"You're not going to die."

"Says the woman planning on staring at me all night to make sure I don't stop breathing."

"It reminds me of when you were a baby. With all you kids, I used to check on you two or three times in the night to make sure you were still breathing. Well, maybe not just when you were a baby. I think you were about three or four before I stopped thinking you might die in your sleep." She chuckled to herself. "Mothers do that because they're afraid of SIDS, but I don't think that's the only reason. Sometimes it's just so hard to believe you actually created life. It feels like that little light might blow out any minute. It just can't be real."

Patrick stared at the ceiling and listened to her speak. He didn't care what she said. He wanted to hear her voice. He knew what she meant about life feeling fragile. It felt that way to him now. Death lurked everywhere. He could drown himself in a few inches of water. He could smother himself with a pillow. Stab a pencil into his neck. The most insignificant, harmless thing could end his entire life. How do so many people live to be old?

How has the human race stuck around so long? Every single one of his ancestors had to stay alive long enough to make a baby. The odds of him existing at all were astronomical.

"Are you okay, Patrick?" Mom asked. "You haven't said anything for a while."

"Well, I'm not dead, if that's what you mean."

"Don't be cute."

She ran her fingers across his cheek in a way she hadn't done in a long time.

CHAPTER THIRTY-ONE

Amanda put her hands on David's shoulders, but he didn't react. He stared at his phone. "I got a few hours of sleep," Amanda lied. "I don't think I can go back to sleep. Why don't you go lie down?"

He reached up to put his hand on hers, but continued to stare at his phone.

"Honey, who are you expecting to call at this hour? The kids are safe in bed."

Amanda had a passing moment of déjà vu, but couldn't place the forgotten memory.

"You're not going to like it," David said. "You're going to say a conman took advantage of me. And you might be right. But I don't care. It's just money."

"What?" she asked.

"The estate lawyer I met in New York, he's a medium, I guess you'd say. He can speak to the dead. Rachel's message to me was delivered after she had already died. So I hired him to consult with her again, and get advice on how to stop the killing spell."

"You have got to be kidding me."

"Judge me all you want," David said. "It's something. What are you doing to stop the spell?"

"There's no reason to snap at me," Amanda said, taking her hands off his shoulders and sitting in the chair next to him. "How much did he charge?"

"Don't worry about it."

"David…"

"The way he described talking to the dead… it sounded right. I think that's something dark wizards can do." David pressed his clenched fists into the table. "We have a special relationship with darkness, and I think that means we have a special relationship with death. We're closer to it maybe. Or we can understand the language of death. I don't know. But I really do believe him."

"I don't think dark wizards can talk to the dead. None of us can."

"I can."

"What?"

"Crystal."

Amanda would always hate the sound of that name on his lips. She rubbed the side of her eye to calm a twitch.

"She helped me find Evangeline last year," David continued, not looking her in the eye. "At least she helped steer me in the right direction. It's… vague. Hard to explain."

The whole concept made Amanda want to vomit, for several reasons. "You're talking to your dead girlfriend?"

"She's not my girlfriend… and she's dead. She only shows up to help with our kids."

Amanda bit her lip so hard she thought she might taste blood.

"We don't have time to fight about something this ridiculous," David said, apparently feeling her anger without looking at her. "She's dead."

She didn't want to fight about it either. She didn't want to think about it. She hated him for saying her name aloud.

"For what it's worth," he said, finally looking at her. "If she was alive, I would have no interest in her. She changed. And I don't like the person she became. When I chose you, I made the right choice."

"Of course you did, you asshole. Don't say that like it was in question. Did you have doubts?"

"No, I…" David put his face in his hands.

"Go to sleep."

"I am not sleeping until we figure this out."

"We'll sleep in shifts."

"You need your sleep. You're still healing."

"I'm *fine*, David. You, on the other hand, look like shit. Go to sleep."

"Maybe I should," David said. "That's when the dead speak to me."

"Those are dreams, David. It's not real." Amanda grabbed a lock of her hair and pulled on it.

"I honestly do not understand how a living, breathing witch can be so closed minded. Just open your mind an inch." David posed his fingers to demonstrate an inch—as if a visual representation of measurement would help. "Your son is about to die a supernatural death. Can you at least consider supernatural solutions as well?"

"To be fair, we're not one hundred percent sure this killing spell is even real. It sounds so far-fetched."

"What is wrong with you?" he shouted, standing up.

"You'll wake the kids," she said.

"How can just stop believing in magic when you don't like it? You have this uncanny way of actually changing your belief system based on what's most convenient for you at the time. And you're not bullshitting it either. You genuinely believe different things based on the circumstances. It would be fascinating if it weren't so fucking annoying."

"Oh fuck you. Am I such a terrible person for not wanting to believe in some kind of mystical darkness hovering over my children, just waiting to swoop down and strike? Does that make me crazy? To have a little bit of hope this might be a false alarm? How dare you yell at me? You do the same shit all the time. You refused to believe I was going to die, and you kept telling me to have hope, and it annoyed the shit out of me."

"I'm sorry," David said.

"It's okay. Just go to fucking bed like I asked you to. You're tired and stressed and you're being a shithead."

"Can I trust you to watch them tomorrow? I have some things I need to do."

"How could you even ask me that? Of course you can trust me. I can keep an eye on them as well as you can. And what the Hell do you need to do?"

"I don't want to leave them, but I can't sit in this house waiting for them to die either. I need to act. I'm not going to let this happen without giving it the fight of my life."

David chugged his cold coffee, caring only about the caffeine and not the taste. The cold dregs sat heavy in his stomach, but he didn't care. He poured himself a bowl of cereal but couldn't bring himself to eat it, and left the soggy mess in the kitchen sink.

Amanda watched him with her arms crossed. He could understand her annoyance—that he would bail at a time like this and tell her nothing. But he didn't have time to worry about that. He needed to attack this at every angle. He had called Mr. Sherman. Now he had two more people to contact.

"You said I'm not doing anything to help," Amanda said. "But that's not true. I'm praying. I've been asking God to spare our children almost constantly since we found out. It might not be much, but it makes me feel better. We can't stop a killing spell, but God can."

David ignored her and shoved his wallet and cell phone in

his pocket.

"If you're going to wander around aimlessly hoping for answers, will you also buy more bread and coffee filters?" Amanda asked. "And will you bring me my handgun out of storage?"

"Sure," he said, not really hearing her. "Bread, coffee, gun."

"Coffee *filters*."

"Wait," David said, grabbing his keys. "I'm not bringing a gun into this house. Are you insane? Are you trying to kill our children?"

"I'm trying to protect them and I'd feel more comfortable if I had a weapon."

David glared at her, unwilling to waste time giving her the lecture she deserved. On the outside of the apartment, he squeezed the doorknob as if unwilling to let go. Should he go back and tell Patrick and Evangeline he loved them? The idea made his chest hurt. He couldn't say a final goodbye every time he left the house. He didn't have the strength.

David got behind the wheel of the Escalade and dialed a number on his cell phone.

"Holiday Inn Express Baton Rouge," said a friendly woman in a heavy Louisiana accent. "How can I make your stay wonderful?"

"Transfer me to room 205."

"Hold please."

"Hello?" Zander asked in a groggy voice.

"Don't hang up," David said. "It's a matter of life or death." The words sounded so over-dramatic and cliché, but unfortunately they were true.

"Mr. Vandergraff?" he asked, sounding much more awake. His voice no longer had the syrupiness of sleep and now had a crisp terror about it.

"Yes."

"How did you find me?" he asked in a choked whisper.

"This is… this is the hotel room phone. Are you here?"

David could imagine him getting up to check the locks and peer out the window.

"No, I'm in Houston. I'm not going to hurt you. I'm only asking that you listen. I need your help."

David didn't hear a click, so he continued.

"I made a mistake," David said. "Well, I made a *series* of significant mistakes I would like to apologize for. I'm sorry I hurt you. And I'm sorry I imprisoned you. And then banished you. And…" David felt like adding something about how he deserved it, and about how David knew his terrible secret. He knew he hadn't misjudged him at all. But he had to trust Rachel's message. He had no other option.

"Okay," Zander replied tonelessly. "So you really are a wizard, aren't you? That's what you meant by *banishing* me. It was some kind of curse that sent me away." Despite his evocative and direct question, his voice stayed flat.

"Yes. I'm a wizard. You're a wizard. And so was your aunt, and that's why I'm calling. Like I said, I made a lot of mistakes and one of them was ignoring your aunt's messages. She said you were supposed to save my baby girl. I should have listened. And now I'm asking you to come back to Houston."

"I thought you banished me."

"Well, my son did. You can still come back. You can fight against the spell. I can tell you're a powerful wizard. If you really want to come back, then you can. It might be difficult and uncomfortable, but you can." David cringed at his own words. It takes serious determination to fight against a fresh banishing spell, especially one created by a fall equinox wizard. He could fight against it, but David knew he had no motivation to do so.

"I'm not asking you to do this for me," David said. "I'm asking you to do this for my children. I have reason to believe my son and daughter are in serious danger. When I sent you away, I had no idea my daughter would need saving, so I didn't take the message seriously. I was wrong. And so I'm asking you to come back—not for me—but for my daughter. Please."

"What am I supposed to do though? How do I save her?"

"I don't know. I'm trying to find out more. Just come back and do what you were already doing. Stay close to her, but out of sight."

Zander didn't respond. David could hardly believe his own words either. He asked a child killer to stalk his daughter. *Pleaded* with him to do so.

"I won't approach you. I won't talk to you," David continued. "I promise. Keep your distance from her, and I'll ignore you completely. I won't hurt you. I only care about the safety of my daughter… I'll pay you if you want. Hell, I'll give you my entire half of the inheritance. At least what's left of it."

David meant every word, but he had a fleeting moment of grief for the future he envisioned. He thought about tearing down their dream home or finishing it to sell it to some other family.

"I don't care about that," Zander said. "I don't want the money. I *hate* the money," he added, his voice sounding heavy again, but now with tears.

"Okay, then do it for my daughter. Do it for your aunt. It's clearly what she wanted you to do. Her final legacy."

Zander hung up the phone.

"Dammit," David said. "Fine," he said to the empty car. "I'll figure something else out."

Zander's message had been only one of two. He had his own instructions. *Sacrifice.*

CHAPTER THIRTY-TWO

Samantha sat on the curb and stared at Patrick's car. The hotel was walking distance away from their apartment and she couldn't stand not knowing what was going on. When it came to the Vandergraffs, she didn't know if she felt love or hate, if she wanted them to live or die, but she knew she cared what happened.

She thanked God every night for a safe, clean bed, but that didn't stop her from hating that tiny room. Once she had gotten over the hunger and exhaustion, she had more space to feel grief. She could only think of Imogene and every time she thought about having to go on living her life, she couldn't breathe. The hotel room represented a miniature version of her entire future. Sleeping. Eating. Showering. Watching television. And nothing else. Surviving day to day all alone.

So, instead she stalked the Vandergraffs. She hated them too much to talk to them, so she hung out next to Patrick's car. That way she could keep track of him. Death could find him in his bedroom, but it seemed like the safest option. David had taken their Escalade, but no one else had left the apartment, even though it was Tuesday. Hit by killing spell seemed like a good excuse for a sick day though. Who would want to spend their last days learning chemistry or running around in futile circles around the track in gym class? She didn't miss school. The only thing she had liked about it was Emmy anyway.

A gust of wind caused tiny pink petals to shower down on her from a nearby crepe myrtle. Something changed with the wind. The birds and frogs that had been silent in the urban concrete-scape now sang—or screamed. The trees sticking up from between cars swayed and shuddered in unusual patterns as if moved by a force other than wind. It felt as if the whole parking lot came alive.

Samantha stood up and walked between the cars, balancing on the yellow stripes in the parking lot. And that's when she saw him, leaning against a very fancy car, looking up at the apartments. She followed his gaze to see he looked toward the Vandergraff's apartment.

"Hi," Samantha said.

He startled and turned toward her. He was tall with shiny black hair and kind eyes. And although equinox wizards were hard to read, there was no question about him. Despite the dark clothes and overall gloominess, he screamed springtime.

"What are you doing?" Samantha asked, a strange and nosy question to ask a stranger.

"Uh." The man looked at the asphalt as if he didn't know the answer. His head appeared weighted as if he couldn't hold it up for long.

"Are you watching the Vandergraff's apartment?" Samantha asked.

"Uh…" he said again. "No."

"Are you sure?"

Samantha looked back at their balcony, directly in his line of sight.

"Are *you* watching their apartment?" he asked.

"Me?" Samantha asked, and felt dumb. Who else would he

be talking to? "Well, yeah. I am. But I know them," as if that explained everything. "Who are you?"

"I'm just some guy," he said.

"That's a really weird way to answer that question," Samantha said. "Usually people give a name. For example, I'm Samantha."

"I'm Zander."

"Do we know each other?"

"I don't think so."

"You sure? Your name sounds really familiar. Do you know anyone from the Carthage family?"

"I don't think so," he said again. "I'm not from around here."

Samantha thought she did recognize a hint of an accent that was different but familiar at the same time.

"Okay," Samantha said. She looked back toward the Vandergraff's apartment. He had barely taken his eyes off of it long enough to look at her, and although she had stalked them too, she felt compelled to see whatever he found so fascinating about the empty landing.

"So… you know them then?" he asked. "The Vandergraffs."

"Yes."

"Please don't tell them about me."

"I don't have much to tell at this point. You're not exactly an over-sharer."

He nodded, and actually looked at her now, holding up his head that weighed a thousand pounds.

"You know…" Samantha said. "If you're stalking them, you can tell me. Because I'm stalking them too."

"Are you a witch?" he asked.

Samantha looked around to make sure they were alone. Wizards don't ask each other that question. For reasons of discretion, but also because they didn't need to. Wizards had no trouble sensing each other.

"Yes," she said. "Of course."

He widened his eyes in disbelief, which didn't make sense because he had asked the question.

"Why are you watching them? Are you here for the same reason I am?" he asked.

"Hard to say, you forgot to tell me your reason."

"I'm not sure what my reason is."

Samantha gasped, calling Zander's attention back. Her heart thrummed against her rib cage. She knew why his name sounded familiar, and why his accent seemed familiar. Maybe a long shot, but how many spring wizards named Zander from Louisiana could there be?

"Do you know Imogene Grey?" She had asked that question so many times in the past weeks, with no recognition, she didn't expect the blast of recognition in Zander's eyes. He walked closer to her, so he stood only about a foot away. Yes, definitely springtime. One hundred percent. Compared to him, she felt like the dead of winter.

"What did you say?" he asked. Despite the fact he advanced on her, he didn't seem frightening. He might look frightening if she didn't know better, but he had an overpowering goodness radiating from him, much as Imogene had.

"I asked if you knew Imogene Grey."

"Why would you ask me that? Who are you?"

"I thought maybe you were the Zander she talked about. Her best friend that was taken away. Are you?"

He nodded, his mouth agape.

"Oh my God," Samantha said. She ran at him and hugged him as if they were old friends and not complete strangers. He didn't seem to feel so warm to her, and barely touched her back when she wrapped her arms around him. When she looked back at him, she blinked away tears. It felt as if a piece of Imogene had survived. Someone else remembering her made her seem more alive. He filled in all sorts of gaps. He had known Imogene for longer, and had different memories, new to Samantha. It would be like talking to her again and learning new things about her.

"I don't understand," he said. "Who are you?"

"I'm sorry… I met her after you. We were together in Metarrie. We were close."

"Did she really die?" His question dripped with all that weight that pressed his head down.

Samantha nodded, swallowing back tears. She couldn't bring herself to say the word.

He sighed, but didn't seem surprised by her affirmation.

"It's so crazy you're here," Samantha said. "That can't be a coincidence. Magic brought you here."

"I've been having a difficult… and weird… few months," he said.

"Okay. You want to tell me about it?"

"Um…" He reached into his jeans pocket and pulled out a piece of paper. It looked like a cocktail napkin he had carried around for several years. "I'm here because of this." He handed her the note like he thought it might explode if he moved too fast.

"Save his baby girl," Samantha said, reading the handwritten note. "What does that mean?"

Zander shook his head, and he took the note out of Samantha's hand and folded it back into his pocket.

"Does that mean Evangeline?" Samantha asked, connecting dots. "Are here to save her?"

Zander didn't reply. He frowned so deeply, Samantha had trouble imagining what he might look like if he smiled. "I don't know," he said finally.

"That's it. You're the answer. Are you like Imogene? Can you reverse death?" She gasped after she said it, appalled at her own words. That question should not be asked aloud, especially outside in broad daylight.

She expected him to slap her for uttering such blasphemy aloud, but he pinched his lips together and shook his head.

He told her more than he had probably intended to by not freaking out at the suggestion. He had considered it a normal question, like whether or not he could whistle or roll his tongue.

"We can test it," she said. She could hardly believe it herself when she walked around the fancy silver car and climbed in the passenger seat. But she felt as if she already knew him.

"Excuse me," Zander said, bending down to look at her through the window. "What are you doing?"

"I want to take you to the lilies," she said.

"What?"

"I'm sorry, I know that wasn't an explanation."

"I need to stay here."

"But you don't even know why. I know why. I know lots of things. About magic. About everything. And I'll tell you."

Samantha knew she had said the right thing. He opened the door and climbed in the driver's seat.

CHAPTER THIRTY-THREE

David had changed his mind and stopped off at the storage unit to get Amanda's gun. He thought it might come in handy for the next conversation he planned to have. He eyed the locked box sitting in the passenger seat.

"In five hundred feet, take a U-turn," said the mechanical female voice on the GPS. David turned it off. The GPS had asked him to make several wrong turns and had also politely suggested he turn the wrong way on a one-way road. Amanda had mentioned something about a repulsion spell around the Prescott's house, and it seemed to impact his electronics. The check engine light popped on.

"You're fine," he spat at the car, pounding the dashboard with his fist. "Pull it together."

David wiped sweat off his forehead with his hand and adjusted the vents of the air conditioner. He had hoped to use magic to track her down. He could use her obnoxious brightness to her advantage. However, the repulsion spell seemed to work by blinding him, flooding his magical senses with ambient heat from all angles. And the heat made him groggy. He wanted to head back home and climb under the covers in a dark room.

Even pulling over and closing his eyes sounded appealing. But he knew if he fought against his instincts, he could push through the repulsion.

David pulled in front of the Prescott's house as he had a year ago, but this time, the driveway was empty and the windows were dark. Perhaps John and Thea were at work. But he had guessed they wouldn't return to work only days after the death of their daughter.

He didn't want to confront John… or he did, but not now. However, he could use him to his advantage. Hold a gun to his head until Thea gave him the answers he wanted. And if she didn't… well, he might pull the trigger.

David parked by the curb and walked out onto their lush green lawn. Their house reminded him of an over-sized gingerbread house, draped with vines. Thorned rose bushes flanked the front of the house and as he got closer, he had the only slightly irrational thought they might reach out their thorny tendrils and strangle him, like deceptively beautiful sentries. When he made it to the front door, the roses didn't grab him, but the overpowering sweet smell made him want to retch. It felt as if someone shoved rose petals down his throat and he choked on them. They had a large bronze sun hanging on their front door like a wreath, an oversized mat with "Welcome" in large letters, and a garden gnome dressed in Texas A&M gear. The gnome stared at him from the bushes threateningly.

The ambient heat increased around the house. The temperate spring day should have felt glorious, but he thought his T-shirt might melt into his skin. The heat made it difficult for him to sense any wizards in the house.

He felt as if he was being watched, and he eyed the Aggie gnome, who remained made of porcelain and not moving.

He felt a sting on the back of his neck and grabbed the spot. The back of his skull and his shoulders filled with poison, contracting and throbbing.

Clutching his neck he turned to see a ghostly girl standing on the red-brick path. She made his hair stand on end. Something felt so *wrong* about her. He wondered if he saw Julie's ghost—a demon version of the once vibrant and beautiful girl. He made the mistake of looking at her dark eyes, and the "bite" hit him in the face now, as if she shot invisible poison darts at him from her eyes. His entire face burned and he worried it had erupted in blisters.

Then he froze in place, the pale girl staring at him without blinking. Darkness had encroached on the edges of his vision. He had tunnel vision now, only able to see the little girl's black eyes. Numbness replaced the pain in his neck and face. He became paralyzed, but he didn't fall, he just lost control of his own faculties. He watched his hand move without his command, reaching around his back. His unruly hand clasped the gun he had stuck in his belt and pulled it out. He turned off the safety and decisively brought the gun to his own temple.

"Leona."

David couldn't move his head, but he heard Thea's voice and saw the demon girl look away from him. As she looked away, he felt a tingling sensation in his fingers and he dropped the gun with a clatter. He regained his faculties, his whole body burning as his nerves sparked to life. He kneeled down on the hard red brick and wiped his face with his hands, half-expecting to find nothing but a bloody mass of flesh where his nose used to be. He wiped blood from his nose, but his face and skin appeared intact.

He remembered the gun and reached toward where it had fallen, but he hadn't reacted quickly enough. Where the gun once lay, he saw Thea's muddy feet. She held the gun in one hand and held a garden spade in the other. Her hair looked less shiny and she had dirt all over, like she had worked in the garden for two days straight and hadn't stopped to shower or sleep.

"Go inside, Leona," she said, addressing the *thing* on the

path in front of him. "Now."

The girl padded away, through the gate into the backyard.

"You're welcome," Thea said. "I just saved your life." She examined David's gun. He wished she would put the safety back on. He had no intention of using the wretched thing or even taking it out. He didn't trust he could defend himself with magic. He had been right, although the gun hadn't helped either.

"What was that thing?" he asked.

She glared down at David. "My daughter."

"The missing one?"

"What do you want?" she asked.

David stood up, testing his balance. Now the girl had left, he had control again, but he felt as if he might vomit or pass out at any minute. An unnatural amount of sweat poured down his forehead, stinging his already burning eyes.

"I'm sorry about your daughter," he said, hoping he sounded as sincere as he felt. He used his shirt to wipe the sweat off his face, forgetting about the blood and ruining his white shirt.

"I've heard those words a lot in the past few days," Thea said. "But you're the first to come to call with a gun instead of a casserole."

"I'm not here to hurt you. The gun is for my own protection. I know how easy it is for you people to kill winter wizards. Like stepping on an ant."

She smirked. "I know it won't matter, but I am sorry your brother died. It was a horrible accident."

"No. You don't get to push it aside like that. He murdered him. Your husband is a murderer. And the only way to make it right would be to shoot your husband right between the eyes."

"Is that why you came?" she asked, caressing the gun in both her hands. "He's not here. He doesn't live here anymore."

"Why not?"

"That's really none of your business."

David wiped his face again. At least the bleeding had stopped.

"Or perhaps you came to finally kill me," Thea said. "That would be kind of you. A much better gift than a casserole in any case. A mercy killing."

"I didn't come to kill anyone. I came to ask for help."

"Help?"

"We have something in common, Thea," he said, using some of his rehearsed talking points, although his words sounded less powerful while dripping in sweat. "Something important."

She narrowed her eyes.

"We love our children," David continued. "We would do anything for them. You proved that. There was a prophecy. You believed a Vandergraff was going to kill a Prescott. And to save your children and your husband, you were ready to die. You begged me to kill you. And it worked. A Vandergraff didn't kill a Prescott. In fact, a Prescott killed a Vandergraff. I just want to know how you did that? How did you change the prophecy?"

She scoffed. "What makes you think it worked? You didn't kill me, you ass. So it didn't work. It's still going to happen. Unless you've changed your mind and want to end it all right now… but what the fuck does it matter? I've done *everything* to try to protect my family, and my sweet baby girl…" She inhaled and made a noise between a sob and a hiccup. "My baby girl dies in the most random, Mundane way I can imagine. Do you know what that means? It means nothing we do matters. Wizards are a great cosmic mistake God is hell-bent on fixing."

She stood in front of him with her eyes closed, tears leaking out the corners. He could have snatched the gun then, but he chose not to. While he stared her, he realized something. Thea thought Julie's death was random, which meant his children were safe from vengeance. It also meant she was wrong… or she had been right the first time. A Vandergraff had killed a

Prescott. Evangeline killed Julie. A small part of him wanted to tell her the truth. He wanted her to know Julie hadn't died a random death. She died because she tried to save someone, a stranger she had never met—the spring equinox witch. But he knew he couldn't.

"Thea." He said her name to call her attention back. "Thea."

"What?"

"You believed you could prevent the death of someone you loved… by dying yourself. How does that work?"

She looked up at him now, seeming to see him for the first time through her swollen eyes." Whose death are you trying to prevent? Is it one of your children?"

David knew he couldn't say much without giving away the truth behind Julie's death too. "Let's just say, I'm in a similar situation."

"Is it Emmy?"

"Uh… no, actually. Why? Do you have reason to believe something is going to happen to Emmy?"

"No, nothing like that…. Never mind."

"Listen, I don't need you to hold my hand and walk me though it or anything, I just need the basics. If I'm going to die, I need to make sure it counts. I don't want to die and have it not matter. I need to get this right, and…" he laughed a strained, airy laugh pointing at the gun in Thea's hand. "I only have one shot."

Thea glanced at the gun in her hand. "I thought you said it was for your own protection. You mean to use it on yourself?"

"Not here, not now. I have affairs I need to get in order. But if I did… if I killed myself, would it make a difference? How do I make sure I'm dying so another can live?"

"What does the prophecy say?"

"There is no prophecy."

"Then how do you know someone you love is going to die?"

David hesitated, and then risked giving her a bit of the truth.

He needed to get this right.

"A killing spell has been cast, but is not yet completed."

Thea cringed, which made David's stomach knot.

"I don't know about killing spells."

David interrupted her before she could go on to say something self-righteous and obnoxious about how her kind doesn't mess with dark magic and he should be the expert. "I'm not asking you how to cast one. I'm asking you how to stop one."

"You can't."

"I don't believe you."

"Once the energy is out in the world, it has to go somewhere."

"Right… but how do you get it to go somewhere else?"

"You want to take the bullet," she said.

"Yes."

"Well, there is always sacrifice."

David nodded, wanting to shake her. "Yes, that's what I'm trying to do."

"No, I mean the magic."

"What do you mean?"

"I don't understand how you know so little about magic."

"It's a long story. Just explain it to me."

"Sacrifice is more than a word. It's a magical concept. There are some acts that have so much power they have inherent magic."

"Is it a spell?"

"Not exactly. A wizard's sacrifice releases magic naturally. Like how a talisman provides protection. Wizards have greater power to influence their world than Mundanes do, and even our feelings… love, hate, hope, fear. They're infused with magic whether we want them to be or not. That's how a talisman can protect someone simply by loving them. A sacrifice works the same way. You can create a powerful protection by sacrificing yourself for someone you love."

"But how do I do it? How do I take the bullet if I don't know how they'll die?"

Thea shrugged and looked back toward her house as if she had heard a noise, and then turned back to David.

"You have to wait for an opportunity, I suppose. You're a wizard. Lead yourself to the place you need to be."

"I…" David shook his head.

"I hope it works for you, David. I do. And once upon a time, I would have assumed it would work. Love conquers all, and all that. But now, I don't know. I don't think any of it matters. Good. Evil. Love. Hate. Maybe it means something to the Mundanes, but not to us. *All* wizards are evil. Perversions of nature. We'll all pay for it and it doesn't matter what we do."

David thought of what Amanda had once said about "why do bad things happen to good people?" She had said it was a stupid question. And once she said it, he agreed with her. He couldn't judge a woman who had lost her daughter, but he wondered if dark wizards were more resilient than their light counterparts. When something tragic happens to Thea, she loses faith in all things. Everything must be good all the time, or everything was bad. David didn't think like that.

David didn't assume things would always be bad, quite the opposite. He believed in good. But he also always assumed things would be hard, perhaps horrifying. He didn't wonder why, he just knew that's how life was. And that's what made the "good" so much more beautiful. It didn't come easy.

"Maybe," David said finally. "But I don't care. Just like you, I'm not going to let my children die without doing everything in my power to stop it, including trying the impossible and preposterous. Maybe it will work, maybe it won't. I still have to try."

He backed away from her, wary of turning his back to her, and the little girl who probably hid out of view.

"Thank you, Thea. That was helpful," he said, continuing to back away. "I'm sorry I bothered you."

"Wait. Come inside. I'll teach you some protective spells."

CHAPTER THIRTY-FOUR

Patrick paced through the living room and kitchen, unable to stay still for more than a moment. Amanda thought he inched closer and closer to the front door with enough weaving and back stepping to try and throw her off. He should know better than to think he can sneak out of the apartment right in front of her face, but if wanted to leave, she couldn't stop him. And that terrified her.

"Can you please stop circling around me?" Amanda asked for the forth or fifth time. "Sit down. Or at least pace in your room. You're driving me crazy."

Patrick ignored her. He swiped too close to the television. The television—one of the many things in the house that could kill him. One hard knock on the entertainment center and the massive screen would crush him.

Amanda walked past him and knocked on the bathroom door. Evangeline had hid out in there for the last half hour.

"Eve, would you please come out? It makes me uncomfortable not being able to see you." After she didn't reply, Amanda switched tactics. "If you don't come out right now, I'm going to take Anabel Lee and your books. Every single last one."

"You're going to kill the lizard?" Emmy asked from over the laptop.

"Of course not," Amanda said. She spoke back to the closed door. "I'm not going to kill the lizard."

"Are you going to burn her books and make her watch?" Emmy asked.

"Emmy, just shut your mouth. Or better yet, help me. Why don't you come talk to her? Any of you. She hates me the most."

"No, I'm not speaking to her," Emmy said. "This is mostly her fault."

"Xavier?" Amanda prompted.

He shrugged.

"Okay, according to the internet, here are the most common ways to die in your home," Emmy announced, looking at the screen. "Falls. Poison. Burns. Choking. Drowning."

"That's not helpful," Amanda said.

Amanda couldn't help having the terrifying visualization of Evangeline drowned in the bathtub, already dead a few feet away. She knocked on the door again.

"Could you please at least say something so I know you're not dead?" she asked. "I'm not kidding. And if you don't, I will find a way to break down this door. Say something, right now," she shouted. "Please, honey, I'm just worried about you." The bad cop good cop routine didn't work well with only one cop. She sounded insane. "Where is your father?" she muttered to herself.

"Eve, could you please just—"

Amanda heard Evangeline give the door an aggressive kick as proof of life.

"Thank you," she said.

"I could have told you she was alive," Patrick said. "Can't you feel her magic in there? That would be gone if she was dead. That's what it was like with Julie."

"Did you know you can get struck by lightning inside your

house?" Emmy asked, her eyes on the laptop screen. "During a storm you're not supposed to use hair dryers or take a shower."

"I have to get out of this apartment," Patrick said.

"Don't you dare," Amanda said.

"I cannot stay in here," he said. "I hate this apartment. I hate the color of the floor. I hate the way it smells. The whole place smells funny."

"I think that smell is coming from you," Emmy said.

"I'm serious. It smells like old dryer lint. But not in a good way."

"You know, maybe we *should* vacuum out the lint traps," Amanda said. "Those can catch fire."

"I have to leave," Patrick said.

"Please don't," Amanda said.

"What if I stand on the landing out there?

Emmy gasped as if he had suggested base-jumping.

"Go on, Emmy," Patrick said. "Tell me all the ways I can die standing on a landing. I could fall down the stairs. Drive-by shooting. Killer bees. Volcano erupting in the middle of Houston."

Patrick opened the front door and took a large dramatic step outside and then slammed the door again, glaring back in at them as he did so.

Amanda took a large, shaky breath. She could see his silhouette through the blinds. He had kept his promise to stay close.

"Emmy, maybe you should leave," Amanda suggested.

"I didn't do anything," she said, throwing up her hands in protest.

"I don't care. You're just one more person in this apartment. You can take my car."

"Really?"

Emmy didn't move, she stared at the keyboard.

"Did you hear me, Emmy? I said you can take my car. In

fact, I'll give you my keys and my credit card. You can go shopping."

Emmy looked at her, her face surprisingly morose for someone who had won the teenage lottery. "But what if they die while I'm gone?" she asked.

The familiar scent of her mother's garden filled Caroline's mouth with bile. The flimsy repulsion spell around the house had done little to keep her away. The offensive magic had been about as bothersome as a lone mosquito buzzing around her ears. Summer wizards were terrible at negative magic—repulsions, banishments, and the like.

She didn't stay away because of the repulsion, she stayed away because she had no reason to come back to this wretched house. Not until now.

Her mother had gone into the house with the winter wizard and Luke was at school. She knew the winter wizard would distract her mother—vigilantly watching out for evil, but looking in the wrong place.

She let herself in the back door. The inside of the house gave her a stronger lurch of nausea. Even days after Julie's death, everything looked so perfect. Clean, uncluttered, and decorated like a model home—nice to look at, but useless. However, she could use the artificially fresh smell of lemon floor cleaner to her advantage. She summoned protective energy around herself, visualizing impenetrable wings sprouting from her back and then growing to form a sphere around her body. The cocoon would mask her own energy… and protect her from dangerous intrusions. She took a deep breath of empty air, the smell of lemon gone, and she knew her spell had worked.

Despite the cloaking, she tiptoed up the stairs, wincing at the sound of each familiar creak and groan of the wood. She reminded herself it didn't matter if they caught her. Neither her mother nor the winter wizard could do anything to hurt her. She had summer and winter magic brewing inside her that originated from the solstices, far stronger than anything those flat, one-sided wizards could muster.

She found Leona in Julie's room, playing with the old dollhouse that had gathered dust. Caroline smiled to herself as she spotted what she needed sitting on the dresser, and she pocketed it before speaking.

"Don't you think you're a little old to be playing with dolls?"

Leona startled, dropping one of the tiny figures. Caroline gave her shield another inspection. The air felt empty.

She had experienced too many attacks to underestimate her youngest sister. Only Leona could bring Caroline to her knees. She had relished the day they sent Leona away. She looked at the fragile, white skin of her neck and imagined slitting her throat open. She would feel better knowing Leona didn't exist anymore.

But things had changed. Caroline had the magic of three events, and she could muster a shield that could withstand even a siren's magic. Her theory proved true. Leona stared her down, her black eyes turning darker. Caroline knew an impressive onslaught of pain rocketed in her direction. Even startling Leona could have resulted in an unintentional attack. And she could tell she hit her with her nastiest, and quite intentional, defenses.

Caroline smiled at Leona. "Relax. Your magic isn't going to work on me. But that's good, right? Finally someone you can talk to without accidentally killing or maiming them. I mean, that's what you always wanted, right? A friend?"

Leona didn't answer. She picked up the doll she had dropped and placed it back in a tiny armchair.

"You know, it's much more fun to play with the real people," Caroline said. "But you know that. No one is better at that than you. Not even me."

"What are you doing here?" Leona asked, looking at the dolls. "Mom said you couldn't come in the house."

"What can I say? I guess it was just the lure of the siren," Caroline said, chuckling at her own play on words. "I need you to come with me now."

She shook her head. "I wouldn't try that if I were you," Leona said, her eyes burning with darkness again.

"Oh really? Take your best shot. Or is that not what you've been doing already? I mean, don't go easy on me. Give me the good stuff."

Leona turned away from the dollhouse and sat in Julie's pink sofa chair. She crossed her arms as if daring her to try and take her. "You made a good shield," Leona said. "But you can't keep it up forever. If you try to hurt me, you'll regret it."

"I don't want to hurt you, baby girl. I want us to be friends." Caroline smiled, hoping she looked sincere. She had bested Leona and it felt better than any drug. "How many days before they send you away again?" Caroline asked. "Probably it will be soon, right? They let you come up to say goodbye to Julie, but then it's back to that "school," she said with air quotes.

Leona stared at Caroline's feet, perhaps trying to attack at another angle—melt off her toenails. But Caroline didn't feel so much as a tickle.

Caroline pulled the trinket out of her pocket, the one she had taken from the vanity. A delicate crystal bird hanging from a string. The wings caught the sunlight and rainbows danced on the wall behind her.

Leona's eyes went wide. She reached for the little bird—her talisman.

Caroline held it out of her reach. "I don't understand why you chose such a fragile object as your talisman." She let the bird sway back and forth. "Just one little mistake and it would break. Seems a little foolish to me."

Tears spilled out of the corner of Leona's eyes. "Give her

back," she said.

Caroline smiled again, pleased with the reaction. Object talismans could hold a shadow of a person's magic, but other than that, they served a symbolic purpose. If Caroline dropped the bird and crushed it under her foot, it might cause Leona some magical pain. A jolt of grief perhaps. But no real damage. But she remembered how attached Leona had been to her bird, carrying it in a little pouch around her neck. And when she thought no one was looking, she would speak to it, as if she believed it was real.

"Give it back," she said again, crying like a girl much younger than thirteen. Perhaps frozen in time away from the world, she hadn't gotten the chance to grow up.

"If you come with me and help me, I won't hurt your friend."

Leona nodded. This would be easier than Caroline had expected. But her precious parents had done most of the work for her. Give a lonely, isolated child a chance to belong, and she would do anything for her.

"Come now, out the back door, while Mom is still talking to that man."

Samantha stepped out of Zander's car, marveling at the luxurious interior. How did this man have so much money? Didn't he grow up in foster care too?

A light rain fell, and she worried that might scare him off, but he didn't to mind it. The gentle curtain of rain dusted them with water droplets in their hair and eyelashes. Zander followed Samantha toward the patch at the back at the property where she had planted the lilies. She had marked the spot with a circle of white rocks. The ground inside remained as empty as ever. No green tips peeked out of the ground. The spot looked especially desolate. Even weeds had refused the spot where she had planted the bulbs and the soil looked pale and dry, even as the rain fell.

"There," she said. "That's where I planted the bulbs that were hit by the killing spell."

"I don't understand," Zander said. "You want me to make your flowers grow? I thought I was supposed to save the girl."

"These lilies were killed by the same spell that hit Julie, Patrick, and Evangeline. I tried to use my own spring magic to make them grow again, but I can't. Maybe you can."

"Why could I do something you cannot?"

"Because you're better than me."

"You don't even know me."

"Just try."

Zander kneeled next to the spot, his expensive jeans sinking into the mud. He didn't seem to notice. He placed his hand over the bare patch and listened to the ground. He reminded Samantha of a doctor listening for heartbeat with a stethoscope. He took his hand away and shook his head.

"The bulbs are dead."

"I know…"

"No, they're really dead. I've only done this once before, so I'm not an expert. But I know I need something to work with. If a bit of life is hanging on, I can find it and make it stronger, like fanning a flame. I don't know what that little light is. It does seem to hang around for a while even after the heart stops, but it doesn't stay forever."

Samantha wiped away the water droplets that had collected on her eyelashes. The rain grew heavier now, and water ran down her face.

"But your friends aren't lily bulbs," Zander said. "And they're not already dead. You said you were a witch. You must be able to see it—the life in things. There is life in plants and insects and to a smaller extent, even non-living organic matter—like rocks and water and air. But it's nothing like the fireball of life inside a human being."

"So what are you saying?"

He wiped water off his own face too. "I'm just saying you shouldn't lose hope because the lilies are dead. I don't think it means what you think it means." Zander raked his hands through the grass and small purple flowers bloomed in the wake of his fingers.

Holy crap.

Zander cocked his head to one side, as if he had heard something Samantha hadn't. He stood up, not stopping to knock the mud off his jeans or his hands. He looked toward the road and Samantha followed his gaze wondering what she had missed.

"Zander?"

He didn't respond or even look at her, but walked toward the road. A painful ball of familiar fear swelled in Samantha's chest. This reminded her way too much of her last moments with Imogene.

"Stay away from the road," Samantha pleaded.

Samantha grabbed his arm and dug her nails into his skin. She pulled her entire body weight backward to try and stop him. He had about eighty pounds on her, but he should have at least reacted. He continued to walk toward the road like a zombie.

She jumped on his back and wrapped her arms around his neck. Maybe she could strangle him until he passed out. At least then he wouldn't make it to the road. At least, her arm wrapped around his neck caused him to notice her presence. He pulled her arm away as easily as someone removing a scarf.

"Everything will be okay now," he said. He turned to Samantha with a lazy smile. "Look."

He pointed toward the road. Samantha screamed.

Imogene stood on the edge of the road, looking as she had when she saw her last, as if she had finished running across that highway and now waited on the other side. She gave them a tight-lipped mischievous smile, which looked wrong. Imogene always smiled all the way—with her teeth showing and eyes sparkling. Samantha's skin felt too tight and her body felt too dry. The oxygen in the air dried up and she took a wheezing breath.

She grabbed Zander's arm again. "That's not Imogene," she said, her voice a choked whisper. "That's not right…"

He ignored her and continued to move toward the road. The unknown demon that looked like Imogene shook her long black curls, and Samantha noticed her hair stayed dry—untouched by the soaking rain and humidity.

"Zander, please. I wish she was real too. But she's not."

"Why don't you believe what's right in front of your face?" he asked.

Samantha shrieked again, when she turned to see Imogene was *right in front of her face.* Somehow she had managed to advance on them in the millisecond Samantha had turned her gaze to Zander. Samantha dug her nails into his bicep and noticed she had drawn blood, but he didn't flinch.

Now closer, she noticed more things wrong with Imogene's hair than the lack of rain. It turned white, and not strand by strand like when you grow old. The tips of her hair had become white and straight and the white death crawled all the way to her scalp. Then her skin grew pale too, turning nearly translucent. Only her eyes didn't lighten, they turned black. And then a different girl stood in front of them, one Samantha hadn't seen before. Her hair had now turned wet from the rain and stuck to her neck and shoulders. Amanda had never seen hair that light. She looked alarming. And her black eyes seemed over-large and throbbing. Samantha could see the veins in her neck and chest behind her translucent skin.

The girl reached her hand to Zander. Samantha didn't know if he didn't see the transformation or if he didn't care. He took her hand without hesitation.

"No," Samantha said, continuing to pull on him. "That's not right," she said again.

The girl took her eyes off Zander for a moment to look at Samantha. Her black eyes bled out of the sockets. The frogs in the nearby pond screamed and cicadas joined the terrified chorus. The blackness of her eyes covered her whole face and then bled out into the air, reaching toward Samantha with demon fingers. Samantha tried to move, but she couldn't. Her heart beat out of control and her blood rushed too quickly. Somehow she could feel every cell in her body. She could sense all her organs, and they all seemed to boil, and then everything went black.

CHAPTER THIRTY-FIVE

Amanda advanced on David as soon as he came through the door. She wanted to slap him and hug him simultaneously.

"Where the Hell have you been?"

"Did Zander come here?" he asked under his breath.

David tugged on his wet shirt and Amanda noticed a smudge of blood. She grabbed him by the hem of the shirt, examining the stain. "What happened to you?"

"Nosebleed. It's no big deal."

"Are you sure?"

"Yes, I'm sure. Now what about Zander?"

"Of course he didn't come here. Are you expecting him? Please tell me you didn't invite him to our house."

"God no. I just told him to come back to Houston, and my PI just called me and told me he did. His credit card showed him at a Sonic in Beaumont. He's on his way here like I asked."

"You've been gone all day. I hope you have more to show for it than getting Zander Colter to eat at a Sonic in Beaumont."

"We can't talk about it right now," he said, looking over at Patrick and Emmy in the kitchen.

"Did Mr. Sherman call you back?" she asked.

"No."

"But you seem… better. Less worried," Amanda said. "You have some kind of plan. Am I right?"

"Later."

Amanda's entire body seized as she heard the whoosh of a flame and Patrick cry out. She ran to her son and pulled him away from the stove.

"I'm okay. I'm okay," she said. Despite his reassurances, Amanda could feel the fear radiating off his skin. His voice shook.

She pulled him into an aggressive hug.

"Mom, I'm fine," he said, squeezing her back. "You're kind of squishing my organs though."

"What happened?" David shouted. "What the Hell happened?"

"I turned on the burner and it just shot out at me. I think I lost a few arm hairs, but that's it."

"Why were you using the stove?" Amanda asked. "Are you trying to get yourself killed?"

"It's just the stove," Patrick said. "I was going to get the water boiling for the pasta. I'm trying to help."

"That's not helpful, Patrick. Scaring the crap out of me is not helpful. Go to your room… and crawl under the covers," she said, her voice breaking.

"Mom, please don't start crying."

"Just get out of the kitchen."

"Okay," he said and moved to stand alone in the middle of the living room.

"I can't," Amanda said, pointing at the pot on the stove. The thought of making dinner made her want to cry all the more. "I can't do it."

"I'll order pizza," David said.

"I can't get Evangeline out of the bathroom," Amanda said.

"I can't get Patrick to stay inside the apartment and away from the stove. I just can't handle this."

"I know."

"This is all so unfair."

"If it helps, I think I can get Evangeline out of the bathroom and keep Patrick in the apartment."

"How?"

"Magic. Repulsion for Evangeline. Confinement for Patrick. They're stronger than me, so if they know it's happening, they can fight against it. But if I'm careful, subtle, then they won't realize they're being manipulated."

"Good. Do it."

A few minutes later, Evangeline walked out of the bathroom holding her lizard and walked over to the rest of them at the kitchen table. David shot Amanda a look she deciphered to mean, *be cool*.

"Thank you for joining us," David said.

Evangeline didn't say anything and sat in the chair next to him.

"Pizza is coming," he said. "Are you hungry?"

Evangeline put Anabel Lee on the table and looked at Amanda as if daring her to tell her to take the lizard off the table, as she had so many times before. Amanda said nothing.

"Something's wrong," Patrick said.

David thought he might have caught him. "What do you mean?"

"I sent him away. Why is he back? He shouldn't be back."

"I think he went crazy," Emmy said squinting at her brother.

"Patrick, can I speak with you in your bedroom real quick?" David asked.

Patrick got up too fast, and his chair teetered, causing David's heart to skip. He only had to trip and hit his head on the edge of the counter... that might do it.

He followed him into his room and closed the door.

"Are you talking about Zander?" David asked.

"Of course I am." Patrick paced around the room in increasingly small circles, and David thought Emmy might have been right about Patrick going crazy. "He shouldn't be here. I sent him away."

"You can tell he's back in Houston? Is he close? Is he outside?"

Patrick shook his head like a horse trying to shake away a fly. "I don't know. I don't have his exact coordinates. It doesn't work like that. But yeah, in Houston at least."

"I asked him to come back."

"What?"

"It's complicated… but he got a message from his Aunt Rachel." David left out the part about her being dead when she shared the message. "It said, 'save his baby girl.' And I thought maybe it meant Evangeline. If not, well, it's the best idea I have. I just asked him to come back to Houston. Be close by if… you know, fate calls him or whatever."

"You're so stupid."

"Excuse me?"

"You've killed us all, you know. Not just me and Evangeline. Everybody. We're all fucked now. And of course it happens now, when there is nothing I can do about it. I can't even go into the fucking kitchen without almost dying, I can't exactly stop her. I probably wouldn't even make it there, and if I did, I'd die right away."

"Patrick." David grabbed his arm to get him to stop circling and look at him. "Just tell me what you're trying to say."

"It's not your fault," Patrick said. "Not really. You're just a pawn."

"Okay…"

"He's the spring."

"Who's the spring?"

"How many steps back do you need me to take before you understand what I'm telling you? Do you need me to describe the seasons? Explain what magic is?"

David bit his lip and squeezed Patrick's arm again. David felt as if Patrick needed anchoring or a current would pull him out to sea. "I'm sorry," he said. "I know you see the world differently. I'm sorry I can't see it too."

Patrick looked up at him. "I didn't mean… I'm sorry," he said. "I know I'm being an asshole. I'm just stressed."

"Stressed is probably an understatement."

"Yeah."

"You're saying Zander is the spring?"

He nodded. "The spring equinox. Just like Imogene was. It's like he appeared out of nowhere as soon as Imogene died. He just shows up in the stupid storage shed."

David thought about mentioning that Zander didn't materialize in the storage shed, a complicated string of events led him there, but he knew Patrick wouldn't care.

"So I sent him away. Trying to save him. And trying to save us. Trying to keep Caroline from taking his magic too, and having magic from all four events, because that would make her invincible. Immortal maybe. Not a wizards like you, not even a wizard like me. She'd have power humans should not have. Power that wouldn't go unnoticed by the Mundanes. It could wreck the whole balance of the world. But it doesn't matter now. I'm going to die. I can't beat her. And I should have known as soon as Zander showed up. An innocent girl died, and it didn't even matter. She just called a different spring equinox wizard. And pop. He shows up in Houston. I send him away, and he just comes right back. He's probably knocking on Caroline's door right now because his car broke down a block away."

"I had no idea he was the spring equinox. How is that possible? I thought for sure he was a winter wizard, a dark wizard. He's evil. He killed a child."

"I don't know how you couldn't see it. It's pretty obvious what he is. You should have at least been able to get the season right, it's not like he's on the cusp."

"But are you sure Caroline is back in Houston?"

"Yes, I'm sure."

"Is Jude with her?"

"Yes."

"How do you know that?"

"Don't even worry about it. I'm done involving other people in my problems. I let Julie and Evangeline help me, and I got them killed. I got Imogene killed. I probably got Zander killed. I'm done killing people. No one else is going to die because of me."

Patrick's face contorted into tears and it made David want to cry too. He hugged Patrick and wanted to keep him right there in his arms. That way anything that wanted to kill him would have to go through him first. He could soften the blow.

"I know you think you're responsible for everything and everyone, but you're not. You're just a kid, okay? It's my job to take care of you, so let me. You're not alone in the world."

David heard a crash and Amanda shout and released Patrick to shoot back out the door. Evangeline had blood running down her arm and Amanda wrapped her hand in a dish towel.

"I broke a glass," Evangeline said with a shaky voice. "I didn't mean to. It was an accident."

"It's okay," David said, impressed with his own forced calm in the sight of so much of his daughter's blood. "How bad is it?" he asked Amanda. "Let me see."

He took Evangeline's hand and pulled back the bloody towel. She had a deep gash in her palm several inches wide and seemed to have already spilled a gallon of blood. It trickled down her forearm and pooled onto the linoleum.

"She needs stitches," David said.

"No," Patrick said, from behind him. "The magic is getting

restless. It wants to drive us out, get us in a place where it's easier to kill us."

"She needs stitches," David said again, holding her towel-wrapped hand.

"There is that urgent care place not far away," Amanda said. "That would be safer than going to the hospital."

"Okay. I agree."

"Don't take her out of the house," Patrick said.

CHAPTER THIRTY-SIX

While David waited in the waiting room with Evangeline, he called Zander. He didn't want to call him right in front of Evangeline and prompt questions, but he couldn't leave her side.

"Hi. You've reached Zander's phone. I'm sorry you missed me but leave me a message and I'll get back to you soon. Have a great day."

"This is David Vandergraff. Please call me back or text me."

Evangeline didn't ask who he had called. She huddled over her hand.

"Are you cold?" David asked.

She shook her head.

"They have the AC on too high."

David looked at his phone to check the weather. "It's supposed to rain again."

"Dad, don't let Amanda kill Anabel Lee."

"She would never do that, honey."

"She hates Anabel Lee."

"Maybe. But she loves you, so she wouldn't hurt your lizard."

"Will you take care of her after I'm gone?"

David bit the inside of his cheek. He wanted to tell her she would not die, but he knew she wouldn't appreciate that any more than Amanda had.

"Of course I will," he said in a strained voice.

"You'll feed her and clean her cage?"

"Yes."

"I love you," she said in a whisper.

"I love you, too," he said barely able to form the words. "Very much."

David's phone dinged. A text from Zander.

Hello.

Are you in Houston? He texted back.

Yes.

Ok. Thank you.

How r u?

David stared at the text. Something felt off.

Been better.

That's too bad. How is Mom?

"Evangeline Vandergraff?"

David continued staring at the screen.

"Dad, she called my name."

"Right."

He stood up mechanically and followed Evangeline and the nurse, staring at his phone.

"Sir, did you hear me?" David looked up to see they had made it back to the exam room.

"I'm sorry," he said.

The nurse gave him a look that dripped with judgment. "Has she ever had a tetanus shot?"

"I don't think so. No."

"Okay, honey," the nurse said. "The doctor will be here soon."

Jude? David texted back.

He waited, staring at the phone, but the typing bubble never popped up.

Why do you have Zander's phone? He texted back.

Just holding it for him. Why are you texting him?

Where are you?

Where are you? He parroted back.

Are you okay?

I'm excellent.

"Who are you talking to?" Evangeline asked.

David put his phone back in his pocket. "I'm so sorry, honey. I'll put it away."

The nurse peeked back in the door. "Mr. Vandergraff, there is a girl here asking for you. She says she's your daughter. Can I let her back?"

"What is she doing here? Yeah, sure, send her back here."

The nurse waved to someone David couldn't see, and then Samantha came through the doorway. Her hair was limp and damp and she had grass stains on her skirt. She smiled at the nurse and then closed the door behind her.

"You're not Emmy," David said.

"I know," Samantha said, further stating the obvious. "I lied."

"What are you doing here?"

"Are you okay?" Samantha asked Evangeline.

Evangeline had her bandaged hand cradled close to her chest and she scowled at Samantha.

"No," she said. "But you know that."

"I came back to the apartment and saw you leaving with her. She was bleeding, so I followed you."

"Followed us how?" David asked. "Do you have a car?"

"I… borrowed one."

"I'm not dead yet," Evangeline said. "You can leave."

"I get why you might be pissed at me, but it's not really fair. I'd say we're pretty much karmic equals. Actually, you're much worse. You cast the same spell I did, but you cast the one that killed Imogene too. None of this would have happened if it wasn't for you."

"Please leave, Samantha," David said.

"You don't have to protect me from the spring witch," Evangeline said. "She can't do anything to me."

"Are you sure?" Samantha asked. "I thought I destroyed you," she said. "Isn't that why you're mad at me in the first place?"

"You have no business here," David said. "I gave you money. You can just leave."

She scoffed. "I appreciate being able to eat dinner every night and sleep in a clean bed, I really do. But beyond that, I don't care about money. You can't pay me to go away."

"That's not what I'm doing. Although, if I could get you to at least leave this room, that would be great."

"I know I made a mistake," Evangeline said. "But it's not my fault Imogene died. It's Caroline's fault. Do you even know who she is?"

Samantha paused. "Yes."

"No, you don't," Evangeline said. "Not really. We were trying to protect the spring witch. We were trying to help her. And you just assume our spell didn't work. But I'm not so sure. Maybe she died happy instead of being tortured. Maybe we directed her fate down the best possible path. It might look like a bad path, but you don't know it wouldn't have been worse if she had stayed alive. Maybe you should be saying thank you."

Samantha's cheeks flushed and she pursed her lips as if she might spit. "You make it really hard for me to care whether or not you live or die. But I care about the other people in your family, and I know they wouldn't like it." With her face reddened, she looked at David now. "I think I know how to fix this… but there is a problem."

"I'm listening."

"I met this guy named Zander—"

"Okay, let's go outside," David said, and he herded Samantha back out the room while Evangeline glared at him. "Waiting room, go. I don't want to leave her for long."

"What's the problem?" Samantha asked when they'd made it down the hall.

"How do you know Zander? When did you see him last?"

"I don't know him, not really. But I met him today. He's a spring equinox wizard, just like Imogene. The only kind of wizards who can reverse death are spring equinox wizards. And it's not like they're running around everywhere. I've only met two in my entire life, and I've met lots of spring wizards. Even meeting two sounds like a lot. And the fact that he's here, in Houston right now. Not just in Houston… but was at your apartment complex—"

"He what?"

"—It can't be a coincidence. It is fate's way of helping you out. Fate or God or a spell, or something. Whatever it is wants Evangeline and Patrick to be okay. I mean, it's like he was waiting out there like a guardian angel, ready to swoop in."

"It's not a coincidence," David said.

"I know right?" Samantha said, misinterpreting his statement. "But… I lost him. I don't even know how to explain it. This scary girl showed up. Or she looked like a girl. Something was really messed up about her. And I passed out and then when I woke up, he was gone. He left his car, so I took it. I… I don't know what to do. You need to help me find him again."

"Can I see your phone?" David asked.

"I don't have a phone."

"Do you have any way of contacting this Zander person?"

"Yes, he gave me his phone number."

"Can I see it?"

"His phone number?"

David nodded.

"Sure. You should call him." Samantha reached into her tiny burlap purse and brought out a napkin with a phone number on it.

David snatched the napkin out her hand and ripped it into as many pieces as he could, leaving a pile of frayed napkin on the carpet.

"What are you doing? Stop."

"Do you remember his number?"

Samantha shook her head, gaping at the pile of shredded napkin.

"Good," David said. "Forget he exists. Do not try to contact him. And never, ever call him. You should ditch his car too. Just leave it."

"I don't understand."

"I know. I'm just asking you to trust me."

"Why wouldn't you want his help? I always thought you were a good dad. I assumed you would be willing to do anything to save your kids."

"I am. And I have enough to worry about without worrying about you too. So I'm asking you to please leave."

"I can't."

"Why not?"

"Because I have nowhere else to go."

"Sir," the nurse said. "The doctor is ready to do the procedure. Do you want to be with her?"

"Yes," David said. "Just go back to your hotel," he said to Samantha. "Please."

David went back into the room, where Evangeline looked as if she tried not to cry, and not succeeding. They had a needle sticking into the skin near her cut, presumably administering the local anesthetic. David took her other hand.

"It hurts now, but once the medicine takes effect, you won't feel it at all. Just hang on." He squeezed her hand again and she sniffed. He hated seeing anyone he loved cry, but Evangeline proved especially disarming. She had the disposition of a porcelain doll, still and unmoving, but also breakable. And now he watched her break.

"Just take some deep breaths, sweetheart," the nurse said.

David's own eyes felt heavy with tears, because he had to watch his daughter in pain, but also because he knew he had found his best chance to cast the spell Thea had taught him. Evangeline was as vigilant as a jungle cat and as quick to strike. But right now, she felt nothing but pain. He could be in and out without her noticing.

When Thea had described the protection spell, she had said it required hours of meditation, perhaps days. But he didn't have days, maybe not even hours. Zander had been his last hope—the only other thing that might work. And now, he had lost him too. What if Caroline came for them next? And now with the power of all four events? Time had run out.

Thea had also said winter wizards couldn't handle spells like this. "It's hard to see in the dark," she had said. Dark wizards were so consumed by their own darkness, they couldn't see past their own nose. Her statement held some truth, but it dripped in bias. Even the dead can see love. And that's all he needed.

David continued to hold her hand, but he let the rest of his body relax as much as possible without falling to the floor. He focused on releasing the decades of tension in his neck and his jaw. He tried to unravel the knots of fear in his gut that had lingered there for as long as he could remember. The sound of the doctors and nurses speaking became muffled. And then he could only hear Evangeline's heartbeat.

As Jess had said when she "read"' Evangeline, the darkness surrounded her. And it didn't seem like an outside force he could suck away. Doing so would be like trying to remove a germ by sucking out all of someone's blood. She had the darkness in her veins and her spiritual energy appeared like black smoke. He couldn't tell what energy was the killing spell, and what part was Evangeline. Amanda had nearly killed herself trying to suck out Jude's darkness, and he hesitated, but then he realized how foolish that was. If his plan worked, he wouldn't live long enough to die of cancer.

Then he remembered what Jess had said about "death being behind her," and he expanded his focus. Then he thought he found it, a lump of darkness on her back, hovering over her heart. That had to be the spot. Her own darkness flowed through her symbiotically, as blood through veins. This seemed more like a parasite. Thea had described magic like a living creature and this supported that. People couldn't "see" the germs making them sick, so they once didn't know they existed at all. He had similarly missed this invisible affliction.

Thea had described envisioning a circle of light around the child, a protective cocoon filled the child with light and burned away the parasitic curse. Light repels demons, she had said. He knew this would not work for his children, at least not this one. Instead of heat, he had to freeze off the parasite.

He envisioned her in a dark cocoon, like a womb—but with cold, clean darkness like the water from the pools of a cave. Her body suspended there, deep underwater, deep under the earth, untouched by sun or air. No living thing could reach her or harm her while she waited in her tomb—not a tomb of death, but one of protection. Not a place to die, but a place to wait.

Evangeline gasped and David gripped her hand tighter.

"It's okay, dear," the nurse said. "Almost done."

David understood her gasp hadn't come from the pain in her hand, but from his spell. But he didn't know what it meant. He thought her hand felt colder, and he used that sensation, grabbing it so he could intensify it.

Even the doctor looked up at her. "Can we take her vitals?" she asked.

David did his best to ignore the Mundanes. He was close. She was in her protective cocoon. Now he had to lure the killing spell.

He spoke the words in his mind.

If I had made a different choice in my life, Imogene Grey would still be alive. If I had not cheated on my wife, Imogene Grey would still be alive. If I had never been born, Imogene Grey would still be alive. I, David Vandergraff, killed Imogene Grey, and I take full responsibility for her death.

His spell had three parts—protection, meeting the conditions of the spell, and sacrifice. Three powerful angles of attack. Now for the last part.

I, David Vandergraff, having the option to live, choose to die to spare the life of my daughter, Evangeline Vandergraff. I fear death more than anything. Losing my future—the opportunity to grow old with my wife, to see my children grow into adults, to meet my grandchildren—is the worst thing I can imagine. But I willingly choose death, in return for my daughter's life.

He worried he hadn't meant it, which would water down the magic. Sacrifice needed to be as decisive as jumping in front of bullet to save someone else. It had to transcend general sense all parents have that they would die for their child. It had to be a real, tangible act.

Then he saw death coming for him. A cloud of darkness like pure, unadulterated fear, seeped into his skin hungrily. He had to hold his breath to keep himself from crying… and to keep himself from begging God to take back his words.

"Her vitals are fine," the nurse said.

The doctor gave Evangeline another clinical glance. Who knew what the Mundane had sensed while the epic encounter with death had taken place in front of her nose.

"All right," she said. "I'm all done. You'll have to come back in one week to have your sutures removed. If they come loose sooner, come in right away. And also come in if you notice any oozing or painful redness around the wound site. Okay?"

She squeezed Evangeline's shoulder.

"Are you all right?" the doctor asked David.

"I just get a little queasy around blood."

"Why don't you sit down? I don't want to come back in here because you passed out and cracked your head open," she teased.

The doctor and the nurses left the room, promising to come back with discharge paperwork.

"What did you do?" Evangeline asked him.

"Oh, nothing. I was trying a pain reduction spell. Did it work?"

"A little bit."

CHAPTER THIRTY-SEVEN

David sat in bed with his laptop. It was his turn to sleep, but he needed Amanda to sleep so he could sneak into Patrick's room and cast his spell again. If he could do it in an exam room in front of Mundanes, he thought he could do it in a dark room with Patrick asleep.

He had held his breath all the way home from the urgent care, scared he would end up getting Evangeline killed if the killing spell took him in a car accident. Now every twitch and ache might be the harbinger of a heart attack. Irrational fears about miscellaneous pains may not be irrational anymore. But most of all, he tried not to think about it, and as a master of denial, he had done well.

However, the e-mail that popped into his inbox threatened to break his composure. An e-mail from Mr. Sherman with a large attachment—one that contained his last will and testament for his review. David couldn't look at the attachment. He couldn't make it real and fall apart.

In a moment of unexpected morality, Mr. Sherman hadn't charged him for a new message from Rachel, because he had been unable to obtain one. "She might have passed on," he said.

278

However, this had made his first message seem all the more plausible. He could have taken the money and made something up, but he didn't.

Amanda came out of the bathroom and rubbed lotion on her hands, keeping her eyes on David the whole time. An odd silence passed between them. She averted her eyes and looked at her hands as she continued to wring them even though the lotion must have absorbed by now.

"You figured it out, didn't you?" She looked up at him again, her shoulders slumped and her eyes red.

"Figured what out?"

"Rachel's message… sacrifice."

David's lips felt numb. He had spent the day reworking his will with Peter Sherman, but it hadn't seemed real. He had created a will before. He had discussed guardianship with Jess and Carson. That had been more than fifteen years ago… but he had done it.

If Amanda figured it out. If he had to say the words aloud. It would be real. He didn't think he had the strength to face it. He had to keep it at arm's length. A distant general sense he would die, like all people do.

David's lack of response gave Amanda her answer. Her face contorted into sobs. Tears flowed down her face and she held her bony elbows and shook. He had never seen her cry like that, and he dove out of bed and pulled her into a firm hug. He cradled her head against his chest.

"Why are you crying?"

She pushed him away from her then. "You promised to stop lying to me. So stop."

His lips felt numb again and he bit them so he could feel them. He looked back at his laptop, and then at the floor. "There is magic in sacrifice. I talked to Thea Prescott… I know that's weird. But she tried it before, I knew she would know."

Amanda shook her head as he spoke.

"It's a simple spell." He rubbed the back of his neck as he spoke. "It's a choice really. A powerful choice. It can divert a killing curse."

Amanda put her face in her hands and breathed deeply. "There has to be another way."

"I don't know of one. Neither does Thea Prescott, or Peter Sherman. Even in death… Rachel also knew. It's the only way. Otherwise she wouldn't have sent me that message."

"Where is the fucking coward I married? You're just going to *die*? That's your solution? Aren't you afraid to die?"

"I don't think I've ever been more afraid of anything. Well, that's not true… I'm more afraid of watching my children die."

"I survived months of chemotherapy and beat cancer, just to live a few more months."

"What are you talking about? I'm going to die, not you."

"For someone with an MBA, your math is terrible," she said with a shaky laugh. "Which of your children are you planning to save? Patrick or Evangeline? Are you prepared to make that choice?"

"No. No. I can do both."

"David, I figured this out too, maybe before you did. My mom always said the only force that can overcome dark magic is love. And I always thought it was mind-numbingly cliché and sentimental. I didn't take it seriously. But, I think it was more than a stupid thing she said. It was the only, and the most important, magical lesson she ever taught me. You're right. Sacrifice will work. It's the only thing that will work."

Amanda crawled under the covers next to him. She closed his laptop and took it away from him, placing it on the side of the bed. She rested her head on his chest as she might on any other night, not as if she had said she planned to die.

"How can you be so calm?" he asked. He hoped she had a good answer. Perhaps he had missed something. She had some secret understanding about how this would all be okay.

She intermingled her fingers in his. "I don't see any point in being hysterical," she said. "I've been preparing for death for a long time now. For ten months, I've lived with the knowledge I could die before my next birthday. I'm not saying that makes it easy for me, but I have had time to go through the stages of grief."

David took in a sudden intake of breath. She pressed her face into his shoulder.

"If you think about it, nothing has really changed. I've always believed I would die for my children, and I know you have too."

"Every parent thinks that. But few of them actually have to make that choice. It's not the same."

"I'm just saying we already made this choice. There *is* no choice, really. Not for me. I couldn't live a life knowing I could have saved my children, and I didn't."

"Amanda," he whispered. He didn't know why they whispered, but they spoke softer and softer as they went along. He found he didn't want to look at her. He couldn't handle this moment, not while looking into her eyes. "You can't die. We can't *both* die. What would happen to the kids?"

"They would live," she said.

Amanda circled the wedding ring around his finger and they both watched it turn.

"We can't abandon them like that."

"Babe, remember this is a last resort. There is still a chance it won't happen. We're not going to head out and drive our car into the ocean on purpose. We just need to be ready… if fate calls us."

"And if it doesn't?"

"We just have to be vigilant. And have faith."

"This is unfair."

"We already had a life that was a thousand times better than what most dark wizards get. This is the only way dark people can be good. By loving. By sacrificing."

"By dying. By ridding the world of us all together."

"You know that's not what I mean."

"Yes, it is. You think that's the only way we can do right by the world… by leaving the world.

"I should have died already." She untangled her hand from his and smoothed out the blanket. "There is something I want to tell you. Something that's been weighing on me." She wouldn't look him in the eyes. "I know I get so mad at you when you're not honest with me. I know I'm a hypocrite. I just… I was so ashamed."

"What?" he said, his stomach tightening, although he couldn't imagine how this conversation could get worse.

"Caroline saved my life. She came to me at the hospital and cast a spell to take away the cancer."

David waited for the terrible catch. "That's it?" he asked finally.

"That's *it*?" Amanda echoed. "Did you not hear what I said?"

"Why did you think you needed to keep that a secret?"

Amanda shook her head at him.

"What?" David asked. "I suppose you think it was selfish or something? Because she got all her power through prax portentia. And then she used it to save your life. All that darkest of dark magic, coursing through you."

"Yes, exactly," she spat back. "It was selfish."

"No, it would have been selfish of you to deny her. It makes me angry to think you even considered it."

"You don't know what you're talking about."

"No, *you* don't. You don't get to die, and leave me. It's not your choice because it's my life too. I can't believe you would have even considered not doing something that would save you." David knew this didn't make much sense. He couldn't even say why he felt so angry. But the thought scared him. The thought that she could have said no to Caroline and today she would be dead. He knew she might die tomorrow, but the thought she would have died sooner… that he might be lying in bed contemplating his death alone… was unacceptable.

"Why do you even care so much?"

David didn't understand the question. He shook his head at her. "Why do I care if you live or die?"

"Well, yes. Even if I am your talisman, why do you think you would die without me?" She paused. "Why do you love me so much?"

"What? After twenty years of marriage you want to know why I love you?"

"Yes." She barely opened her mouth when she said it.

"Amanda… you can't be serious."

"I don't think you really see me David. You see someone else, someone you thought I was. Some sweet little woman who goes to PTA meetings and church, whose life is pointless without those things. You don't see me for who I really am."

David laughed, and Amanda glared at him. "I'm sorry," he said. "I'm not laughing at you. That's just the stupidest thing you've ever said."

She continued to glare.

"I don't think you're sweet, Amanda. Or nice. Or good. And certainly not some kind of cliché little good wife. Is that really what you think I want?"

Amanda didn't reply.

"I see you for *exactly* what you are," he said. "I always have. Magic or no magic. Do you think that's why I wanted you to go back to church? Because I wanted you to put on pumps and a cardigan and participate in bake sales?" He chuckled again. "Because it's not. I just thought… it doesn't matter what I thought."

David took her by the shoulders and looked her straight in the eye. "Amanda, you're despicable. And I love you."

Her face broke into tears. He pulled her into his arms and stroked her hair. He had to hold his breath again so he wouldn't cry too. She had seen him cry plenty of times, but he knew if he cried this time, he might break the fragile strings keeping him from falling apart.

He couldn't handle this conversation anymore, so he kissed her. He could taste the salt of her tears intermingled with cinnamon toothpaste. He considered he might never taste her again, but then pushed the thought away. He didn't have the strength to think like that.

Making love to her might be the best way to forget, so he kept going. Kissing her. Touching her. Sliding insider her. Anytime he thought about making love to her for the last time, he shook the thought away and concentrated on nothing but how good it felt to be inside her.

Afterward, she laid her head on his chest. The stillness made all the fear come back. He continued to try and distract himself. The smell of her hair. The softness on the inside of her hand. He would miss her toenails poking his feet. Why did God have to make life so fucking wonderful, if He would just take it all away?

"You know, I could take us anywhere," she said. "Well, maybe not anywhere. But any good memory you have of us. I probably have it saved. Anywhere you want. First kiss. First time we had sex. Our wedding. Our honeymoon. Or back at school, that rainy day when we had sex in the library."

"That was a good one."

"Or our kids," she said, her eyes welling up with tears again. "That baby smell. That little laugh. Those teeny tiny toes. Or the first time I felt life moving inside me." She laughed a bit as she blinked back tears. "Well, I guess that last one is just mine."

"No. I don't want to relive anything." He wiped the tears away from her eyes with his thumb.

"You're right, it would hurt too much."

"Yes, but that's not why. I don't have the time to live in the past. I don't want to waste any of the present. Your saved memories are amazing, but they are still not as good as having you right now."

He interlocked his hand into hers, taking the time to run his along the back of her palms and across her knuckles, experiencing every single part of her. His hands shook as he did so, and she squeezed them to keep them still.

"I'm afraid to fall asleep," Amanda said. "What if I don't wake up?"

CHAPTER THIRTY-EIGHT

The next morning, David and Amanda ate breakfast silently with Evangeline and Emmy while the boys continued to sleep. All five of the family phones erupted in an alarm simultaneously, interrupting the silence. A low-pitched single note repeating at unnatural volume.

"It's a flash flood warning," Amanda said, looking at her phone. She placed the phone back on the counter.

"That's probably the same storm that hit Austin last night," Emmy said. "The news said a wall of water forty feet high washed out an entire neighborhood. There are like twenty people missing. One whole family got washed away."

"That doesn't sound true," David said.

"Watch the news, Dad," Emmy replied. "Why don't you ever watch the news?"

"I said it was just a flash flood warning," Amanda said again. "We get these all the time. Just about anytime it rains. We don't live near a river. It's fine."

Emmy flipped through the channels as they talked and she stopped on a man in front of a radar map full of ominous red blobs of storms.

"Look," Emmy said. "There are like five tornadoes going on right now."

"That's ridiculous," David said.

"I'm not the one saying it. The man is saying it," Emmy said, pointing at the television.

"Those are nowhere near us," Amanda said, grabbing the remote and turning off the television. "Everyone needs to relax."

"I know you're not going to let me do it, so can you please move my car under the covered parking so it doesn't get hailed on?" Patrick asked Amanda.

"I'll do it," Emmy said.

"I'll do it," Amanda said.

"Why?" Emmy asked. "I'm no more likely to hit by lightning than the average person."

"I'm not sure that's true, Emmy."

"Let Emmy move the car," David said. He meant to say it casually, but his tone chilled the room. He stared Amanda down while Emmy stared at him.

"Why?" Emmy asked.

"You really want to question it?" David asked. "Do exactly as I say. Take the keys. Walk down the steps. Go directly to his car. Do you know where it's parked?"

"Is it really necessary to outline every single step I need to take? Did you think I would somehow forget I needed to walk down the steps first? Seriously, the paranoia level in this house is stifling."

When Emmy opened the door, the smell of rain and cool air washed into the apartment. David thought he could sense the electricity of the coming storm, as if the electrons in the air moved too fast and might strike any of them at any moment. Without thinking about it, he pulled Amanda away from the door, as if he believed a lightning strike might somehow come down from the heavens and defy physics to take several sharp turns directly into Amanda's heart. He wished he could call himself paranoid, insane even.

"Come here," Amanda said, and she now pulled him into their bedroom and closed the door.

"You need to relax," she said. "They're going to suspect something."

"I'm just being cautious. If the sacrifice spell worked, then you and I might be the ones with death hanging over our heads. People who are marked to die shouldn't go outside in lightning storms. If we have to die, we can at least delay as long as we can. Hell, isn't that life. Isn't that the whole fucking point? Doing everything we can to delay death as long as possible? That's what everybody does. We might have less time than before, but it's still the same."

"Delaying death as long as possible is not the point of life. And you know that, or you wouldn't have made this choice."

Every single moment seemed more precious than ever before, as those moments counted down, his senses heightened, as if to take in greater and greater amounts of his world in each second. He could feel individual strands of her hair against his fingers. He could smell her skin, and her soap, and her lip gloss. The thunder boomed more loudly, and he could feel the vibrations through the soles of his feet. Life fought. Every ounce of it—every sensation, every emotion—screaming to hang on.

Emmy opened the door without knocking stuck her head in. "Well, I'm alive. I thought you might want to know." She ran her fingers through her wet hair. "Mom's car is already under the cover, but I need to move the Escalade now. Dad, give me the keys. I only saw one spot left, I have to hurry."

The lights flickered and then went out. He heard Emmy take a sharp intake of breath.

"It's no big deal," Amanda said. "We'll just get the flashlights. Light some candles."

"I'm on it," Emmy said, leaving the room.

Although the clouds obscured the sun, enough daylight remained to illuminate the room. An eerie greenish light filtered in through the windows, punctuated with flashes of blue-white lightning.

They left the bedroom and met Evangeline in the living room.

"The lights went out," Evangeline said in strange toneless voice. David knew her flat drone didn't mean she felt nothing, it meant the exact opposite. She had her arms crossed in the same protective stance she had used constantly for the past few days. She clutched her own elbows like the handrails on a lifeboat, the only thing keeping her from tumbling into the ocean.

She looked as if she might bite anyone that got close to her, but David pulled her into a cautious hug. She didn't unlatch her arms, but she didn't fight him either.

"It's okay," he said. "You're going to be okay. It's just a little rain."

She released her grip around herself, holding onto her forearms instead of her elbows. "What do you mean?" she asked.

David wondered if he'd somehow said too much. Even those simple statements had given something away. Twenty-four hours of banning her from doing anything remotely dangerous—including taking a shower and using the microwave—and now, "you're going to be okay?"

He gave her another quick hug, but didn't risk saying any more. She let her arms drop at her sides and she stared at him with those piercing green eyes. But she didn't speak.

"No candles," David said. "Put that out before you burn the apartment down."

Emmy blew out the one candle she had lit.

David's gut lurched. Despite the blaring alarms and the thunder shaking the dishes in the cabinets, Patrick hadn't come out of his room.

"Patrick?"

"I checked on him five minutes ago," Amanda said.

As soon as David had his hand on the knob of the boys' room, the door opened and Patrick stared out at him.

"Jesus, Patrick," David said and he pulled him into a hug.

"Dad," Patrick said. Without any more explanation, David could tell by the tone of Patrick's voice, something was very wrong. His already racing heart took an extra irregular beat.

David released Patrick and looked at him.

"Xavier won't wake up," Patrick said.

Amanda gasped. David pushed Patrick out of the way and directed his attention toward his other son. Amanda muttered something about not checking on Xavier. But why would she?

As Patrick had said, Xavier was pale and unresponsive, but he didn't feel cold. His skin burned David's fingers. And David had no trouble finding his pulse. His heart thrummed so fast his veins vibrated.

Amanda grabbed for him too, and David pushed her away, unsure of why.

"Call 9-1-1," he breathed to her, and she disappeared, following his command.

David grabbed Xavier by the shoulders and shook him. Xavier didn't open his eyes, but he did take a labored breath. "Wake up," David shouted, as if he was dragging and might be late for the bus.

"What happened to him?" David shouted at Patrick.

"I don't know. He was just like that."

David swatted Emmy's hand away, as she reached out to Xavier too.

"For how long?" David continued to shout even though Patrick kneeled right next to him.

"I woke up when the alarms went off. I went the bathroom and brushed my teeth."

"You brushed your teeth before you called me?"

"No, I didn't know anything was wrong. I thought he was just still asleep."

"They're on their way," Amanda said, appearing in the doorway again, holding her phone. "Is there any chance he ingested some kind of poison or a drug overdose?"

David put out his hands to show her the room. "Christ, Amanda, I know as much as you do."

"They were asking me," Amanda explained. "We don't know. We don't think so," she said into the phone.

"What's wrong with him?" Emmy asked unhelpfully.

"I don't fucking know, Emmy," David said, immediately regretting shouting at her.

Xavier waited far too long between breaths, and David kept shaking him and shouting at him. When the paramedics arrived, David nearly collapsed as he got up. The panic had grown so intense he was dizzy.

He clutched the side of the gurney and let the paramedics drag him into the ambulance too. He rode in the back and watched while the young woman attached tubes and wires to him. David's muscles relaxed slightly, knowing he was in the hands of someone he could do more than yell and shake him and he appreciated being able to see his heart rate in bright, glowing green. Still beating. Still beating.

"Does he have any medical conditions?"

"No, he's healthy. He's seventeen."

"Allergies?"

"No."

"Medications?"

David recited the names of two different anti-depressants.

"Did he eat or drink anything unusual? Take any drugs, legal or otherwise?"

"No, I mean, I don't think so. I don't think he's even left the house in a few days."

"We'll give him a blood test when we get to the hospital, but that takes time. The sooner we know what he took, the better."

"What he took? You think it's a drug overdose?"

"That's my best guess based on his health and his symptoms, but I don't know without a blood test. Does he have a history of drug use?"

"No."

"I'm not the police, I just need to know so I can help him."

"I told you, no. If he's on drugs, I had no idea."

The paramedic examined the inside of Xavier's arms, presumably looking for track marks.

CHAPTER THIRTY-NINE

"You can't make me stay," Evangeline said.

Amanda had her body blocking the doorway with a hand on each side of the door frame. She pursed her lips and shook her head.

"Don't make me curse you," Evangeline said.

"Leaving the house won't help Xavier. Dad is with him. The doctors are helping him."

"Mom, you have to step aside," Patrick said. He stood next to Evangeline, looking especially tall compared to her.

Emmy surprised Amanda by taking her side, at least in positioning. She interlocked her arm around Amanda's elbow, blocking the door with her.

"Emmy, don't," Amanda said. "I don't want you to get hurt."

"We're not going to hurt you," Patrick said. "We're just asking you nicely to get out of the way."

"Patrick, you're supposed to be the smart one," Emmy said. "Isn't it obvious what's happening here? You said yourself the magic was getting restless… trying to draw you out."

"Get out of the way," Evangeline said again.

"Emmy, get out of the way," Amanda said.

"Mom."

"Better yet, go to the hospital," Amanda said. "You can text us updates. That would be nice, wouldn't it?" she said, addressing the other two. "Emmy can be your eyes and ears."

"Yeah," Emmy said.

"Go," Amanda said. "Take the keys. Now."

"Okay," she said. "I'll… which car?"

"I don't care, Emmy. Just go."

"Okay," she said again under her breath, taking the keys out of Amanda's purse on the side table. She ducked under Amanda's arm and darted down the stairs.

Evangeline shook her head. "Why did you do that? What if she dies?"

"Well, there's no greater chance of that than usual," Amanda said. "I can't live my life assuming *all* my children might die any minute. Two of them is enough for me."

"You don't know," Evangeline said with a wavering voice. "Xavier might die. *Why?* We must have done something wrong with the spell. It's not hitting the right people. What did I do wrong?"

"I think it's my fault," Patrick said. "I shouldn't have been sleeping in a room with him, not when death is so close to me."

"Are you listening to yourself?" Amanda said. "Death isn't like the flu. He didn't *catch* it from you. To answer your question, Evangeline, your spell is working perfectly. Your sister is right. This is only happening to draw you out."

"That doesn't matter," Patrick shouted. "If Xavier dies just to make us go out in a storm, that doesn't make him any less dead."

"He's not going to die."

"You don't know that," Evangeline said.

"I'm going to die anyway," Patrick said. "And I'm tired of being stuck in this apartment. I'd rather die knowing I was there for my brother when he needed me than waiting to die in a freak kitchen accident here."

"No," Amanda grabbed the door frame tighter and the edges dug into her palms. She knew she couldn't stop them from leaving. They didn't want to curse her, but they would… eventually. Or Patrick might knock her out of the way. But this felt like the right moment to strengthen the existing magic by demonstrating clear, symbolic sacrifice. "I don't care if you curse me or hurt me," Amanda said. She said the next part in her head, knowing they would recognize a spell when they heard one. *I, Amanda Vandergraff, will endure any pain, up to and including death, in order to protect Patrick Vandergraff from pain and death.* As Amanda spoke the words in her head, Patrick moved closer. *I willingly and knowingly sacrifice myself so he may live.*

"Mom, last chance. I'm asking you nicely."

"Not moving," she said. "Like I said, I don't care if you hurt me."

"I told you I wasn't going to hurt you and I'm not," he said. "That's good."

"I'm going to put you to sleep. It's not going to hurt."

At first, Amanda thought he meant death, but Patrick would not kill her to get her to move out of a doorway. No matter what happens in his life, she knew he would never do that. He was a good man.

"I love you, Patrick."

"I love you, too."

Patrick put his thumb under her chin and his middle finger on her cheek bone. She felt intense pressure, but as he promised, it didn't hurt. Darkness filled her vision and her legs buckled under her.

David stayed with Xavier while they monitored his vitals and ran tests. Everyone asked him the same questions. The ambulance ride to the ER had roused Xavier. He teetered on the edge between falling into a deep sleep and absolute terror. He shrunk away every time someone tried to touch him. David felt the need to keep explaining. *It's okay, they're just taking your blood pressure. It's okay, they're just taking your pulse. It's okay, they're just taking a blood sample. It's okay. It's okay. It's okay.*

"Why did you bring me here?" he asked when they had a moment alone. Or as alone as you can get in an ER. Xavier hated going to the dentist. He had gone once and then refused to go again. He made a motion to rip out his IV and David grabbed his hand to stop him.

"It's okay," he said once again. Each time, the statement seeming more and more meaningless. "It will hurt much more if you rip it out."

Xavier then pulled the pulse monitor off his finger, and David put it back on.

"If you take that off, the machine will start beeping, and they'll just come in here and put it back on." He knew the drill after spending so much time at the hospital with Amanda. He knew the purpose of all the wires and gizmos, but that knowledge didn't comfort him. He hated hospitals all the more for having spent so much time in them. The whirring sound of a blood pressure cuff made his hair stand on end.

"I want to go home," Xavier said. "Why won't you take me home?"

"Because you wouldn't wake up," David said in a strained voice. "They think you had a drug overdose… did you? Did you use drugs?"

"No."

"Xavier, please don't lie to me. If the answer is yes, I won't be mad. I just want to make sure you're okay."

"I didn't use drugs," he said again and closed his eyes as if the few sentences they had exchanged had drained him.

A woman in a white coat pushed back the curtain and David saw the muscles in Xavier's forearm tense.

"I'm glad to see that you're alert," she said. "How are you

feeling?"

Xavier didn't respond. He had his lips pressed together so hard, they turned white.

"I'm Doctor Farady," she said, checking his file. David prepared himself for the onslaught of predictable questions every single person at the hospital had asked him.

"He's not on drugs," David said. "He said he wasn't, so he isn't. He's not a liar."

"Well," she said, looking at his chart. "That does seem to be the case," she said with practiced sweetness. "Your blood test came back negative for common recreational drugs."

"I told you that," David said. "I said it over and over but no one believed me."

"It's not personal," the doctor said. "We have to make quick treatment decisions. And we have to make our best guess based on what we see."

"So I can go home?" Xavier said.

She smiled tightly. "It's wonderful you're not using drugs, but I'm afraid that simply means we need to do more tests to determine what's really wrong. We'd like to admit you and continue to monitor you."

"No," Xavier said. He dug his fingernails into David's forearms.

"Can he go home and come back tomorrow?" David asked.

"According to his chart, he was unresponsive only hours ago. I don't think it's safe for him to go home just yet."

"You have no idea what's wrong with him do you?" David asked.

"Based on his symptoms, I would have guessed it was a reaction to a substance also. And not necessarily illegal drugs. It could be a side effect of a legal or prescription drug or a reaction to some other substance in his environment. We can test for a lot of the common possibilities, but if it's something more uncommon, we need your help determining what it might be.

There are hundreds of thousands of possibilities."

David glanced back at his son, and David could see his heart rate increase on the monitor. He wondered if the doctor had gotten too close to the truth. In any case, Xavier hid something.

"We'll let you know if we think of anything," David said.

"All right. Well, your fever is down, which is good. Your blood pressure and pulse rate are still too high, but at least they're stable. I'll have someone come and take you up to the pediatric unit. I promise, it's very nice. Lots of movies and video games. Whatever you want."

The doctor disappeared behind the curtain. They got about thirty seconds of her time and then she moved on.

"Where are Patrick and Evangeline?" Xavier asked.

"At home."

"I don't want them to die because they came to see me."

"I'll take you out of here right now," David said. "But only if you tell me what's really going on."

"I don't know what you want me to say. What do I have to say so you'll let me leave?" He scratched at the tape on his IV. "The woman just said I passed my drug test. How can you still not believe me?"

"The doctor said they only test for common substances, you could have reacted to something more uncommon. Then I realized how silly I had been to even consider you might use the *common* substances this Mundane hospital tests for. You wouldn't do that."

"If I tell you, you'll really let me leave?"

"I said I would, so I will."

"How will we get out?"

"It's not a prison. We can leave."

Xavier picked at the tape around his IV.

"Don't get ready to go just yet," David said. "You haven't told me anything. What did you take? What is it, some kind of potion? Where did you get it?"

He pointed to the handwashing station by the bed.

"What are you pointing at?"

"Water."

"I don't understand."

"I told you what I was taking. You have to let me leave."

"Is that some kind of joke? It's not funny."

Xavier looked as if he needed all of his energy to keep himself from ripping the IV out of his arm. He didn't look like he was making jokes.

David placed his hand over the spot on his arm with the IV. "Just relax and explain."

"It's really not a big deal. It's not like Mundane stuff. It's not real. It can't hurt you."

"Apparently it can, because it did," David said.

"I must have messed it up somehow. I don't know what happened."

"Please… just back up and explain. How did you make water do this to you?"

"Some wizards make complicated potions with all these ingredients, but that's kind of a spring wizard thing. It's best to use simple substances like water. Salt sometimes. Or oxygen. Haven't you ever heard of an oxygen bar?"

"I have but…"

"It's a wizard thing. They can imbue the oxygen with magic. And if the heath inspector or whoever wants to check it, they only find oxygen."

"And you did that with water?"

"Yeah."

"How does it work?"

"How many more questions do I have to answer before you take the IV out?"

"Jesus, Xavier. Fine." David turned off the IV machine and pulled the tape off of Xavier's arm. There was one good thing about hospital experience. He had seen this done plenty of times. "This might sting a bit, but it will be quick."

"Okay."

David pulled the IV needle out of his forearm. Xavier pulled his arm back as soon as he could and cradled it against his chest.

"I'm not trying to torture you with an IV needle to get you to talk, I'm asking you to talk. I'm also not trying to threaten you by making you stay at the hospital if you don't talk. If I am satisfied I understand what's wrong with you, we can leave. If it's a magical issue, there is no point making you stay here. That's all I'm trying to do. Okay?"

"Okay."

"How do you turn water into a potion?"

"You use a tiny bit. Like one drop. And you imbue magic into the water drop. You picture all the little molecules and you picture them changing colors and moving. They don't really change color or anything, you're just attaching your magic to the molecules. Then you put the droplet on your tongue or rub it on your wrists."

"How did you learn how to do that?"

"My mom. I mean, she didn't teach me how. But I saw her do it. And she did teach me how to do other stuff with water, like turn it to poison. It's the perfect way to kill someone because it's untraceable."

David winced. How could Crystal think it was appropriate to teach their children how to turn water into poison?

"So you're poisoning yourself? On purpose?"

"No, it's not poison. I'm just saying I could do that."

"Well, then what does it do?"

"I don't know. Makes you feel good I guess. You just don't care about stuff. It doesn't hurt you if you do it right."

"Samantha's parents died from magical drug use. You know that right? You're not going to be able to convince me it's as harmless as regular water. You need to stop. Immediately."

"I don't know."

David scoffed. "You don't know? Well, I think you need to figure it out. I have to trust you on this, Xavier. I don't exactly have a choice. I can't take away water."

Especially not today. Even in the afternoon, the clouds had muted the light seeping in from the windows and water rushed down the glass. Damn water.

"I'm sorry," David said.

"For what?"

David shook his head. "I haven't done anything to help you. I feed you and clothe you and give you shelter… and even that has been tough sometimes. But beyond that, I really don't know what I'm doing. And I think I'm just too chicken shit to try."

Xavier didn't say anything, but David had gotten good at interpreting his looks. He had his head cocked and his gaze shifted downward, which meant he was listening. Unlike most people who felt the need to speak to fill a silence, Xavier did not. If he didn't have anything to add to a conversation, he wouldn't speak.

Xavier looked up at him, which David interpreted as Xavier wondering why David had stopped speaking. "What do you mean, you're too chicken shit to try? Try what?" he asked.

"Sometimes I think I should talk to you about the things that have happened to you. That I should do more than just ignore it. But I'm just afraid. I'm afraid I'll make things worse. And I think I'm just afraid to hear it. It's easier to ignore."

"Well, I don't want to talk about it. And I don't think I need to talk about it. I don't understand how that's supposed to help."

"I guess I don't either. I just don't know what else to do."

"You don't have to do anything. You don't have to worry about me all the time. I'm fine."

"That's hard to believe while you're lying in a hospital bed."

Xavier swallowed and coughed like his own saliva had irritated his throat. And then he looked at David and didn't say anything.

"How did you do it? How did you get to be fine?"

"I don't know that I am."

"You have a wife and kids and your own business. If I could end up like you, I'd be happy."

David tried to suppress a smile. "I don't know if I should be touched… or concerned. I think you can do better than me."

"I'll skip the affair and secret family."

"That's a good idea."

"I'll stop doing the spell. I don't think I can do it all at once, but I think I can do it gradually. Maybe just only at school. I don't mind being at home."

"If there is anything I can do to help…"

"I do have one question."

"What's that?"

"Do you think it's worth it?" Xavier asked.

"What?"

"I don't know. Trying, I guess. Do you think I can be normal? Or is there no use in trying?"

The million dollar question. "No, I don't think you can be *normal.* But what's the fun in that anyway?"

Xavier smiled. "You know what I mean."

"Of *course,* I think it's worth it. I know it's worth it. And of course I think you can live a good life and be happy. I'd bet my life on it."

"Hey." David jumped in surprise. As they had talked, David had generated a magical bubble of privacy around them and didn't expect it to be broken. Jess Oppenheimer dropped her wet umbrella by the wall and shook water droplets out of her auburn hair.

"What are you doing here?" David asked.

Jess scoffed. "My nephew is rushed to the hospital, and I'm not allowed to come visit?"

"Nephew?" David asked. "Have you ever even met?"

"Hi, I'm Jess," she said to Xavier. "How are you feeling?"

"Fine," he said.

"David, could I speak with you privately?" Jess asked.

"Why?"

"It won't take long," Jess said.

"We're still going to leave, right?" Xavier said.

"Yes, we're going to leave," David said, getting up. "One minute."

David stood up and followed Jess around the corner. He reasserted his protective bubble so they could stand amongst the passing nurses and doctors in the hallway without notice.

Jess examined all the nearby staff before she spoke, her gaze darting toward every movement around her.

"Is something wrong?" David asked.

"It's important you don't tell anyone I came to see you," Jess said.

"Why?"

"Because what I am about to do is against the law."

"I don't understand. Are you planning on stabbing a nurse or something? Stealing prescription meds?"

"*Wizard* law, David."

"We have laws?"

She brought her voice down lower. "I have some concerns about the events of the next few hours," she said. "Serious concerns."

"Oh… good."

"Why is that good?"

"Because it's close enough you can see it now, right? The future? You know how it will happen so we can prepare."

"I hope I'm wrong," she said, grabbing his wrist. "I want you to understand I could be wrong."

"It's okay, Jess. You're here to tell me I'm about to die, aren't you?"

Jess let go of his wrist and shook her head. "No…"

The monster of fear that had been redirected toward Xavier

thrashed again, making his stomach burn.

"What do you mean… no?" he asked. "It's me. *I'm* going to die."

"I… I don't think so. Not today… why do you think you're going to die today?"

David's breath caught in his throat and he had to fight to get his words out. "Then… why are you here?"

"It's Evangeline. Evangeline is next. It's going to be soon. She's going to drown. I can see it so clearly. Her pale skin in the dark water. At first, she doesn't seem to be fighting it, she just floats in space, but then all of a sudden, she gets scared. She thrashes, but she can't find the surface. She doesn't even remember which way is up. She kicks her legs frantically, reaching out for the surface, but it's the wrong direction. Her hands never find the air. She drowns."

David grabbed her by the shoulders. "You're wrong. I cast a sacrifice spell. *I* die. She lives. You can see it on me, right? The death behind me? Like it was on Evangeline?"

"No," she said. "Nothing is different about you. You're not marked."

He continued squeezing her shoulders, hoping to shake different information out of her. "No. No," he said. David released Jess's arms.

He grabbed his cell phone and dialed Amanda. He knew Evangeline would never pick up hers.

You've reached Amanda Vandergraff. Leave a message.

"Amanda. Amanda. Amanda. Pick up the damn phone. Amanda!" David ended the call and looked at Jess. "Why isn't she answering?"

An unfamiliar number flashed on his phone, but he still picked up and said, "Amanda?"

"No," said a different female voice. "This is Samantha. Samantha Carthage."

"Yes, I know who you are. What's up, Samantha?"

"Patrick and Evangeline left the house?"

"What?"

"I've been watching the apartment, and they just left."

"Was Amanda with them?"

"No. I'm following them. What should I do?"

"Did you try calling Patrick?"

"It went straight to voicemail."

"Where are they?"

"Driving north on Gessner."

"Dad?" A sopping-wet Emmy stood behind Jess, her blonde hair sticking to her cheeks.

"Keep following them. I'll call you right back," he said and hung up the phone.

"What's wrong?" Emmy asked. "Is Xavier okay? Where is he?"

"Emmy. Are you here by yourself?"

"Yes, but Mom said that was okay. She told me to take the car."

"So Evangeline is still at home?"

Emmy hesitated. "She was there when I left."

Jess shook her head.

"I need you to do something for me," David said to Emmy. "Will you drive Xavier home?"

"So he's okay?"

"He's good enough. I promised I would take him home, but I need you to do it."

"What's wrong, Dad?" Emmy asked. Her blue eyes staring him down through the passing scrubs of oblivious Mundanes.

"Nothing. Well, nothing new."

"You and Mom keep asking me to drive the car," Emmy said.

"So? Isn't that a good thing?"

"It's weird," she said. "You guys are acting weird."

"He's right behind that blue curtain. Go talk to him."

"Are you sure you're okay?"

"Everything is fine, Emmy."

She looked so grown up, more like Amanda than ever. Her eyes lingered on him for a few moments longer, and then she retreated behind the curtain.

CHAPTER FORTY

Patrick headed to his car with Evangeline in tow, thinking the whole time he had made a mistake. Water soaked his new running shoes. That shouldn't happen, not in their apartment complex parking lot.

He got in the driver's seat of this car and closed the door against the deluge.

"I really wish you wouldn't come," Patrick said.

"But you know I'm going to," Evangeline said, fastening her seatbelt. "So there is no point arguing."

Patrick hesitated, watching the long streams of water flow down the windshield and wondering if his wipers could keep up.

"Drive, Patrick," Evangeline said.

"She's right, you know. Going to see him doesn't help anything."

"Please," Evangeline said.

Patrick turned the key in the ignition. Evangeline grasped the side of the door with one hand and dug her other hand into her thigh. He knew she was more frightened than she let on.

He turned on the windshield wipers and the headlights on. He looked at the clock. 3:14 p.m. Still early, but it looked dark out. A blanket of dark gray covered the sky, as if darkness and death prepared to suffocate them, regardless of the time of day.

Patrick pulled out of the apartment complex and let out a long exhale. Xavier was at Memorial Herman Southwest. He could avoid the highways by cutting through the neighborhood. He didn't want to risk getting on the Freeway.

However, as he drove along Gessner, he thought he might have made a mistake. This would take forever. He slowed down as they drove through a large puddle and he could feel his wheel losing traction.

He exhaled again on the other side of the puddle. His wrists hurt from grasping the wheel. "We're almost there," he said to Evangeline.

She scratched her leg and looked as if she might draw blood.

"In driver's ed, they explained how much more force you get in an accident with an increase in speed. And basically, it's really hard to die in an accident when you're going as slow as we are."

She nodded, staring out the window.

Despite his calming words, he felt so tense that his butt might not be touching the seat. He might have levitated. The rain and the thick current of water made it difficult to see the lines on the road.

Why did he do this? Was he a slave to magic? The killing spell compelled him to curse his mother so he could put himself and his little sister in mortal danger. When he left the house, it had felt like the obvious choice. Xavier needed them. How could they not go?

Now, as he watched small rapids rushing into the gutters he saw the urgency to leave the house had been an illusion. Understanding how spells work didn't help. Knowing the future didn't help. Common sense didn't help. The magic perverted his thinking and compelled him to act. Now he was stuck on a flooding road, and it was too late to turn around.

"What are you doing?" Evangeline asked.

Patrick had put on his blinker in preparation for an exceedingly slow and cautious lane change.

"I'm pulling off the road," he said.

"Why?" Her voice sounded muffled, as if already under water.

"Why do you think? The roads are flooding." His voice also sounded muffled, and oddly calm. "Maybe we can fight against the spell, maybe we can't. But not fighting isn't an option. I'm not going to just give up and drive into the river."

"But you are," Evangeline said, her voice quieter now, as if he might have imagined her speaking at all.

"What?"

"I don't want to die," she said. Her almost imperceptible voice wavered with tears. "Please, Patrick."

The terror in her voice shook him out of his stupor. He realized how disoriented he felt. He had turned off the main road into a neighborhood. The sound of the rain increased and he noticed small white pebbles bouncing on the black asphalt in front of him. Hail. But was that asphalt? Something was wrong.

He felt Evangeline's small hand clutching his forearm. With the power of foresight, he expected he would get a barrage of warnings before he died. Visions pelting him with the intensity of a fire alarm. But instead of panic, he felt paralyzed. Sliding into death with no fight at all.

The steering wheel locked and he felt the traction of the tires give way. Then it all happened fast.

He could tell by the houses on either side of them they were on a road, but it appeared Brays Bayou had spilled over it's banks and the water rushed into the neighborhood. If he had felt paralyzed before, it was nothing compared to how he felt now. The car was paralyzed. The steering wheel wouldn't move. He couldn't turn the wheels. And he couldn't get the door open. The engine had died and all the internal lights had shut off, but the car continued to move, propelled by the water.

"No," he said.

Evangeline shrieked and pulled her knees to her chest. Patrick felt it too. Water. It had seeped in surprisingly quickly, flooding the floorboard up to his ankles. For God's sake, the water couldn't be that deep. A foot maybe? Two feet?

"What do we do?" Evangeline said.

Patrick continued to clutch the useless steering wheel as a current grabbed the wheels so they moved backward... closer to the bayou itself.

He looked at her, crouched on her seat, looking at him expectantly, as if would have an answer. She looked ready to pounce. Ready to fight. And he hadn't been. He had wanted to fight against the spell to the last second, but he hadn't. He had sat and watched as his car swept toward the bayou.

"Hang on," Patrick said.

He twisted his body around, so his feet faced the driver's side window and he kicked with both feet as hard as he could. His jangled nerves seized with an extra flash of pain, but he broke the window. The entire pane popped out and crashed into the water. One tiny bit of luck. He had considered a piece of glass might fly out and hit him in a crucial artery.

"We're getting out of the car," he said. "You go first. Or no... I'll go first."

"I can't," she said.

"Yes, you can. We have to get out before the car tumbles into the bayou. It's still shallow here. You just have to hold on to me."

When she came to live with them, she didn't know how to swim. Dad had encouraged her to learn, but she said she was too old to take swimming lessons. Patrick figured she didn't want to wear a swimsuit in public and show off her scars. In any case, Dad hadn't pushed the issue. But it had always bothered Patrick. That's the reason why he became a lifeguard. He knew this day would come, and had known for almost a year. The details had always been fuzzy, but he had had enough visions of her drowning to know it would come up, sooner or later. So he had prepared himself. Even so, he was still surprised to be right.

She shook her head again. "You should go," she said. "I'll be fine right here."

"Don't be stupid," he said. "You know I'm not doing that."

The car was moving. There was no time. He could see the image of the Gessner Street bridge looming closer, the water alarmingly high. The bridge usually stood twenty feet or more over the concrete spillway. And now, the rapids licked the underside of the bridge.

"Trust me," he said. "Take my hands. I won't let go."

Patrick grabbed both of Evangeline's hands and crawled out of the window feet first. The water felt colder than he expected, and deeper. He couldn't find footing. Evangeline whimpered as Patrick dragged her across the driver's side seat. He grasped her wrists with his full strength and he knew he hurt her, but he couldn't worry about that.

The rushing current pulled his body at a different rate than the car, and his strongest grip couldn't hold. Her small wrists slipped out of his hands. It only took seconds for the car to rush away from him, well out of his reach. The water rushed through the open window.

"Fuck," he screamed, punching the water. The water knocked him off his feet and dragged him too. This was harder than he expected. The water was about chest deep, but it moved so fast. He couldn't swim against it.

The car continued to move away from him, with Evangeline inside. He grabbed onto a tree branch and watched as his car tumbled into the spillway and out of sight.

This couldn't be happening. Even after all the visions and the impending killing spell, he couldn't believe it. Part of him wanted to let go of the branch and let the water take him. He could follow her that way and try again to get her out of the car. He lost one shoe, and then the other. And the socks followed. He didn't know how much longer he could hold on anyway. His arms and shoulders burned with the effort.

He considered letting go and hoping his body could withstand the rush of water toward wherever Evangeline had gone when he heard shouting.

"Grab on." A group of people had approached the bank and one of them held a rope. "Take it," the man shouted again.

Patrick grabbed the rope with one hand, and then the other, afraid the rope would slip out of his grip as Evangeline had. However, he felt his body moving toward the bank. They pulled him out.

As soon as he felt ground under his feet, he clawed his way out of the water, ripping up the lawn under the edge of the bank. The man grabbed him by the arms now and dragged him further from the water. Now on land, the rain continued to plummet down on him. He had trouble focusing on the people around him and was shocked by a familiar voice and a wave of familiar magic.

"Patrick." Samantha wrapped her arms around him. Drenched and covered in mud, she smelled of the bayou water.

"Come out of the rain," said the man who had pulled him out. Or one of the men. There were four Mundanes there with Samantha, three men and one woman. The man who addressed him was sunburned and balding.

"My sister was in the car," he said to the strangers and Samantha.

"I know," Samantha said. "They called 9-1-1. Someone will come rescue her."

Patrick trembled, colder than he should be in a Texas spring. He should go inside and dry off, but that would mean forgetting Evangeline was out there somewhere, drowning, or already drowned.

"I told her I wouldn't let go," Patrick said.

Samantha tugged his arm and helped him stand. He continued to shake.

"Come on." The Mundane woman in her sixties with long gray hair took Patrick's other arm. "Come inside," she said.

Something sliver caught his eye. A car, parked too close to the edge of the water. And not just any car. A brand new silver Tesla.

"He's here," Patrick said. He shook the woman and Samantha off of him and moved toward the car, pointing. "He's here. Maybe he can save her."

Samantha stepped in front of him and pressed on his chest with her hands. "Who is here?" she said softly, like he was a crazy person.

"You don't know him. A spring equinox wizard. He can save her."

Samantha glanced at the car and then back at Patrick. "I drove that car here. I followed you and Evangeline as soon as you left your house. I was afraid something would happen to you… and it did. When you went into the water, I started banging on doors until someone would help me. These people did. And they called 9-1-1 too."

"That doesn't make sense. Why do you have Zander Colter's car?"

"I don't know where he is. But I don't think he's coming."

"I know where he is."

"You do?"

Patrick nodded.

CHAPTER FORTY-ONE

Anytime Amanda woke up in a hotel, it would take her a few moments to remember where she was. Waking up on the floor in the muddy entranceway of their apartment felt like that, but far more intense. It first took her several minutes to orient herself. This apartment had never felt like home to her, and her instincts had the same reaction. She must be traveling. In between one place and another.

Then when she could give the room a name, it took another few minutes to remember how she had gotten there. The memory of Patrick's face right before he cursed her floated into her mind and the fear came with it. The opposite of waking from a nightmare. She woke *into* one.

She sat up. She felt lightheaded, but otherwise seemed uninjured. The sky out the window had an odd grayish blue and told her nothing about the time of day. She had no idea how long she had slept. The clock on the kitchen stove didn't help either. They must have lost power because the digital display flashed 12:00 over and over. She might have fallen into a rabbit hole where time didn't exist. What if hours had passed? Days? And none of the people she loved had come home to wake her.

314

In a cursed sleep, she must have been able to dream, because the image of Caroline's face and the sound of her voice echoed clear in her mind. It felt as if they had just spoken. A dream would be the only explanation.

"Bananas?" Amanda whispered to the empty apartment. "Caroline and I were talking about bananas?"

The strange memory seemed clear to her. She closed her eyes and shook her head as if she could shake out the intruding thoughts. And that's what they were… intruding. Foreign. She had a memory that didn't belong to her.

It took her a few more minutes to realize what must have happened. Either intentionally, or unintentionally, Patrick had passed one of his memories to her when he cursed her. With a lurch, she realized he had meant to share the memory. The fastest way to send a message. He had a memory about Caroline he needed someone else to know… so it wouldn't die with him.

Still sitting on the floor, she cajoled the memory forward instead of brushing it away. She had plenty of experience with memory magic, but she had always remained in control. This time she had to succumb to an intruding presence and allow the offending memory to take control of her senses while all of her instincts pushed it away. She had to tiptoe in and out a few times before she could immerse herself.

She found herself in Patrick's mind. Patrick's body. Patrick's life. Although disorienting, it also felt precious. Few parents got to experience such a powerful closeness to their children—actually *being* them.

Although she almost wished she had never gotten the chance. She didn't like how it felt to be Patrick. He felt anxious. Scared of something unknown and unnamed. An ambient fear coursed through his body like a physical substance. Thick and visceral, as if she could squeeze the anxiety out, and she wished she could.

She had expected to feel youthful and vibrant, like when she visited her own young self. And she might have felt that way, instead of distracted by unexpected twinges of pain. A mild, but constant tingling in his extremities. Amanda didn't know Patrick suffered from chronic pain. He hadn't said a word about it. Amanda guessed the pain lingered from the torture that Caroline had put Patrick through. A constant, gnawing reminder.

Patrick's magic also felt foreign—like seeing a new color for the first time. Hitching a ride in his memory, she only had a subtle sense of the fall magic, but she didn't like that either. As much as she had resented being a winter wizard, her magic felt so much *quieter* than Patrick's. The fall magic squirmed like an animal living inside his head, churning through thoughts and images that all moved too quickly to make any sense, and perverted into an extra fourth dimension. She could hardly describe the sensation, let alone make any sense of what any of it meant.

After discovering her new body, the rest of the scene materialized. The smell was so familiar, it bothered her she couldn't pinpoint it, like a name on the tip of her tongue. As bits and pieces of florescent lighting and colorful signs came into view, she could define the scent. The grocery store. A mix of produce with a hint of pesticide and laundry detergent blended with thousands of other vague smells.

"You're buying bananas?" asked Patrick. "In your house somewhere, do you have one empty plastic H-E-B bag filled with more plastic H-E-B bags? I'm not going to lie, that kind of blows my mind."

And there she was. Caroline, leaning on her grocery cart and looking away from Patrick, examining a mango and then putting it back. She had pulled her hair back in a messy ponytail and she had circles under her eyes. She didn't appear to be in control of the situation, taken off guard. Amanda guessed Patrick had tracked her down and then ambushed her in the grocery store. The image of the store around Caroline blurred and faded in and out, but the sign above the produce section looked familiar. Could she be shopping in the grocery store less than a mile from their apartment?

"It's really weird seeing you act like a human," Patrick continued. "But I guess it would be stupid to think you didn't have to go to the grocery store. You have to eat. You need toilet paper. Shampoo. Stuff like that. Everybody does."

"Go away, Patrick," she said, ignoring him and pushing her cart away from him.

"I'm curious," he said, following her. "How well did my repulsion spell work? How far did you have to go? How long did it take for you to be able to come back?"

He followed her to the bakery section. "I'm very patient, Patrick. And not easily distracted. It doesn't matter where I went or how long I was gone." She poked a bag of tortillas but didn't pick it up. "I think it's rather presumptuous and arrogant to assume I only left because of your spell, and only returned because the spell wore off."

"You know, you look really tired. Are you getting enough sleep? And you've got a little something on your T-shirt there." He pointed to a small orange smudge on her T-shirt. She slapped his hand away from her and with the slap came a pain that radiated behind his eyes. His knees nearly buckled, but he knew she had only given him a taste. A warning shot. However, it reignited the trauma of what Patrick had experienced before. His body filled with adrenaline.

"Thank you for your concern," she said. "I'm fine."

"I actually wanted to thank you," he said. His voice had a haughty sound, but Amanda knew him well enough to know he faked the confidence. Although she didn't have to guess. She could *feel* his terror. "I hadn't met many others of our kind. I didn't know much about what we could do, but I learned a lot from you."

"There's no point in avoiding using words like 'wizard' and

'magic.' The Mundanes are too stupid to get it even if we wave in their face." Caroline stopped in front of a man in a red H-E-B shirt. "Excuse me, sir, can you tell me where I can find the batteries?"

"Sure. They're on a display in front of aisle nine."

"Thank you. Oh, and also, I wanted you to know I'm a witch." She pointed to Patrick, "And he's a wizard. We practice magic."

The man looked at Patrick and then back at Caroline and smiled. "Okay. That's nice," he said.

"Thank you. It *is* nice." She continued pushing her cart. "See Mundanes aren't paying attention to us. And even if we push it right in their face, they think we're crazy. It's really hard to break through the boring and stupid of Mundane life. So there is no reason to believe I won't curse you in the middle of the grocery store. There are lots of reasons why a man might crumble to the floor in pain at the store. Kidney stone. Heart attack. Brain aneurysm. Easy. There you go. There is another lesson for you. What else do you think you learned from me?"

"I learned to look at the big picture. You're right, fall wizards are patient. And focused. Others are so easily distracted by what's right in front of their face. I can see beyond that. The question is… can I see more than you? Am I two steps ahead of you now?"

"I guess you must think you are if you're here gloating. But if that's true, then you've turned quite dark. If you've been two steps ahead this whole time, then you knew your spell would kill Imogene. You might have even known it would kill Julie, and it could still kill you and your own sister. But you cast the spell anyway. Just to put a minor stumbling block in front of me." She applauded. "Bravo. That was either incredibly stupid or pure cold-blooded evil. Which one are you?"

Amanda felt an extra jolt of fear in Patrick's gut, and she could guess why. She knew *so* much. She looked into his eyes and gave him a tight-lipped smile. Amanda could tell she relished in the return of control.

"I'm smart enough to know that I don't have control over everything that happens in the world," Patrick said, the feigned confidence in his voice lessened. "You think you have more control than you actually do. And that's dangerous."

"Patrick, I know better than anyone that fall wizards like to hear the sound of their own voice, and I'd genuinely love to talk you in circles, but I'm a little busy."

She pushed her cart toward the checkout lane.

"Hang on, you're clearly not done with your grocery shopping. No one gets a big cart and buys just bananas and batteries. Don't let me interrupt your normal, human errands. I think it's fascinating. You're sure this is all you need? Milk? Bread? Eggs? Anything else?"

She laughed. "This weird intimidation thing you're trying is really cute. It is. Are we done?"

"As strange as it is to see you buy bananas and batteries, I already knew you were human. You're no comic book super villain. You're just an angry little girl who was the black sheep in her perfect family, who was born with a malfunctioning brain that can't fully process empathy. You're human. You have human fears, human desires, and human weaknesses. And you're right, we're not so different. We both have things we care about."

"I hope that made you feel better, but your brilliant deductions are really rather obvious." She turned away from him so decisively that she almost took down the sunscreen display with her cart. "It was nice seeing you, Patrick."

"You too, Caroline."

As she turned around, Patrick took his chance. He grabbed her head, his palms pressing into her temples, and his fingers digging into her scalp. He knew he had less than a second before she fought back. If she could deliver as much pain as she had when she had him bound and defenseless, he didn't want to think of what she would release when she felt threatened. As a novice to this particular spell, he wished he had lots of time, not a millisecond. He reached into her mind, grabbing anything he could like a kid scrambling for candy after a piñata bursts. He found the image of the home she had hidden with magic before she sent the witches version of a poison spray into his face. He felt as if his eyes had exploded and globs of eye goo and blood poured out of this face. As she clutched at his face, he realized the feeling was an illusion. His eyes remained intact, but he couldn't see.

The people in the grocery store threatened to call the police since he had attacked a woman in front of everyone, but he sent waves of repulsion spells at anyone who tried to get near him. Half blind and feeling brain cells pop one by one, he defended himself on pure instinct.

Bright, white fuzz obscured his eyesight, but he could make out bits and pieces. He felt the rush of warm air and heard the sound of the automatic door wooshing and went toward it, and the bright sunshine blinded him. He nearly got hit by a car as he veered toward his brand new car. He couldn't work his keys, so he crumpled down and sat against the side of the driver side door. He blinked furiously even though the sun hurt his eyes more. His sight gradually returned. Apparently, she didn't like him looking though her thoughts, so she made him blind.

As the image faded, and she transitioned back into the present, and began to smell her real surroundings. Their apartment did smell funny. Like old dryer lint, but not in a good way. She wondered if that's what evil smelled like—old dryer lint. The ridiculousness of the thought reminded her she still sat on the floor, thinking about how evil smells, when her children and husband were in danger.

She reached up and grabbed the doorknob and used it to help her pull herself up. Fall wizards were best at noticing the nuances of fate and time, but Amanda could sense she stood at a crossroads. She could do any number of things that might make sense. She could go to the hospital to find Emmy and Xavier. She could drive around looking for Patrick. She could track down David. She could stay here and wait for them to come back, calling and texting for updates. Any one of those things could be a rational choice. But her magical instincts pointed in her a different direction.

She had the image in her head. A surprisingly normal looking townhome. She could see the numbers on the house, and she knew where to find it. The path she needed to take illuminated in front of her. She would find Caroline and kill her.

Leona watched Caroline as she watched Zander. Caroline had asked her to lead him into her house and have him sit on the couch. Leona kept him in a state that she thought of as "hammock." She could manipulate emotions best when she visualized an action or a place. Words alone didn't mean anything. The actions mattered. She had given Zander the emotional state of swinging in a hammock, looking up at the sky. Obviously, it worked. He had his arms spread over the back of the coach and lounged complacently.

He didn't seem to care why he sat in a stranger's house. And it didn't worry him that Caroline had stared at him and walked in circles around him for almost thirty minutes. She looked as if she walked around a fence looking for weaknesses, a point of entry.

"Okay," Caroline said. "I'm ready. Let him go."

Leona rocked back and forth in her cross-legged position on the floor by Zander's feet.

"Did you hear me?" Caroline asked.

"You're not supposed to hurt spring wizards," Leona said.

"Are you going to tattle?" Caroline mocked. The glass bird appeared in her hand suddenly as if she performed fake Mundane magic. "I could always practice with you first."

"Don't hurt the bird," Leona said. "She didn't do anything to you."

"You really are bat-shit crazy, you know that?" Caroline dropped the bird, but it hovered under her palm, suspended.

"No! I'll release him," Leona said. "Stop it."

Leona watched Zander's body tense and he sat up straighter, the sense of peace on his face disappearing as his brows furrowed.

"Where am I?" he asked.

Caroline sat next to him on the couch and smiled. "Don't you remember?"

"No… what did you do to me? Where is Samantha?" He glanced at Leona and back at Caroline, shifting in his seat.

Leona wished boys wouldn't be so stupid. She knew if she and Caroline looked scarier, he'd run or attack them. He'd save himself. But they didn't look scary at all.

"You were telling me about how you grew up in foster care, remember?"

Zander shook his head.

"But you didn't enter foster care until you were like eight years old, right?" Caroline continued.

"Yeah…"

"I bet most people just assume your mother is dead, don't they? And it's just easier not to correct them."

Zander leaned away from her, but didn't make any movement to leave.

"But your mother is not dead," Caroline said.

"No," Zander said. "Not that I know of anyway. How did you know that?"

"You'd think that would really mess someone up," Caroline said. "Your mother just decided she didn't want you. And it wasn't even like she dropped you off as a newborn at a fire station. She had you for eight years. She knew you. She had a relationship with you. And then she just didn't want to look at you anymore. That must really suck. It makes me wonder why you're not angrier. You just don't have that rage about you. You have every right to be angry."

"Who are you again?"

"But I see when I tell that story, it doesn't make you angry. Instead, it makes you feel profoundly sad. Heartbroken."

Caroline cocked her head to the side like she tried to feign empathy. Or maybe she did feel bad for him, Leona had never understood Caroline. She didn't know what she thought or what she planned to do.

"Your friend Imogene's story is really sad too. Tragic. I did some research on her. It's such an insane thing. Her father, mother, brother, and sister were all murdered right in front of her. And they never figured out who did it, or why. They didn't steal anything. And they never understood why Imogene was the only one spared. Her sister had been a baby when it happened. They shot her in her crib. Why would they murder a sleeping baby but not touch a hair on Imogene's head? Odd, right?"

"I didn't know that," Zander said. "That's… horrifying."

Zander's real empathy made it more obvious Caroline had faked hers. His face had turned pale and he looked as if he might pass out or throw up. But Leona wished he would stop worrying about babies that died over a decade ago, and worry more about what happened in this moment.

"Of course, the Mundanes wouldn't have gotten it, but I think it's pretty obvious why Imogene was spared. Rules are rules, right Leona?"

Leona didn't respond. Instead, she brushed up against Zander's legs, like a cat protecting her master, and he flinched.

"When they found little Imogene, she was holding her dead baby sister, rocking her like she thought she was just sleeping.

Can you imagine that? Try to imagine it."

Zander's face turned paler and he looked either angry or nauseous, or both. "Something is wrong with you. You talk about it like you don't care."

Unbothered by his accusation, Caroline smiled. Leona knew she had found whatever weak spot she had looked for. Despite seeming squishy and harmless, spring wizards don't break easily. No matter how dark the winter, spring always comes again. They always have hope. It takes something horrific to shake a spring wizard. Something even the most positive person couldn't see without losing a bit of faith in the world. Some things you can't unsee. They leave a permanent mark.

Caroline slid her hand into his as if they were boyfriend and girlfriend. Zander tried to pull away, but his body seized as if he sat in an electric chair. His eyes rolled back in his head and he made an odd wheezing, hissing sound. He should have tried to run.

Then Caroline stood up, and he collapsed onto the couch, shaking.

"Take him into the bedroom," Caroline said.

"Why?"

"Just do it."

"I don't think he can move,"

"Goddammit, Leona. Drag him if you have to." Caroline moved to stand next to the door and sniffed as if she could smell someone coming.

Chapter Forty-Two

David would expect to have trouble driving during a significant thunderstorm, but this was worse than usual. Fifteen minutes ago, Samantha had called again and said floodwaters had swept away Patrick and Evangeline's car. The sound of Samantha's small, distant voice grew louder and louder, reverberating in his head. Six words. *Their car went into the bayou. Their car went into the bayou.*

Those six words drowned out all other sensation. His other senses he needed for driving malfunctioned. All his energy directed toward surviving the sound of those six words. It took every last flicker of light left in him to maintain enough hope to keep driving instead of stopping and breaking apart. And he felt as if he tried to warm the Artic with a tiny candle.

Amanda didn't pick up her phone either. He worked hard to ignore that niggling fear of wondering *why. Their car went into the bayou.* He knew he didn't have the space to fear for Amanda too. *Their car went into the bayou.*

His phone rang again and he nearly skidded into oncoming traffic. Another number he didn't recognize. "Yes," he said.

"Patrick is okay," Samantha said.

Tears spilled down his cheeks, making it harder to see. His energy felt as if it went from cold to hot in a disorienting flash, the relief melting his frozen insides. But yet, the relief felt hindered. False. The sentence had missed something important.

"Evangeline?" he asked, in a choked whisper.

Her silence told him everything he needed to know. A brief pause—perhaps two or three seconds, but an eternity of grief and fear shouted through the empty space.

"I don't know yet," Samantha said. "She's still in the car."

"What do you mean?"

"The car went into the spillway at Bray's Bayou. She was still in it. David, we called 9-1-1. I'm sure someone is rescuing her right now."

"Can you do me one favor?"

"Sure."

"Don't let Patrick go after her. I don't care if you have to curse him or tie him down or hit him over the head with a lamp. Keep him safe, okay?"

"I promise."

David hung up the phone without saying anything else. His pulse had become loud, thrumming in his skull like the heavy chime of a grandfather clock. The rain had also become loud. The tunnel vision that had made it hard to focus on his surroundings might work for him now. Thinking wouldn't help him now. Thinking meant fear. Thinking meant grief. Thinking meant doubt. He couldn't have any of those emotions diluting his magical senses. He needed to focus on only one thing—Evangeline.

The hospital was not far from Bray's Bayou. He knew where it crossed the road, so his non-magical reasoning led him there. He was grateful he had recently cast the protective spell on her, not because it had worked, but because he had paid closer attention to the nature and energy of her magic than he ever had before.

As he drove closer to the bayou, he prayed in the only way her prayed these days—pleading. *Don't do this to me, God. Keep her safe.*

David slowed the car when he saw a barricade and flashing lights ahead. He could assume the flashing lights meant the water rescue had already begun, but he couldn't feel her presence here. He felt pulled further downstream.

He went further west down Bissonette, alarmed at the thick rush of water already on the roads. A lawn chair floated down the side of the road near the gutters. He stopped suddenly before getting on the frontage road of Southwest Parkway… because there was no frontage road. Water had overflowed from the bayou and crept up the road. The scene in front of him appeared bizarre and alien. This familiar landscape had turned into a lake.

David hadn't understood why Patrick had chosen a bright white car. Why not black or silver, or even red? No, Patrick wanted white, and it had been the perfect choice for this moment. David got out of the car and stood at the rising bank of the new lake in the middle of the city. The clouds continued to make the midday seem dark.

But he could see her. Alive.

The car had gotten caught on the pillars holding up the overpass. Water rushed into the open driver's side window, but Evangeline had made it to the roof. Despite her dark hair and the dark water and dark skies, he saw her right away because of the bright white car roof she stood on, clinging to the pillar.

"Evangeline!"

He couldn't tell if she had heard him over the rushing water. But perhaps she could see him, or sense his magic. Anything to give her hope. *Don't let go.*

He got out of the car and called 9-1-1. The operator said someone would be there right away, but David worried it wouldn't be fast enough. Water rescues happened all over the city so he couldn't count on an immediate response.

He didn't know how he could save her, but he knew he couldn't watch her drown, not when he had gotten this close. He knew he couldn't swim out and get her. The water would pull him under and he would drown before he got to her.

He felt water around his ankles. He was no longer at the edge of the water. The flood had continued to creep up the frontage road and now rushed around the wheels of the Escalade. He knew he had a chance to retreat. He had to run toward dry land. Abandon the car. But the dirty brown water now covered the white hood of Patrick's car. Evangeline had her arms wrapped around the stone pillar and continued to hang on against the rising tide.

So instead of running to dry land and waiting for help, he did the wrong thing. The foolish thing. Despite recognizing his foolishness, he also knew he made the right choice. He had never felt more certain of anything.

He climbed back into the Escalade and shifted it into neutral. The water continued to rise around his tires and caused him to glide forward. He knew once the water took him, he would have no control over the vehicle, at least not with the steering wheel.

Since his Mundane senses would do nothing for him, he ignored them. He let go of the wheel and closed his eyes. He thought of Evangeline as he had when casting the protective spell. Finding her energy, drawing himself closer to it. In any other situation, he never would have been able to do it. Perhaps so close to death, he already had the keen perception Mr. Sherman had mentioned. He could ignore all the details. The cold water up to his knees. The sound of the undercarriage of the car scraping against the guardrail of the road. The dank, oily smell of the flood water.

He could see her there, even with his eyes closed. Aggressively flickering in the darkness. Refusing to succumb. A powerful fire of magic, dark and spectacular. A raging wall of black fire crawling up the pillar of the bridge. His daughter.

He didn't need his Mundane senses to see her. He had never seen her so clearly. He had never once noticed the awesomeness of her power. She was at once a scared little girl clinging to life and a monster far more horrible than the storm that threatened her. His baby girl.

He felt himself getting closer to her, and he reached for her, although he couldn't say if he reached with his arms or some other sense he couldn't describe.

At the last moment, he opened his eyes, in enough time to watch the Escalade wedge between Patrick's car and the pillar. The two cars crunched together with a screeching and scraping sound. The water rushed around Evangeline's legs up to her knees now. He sat in his open window and reached a hand out to her.

For the briefest moment, her pale face broke into a tiny smile. Her hand felt cold and small, but she gripped his hand tightly. Then the two cars lurched again and Evangeline released his hand so she could grab onto the top edge of the window of Patrick's car. The pressure of the Escalade had caused Patrick's car to break free from the pillar and she moved again.

He had never hated God so much. How could he get so fucking close and still lose her? He had gotten close enough to touch her. Two more seconds and he would have pulled her into the cab of the Escalade.

He watched helplessly as only her head bobbed over the water, riding on the submerged car. The bright white roof emerged from the water and then the nose of Patrick's car shifted upward and he watched, thinking she would flip, but instead the car's front wheels became trapped on the tangled metal of a guardrail. She scrambled toward the front of the car, moving to the front windshield that emerged from the water. The white roof turned red and blue in a pulsing rhythm and

David first thought his eyes had failed him. A fire truck sat on the edge of the water, only a hundred feet or so from where Patrick's car had caught.

Now they would see her. David saw movement on the bank. Men and women in neon yellow lift vests and a bright red raft. He let out a long breath, ignoring the feeling of the cold water now at chest height.

God did seem to have a plan for Evangeline when he lost his grip on her. The force of his car had pushed hers to the perfect spot to be rescued. God had answered his prayer.

The water reached his neck and he became more aware of his own surroundings—his human senses refiring. The rush of the current turned the Escalade on its side. Then he didn't know which way was up. The car tumbled and crashed into one of the other pillars. As he crashed, for a moment he thought he looked at the night sky, staring into the eyes of the moon.

This is it. This is really happening. When the water had crushed the Escalade into the pillar, it had crushed him too. He felt too numb. He couldn't get his arms to move and he wondered if he'd already left his body. As soon as he thought about his body, he felt the pain. He could taste blood filling his mouth, and along with strange foreign objects—a few lost teeth. He couldn't understand where his body existed in space. His broken body remained wedged against the pillar in the mess of glass and metal that used to be the Escalade. He looked down at his arm and realized why he couldn't move it. He could see his own bone. Death would be cruel. He wouldn't die right away. He would have to wait to drown or bleed to death.

As perhaps a tiny act of mercy from God, the water rose, rushing into his mouth, a sensation more terrifying since he couldn't move his head to raise it above the water. Then the water covered his head. He again thought maybe he could see a hint of blue moonlight filtering through the water, saving him from complete blackness. The last sad little light he would ever see.

He tried not to think about his children. About how he would never see them again. He wouldn't see them grow up. He would never have a margarita on his back patio. He would never watch his grandchildren play in the bluebonnets.

He knew he should let go. Stop holding his breath. The pain made him want to scream. At least in death, the pain would stop. As he had said to Amanda, sacrifice can't happen without giving something up… without feeling terrible pain. The more he lost, the more powerful his sacrifice. He could feel it happening. Fate shifting. And he could see his grandchildren playing in the bluebonnets. He wouldn't be there… but they would.

Then he imagined Amanda's face. He thought of how her flowery face cream smelled. He thought of the way she tasted. The sound of her voice. As a living man, he would never experience it again. He didn't know if she waited for him in death, or if he would find nothing but darkness. But even the smallest chance of seeing her again in death seemed better than a life without her.

"Breathe," she said, her voice somehow coming from inside him and outside him at once.

Darkness had enveloped him and he thought he could see the phantom moon on the back of his eyelids. He thought of their first family ritual on the winter solstice, when he first understood the beauty of darkness. Perhaps he had grown too numb—or perhaps so close to death, he had never been further from fear or so close to truth—but the darkness no longer frightened him. It was peace. It was home.

He focused on Amanda's image in his mind. On the sound of her voice. On the feeling of her magic radiating around him. As he prepared to take his last water-filled breath, he prayed. *God, I don't care where you take me. Just take me to her.*

CHAPTER FORTY-THREE

When Emmy pulled into the apartment parking lot, she didn't see Patrick's car, but she didn't say anything about it to Xavier. Breaking the heavy silence in the car felt impossible, so much so, she suspected Xavier had cast a silencing spell on her. She knew he didn't use magic unless absolutely necessary, and apparently Emmy shutting up was absolutely necessary.

She left her wet sandals in the car and stepped onto the wet asphalt barefoot. She and Xavier wandered inside, both oblivious to the rain soaking them. Normal people would run inside or hold jackets over their head. Emmy never understood why people freaked out so much about getting wet. Witches were the ones that were supposed to melt, and clearly, she did not.

They walked into the empty apartment, dripping more water into the puddle that had already accumulated by the door. The dim green blinking light of the 12:00 on the stove clock cast an odd glow on the ceiling. Nobody here. But she already knew that. She could feel the absence from the parking lot.

Drenched, she shivered in the air-conditioned apartment.

She couldn't remember it ever seeming so quiet in this room. She cried even though she couldn't say why. Although she could think of a few good reasons.

"You can talk now," Xavier said with a scratchy voice.

She looked at him, and rubbed her arms, tears spilling.

"I'm sorry," he said.

He seemed to think the silencing spell had upset her, as if she suffered from an acute lack of talking.

"What should we do?" Emmy asked.

"You look cold. I think you should go change into dry clothes."

Emmy knew Xavier knew that wasn't what she meant.

"What if they never come back?" Emmy asked.

"They'll come back."

She didn't think he believed it. He said what he thought he should say.

"But you'll stay, right?" Emmy asked.

"Where would I go?"

"I don't know… beyond the veil."

"I don't know what that means."

"Me either."

"I'm tired," Xavier said. "If I go to sleep, will you be gone when I wake up?"

"No," Emmy said. Once she would have rather died than stay home while the people she loved were in danger. But now she understood why Xavier preferred to check out. She felt ten years younger than she did yesterday, although even her five-year-old self had more courage. Maybe something had broken in her. Or she had a limited amount of bravery available and had already used her lifetime supply.

"Good," Xavier said.

Chapter Forty-Four

Leona tugged on Zander's arm, trying to get him to move. In theory, she could make him do whatever she wanted, but only if physically capable. She couldn't make a man with a broken leg dance in a ballet… at least not well.

"Get up," Leona whispered, funneling the force of her magic into her words. "Everything is fine. You're not hurt. You can walk."

Her magical encouragement did seem to help. He propped himself up on one knee, and then pushed himself up to standing.

"Fuck," Caroline said.

Leona froze, first thinking Caroline was angry at her, but she seemed concerned about something else. She ran into the kitchen toward the back door. Then she ran into the bedroom, all the while not paying much attention to Leona and Zander.

"Come on," Leona said, this time pulling him toward the front door. She didn't have a plan beyond that, but maybe with Caroline distracted they could make a run for it. "Everything will be fine if we go outside," she said, although it's hard to project a feeling of complacency when she felt so far from it. Her hands felt sweaty on Zander's elbow.

But Zander nodded drowsily, and so she must have convinced him. The front door clicked open, far too loudly, but Leona didn't look back. She dug her nails into his arm and pulled him outside. If Caroline hadn't heard the lock, she would hear the deluge of rain.

"Run," Leona commanded.

He didn't move and instead stared up at the sky and held his hand out to feel the rain.

"Run," Leona said again.

He looked her in the eye and shook his head. Leona stared at him with her jaw agape. She didn't get this man. So suggestible up until this moment, but now he defied her.

Leona heard the front door swinging behind her, and she turned long enough to see a glimpse of blonde hair before the intruder closed the door behind her.

Amanda's misdirection spell had worked, sending Caroline away from the front door. She had expected to have to break in one way or another, but Zander and the strange girl walking out and leaving the door open felt like the luckiest thing that had happened to her in a long time. Or maybe it was magic. Was there a difference? In any case, she got what she wanted.

Caroline and Jude's townhouse felt warm and smelled of beef stew. She saw Jude's shoes by the front door. She nearly screamed when she felt something on her leg, and then saw a tabby cat. It had an odd breathy meow and squinted at her with yellow eyes before deciding Amanda didn't interest her and stopped to lick her paws.

Between the cat, and the shoes, and the dish in the Crock-Pot, she lost of all her previous certainty. It was all so *normal*. So wholesome. At least, she did not sense her son's energy in the house. She didn't think so. The energy in the townhouse had a glaring, disorganized quality that left Amanda with a foul taste in her moth. Caroline's magic was dirty—tainted with the magic she had stolen from others. And as such, her magic never seemed pure or clean.

Amanda clutched her hunting knife. She had chosen the weapon deliberately. Caroline would not fear a weapon so Mundane, and she would assume if Amanda did choose a Mundane weapon, she would choose a gun. A hunting knife—a universal weapon that could take the life from man, beast, and wizard alike, with no regard toward so-called power. Caroline wouldn't expect this.

Amanda felt the curse hit her a second before she saw Caroline emerge from her bedroom. She glowed in Amanda's vision. Amanda couldn't explain or replicate the spell that vibrated through her body. It felt like death. It felt like nothingness. The end to life, and worse, the end to love. Caroline had taken away her greatest weapon against Amanda… hope. With the death vibrating through her body, Amanda no longer had those lingering doubts, or fantasies about Jude and Caroline as a happy, normal couple.

Amanda heard, rather than felt, the knife clatter out of her hand. Caroline's spell had hobbled her, left her defenseless. Nothing would stop Caroline from picking up the knife and slitting Amanda's throat. Amanda guessed that Caroline meant to frighten her with the feeling of death surrounding her, but instead it calmed her. In the many months of near death during her cancer treatment, she had gotten close to acceptance. She had tried to hide it, but she knew she was more like Jude than the rest of her family. And if she had to die to save the others, then she would. She had less value than them.

Despite how hard she tried to do what God wanted of her, she had failed at ever becoming a good person. She didn't want to fight it anymore.

"What do you want?" she thought she heard Caroline say.

The curse lessened. Perhaps Caroline wanted her coherent enough to answer. Amanda had fallen to her knees. The knife on the floor lay within her reach.

"What do you want?" Caroline asked again, her voice harsh.

For the first moment, she looked like a lovely young woman, but she lost that illusion quickly. Her eyes lost their sparkle, turning dim and cold.

Caroline grabbed Amanda by the hair and Amanda shot a curse at her. Unfortunately, her lack of experience with magic would prove dangerous. An odd blue flame shot at Caroline and also hit the drapes behind her. Caroline screamed and Amanda thought she could smell burning flesh and hair. Amanda looked up at her and saw her flame had grazed the side of Caroline's face and had burned off some of her hair.

Caroline grabbed her by the neck and strangled her. She had far more strength than Amanda expected and she guessed magic played more of a role than Caroline's delicate fingers. Amanda's throat burned as she desperately tried to get oxygen. Her nasal passages swelled shut. She reached for the knife, but her hand couldn't find it.

Suddenly, Caroline screamed and released Amanda. Amanda wheezed in as much oxygen as she could, white lights popping in her vision. When she finally managed to breathe, she inhaled a thick chemical-scented smoke.

Caroline continued to scream, like an animal. Amanda saw the skin on her arms peeling off in large sheets, and more and more blood oozed from her skin. *Christ… did she do that?* As dark as Amanda knew she was, Amanda couldn't imagine something so horrible, let alone inflict it upon another person.

The same little girl she had seen in the front lawn looked down on Caroline as she grasped at her arms and screamed and cried. Caroline choked on her own sobs and then vomited. The window panes on either side of the front door shattered and the glass shot in toward all three of them. One piece landed in

Amanda's neck. The pain did not bother her as much as the amount of hot blood running down her arm.

Amanda thrust the knife into Caroline's heart. An odd moment of combined compassion and wrath. Amanda had never seen anyone in so much pain, and she felt compelled to put an end to it. She had expected the plunge to be difficult. She thought she might hesitate, and have trouble breaking through the muscle and sinew to the heart, but the knife slid in effortlessly. Caroline's warm blood spilled out onto Amanda's hand. So much blood. Caroline collapsed into her and Amanda could sense her agitated energy fading, and it felt like a great release. Everything she had held back in herself, and everything that needed to happen to bring justice, in one glorious warm moment of gushing, spilling blood.

"Run," Amanda said to the little blonde girl, but her voice came out in a choked snarl. However, the girl seemed to understand because she followed the command, heading toward the front door.

Amanda lay Caroline on the floor and pulled the knife from her chest, which caused an even greater eruption of blood. It poured from her chest and flooded the tile. Amanda's knees felt warm as the blood pooled around her.

Amanda felt warmth on her cheeks and found tears, but she didn't cry with the remorse she had expected, but with relief. She had prepared herself for a sacrifice, decimating her soul to save the people she loved. But it didn't feel like that. It felt like pure, selfish, pleasure.

"Sophie," Caroline said.

Amanda leaned in closer to her lips. "What?"

"Sophie," she said again, in desperation. Her voice dripped in fear, but Amanda didn't understand her declaration.

"Sophie," Caroline said again. The pointed toward the bedroom and her arm went limp. The sparkle in her eyes faded. Amanda could no longer feel that dirty, angry energy that surrounded her. She was gone. Nothing but flesh and blood.

Amanda's eyes burned. The insides of her nostrils burned. And her lungs burned as if she breathed in the flames. The blue fire had moved faster than normal flame and it surrounded her. She felt more tired than she ever had before. With each heart beat, another river of blood spilled from her neck. She clutched at her wound, although her hands alone had no chance of staunching the bleeding.

Then she heard something strange. Foreign, and unexpected, yet familiar. A baby's cry. The cry was urgent and hearty as if the child had screamed for some time, but Amanda hadn't heard her. A silencing spell, perhaps?

Sophie.

She wanted to believe the sound was an illusion of an oxygen-deprived mind. But she noticed things in the smoke-filled room that she hadn't before. Strange, colorful shapes on the floor. Scattered toys and teethers. A tiny pink sock. Amanda clutched the sock. So small, she could barely feel it in her clenched fist. The last thing she would ever hear would be the sounds of her baby granddaughter burning to death one room away. The God she had loved all her life would never allow such a thing.

"Sophie," Amanda called. Her voice sounded raspy and almost inaudible. "Sophie," she said again—the word masked in a fit of coughing—a sick mirror to Caroline's dying moments seconds ago. The crying continued, and it seemed the wail became weaker.

No. No. No. No. Please, God, no.

"Hey," Amanda said, trying to yell back to the girl who had left. Had she known about the baby? Had anyone known? Caroline excelled at hiding things she didn't want found "Zander," she tried also. He had to be close. But she knew he wouldn't hear her pathetic cries.

Amanda found an extra pocket of strength and pulled

herself up to a crawling position. She could feel the warm blood spilling out of her, leaving streaks behind her as she crawled toward where she thought she heard the crying.

The sound had been no illusion. She crawled her way into a bland nursery with gray carpet and gray walls, or perhaps the smoke made it look that way. She could see a mass of pink blankets in the crib, unmoving. The flames hadn't found their way into this room, but her room had filled with smoke. *Cry, dammit. Please cry. Let me hear you cry.* She wanted to plead the words aloud, but she couldn't stop coughing long enough to speak. Blood splattered from her mouth onto the carpet.

She made it to the crib and pulled herself up by the bars.

"Sophie?"

She saw the sleeping face of the most beautiful little girl she had ever seen. Probably about six months old. She had long eyelashes and wispy curls of blonde hair.

"Wake up, baby girl," she croaked. "Please wake up. I'm sure someone will be here to get you soon." She fished out her tiny hand from the blankets and squeezed it. "Please wake up."

God don't do this. Please don't do this. I've already given the only life I have to give. How could you?

The smoke in the room thickened, and Amanda's breaths became more and more shallow. She felt so tired. But she wanted to hold the baby before she went to sleep. Amanda pulled herself up to standing and reached in and gathered the still child in her arms. Her blood spilled onto her.

"Don't go to sleep," she whispered, reminded of all the times she had held a baby and whispered the opposite. She sunk back down to the floor with the baby in her arms and in her weakened state, she did what came naturally, she sang the lullaby she had once sung to her own children. It came out as nothing but undulating wheezes, but she heard the words clearly in her head.

All night, all day,

Angels watching over me, my Lord.

All night, all day,

Angels watching over me.

Now I lay me down to sleep

Angels watching over me, my Lord.

Pray the Lord my soul to keep

Angels watching over me.

The words rippled through time, back to when she was a young mother, and back further to when she herself was an infant. And perhaps rippling through the future as well. She had the feeling of living her entire life, and the life of the future she would never have, in the space of that song.

She lay on the floor now, next to Sophie. *Please God. Please.* She couldn't formulate a prayer any more complex than that. She pleaded. So close to death, she didn't care at all. She only wanted Sophie to live. Nothing else mattered.

The last thing she saw was two strong hands reaching through the smoke to collect Sophie. She could sense Zander's presence even though she had never met him. He radiated life. He *was* life. "Save the baby girl," she said.

She thought she could hear him speaking to her, but with Sophie safe, Amanda was ready to sleep. *Thank you, God. For everything,* she prayed silently and fell asleep humming her lullaby.

Zander's head ached and he couldn't stop coughing long enough to breathe. He would take the baby out and then go back for the woman. He feared he was already too late. There had been so much blood.

The child didn't squirm or cry in his arms. The memories of that other similar night crept along with him like ghosts. The baby in his arms, and the baby he couldn't save flashed back and forth in his vision. He made it out to the lawn, and fell to his knees, unable to control his coughing.

Leona reached toward the child. "Oh my God," she said. "Oh my God. She had a baby? Is that why you wouldn't leave?"

Zander pushed her away. "Don't… take…" he could barely make words, but he shielded the infant with his body like a bear protecting his cub. He could hear sirens. They would take the baby and it would be too late.

"She's hurt," Leona said. "The blood."

"Not… her… blood."

He pulled the baby into his chest, trying to surround her with as much of his life as possible. He grabbed Leona by the wrist and pulled her against the baby too, surrounding her in their magic on all sides.

Leona didn't stop him, and she looked in his eyes from inches away with a look of terrified understanding. "Is she dead?"

Zander shook his head. Even making the statement could cancel out their magic. Even a force as powerful as life felt like a tiny whisper in the face of death. "Alive," Zander said, nodding his head. "Think alive."

Leona nodded.

He tried to ignore the sharp pains in his head, the burning in his lungs, and the stinging in his eyes. He had struggled to summon life on that playground years ago and this was harder. He was exhausted, aching, and terrified. He didn't feel like he had any control over the life force. He struggled to hang on to his own. Summoning life felt like warming the world with nothing but a flickering candle.

The sirens grew louder, and he could see flashes of blue and red in his periphery. He didn't have time. They would take the baby and she would stay dead forever. No, it couldn't happen like that. His aunt asked him to do one thing… the woman inside asked him to do one thing… save the baby. If he didn't, none of this would mean anything. All this death, all this suffering, useless.

He pushed all those thoughts out his head. He envisioned his flickering candle growing brighter. So bright, it washed out everything else but blinding light, encircling all three of them. The vision brought on the actual feeling… a warm, vibrant sensation that brought a new dimension to the world around him. Colors looked deeper. He could breathe again as if the oxygen in the air had multiplied. The pain in his head lessened. He knew it worked, he at least summoned up enough life to heal himself. But he didn't know if it would be enough.

Then he heard the most beautiful sound he had ever heard. A tiny cough. And then a wail.

EPILOGUE

They held the funeral on May 17th, the night of the new moon. Aunt Jess probably didn't plan it on purpose, but Patrick appreciated the darkness because it provided a certain amount of privacy, and space. Ever since he had learned of the death of his parents, Patrick had felt nauseous, living in constant fear he might hurl. Now, walking out onto the beach, his stomach constricted into a tight and painful ball. Sooner or later, he would vomit on the sand and he'd prefer it if everyone didn't watch. Although he didn't know if he'd eaten enough recently to actually throw up.

Evangeline walked behind him and he kept looking back at her to make sure she hadn't disappeared. A strange concern, but she blended with the darkness so well. He thought if she could will herself to disintegrate, she would, and who knew what was possible. She had refused to come, using magic to break all the windows on Aunt Jess's car, and then finally gave in to make Emmy stop crying. Of course, Emmy hadn't stopped crying—not at any point over the past few weeks. Patrick thought she woke up already crying. He had grown so used to seeing her eyes red and wet, he forgot she could look any other way. At least it made her easy to keep track of. He could hear her sniffing as she walked.

They stopped about twenty feet from the surf and the wind made Patrick shiver even in the seventy-degree weather. He clamped his teeth together so everyone wouldn't hear them chattering. In the moonless night, Patrick couldn't see the horizon. The ocean and sky blended together into one expanse of darkness, an angry darkness that roared with wind and waves.

Jess and Carson argued over how to set up the Chinese lanterns. That's how they would release their ashes. It had sounded like a nice idea, but the lanterns seemed ready to blast off into the waves prematurely, thrashing about in the wind. The lantern service was a wizard tradition of some kind and meant only for them. Even their magic-ignorant cousins had to stay home.

There had been a more traditional service the day before. And even though he hadn't even changed his socks since the funeral, he could barely remember it. During the entire ordeal, his skin felt too tight and anything he looked at directly blurred and distorted. Music and voices sounded like nothing more than a ringing in his ears. He had only a vague sense of who had attended, mostly former coworkers of his parents and some people from their old church, none of whom he could name.

He could only clearly remember the conversation he had with Samantha. He had asked her what she planned to do—asked if she needed money or a place to stay. She said that she didn't, but didn't provide any other explanation. Perhaps she lied because she didn't want to worry him, but even in his muted state, he could tell she was hiding something. And when she thought he wasn't looking, she let this tiny smile slip. In that lapse of a few seconds, she looked happier than he had ever seen her before—and at his parents' funeral he found that distasteful and unnatural. He ignored her after that.

Evangeline brushed past him and stuck her toe in the water,

and then retreated again, with her arms pinned against her stomach all the while. Her shoulders must get sore from staying in that position all the time.

"Have you seen the ocean before?" Patrick asked her.

She looked like she shook her head, although in the dark he couldn't say for sure.

"I can't believe we never took you," Patrick said. "What do you think?"

"I don't like it," Evangeline said.

"Okay."

"I don't like the sky in Houston," she said.

"Isn't it the same sky everywhere?"

"No. There are no stars here."

"Well, there are stars, you just can't see them."

"I know that. I'm not an idiot. I'm just saying, the sky is ugly. It's all orange and dirty."

"Yeah," Patrick said. He leaned down, ready to collapse on the sand when he saw a flash of unnatural, grounded lightning accompanied by several shouts and an odd hissing, spluttering sound from Emmy.

Patrick turned to see Xavier advancing on Nathan. Another crack and flash came from Emmy, directed at Xavier.

"What the fuck?" Patrick asked.

"That summer wizard was touching all over our sister," Xavier said. "Are you going to just let him do that?"

"Oh my God," Emmy said. "What is the matter with you?"

"You shouldn't be here," Xavier said to Nathan.

"I'm sorry," Nathan said.

Nathan might not have a choice. Emmy's might have her nails dug into his forearm.

"Shut up," Carson spat. "Shut up. I'm trying to get these fucking lanterns set up. Otherwise, I'm going to chuck your parents into the ocean."

"Carson," Jess scolded.

Carson continued muttering under his breath and Patrick almost laughed. He could picture Carson getting pissed and chunking his sister's remains into the ocean like a football. Patrick felt bad for his aunt and uncle. They got screwed in the will. No amount of money can ease the blow of inheriting four children.

The one good thing that had come out of all this shit—Jude was arrested for the murder of his wife and mother. Of course, he didn't commit that particular crime, but whatever. He was in jail. Hopefully forever.

Patrick popped a chalky antacid and moved closer to Xavier to try and stop him from attacking anyone. Xavier rubbed his fist against his chest and breathed in uneven spurts. He ignored Patrick, a new normal. Xavier had grown cold toward Patrick and Evangeline since the deaths—cold to everyone except Emmy, at least until a minute ago. Patrick didn't know if he could live with Xavier anymore. He radiated blame. Every time he looked at him, his eyes said—*It's your fault.* Patrick already knew that, and every reminder made him feel sicker.

The flapping sound of the unruly lanterns silenced and Patrick saw that Evangeline had taken the lanterns from Carson and Jess. She had one in each hand, and they both hovered completely still. Even her hair didn't move, as if she'd created a tiny vacuum around her to stop the wind. Or maybe a black hole.

"Thank you," Jess said. She approached Evangeline, cautiously as always, and placed the pouches of ashes in their designated spots. "Do you want to light them?" Jess asked. She didn't offer a lighter and Patrick assumed she meant for her to use magic.

"I can't," Evangeline said.

Patrick didn't know if she meant she couldn't emotionally, or if she literally couldn't. He had seen her create light before, but not for a while. Could her magic have grown so dark she couldn't generate flame?

Either way, Jess didn't press the matter. She turned to the others, looking at Patrick first.

"Emmy and Xavier should do it," Patrick said. "I'm not good at that kind of magic. You know they can. They practically set each other on fire two minutes ago."

He stepped back, unsure why he had declined. He might have more balanced fall magic, but he'd had plenty of practice now. He could light a candle with his own two fingers as easily as he could with a lighter or match.

"Go on," Nathan said to Emmy.

Emmy approached, continuing her soft sobs. Xavier put his arm around her shoulder and walked with her toward Evangeline and the lanterns, an un-Xaiver-like show of affection.

Even though Evangeline didn't light the wicks, she held the lanterns—serving a purpose. Patrick regretted not joining in the ritual. He felt separate and cold, as if he watched his own funeral.

He decided to help in another way. His shaking body made magic difficult, and he tensed his muscles to try and keep still, but that made the shaking worse. The grief grabbed him suddenly and he started to cry. The tears made the shaking stop, so he could focus better. He focused on Evangeline and her vacuum spell and harnessed it, widening it until the wind had stopped all around them. The waves closest to the shore became gentle laps against the sand, as if they stood in front of an endless, smooth lake.

His parents could float into the darkness peacefully now. He covered his mouth so the others wouldn't hear him crying in the new silence. Sparks scattered around Evangeline like iridescent snow. Emmy created a light blue flame and Xavier's glowed white with a subtle rainbow sheen.

Once lit, they took the lanterns from Evangeline. They both looked around at everyone as if waiting for a signal. Patrick could only imagine how hard it would be to let go of those lanterns.

"Now?" Emmy whispered.

"Whenever you're ready, honey," Jess said.

Emmy released her lantern and Xavier followed. They rose into the air quicker than Patrick expected. They probably looked beautiful against the tranquil black, but Patrick could only see blurry light blobs through his tears.

Emmy came up to him and wrapped her arms around him. Apparently, he didn't do a good job at crying quietly. He knew she could feel him shaking again, but she didn't say anything, she rested her cheek against his chest.

"I know none of you wanted to say anything, and that's okay," Jess said.

Patrick wished she would shut up. Nothing should happen until the lanterns had faded out of sight. Time should stop.

"But I just wanted you to know something," Jess continued. "Your parents—" her voice broke and she took a few deep breaths and then continued. "They knew they were going to die. At least, they knew there was a good chance. They left you each a letter in their will, and you can read it whenever you're ready. Don't worry, I didn't open them. But they did leave a note for Carson and I as well. Basically, begging us to try and not totally screw you up for a few more years until you leave for college." She sniffed. "I—I thought I knew them really well. But I don't think I really understood them until after they died. They loved you, and each other, so much. And they were a lot braver than I gave them credit for. That's—that's it, that's all I wanted to say. I'm sorry." She sniffed again and Carson put his arms around her.

They watched the lanterns until they disappeared, and continued to stare at the sky for a long time after that. It felt wrong to leave. The ritual symbolized letting them go and then moving on with life, but he couldn't picture life beyond that dark beach.

When the incoming tide lapped at his feet, Carson and Jess herded them away from the shore, back to the parking lot.

Patrick felt numb on the ride home and hardly noticed time passing. When they got back, Jess tried to feed him and he refused.

"Here," she said, handing him something else. An envelope.

It took him a moment to realize what she had handed him. He shook his head, as if she had asked him to take a peanut butter and jelly sandwich again.

"You don't have to read it now if you don't want to. Or ever. Just take it."

Patrick took it to the office where he had been sleeping on the floor. He insisted on letting his other siblings get the few remaining beds and couches. Sleeping on the floor seemed like a lousy penance for what he had done, but it helped him feel a bit better.

He hadn't intended to read the letter right away. Maybe not ever. But he ripped into the envelope without thinking. His vision blurred as if his eyes refused to read the letter. He managed to read a few lines of his father's handwriting.

"... *I loved my life. Despite everything that happened, I still feel like I hit the jackpot. I didn't do anything to deserve all the good that came to me, and I thanked God for it every night. I don't want my death to trick you into thinking that life is bad. Don't ever doubt that your life can be wonderful...*"

With a jagged breath, Patrick refolded the letter, unable to read anymore. He enveloped himself in the second-hand sleeping bag that had become his bed and for once, he didn't think about the future. He only focused on the sound of his breathing, and his beating heart.

ACKNOWLEDGEMENTS

Author's Note: A Taste of Death and Honey was re-published in 2019 through Animus Ferrum press. The new cover was created by Kimberley Marsot and formatting was updated by Dorothy Dreyer.

I have a wonderful life and for that, I owe many thanks to many people. First, I'd like to thank my husband, for loving me just as I am and for supporting me unconditionally on every step of my writing journey. I'd like to thank my mother being a wonderful mother and grandma, and for the magical inspiration and education. I'd like to thank my brother for being an early reader of *Destruction* and for his words of encouragement. I also wish to thank everyone in my extended family. I'm lucky to have supportive and loving relatives all around me.

I had some incredible beta readers for *Destruction*. Their input helped to make the story and characters what they are today. Thank you to Ben Chiles, Charity Bradford, Dana Edwards, Gwen Gardner, Deana Barnhart, and Leah Deane. Your feedback and support meant so much to me.

And, none of this would happen without the support of Curiosity Quills Press. Thank you Eugene Teplitsky, Lisa Gus, Katie Hamstead, Andrew Buckley, Courtney Worth Young, Nikki Tetreault, Holly Erwin, Clare Dugmore, and all the other goats and minions. Of course, I have to thank my brilliant editor Mary Harris. She really helped me make the story stronger. And, the talented cover artist Michelle Johnson. The cover is everything I hoped for and more.

There are volumes worth of people who deserve my thanks for helping to spread the word about *Destruction*—including everyone who participated in my blog tour, cover reveal, and release day blitz. I also want to thank every single person who purchases this book and writes a review. Your support means so much to me.

I also want to thank J.K. Rowling for inspiring my love for magic and wizards…despite her biased portrayal of Slytherins.

Every night I say a prayer of thanks for everything I have. And, I'll do that again here. Thank you God for all of my many blessings. My family. My safety. My health. I truly love all that you have given me I'll do my best to appreciate every bit of it.

ABOUT THE AUTHOR

Sharon Bayliss lives in Austin, Texas with her husband and children. She hates wearing shoes and loves jogging in the rain. She only practices magic in emergencies.

She is also the author of the young adult science fiction novel, *The Charge*.

You can connect with her at www.sharonbayliss.com, www.facebook.com/authorsharonbayliss, and @SharonBayliss on Twitter.

www.ingramcontent.com/pod-product-compliance
Lightning Source LLC
Chambersburg PA
CBHW051627180726
48284CB00006B/1625